ds that she heard heavy, stumbling footsteps on the stairs, followed by a knock on the door. She opened it and immediately stepped back. The man who stood there, slightly swaying on his feet, was tall but rather stooped. He had been, could have been still, a handsome man, but his greying hair and moustache were untrimmed and there was several days' growth of grey stubble on his chin and jaws.

'How's the Missus?' he asked.

'As well as can be expected in the circumstances,' answered Jenny, then closed the door in his face just as recognition dawned in it with the sound of her voice. It was not the heavy reek of stale beer on his breath which had made her recoil, but her immediate recognition of *his* face in the light flooding out from the bedroom.

* * *

Frank brought a cup of tea into her room in the morning.

'You were out late, Mum,' he said. 'Difficult case was it?'

'Yes, very difficult,' Jenny answered. She could not bring herself to tell him of the shock she had had, coming face to face so unexpectedly with his father.

Inheritance

F.V. Dawes

G
Gainsborough Press

This edition published in 1996
by Gainsborough Press
An imprint of Leopard
20 Vauxhall Bridge Road, London SW1V 2SA

First published by Hutchinson 1984
Arrow edition 1987

Printed and bound in Great Britain by
Cox & Wyman Ltd, Reading, Berkshire

ISBN 0 752 90373 X

For my children,
Amanda, Tim and Catherine

AUTHOR'S NOTE

Only the well-known names and historic events in this book are real. The rest is my invention.

CONTENTS

PROLOGUE

This morning we came home from hospital, home being the top two floors of this solid double-fronted Victorian villa just a few minutes walk from Brixton Underground Station in South London. As I look at you, sleeping soundly in the wicker crib which I bought in Electric Avenue market only three Sundays ago, I still find it difficult to grasp your reality: 7 lbs 2 oz of flesh and bone. When I heard your sharp little yowl, before they cut the cord, I started shaking. I was shaking so much that I failed to hold you properly when nice little Nurse Lo laid you against my breast. Your coal-black fuzz looked so strange against my blonde hair and sun-starved pallor, your dark, wrinkled skin suggesting that my womb must be alive with ultraviolet energy.

You frightened me.

If only Malcolm had been there, but he came nowhere near; terrified, I suppose, of his cow of a wife. Apart from the comprehensive school fourth-former in the next bed but one, I was the only female in the Princess Alice Maternity Ward *not* half-buried in chrysanthemums and congratulatory telegrams. No one even remembered to send me a card on my own birthday two days later. My thirtieth.

For the first time I can understand how my namesake Jenny Cole felt when she gave birth to my father in 1916. Unlike me, Jenny was a virgin until she was thirty-five. Times were different and not just because there were no credit cards or plastic bags or launderettes or disposable nappies, and no Pill either.

As an unmarried mother, poor old Jenny was on her own, no midwife calling every day to advise her on the proper care of baby, no official health visitors, no one at all in fact apart from her kind but ignorant landlady to help her overcome the post-natal panic which I now feel.

Having a baby out of wedlock was a terrific disgrace for someone like Jenny, a lady born to privilege. The fact that there was a war on was no excuse; she could not bring herself to confess her shame to her people, as members of middle-class families were apt to refer to one another. Instead she worked nights making munitions at the Woolwich Arsenal to keep herself and little Frank. When the war was over, to provide a settled home for the two of them in hard economic times, she degraded herself still further in the eyes of 'her people' by going into domestic service as a cook.

Listen, Charles, we'll forget about baby talk. You're far too intelligent, I can see, for that koochy-koochy-koo stuff. I have named you Charles after your great-great-grandfather who was an eminent Victorian, a London publisher no less, at a time when this capital city could claim to be the centre of the civilized world. Wrapped in tissue paper in my drawer is the fine Georgian robe of cotton and lace in which he was christened one hundred and fifty years ago in the parish church at Rotherhithe, where the captain of the *Mayflower* lies buried.

Charles Cole was born into the Church of England and became a Catholic when he married his second wife, Kate, since when the Coles have remained through all vicissitudes more or less in the spiritual clutches of the Lady of Rome. I will not choose for you, Charles. The robe will stay in its wrapping.

Just think, you might have been a scion of the great British aristocracy if Jenny had married the man who fell madly in love with her when she was a suffragette. He was a marquess and a bit of a wet to judge from the fact that he let his family's disapproval of Catholics deter him from sweeping Jenny off her feet. Years later, when he finally got around to proposing, he was too late; Jenny had fallen for a working-class hero in uniform. The trouble with him was that he was already married.

Then when Jenny discovered that she was pregnant, with no prospect of a husband, she changed her mind about Captain the Marquess of Broucester. Now *she* was too late. He was a pilot in the Royal Flying Corps, an occupation in which life expectancy was reckoned to be about three weeks, and her letter accepting his proposal arrived at his squadron in France on the very morning that he was shot down and killed on aerial reconnaissance over enemy lines.

Poor, poor Jenny. The 1920s, the period before she and the formidable Irish matriarch who was her mother achieved a rapprochement, are a blank in the family album. The world in those days was less than sympathetic towards bastards.

Bastard. The very word makes me wince as I look down on you in your crib, all fists and feet and funny faces, getting more human and louder by the hour. Your grandfather, Charles, was brought up on the lie that his father died a hero's death in the trenches of Flanders. It is only right that you should know.

Jenny Cole
9 December 1979

BOOK ONE

Inheritance

December 1929

On the 20th inst. at Blackstaff Hall, Westerham, Catherine Cole, widow of the late Charles Cole, in her 91st year.

From the death notices in
The Times.

1

Frank Cole returned to school at Chelwood Abbey at the beginning of 1930 with but one bright memory of the Christmas holidays, and that was a visit to the Adelphi Theatre with his mother to see *Mr Cinders*. This treat came before the summons to Blackstaff Hall, the seventeenth-century manor house high on the North Downs above Westerham where his grandmother lay dying. The old house was already as silent as the tomb and Frank was frightened of the skeletal matriarch who held out her hands to him from the bed.

Now, as he waited with his mother at Clapham Junction Station for the train back to Sussex, he carried in his luggage a record of 'Spread a Little Happiness' which Binnie Hale sang so sweetly in the show they had seen. Everyone was humming, whistling it. Its plaintive message seemed to strike a chord among a people shaken by the tidal wave of financial disaster crossing the Atlantic from Wall Street and depressed by the ever lengthening dole queues outside the labour exchanges.

But that was not the real reason why Frank's record soon became scratchy from over use on the wind-up gramophone in the Lower School common room at Chelwood Abbey. At thirteen, he was in love for the first time, with the adorable vision he had seen from the fourth row of the stalls. A photograph of Her, clipped from the *Illustrated London News* and pasted onto cardboard from a shoebox lid, was hidden at the bottom of his locker beneath his rugby shirts and last term's forbidden copies of *Rover* and *Wizard*.

During his sad Christmas holidays Frank had anticipated his contemporaries of the Upper Third by becoming more interested in sex than in Sexton Blake. Sooner or later it was bound to come out and it happened when one of his enemies wandered into the dormitory to discover Frank alone, sitting on his bed gazing at his cut-out picture of the simpering Binnie.

'My hat, what have we here?' he yelled, snatching it out of

Frank's hands. 'Come and see this, you chaps. Cole's gone sweet on some actress.'

The rest of the form, just off the rugby field, came tumbling through the door, stretching out muddy fingers.

'Oh, gosh. A pin-up.'

'Give it here.'

'Cripes, what a corker!'

Attracted by the din the house master strode in to find a heap of boys writhing on the bare boards between the rows of beds. Frank emerged from the heart of this human pyramid, pink to the tips of his ears.

'Cole again,' snapped the master. 'I might have guessed. What's the reason for this racket?'

The photograph of Binnie Hale, crumpled and torn in the fray, was produced amidst sniggers.

'Is this yours, Cole?'

'Yes, sir.'

'I think Father Nervaux will want to see this.'

'Why, is he sweet on Binnie Hale, too?' asked someone, just loud enough to hear, at the back of the little group. This brought more sniggers, but the house master pretended not to hear as he marched out of the dormitory clutching the offensive object of Frank's affections.

As he expected, he was called to the high master's study after supper, dressed in the school uniform of ankle-length cassock in Lincoln green serge. It was his late grandmother who had insisted on sending him here, after his long illness, to be given a good Catholic education. He had been much happier at Albion Hill Elementary School when his mother was in domestic service as a cook for the Esmondes at Granville Park on the edge of Blackheath. He still kept in touch by letter with Jack Harris, his best friend from those early schooldays.

Father Nervaux gave him a lecture on unhealthy passions, then ordered him to bend over a chair for the ritual 'six of the best' with a thin cane across the buttocks.

'If you feel these carnal desires coming on take a cold shower,' he remarked with a ghost of a smile when he had finished. 'You may go.'

Their mutual dislike dated from their very first meeting at Blackstaff Hall when Frank gave the austere priest the Albion Hill playground version of 'the Freemason's handshake', leaving him with smarting knuckles.

'God, how I hate this place,' reflected the boy as he made his way down the stone-flagged corridor massaging his stinging backside. He might have felt happier had he known that this was to be his last term at Chelwood Abbey, with its refrigerated dormitories, unappetizing meals and cold baths. 'Rich food and warm baths brought down the Roman Empire,' according to Father Nervaux, following the British public-school tradition.

Sitting at a roll-top desk in the front room of her little terraced house in Effra Road, Brixton, Jenny reached out for a bottle of Swan's blue-black ink from which to refill her fountain pen. A tram clanked by on its way to Tulse Hill. It was a Sunday evening in March and through the opened slats of the venetian blinds she could see the congregation filing into the gloomily gaslit Methodist chapel across the road, carrying prayer books and wearing Sabbath expressions. Many of them returned from new homes in the suburbs to worship there.

In a moment the solitary, cracked bell in the tower ceased tolling and with a preliminary wheeze the massive organ pipes burst into the opening bars of 'Jerusalem'.

> 'And did those feet in ancient time
> Walk upon England's mountains green?'

Jenny never went to mass, never prayed, but she loved this hymn and she paused now for a moment, listening to the voices drifting on the evening air while her lips silently formed the words.

It took a conscious effort to concentrate her mind on the task in hand as the gold nib glided across the notepaper with firm, clear strokes:

Dear Father Nervaux,

I write to inform you of a decision I have reached only after long and careful consideration, namely to remove my son from your care at the end of this term. As you know, I live alone but am fortunate in having an occupation as midwife for which I was recently trained by Dr McCall at Clapham Road. Being now secure and settled in this work I feel that both Frank and I would benefit from being together again in our own home. My late mother has left us well provided for financially. As to the boy's education, it was her wish that he should complete it in a Catholic school, however the will does not specify any particular school. I have therefore decided to enrol him at St Wilfrid's Day School for Boys at Sydenham Hill, which has the highest of reputations locally, to commence after the Easter holiday. It remains only to thank you and the masters at Chelwood Abbey for all you have done and to wish you well for the future.

Yours faithfully,
Jenny Cole

Dictating a reply to the young Jesuit priest who acted as his secretary, the high master remarked 'out of respect to your late mother, God rest her soul, a very great Catholic lady, I must express our sadness that we have not been allowed more time to develop Frank's immortal soul.

'He is at times a headstrong boy and his belated baptism shortly before he came to us did not appear to induce a state of humility to Almighty God in him.

'End it "Yours in Christ", et cetera,' instructed Father Nervaux,' and address it to *Miss* Cole – I'll not give her the cloak of respectability. Between you and me, father, I'm not sorry to see the back of that young man. He's a disruptive influence in the Upper Third. *St Wilfrid's* is welcome to him.'

He uttered the name St Wilfrid's in a tone verging on contempt. It was a Catholic school but hardly in the same league as Chelwood Abbey, scholastically or socially. Virtually its only claim to fame was its proximity to that Victorian fantasy in glass, the Crystal Palace, on a ridge south of London overlooking the great city. Yet St Wilfrid's was eagerly sought after as a seminary for the sons of the Catholic bourgeoisie The School was housed in a large mansion built at the time of the Crimean War, a mere seventy-five years previously, and its foundation as a school had yet to attain even a silver jubilee.

What it lacked in acreage and tradition, St Wilfrid's made up for with swank. From the school song ('Then fear not, and veer not, from Duty's narrow way') to the rituals of Speech Day, it did its best to model itself on a minor Anglican public school. Yet somehow it ended up aping the vices without the virtues of schools for young Church of England gentlemen, inculcating in its pupils a sense of exclusivity and class consciousness and a positive dislike of foreigners, without an accompanying sense of responsibility to lead and to serve if necessary.

St Wilfrid's desire for impressive style was expressed in the school uniform, a blue and yellow striped blazer and cap emblazoned with a gold papal cross on a shield and the motto: *Virtus est vitium fugere**.

Jenny was immensely proud when she waved goodbye to her son on his way to St Wilfrid's for his first day, wearing his bright new uniform, with a shiny leather satchel over his shoulder. In his first week he discovered that his posh tailor-made outfit made him a target, not only for the great unwashed of South London but also for those who considered themselves to be his superiors.

Frank found himself living in two worlds – that of his privileged middle-class schoolfellows and that of the dingy back streets of South London where his mother lived and worked as a midwife. The first was a world of detached and semidetached mock Tudor houses, tennis clubs, dancing shoes, vacuum cleaners, gramophone records and MG sports cars. His other world consisted of endless rows of little terraced houses, each exactly like its neighbour, railway embankments and scrap-metal yards, pie and eel shops, pawnbrokers and costermongers wheeling their barrows.

Although separated by only a few miles, the two worlds never met and Frank became vividly aware of the difference when he was invited to birthday tea at the home of Lionel Carter.

Lionel lived in a substantial Edwardian mansion at the edge of Dulwich Village. The door was opened by a maid wearing a cinnamon brown dress with a matching bow in her hair instead of the more conventional black dress with starched white apron and cap. This was an indication of the fact that Lionel's mother, who greeted the young guests in the drawing room, was a suburban pacesetter, very smart and advanced.

Frank knew that Lionel's father was a solicitor who travelled up to the City each morning wearing a bowler hat and carrying an umbrella and a rolled-up copy of the *Daily Telegraph*. Frank told his chums at school that *his* father had been a captain in the army and had died a hero. When they pressed him for details he invented a story about his father leading an attack on a German machine-gun post, personally killing a dozen Huns before he succumbed to a bayonet thrust. The other boys were suitably impressed.

* 'To flee vice is a virtue' – Horace, *Epistles* 1.i.41.

Arriving at Lionel's party, he was introduced to several girls of his own age and younger, all dolled up in pink and yellow frilly dresses with bows in their hair. Despite Mrs Carter's repeated admonitions to mix, the two sexes quickly segregated themselves on opposite sides of the room.

When they sat down to tea though, the guests were obliged to sit where their names had been written on little cards and Frank found himself sandwiched between two girls who blushed when spoken to or, even worse, giggled. Conversation flagged.

'And where do *you* live, Frank?' Mrs Carter asked during one of the long silences.

'Brixton,' replied Frank indistinctly through a mouthful of cake and jelly.

'Ah, Brixton,' said Mrs Carter, managing to make it sound like somewhere on the far side of Tibet.

'Frank's father was killed in the war, knocking out a Jerry machine gun,' said Lionel, as if that explained why he now lived in Brixton.

'Oh, you poor dear,' exclaimed Mrs Carter. 'And is your mother alone in the world? – apart from having you, of course.'

'She's kept very busy,' said Frank, accepting a third helping of jelly from the maid. 'She's a midwife.'

'What's a midwife?' asked the girl on his left, who was about eleven.

'I don't think we need to go into that,' said Mrs Carter hastily. 'If you've all quite finished we'll go back to the drawing room now and start the games.'

Frank loathed hunt-the-slipper and postman's knock. Kids' stuff. While waiting outside the drawing-room door for the embarrassing summons to enter, he went in search of a lavatory but found himself by mistake in the kitchen. The maid, now changed from her smart brown uniform into a drab green overall, looked up from the piles of dirty dishes at the sink.

'Hello,' she said. 'What do you want?'

'I thought you might like some help,' answered Frank gallantly on the spur of the moment.

'Help?' the girl echoed him, laughing. 'Eeeeh, pet – what an idea.'

'My mother used to be in service, like you,' Frank told her, slightly annoyed by her dismissive tone. 'I often used to help *her* when I was just a nipper.'

'In that case,' said the maid, tossing a tea towel towards him, 'I accept your kind offer, since it's Cook's afternoon off.'

As he dried cups, plates and saucers he chatted easily to the girl. She told him her name was Grace and she came from County Durham, one of four girls all put into service as soon as they were old enough. Their father was an unemployed shipyard worker.

'I get ten bob a week and me board at this place,' she said, 'and for that I work all the hours that God sends. Still it's better than being on the dole like me Da, I suppose.'

Frank was captivated by her outlandish accent and her engaging grin.

'You look a bit like Binnie Hale,' he told her seriously.

'Get away, lad. She's a fillum star, ain't she?' The maid was laughing at him, but flattered all the same.

Mrs Carter entered angrily. 'What on earth are you doing?'

'Helping Grace with the washing-up,' explained Frank, somewhat superfluously.

'Come along now,' snapped Mrs Carter, going very red in the face. 'One doesn't help with the dishes. That's what servants are for.'

2

After the birthday party Frank was never invited again to the Carter home. Furthermore, he was aware of a subtle change in his schoolfellows' attitude towards him, as if he were not quite their sort. Noel Hartley said to him one afternoon as they marched side by side in a column of boys returning to school from rugger practice at Crystal Palace fields: 'I say Cole, is it true that your Ma's a midwife?'

'That's right,' answered Frank, on the defensive immediately. 'What of it?'

'Oh, nothing,' said Hartley, who was a prefect and captain of the Second XV and at the age of not quite fifteen had already started shaving. Then he added in a voice loud enough for the younger boys behind them to hear: 'It just seems a rum sort of occupation for one's mater, that's all, being a midwife.'

The Third Formers sniggered sycophantically since it was Hartley who spoke. Few of them were sure what a midwife was, although the more knowledgeable knew it had something to do with 'additions to the family'. Sex education was not a part of the St Wilfrid's curriculum and talk of such matters was confined to whispers in the lavatories and locker rooms.

Although Mrs Cole's profession was the subject of some amusement in the Lower Fourth at St Wilfrid's, in Effra Road it enhanced her social standing. Among her neighbours, mostly hard-working artisans, warehousemen, carters and the like, she was seen to be a lady even if the postman had told everyone about the letter addressed to 'Miss Cole'.

Jenny's was one of the few houses in the neighbourhood with a telephone and she had her groceries and meat delivered to the door. The Coles were also the only family with their own bath, which made them seem very posh. Jenny had this amenity installed, together with a hot-water geyser and a basin, in an upstairs room.

Few of the houses that she visited on her rounds boasted more than a cold tap.

In the Cole household, uniquely in Effra Road, daily baths were the order. Jenny luxuriated in a hot tub with her favourite Condy's Fluid (which always reminded her of the blissful bath she took at her sister's house in Kensington after serving her first spell in Holloway Prison for suffragette agitation) and washed away any lingering odours of the insanitary hovels she was often obliged to work in.

She was a much respected figure in the streets of Brixton in those days, a woman of fifty going about her business on an old-fashioned bicycle with a web of string attached to the rear mudguard and frame to prevent her long navy blue skirt getting caught in the spokes of the wheel.

She always wore a wide-brimmed felt hat, with ribbon tied under her chin to keep it in position, gloves, and in inclement weather a bright yellow oilskin cape. Her black leather midwife's bag was carried in a large wicker basket mounted on the handlebars. Her telephone and her doorbell rang at all hours of the day or night and Jenny was always ready to answer a call. More often than not, Frank let himself into an empty house with a latch-key when he came home from school but his tea was always on the table waiting for him.

He never brought friends home from school, fearing they would scoff at where and how he and his mother lived. Jenny bought him a Raleigh bicycle for Christmas, in the hope that it would encourage him to get out into the country at weekends, but instead he headed towards an even more crowded neighbourhood around the Elephant and Castle where his old friend Jack Harris now lived.

The Harrises had been compelled by declining fortunes (that is, a month's arrears in payment of 7s 6d per week rent) to do 'a moonlight flit' from their little house in Deptford to two rooms in a decaying, bug-ridden tenement off the Walworth Road. Mr Harris had gone into business on his own account as a rag and bone man, touring the seedy streets in a horsedrawn cart, ringing a brass bell to attract customers from their homes. He bought almost any kind of second-hand goods, scraping meagre profits on their resale wherever he could find a market.

Around 'the Elephant', a noisome, soot-pickled ghetto without a patch of green anywhere, Sunday was the liveliest day of the week with vendors of pets and patent medicines, clothes and furniture, books and bedsteads, fish, fruit and fowl shouting their wares in competition with hucksters, tipsters, comedians, distributors of religious tracts and every kind of soapbox orator. Costers with their donkeys jostled with Italian ice-cream vendors, hot-potato merchants, punch and judy men and organ grinders. At every window and barracklike doorway sat whole families, enjoying the raucous melodies and street cries.

Although he had shed the hated St Wilfrid's cap and blazer, Frank still stood out like someone of a different planet as he wheeled his new bicycle through the teeming streets.

'Don't leave that bike of your'n lyin' around unless you want it nicked,' Jack advised immediately when Frank eventually located him in Deacon Street Buildings. 'You'd better bring it inside.'

Frank was astonished at the transformation in his friend. Only a month or two before, he had been the undisputed leader of the Deacon Street Gang, dedicated to eternal battle with Rodney Road Mob, using catapults, bottles, rotten fruit or whatever other weapons came to hand. Now suddenly he had stopped going to the den under the railway arches and cut himself off from everything to do with the Deacon Street Gang and 'kids'.

The reason was that he had reached the elementary-school-leaving age of fourteen, gone into long trousers and become a wage earner. His new status entitled him to two kippers for his tea at six o'clock instead of 'doorsteps' of bread smeared with margarine, jam or fish paste. He had passed the second of four milestones in the lives of boys like him: aged twelve 'fags' (cigarettes), aged fourteen 'long-'uns' (long trousers instead of shorts), aged fifteen 'birds' (girls), aged sixteen 'dole'. There was no shortage of blind-alley jobs such as packing birdseed, baling waste paper or sweeping up in Woolworth's ('Nothing in these stores over 6d' was its proud slogan and the wages of its employees were similarly modest), filling bottles with sauces or pickles and scraping labels off them, acting as errand boy to butchers or grocers, trundling round on a heavy 'Trade-bike' for fifteen bob a week. Most such jobs came to an abrupt end at sixteen when the lad became insurable by his employer.

Jack's older brothers had trodden this path and he had no intention of following them. Already he had found himself a job in the big city on the other side of the river and meant to make something of himself. In some miraculous way he seemed to have grown suddenly taller – perhaps it was the effect of the long trousers. These trousers had knife-edge creases, preserved by placing them carefully under the mattress before he went to bed at nights, a bed which, incidentally, he still had to share with two of his brothers. He had also acquired, on the 'pay as you wear' system, a smart pinstripe suit which was kept folded in brown paper during the week.

Still in short trousers, Frank felt very much the junior beside this new city slicker with his brightly coloured socks and tie and his new haircut, parted down the centre, brushed flat against his head and gleaming with brilliantine. The glasses with one lens blacked out had gone but the slight squint remained.

' 'Ow yer doing then, cock?' inquired Jack as he ushered him and his bicycle into the cluttered room which served as living room, dining room, kitchen and bathroom for the whole family. 'It's so bleedin' crowded in 'ere that even the cat's bin given notice to quit.'

Frank laughed as he answered: 'Oh, *I'm* all right and so's Mum now that I'm home with her.'

'Good on yer, mate,' said Jack, clapping his arm round his friend's shoulders. 'You're a sight for sore eyes.'

The Harris boys, huddled round a table covered with old newspapers and the remnants of a Sunday roast, looked askance at this youth they had not seen for three years and whose voice sounded impossibly 'lah-di-dah' to their ears. Of Mr Harris, hero and victim of the General Strike, there was no sign.

'Dad's out with the barrow,' explained Jack.

'Dahn the boozer, more like,' said one of his brothers.

'And Ma's lyin' down 'aving her Sunday afternoon forty winks,' Jack went on. 'D'yer want a bit of dinner? There's some beef and roast spuds left.'

'No thanks, Jack. I lunched before I set out.'

'Gor' blimey, 'ark at 'im,' exclaimed the oldest brother, putting down his *News of the World*. 'Listen, mate, we eat dinner in this house, not lunch or luncheon, or whatever you call it back at the Palace. I remember you, mate, when you was a snotty-nosed little bugger with the arse 'anging out of yer trousers. You were glad to get a pennorth of crackling from the fish and chip shop then – if I give you the penny – so don't come the old 'Igh and Mighty with me.'

Frank blushed and made no reply. Jack, covering his friend's embarrassment, took him by the arm and said: 'Come on then, let's go down to the caff and 'ave a bit of a chinwag.'

On the stairs down to the street he called over his shoulder: 'Don't mind Bill. 'E just likes to throw his weight about a bit that's all. 'E's all mouth though.'

He led the way to a seedy little café in Walworth Road and ordered two mugs of thick brown tea into which they ladled half a bowl of sugar. They carried them from the counter to a table by the steamed-up window.

'Fag?' asked Jack, producing a twopenny packet of five Woodbines.

'Don't mind if I do,' replied Frank, trying to sound like one of the lads, without much success, and coughing at his first draught on his cigarette.

'I do the football pools now,' announced Jack proudly, at the same time blowing smoke from his nostrils. 'It don't cost much and you can win a fortune. If I win a packet I'll be off to Canada. But just in case I don't, I'm putting five bob a week into me Post Office Savings book.'

'Why Canada?'

'I dunno really. I just fancy it. Better than this dump. I'd buy a ranch and fly me own plane.'

'Sounds great,' said Frank, admiringly.

'All the blokes at work do the pools,' Jack went on.

'What is your job exactly?' asked Frank.

'I'm a copy boy on the *Daily Mail*,' Jack told him. 'I run messages for the sergeant who's in charge of the front lodge. He's a bit of an old sod – 'ates the 'uman race, actually – but he's all right as long as you don't give him no lip, as he calls it. Sometimes he sends me up to put coal on the fire in old Lord Rothermere's office. He's the head of the whole lot. Never says a dicky-bird, never even looks up when you go in. I hate going up there. It can be exciting though – like when the R101 went down. I was on night duty when it happened.'

The R101, the last of the great airships, had crashed in flames near Beauvais in France only a few months previously on an experimental flight to India, killing most of the people on board.

So as not to be completely outdone by his friend's experiences in Fleet Street, Frank remarked casually: 'My mother was a reporter on the *Daily Mirror* when Lord Northcliffe first started it. She often talks about it.'

'Garn,' replied Jack, 'you're 'aving me on.'

'No I'm not,' Frank assured him. 'My grandfather was a publisher and his first wife wrote a famous book.'

'What was it called then, if it's so famous?' demanded Jack.

'*Mrs Cole's Celebrated Cookery*,' said Frank, adding doubtfully, 'Funny thing is she had the same name as my Ma – Jenny Cole.'

Jack hooted with laughter again.

'Mrs Cole's *what*? Never 'eard of it. You're making it up. Now pull the other one.'

'It was published seventy years ago,' retorted Frank huffily, 'at the same time as Mrs Beeton's. You've heard of *her*, I suppose.'

'Well, if you've got all these family connections with the print you ought to be able to pull a few wires,' suggested Jack, impressed despite himself. 'You could become a reporter.'

'Why don't you become one yourself if it's so marvellous,' replied Frank.

'I'd jump at the chance,' said Jack, suddenly becoming very serious. 'There's nothing else in the world I'd rather be, but what chance have I got? No education. No friends in the right places.'

'You can do anything if you want,' Frank told him with all the earnestness of a regular *Rover* reader, 'if you're determined enough.'

'I dunno about that,' answered Jack, doubtfully. 'You've got to know shorthand and typing and . . .'

'You can teach yourself all that from a book,' broke in Frank impatiently. 'Why ever not?'

'It's easy for you to talk,' said Jack, grinding the stub of his cigarette in the jampot cover which served as an ashtray. 'You go to a posh school. You've got to have the right accent, the old school tie, know the people who matter. It's not for the likes of Jack Harris from Deacon Street Buildings, now is it?'

'Had a pleasant day, darling?' asked Jenny, looking up from darning one of his knee-length wool St Wilfrid's socks as Frank came into the back parlour and draped himself over the easy chair by the fire. Without waiting for a reply she went on: 'I can't imagine how you get these enormous holes in your heels. I darned this one only a week ago.'

'Went to see Jack Harris,' announced Frank, ignoring the vexed question of socks. 'They live over at the Elephant and Castle now.'

'Isn't it rather rough there?'

'Yes, it is rather,' he agreed, 'but no rougher than Camberwell. I came through it just now on my way up Coldharbour Lane. I was born there, wasn't I, Ma?'

Jenny nodded.

'Whereabouts though, exactly?' asked Frank. 'I'd like to go and see it.'

'Oh, it's been demolished long since.' Jenny put down her darning somewhat overhastily and got up, saying: 'I'm going to make some Ovaltine. Would you like some?'

Frank followed her into the tiny kitchen and leaned against the dresser, watching her as she put milk in the pan and stirred the mixture with a spoon.

'It must have been rotten, being stuck in Camberwell with me, while Dad was out there,' he mused, out loud.

Jenny bent her head over the gas stove and made no reply, but he went on: 'There was something that puzzled me when we went to Grandma's funeral . . .'

She glanced at him anxiously.

' . . . all those tombstones of the Coles and the Bartons, Grandfather and so on, but not one for my father.'

'It's an Army tradition,' she broke in, 'that soldiers lie where they fall. You remember the line from Rupert Brooke – "that there's some corner of a foreign field, that is for ever England". I think it's the best way to think of it, not to dwell on the frightfulness of it all.'

Then, as she poured the steaming liquid into two cups, she said: 'You know, Frank, I do wish you'd share the company of some of the nicer St Wilfrid's boys out of school instead of hanging about places like the Elephant and Castle.'

'But I *like* it there – the Harrises are such a scream, and Jack was awfully bucked to see me again,' he told her. 'There's no need to worry about me.'

'I *do* worry, though,' she replied. 'I have to worry since you haven't a father to keep you on the right lines.'

'Jack's got a job as a copy boy at the *Daily Mail*,' said Frank. 'He was on duty the night the R101 crashed, the lucky blighter. I'd like to get a job like that. Couldn't I leave school at the end of this term, Mum? I really can't stand that snooty lot at St Wilfrid's.'

'Please stop it,' Jenny interrupted him sharply. 'I've been out on a difficult call today and I'm really too tired to listen to such nonsense. You've got at least two years before you even begin to think about a career.'

'But Jack said . . . '

'I do not wish to hear what Jack said.' She ploughed on with that tightening of the jaw which he recognized only too well. 'Jack Harris is a nice boy and I wish him well, but he hasn't got your advantage of a private education. Education matters, Frank, remember that. So stop daydreaming and concentrate on your maths and Latin. Your last report was a stinker. "Could do well but won't make the effort" – that's the story of your life at Chelwood and now at St Wilfrid's. It just won't do.'

Jenny lay awake thinking over the conversation. Her great fear was that Frank would run wild again as he did when he was a little boy and she had him with her in service at the Esmondes.

That ended with him in hospital and finally with the old trout (God rest her soul) at Blackstaff taking him out of my hands altogether. This time I'm not going to let him go, he is my son. I want him to be somebody, yet it's so difficult living in this seedy neigbourhood.

Jenny's feeling of insecurity was not diminished by a remark from a nosy neighbour in Effra Road a few days later: 'Funny thing, Mrs Cole, but we always thought you was a spinster till the boy come 'ome.'

'Really,' answered Jenny, doing her best to pass this awful woman in carpet slippers, with a dirty apron and her hair in curlers, a cigarette dangling from her lower lip while she talked.

'He is your'n, ain't he?'

'Of course he is,' said Jenny, coldly.

'It's just that I 'eard someone who shall be nameless round 'ere the other day calling you *Miss* Cole,' continued the neighbour with a sly smile. 'Now ain't that strange, Mrs Cole?'

Jenny went on her way, fuming. As a VAD nurse during the war she had met all kinds of men and women and had learned much for which her sheltered, convent-school upbringing had left her unprepared. She remembered still the shock of hearing a woman driver exclaiming after a Boche shell hit her ambulance on the way to Wimereux: *'The bloody thing's bitched my radiator!'* She had never heard a lady swear, or seen one smoke, as her colleagues did in increasingly large numbers. And now, even at fifty, she was still easily bruised by the roughness of the environment she lived in, hurt by the crude innuendo of someone who in her better days would not have dared to speak to her like that.

It was later that day that she saw the 'For Sale' board outside the house in Amen Road. 'House to Let' signs were common enough in those days but few people had the resources to *buy* houses, at least not in the far from golden triangle of Clapham, Balham and Brixton.

Jenny stopped in her tracks and propped her old-fashioned lady's bicycle against the kerb while she peered over the wrought-iron gate. A path of black and white tiles in chessboard pattern led three or four yards to a brown-painted front door with the number 35 set into the leaded light above it.

The flowerbeds on either side of the path were carefully tended, without a weed to be seen. There were lace curtains at the bow windows, surrounded by the ornate stonemasonry favoured by turn-of-the-century suburban builders. A large black cat sat on the whitened doorstep beside two empty milk bottles and stared back at Jenny with wide, disdainful eyes.

She noted that the house was built of red brick with a roof of dark grey Welsh slate tiles. It was end of terrace and consequently boasted a side entrance to the back garden, useful when coalmen came with bulging dusty black sacks on their backs. The privet hedge flanking the front gate was clipped as though to a rule edge, it was so straight.

Across the way from this long terrace of houses in Amen Road was open space, the rolling acres of Tooting Bec, one of those areas of commonland strung like an emerald necklace mercifully across the asphalt of South London from Wandsworth to Peckham. The grass and trees were regularly showered with smuts from the Balloon locos puffing across the commons from Wandsworth through Balham to Gipsy Hill and Crystal Palace, but Tooting Bec was still green enough to remind Jenny of her carefree childhood in that great house on the North Downs, beyond reach of London's smoke and fogs.

Amen Road was, and is, maybe threequarters of a mile long, ending up at its farthest reaches from Streatham Hill in Balham High Road. Its terraces, built between 1898 and 1904, are all exactly alike and indeed similar to all the other terraces in all the other streets round about.

The people who lived there in those days were insurance agents and managers of shoe shops, City clerks and minor civil servants. Their modest salaries did not run to motorcars or foreign travel but they managed an annual week at the seaside with the family (Ramsgate, or more adventurously, Bognor Regis), had season tickets on the Southern Railway into town and considered chicken *à la* king to be the height of culinary adventure. Mr Barratt was only selling up and moving away because he had at last become a partner in the Blackfriars accountancy firm where he had worked for the past thirty years and Mrs Barratt insisted on a better area, since 'the tone of Amen Road has been going down and down'.

They moved into number 35 as newlyweds when the house had just been built. In those days, as Mrs Barratt remarked, most of the houses at 'the better end' of Amen Road had a 'tweeny' or between-maid living in. Now that tradespeople were settling, the Barratts were moving several notches up the suburban scale to a mock-Tudor semidetached at Purley.

A bedraggled girl in cap and apron answered when Jenny

called by appointment with the estate agent at Streatham Hill, bringing Frank with her. Like an earl guiding visitors round his stately home, 'Sir' showed them the front, or 'best' room, dining room, kitchen and hall, complete with hatstand and umbrella rack.

Then he led the way upstairs to view the two double bedrooms, the aptly named boxroom (where the resident drudge slept) and the bathroom – but no lavatory. *That* was outside, reached from the kitchen back door through a glass-paned lean-to where geraniums were growing in pots. The house was heated throughout with coal fires.

'The Conservatory,' announced Mr B. with a courtly wave of the hand. Number 35 clearly was his castle. Frank breathed in the smells of damp compost and fecund foliage and thought it rather like a bit of the Indian jungle, an impression heightened by the eyes of the cat glinting from gloomy recesses beneath the shelves.

But Mr Barratt was now leading them up a path of crazy paving, crossing the rectangle of shaven grass to point out the Rockery, the Rhubarb Bed, the Cox's Orange Pippin Tree and the Olde English Rambler on the fence.

'Takes a ton at a time,' he remarked in passing the coalshed to open the door of another wooden shed, this one with a window. Tools hung in neat rows on hooks in the walls and there was a workbench. A faint aroma of pipe tobacco hung in the air. Mrs Barratt frowned on smoking indoors.

'I'll be taking the vice with me,' said Mr Barratt. He meant the vice on the bench. 'I dabble in carpentry – made a gramophone cabinet last year.'

There was not a woodshaving to be seen.

'I can keep my bike in here, and yours too, Mum,' piped up Frank. 'I'll do all the repairs.'

'I'll be sad to leave,' said Mr Barratt, heaving a little sigh. 'We've had some good times here.'

After they had gone Mrs Barratt asked her husband: 'Is she a widow?'

'I don't know,' said Mr Barratt. 'I didn't ask.'

'You never ask *anything*,' remarked Mrs Barratt testily. 'You did ask our price, I hope?'

'Well, as a matter of fact dear, she offered £285.'

'That's £10 less than we advertised at,' pointed out Mrs Barratt. 'You didn't accept, surely.'

'Well, yes I'm afraid I did dear. She's a *lady*. We'll be leaving number 35 in good hands.'

The lace curtains in Amen Road twitched repeatedly as one removal van left with the Barratts' furniture and another arrived with the worldly possessions of the Coles. These included, the neighbours were interested to note, a yew-veneered upright piano with brass candlestick holders. Jenny acquired this from a saleroom with part of the £10 she had saved herself by driving a hard bargain with Mr Barratt.

She could not play the piano, despite attempts in her childhood to teach her, and she hoped that Frank would make up for this musical deficiency in the family. Alas, he showed no aptitude and the piano stood in the front room at number 35 lovingly polished, but unplayed. Possession of a piano, however, registered impressively on the Amen Road social scale.

Try as they might, inquisitive neighbours discovered very little about the newcomers beyond the supposition that Mrs Cole the midwife was bringing up her son on a war widow's pension supplemented by family inheritance. The fact that she bought the house and sent her son to college indicated that her people must be well off. Jenny kept her distance. She nodded civilly over the garden fence to Mrs Glover, wife of the Prudential agent who lived on one side, and replied with a smile to the hearty 'Good mornings' of Mr Dinnage, the Hoover salesman who lived next door on the other side. But attempts to engage her in conversation were politely but firmly resisted. Mrs Cole seemed respectable and kept herself to herself – Amen Road approved of that. It was a quiet road with hardly any motor traffic along it. Nobody in the entire road possessed a car. The morning milk and coal deliveries arrived by horsedrawn cart. Whistling boys on bicycles delivered newspapers, groceries, the Sunday sirloin.

Jenny and Frank went their separate ways by bicycle – she on her midwifery calls, he in college cap and blazer to school across the urban hills of South London, a journey of panting ascents and rushing descents, especially when he was late.

Despite Jenny's chiding, his attention to his lessons at St Wilfrid's did not become noticeably keener. He was utterly bored by school and had no real friends there, certainly none to compare with Jack Harris. Jenny, naturally enough, worried about him, but was too immersed in her demanding occupation to do much about it. Her change of address made no difference to the ringing of the phone or the doorbell at all hours of the day and night.

The doorbell was rung on that warm summer's evening in 1933 by a young man of about twenty with close-cropped dark hair. It rang again, even more urgently in the few moments before Jenny answered the door.

'Mrs Cole?' he asked, and when she nodded, went on, 'One of our neighbours gave us your address. It's me Mum, see. Screaming the place down.'

'You mean she's in labour?'

The young man looked doubtful.

'Having a baby . . .' Jenny prompted him.

'Yes, that's right, Mum. That's what it is.'

'How old is she?'

'I don't know exactly,' he said, 'but she's over forty.'

'Any brothers and sisters?'

'Three of one,' answered the youth. 'And four of the other. Look, can we hurry?'

'Stay calm, young man,' Jenny told him. 'I will be with you in just a moment.'

She reappeared in just a moment with her old-fashioned upright bicycle with the Gladstone bag in the wicker basket. Despite the heat, her wide-brimmed felt hat was in position secured with pins *and* a ribbon tied under the chin.

'What is your name?' she asked.

'Dawson,' he said. 'George Dawson.'

'And is your father at home, George?'

'He's *never* at home when he's wanted,' answered George savagely.

He was wearing plus-fours, *à la mode*, and the bicycle which he had parked at the front gate was a stripped-down racing machine.

'Lay on, Macduff,' called Jenny, mounting her machine at the kerbside. She had the greatest difficulty in keeping up with George as he led the way into the maze of sweltering back streets between Brixton Hill and Clapham Common. Although it was late evening it was still light and the pavements were crowded with children, playing hopscotch and marbles, girls skipping to rhymes, boys flicking for cigarette cards.

'Slow down, young man, slow down,' panted Jenny. 'You're leaving me behind.'

'Nearly there now,' shouted George over his shoulder.

His home was in a street which looked about the same length as Amen Road, and indeed the houses in it were very similar, too, yet, for all that, it was clearly lower down that unwritten scale of infinite gradations depending on which side of the park, which end of the street, one's job, one's furniture, one's relations, even in the last resort one's number. Number 61, where young Dawson came to rest, was badly in need of a lick of paint and the privet hedge which guarded its little patch of front garden was unclipped and unkempt. Loud screams emanated from the open bow windows upstairs.

Watched by a little knot of curious neighbours and their children, Jenny marched up the path to the front door in the wake of George. In the tiny hallway she paused only to ask him: 'Is there any rickets or tuberculosis in the family?'

A girl of about sixteen butted in: 'No, we're all as fit as fleas. Ma never has a day off except when the stork calls.'

'Get those young ones off to bed,' ordered Jenny, pointing at the children who were fighting and bawling at each other but stopped as soon as she came in. She strode on into the back kitchen where an older daughter was standing in the corner, nervously biting her nails.

'You can get all this mess cleaned up,' Jenny went on pleasantly but briskly. 'And boil some water.'

With that, she squared her shoulders, straightened her dynamic, five-foot-one frame and marched upstairs into battle. The grey-haired woman in the bed stopped screaming when she appeared and whispered: 'Thank God you've come, Sister. The pains have been terrible.'

Jenny carefully removed her hat and its pins before she drew back the thin, much darned cotton sheet covering the woman and examined her, gently feeling the hugely swollen belly and listening to the life inside, bursting to get out.

'Everything seems fine,' she said reassuringly. 'Try to get some rest until the next contractions start. I don't think we'll need Doctor. We'll do it between us, eh, just you and me?'

The fact was that panel doctors who looked after the poor were reluctant to turn out for maternity cases unless there were complications. There was no national health service and no antibiotics. Like the doctors, Jenny was kept out at all hours because of the health problems caused by bad diet, bad air and bad drains. Tuberculosis and diphtheria were the contemporary killers. Jenny had brought into the world too many babies who had died in their earliest years from diseases like croup.

She was bitterly aware that people of her own class bought themselves better health. They kept their own teeth longer and their skin had a bloom. They even smelled sweeter than the people among whom she spent her life. It was not just a matter of buying doctors and dentists and the best hospital treatment, but fresh air and tennis courts and holidays at the seaside.

And food. People like Mrs Dawson had to buy food for their families in the most expensive way imaginable. You could buy a large tin of corned beef for 8d but if that was more than you could afford and you bought it by the slice the grocer would charge a penny - and get anything up to twelve slices from the same tin. Some people were forced from necessity and greatly to the shopkeepers' profit to buy their bread in halfpenny slices.

Dr Annie McCall, who trained Jenny in midwifery at Clapham, wisely stressed the need for fresh fruit and vegetables in the diet of pregnant women. Yet most of them could only afford the 'specs', bruised apples, battered tomatoes and half-rotten potatoes for which the greengrocers charged the highest prices they could get. Similarly, the butcher disposed of his flyblown scrag ends and the fishmonger his smelly herrings left on the slab at the end of the day to those who could afford nothing fresher.

Jenny was reflecting on these inequalities as she drew back the faded, threadbare curtains and opened the sash windows to let more air and the last of the evening light into the stuffy room. As she was doing this, the daughter who had met her at the door came in with a tray.

'Thought you might like a cup of tea,' she said cheerily. She had a mop of dark curly hair and a bright impudent face.

'Has your father come back yet?' asked Jenny.

'Not likely,' answered the girl. 'He'll be down at the Bedford. You won't see him till chucking-out time. Beats me how a bloke who's on the dole finds the readies to go down there every . . .'

'Doris!' Mrs Dawson remonstrated. 'Don't be cheeky. It's not your father's fault that he can't find a job and there's millions like him.'

Jenny noticed that Doris made a wry face as she left the room.

There was still no sign of Mr Dawson as darkness fell and the street lamps went on. It was still oppressively hot. The contractions came and went, with Mrs Dawson groaning and tossing about and occasionally screaming out loud again. Jenny sat by the bed, holding her hand, sometimes cooling her brow with a damp flannel.

It was during one of the quiet periods that she heard heavy, stumbling footsteps on the stairs, followed by a knock on the door. She opened it and immediately stepped back. The man who stood there, slightly swaying on his feet, was tall but rather stooped. He had been, could have been still, a handsome man, but his greying hair and moustache were untrimmed and uncombed and there was several days' growth of grey stubble on his chin and jaws. He was in shirtsleeves and braces, without collar or tie.

'How's the Missus?' he asked.

'As well as can be expected in the circumstances,' answered Jenny, then closed the door in his face just as recognition dawned in it with the sound of her voice. It was not the heavy reek of stale beer on his breath which had made her recoil, but her immediate recognition of *his* face in the light flooding out from the bedroom.

3

The last time Jenny and Will Dawson had been together was seventeen years in the past in room 12 of the Commercial Hotel, Brighton. Every minute detail of that room and its dowdy furnishing was etched in her mind: the flowered wallpaper, the damp patch on the ceiling where it sloped into a corner following the line of the roof, 'No food allowed in rooms, NO PETS' framed in glass, a chipped chamber pot decorated with violets, the large bed with its black iron rails at top and bottom and a tarnished brass knob at three of the four corners. Heavens, how those bedsprings creaked.

Even now, a middle-aged, respectable woman, she blushed pleasurably at the delirious abandon of that afternoon. Her black felt hat hung on the bedpost which lacked a knob, her black silk stockings cast carelessly aside on the floor. My lady, he said. *My lady*. His military hospital blues and red tie were neatly on a hanger marked erroneously 'Grand Hotel'.

Immediately after that he had been sent back to the Front in France, which he had been dodging for weeks, and she never saw him again although she wrote desperate letters to him telling him that she was pregnant. As she leaned with her back against the door that she had just slammed in his face, her mind suddenly seized on that girl with the impudent face. Doris must have been born around the same time as Frank.

So his protestations that Ivy meant nothing to him, that his feelings for her were dead, were false. He continued to make love to her while he pursued me. And he is still making love to her.

These thoughts were terminated by a sharp cry from the woman in the bed, with the onset of still more violent contractions.

This time the baby was delivered, filling its lungs with the warm summer night air and letting out a shrill yowl of greeting. Jenny was too busy swabbing the infant, tying the umbilical cord and disposing of the placenta to ponder on the extraordinary coincidence of coming to this house.

The youth who had fetched her and his sister were waiting anxiously on the landing outside the room listening to the baby's cries.

'It's a boy,' announced Jenny, going out to them. 'A beautiful bouncing boy. Where is your father?'

'Downstairs,' said the young man and, pressing a ten-shilling note into Jenny's hand added: 'Thank you for all you've done.'

She found Will in a barely furnished back room, slumped over a table covered with a piece of well-worn oilcloth. An empty bottle of Courage pale ale was at his elbow. She touched him on the shoulder, noticing as she did so that he was going bald on the crown. The blue eyes which looked up at her – the colour of cornflowers on a summer's day – were filled with tears.

'Jenny,' was all he said, in a flat voice. 'Jenny.'

'You have a son,' she told him. 'A fine, healthy son. Aren't you going to go up and have a look at him? And your wife, what about her?'

'I don't want to see it,' he answered bitterly. 'Or her. It's just another mouth to feed. I didn't want it, neither did she.'

His son came into the room and asked Jenny: 'Will she be all right now?'

'Yes,' she assured him. 'She's rather weak but all she needs is rest.'

'Fat chance of that,' replied the young man, 'with *him* around.' And with that he turned on his heel and left.

'My eldest,' said Will, twisting his mouth into a smile. 'Fine boy, isn't he? A credit to his father. He sells wireless sets, earning good money, so he struts around as if he owns the place. Treats me like dirt. And he's not the only one . . . Those bastards at the labour exchange and their bloody means test. Because the older ones are out at work they've even stopped my miserable twenty-nine and threepence a week. I have to rely on *him* to pay the rent and slip me the odd half crown for a pint and a packet of fags.'

'Ivy shouldn't have any more children,' Jenny told him. 'You were lucky there weren't any complications this time – childbirth's extremely dangerous for a woman of that age. Still, you've got a fine baby son.'

He said nothing but sat staring fixedly at the wall. After a moment or two he started to speak: 'I had it made, you know Jenny. Clerk of Works for old Charley Holmes down at West Wickham, spec building, the bloody cash was rolling in. Two per cent mortgage on our own house, Sunbeam tourer on HP. The car was repossessed by the finance company. We lost face with the neighbours. Couldn't give Holmes' Sweet Homes away, much less sell 'em. Started going to the dogs, literally. I had a bad run of luck at Catford and, expecting it to turn, I – well – borrowed some money from the firm which wasn't mine. Only my luck didn't turn, the auditor popped in one afternoon without warning. Some of the figures didn't tally. Everyone's on some kind of fiddle in the trade – kickbacks, backhanders, materials, time sheets and the like. The old man always turned a blind eye to it. Well, this time he didn't. He put the law onto it and I got six months hard labour. Ivy had no option but to sell up – she couldn't keep up the mortgage repayments with me inside. That's how we ended up in this dump. What chance have I got of getting a job with three million on the dole and me having done time?

'Don't think I haven't tried though. By God, I've tried. I've even walked, yes walked, from here to Surrey Docks to try and get a day's work. Imagine it, forty or fifty men waiting at the gates hoping for just one day's work, and then when you don't get it, trudging all the way home again with empty pockets and an empty belly. Here, take a look at these . . .'

With a gesture that was so dramatic it verged on the comic, he pulled off one of his shoes and held it up so that she could see the holes in the sole, patched with bits of cardboard, and the worn-down heel.

'See?' he almost shouted, shaking the shoe in his hand. 'That's what Will Dawson is down to – shoes mended with cardboard. I've even thought of going to sea. At least it'd be better than hanging around here being sneered at by my son, and rotting. Cadging a tanner for a pint of wallop. Nipping Woodbines in half to turn a packet of five into a packet of ten. Bread and potatoes, and still more bread and potatoes. Ships' biscuit and bully would seem like luxury to a chap like me. But first you need a seaman's book and you can't get one of those till you're in the union. And even if you get in the union and get a book you need a pound note or two to slip between the pages when you apply at the docks office, just to ensure that you get selected.

'Oh, I'm sick of it Jenny. I know I'm not a good father. I should be sitting here of an evening cobbling the children's boots, and me own, or down on me knees polishing the bleeding lino, or something.'

He started to cough violently. It sounded like the legacy of one of those wartime gas attacks but Jenny noticed that the fingers he placed over his mouth were stained a deep yellowy brown from nicotine.

'You must see that your wife stays in bed for a few days,' she said, picking up her bag to go. 'I'll call in and see her and the baby to make sure everything is all right.'

He stood up and looked down into her face.

'How is the boy?' he asked.

'I've told you – a perfectly normal, healthy baby.'

'No,' he said impatiently, 'not the baby. I mean *our* boy.'

'I wonder you have the gall to ask,' she replied softly but forcefully, 'when you never answered one of my letters and left me to fend for myself.'

'I'd like to see him again,' said Will.

'No,' she hissed back at him. 'Leave it. No good can come of him seeing you. Not now.'

'You're as lovely as ever, Jenny, but you've grown hard.'

'Is it any wonder?'

He looked at her speculatively, then asked: 'You couldn't lend me ten bob, I suppose. Fact is, I'm a week behind with the rent.'

She felt the ten shilling note crumpled inside her pocket and remembered the tone of the young man's voice when he spoke to his father.

'I understood you to say that George pays the rent.'

'Half a crown then?'

'For God's sake, Will, what's happened to you?' she blurted out before turning away and stumbling from the house.

Frank brought a cup of tea into her room in the morning before going out to do his paper round.

'You were out late, Mum,' he said. 'Difficult case was it?'

'Yes, very difficult,' Jenny answered him. She could not bring herself to tell him of the shock she had had, coming face to face so unexpectedly with his father.

4

Throughout that summer, while Adolf Hitler rose to power in Germany, and Noel and Lionel played 'I want to cling to Ivy', the hit of 1933, on their gramophones, worried about their acne and drooled over the prettier girls at the tennis club, my father dreamed of being a writer. In the evenings, when Jenny fondly imagined that he was busy upstairs with his Latin grammar, he was in fact scribbling satirical verse, mocking the fad for Surrealism in art:

What is he? A Matisse?
What does it show?
A foot and toes with eye below.

At school he was in constant trouble for letting his hair grow until it curled over his ears and was thick on the nape of his neck. A 'short back and sides' was the accepted hairstyle and anything varying from this was equated with things artistic, poetic or feminine, which any decent chap would avoid. The most serious activities at St Wilfrid's were games and the Officers' Training Corps.

Frank was obliged to take part, and made a point of marching deliberately out of step. He told the others that they reminded him of the youths in *All Quiet on the Western Front* who were persuaded by the patriotic frenzy of their schoolmaster to become cannon fodder in the trenches. They resented this greatly since the novel was about *Germans*, who were still called Huns or Boches and together with Wops, Frogs, Dagos, Niggers and Wogs (almost anyone with a coffee-coloured skin) were regarded as inferior people, collectively known as foreigners. The British were God's elect, of course.

His friend Jack had left the *Daily Mail* after being advised that the only way to break into journalism was by getting a start on a local weekly. He was now on the *South London Mercury*.

'It's only in the composing room, sweeping up and making the tea,' he told Frank. 'I go home stinking of ink. I've been doing some reports of local clubs and leaving them on the editor's desk, but they always seem to end up on the spike.'

Jack had no time for hanging around street corners on Saturday nights with his old pals, eating fish and chips from greasy newspaper, telling dirty stories, talking about film stars, cup chances, goal scores, the pools and racing tips and whistling after the girls. They told him that Smiler had 'gone birding' and that Bert, whose mother was still a dresser in the theatre, had found himself a peach. Jack was looking for a means of escape from those mean little streets and soot-blackened courtyards which were only a couple of miles away from the Houses of Parliament on the other side of the river but which seemed to him to be a wilderness of vulgarity and shoddiness. He found his escape on a racing bicycle, bought on the 'never-never' from his wages and kept in a corner of the Harrises' already overcrowded living room.

He joined a cycling club, the New Cross Wheelers, and discovered the countryside which lay beyond the teeming streets, smoky little factories and railway sidings – the orchards and valleys of Kent. Frank persuaded his mother to buy him a second-hand racer and joined the Wheelers, too. They competed against one another in the time trials that were held on the

Dover Road early on Sunday mornings before the motor traffic to the coast built up.

One Monday morning during assembly at St Wilfrid's, the head announced that he wanted to see Cole in his study immediately afterwards. He sat behind his desk, immensely dignified in mortar board and gown, and regarded my father unsmilingly.

'Why did you fail to turn out for the Second XI against Dulwich College on Saturday?' he demanded.

'Sir, I was out with my cycling club,' answered Frank, more boldly than he felt. 'In training for a twenty-five yesterday.'

'*A twenty-five*?' repeated Dr Pollen, staring at him uncomprehendingly. Cycle racing was a decidedly working-class pastime, not something for the young gentlemen of St Wilfrid's.

'I completed the twenty-five miles in one hour, eleven seconds, sir,' continued Frank, 'my best time yet.'

'Congratulations,' said Dr Pollen icily, no more impressed than if Frank had set up a new record for polesquatting or marathon ballroom dancing. 'Presumably while you are indulging in bicycle racing on a Sunday you have no time to attend mass.'

He pronounced it 'marse'. Frank's silence was confirmation of his mortal sin and the head proceeded: 'I shall talk to your mother about this, Cole. Also I am far from happy with your lack of interest in the school's sporting activities. It's a pity that you don't show the same enthusiasm for cricket that you show for bicycle racing – you could be quite a useful all-rounder if you put your mind to it. Up school, Cole. Up school! Remember that.'

Jenny went back to the Dawson home several times to check on the progress of Ivy and the baby. She was relieved to find that Will was out when she called, but on her final visit he was there. He followed her down the street afterwards and catching up with her at the corner laid his hand on her arm and said: 'Jenny, I have to talk to you.'

'What about?' she retorted, shaking his hand off and continuing to walk on.

'It's the boy,' said Will, keeping pace with her, 'I have to see the boy.'

'What's the point?' asked Jenny. 'You're a stranger to him. As far as he's concerned, his father died in the war.'

'I won't let on I'm his Dad,' persisted Will. 'Just say I'm an old friend – we met before when he was little anyway, probably he'll remember. Please, Jenny. I've got to see him.'

'No,' she said flatly, stopping in her tracks and glaring up at him. 'I won't allow it, and that's my last word.'

A crowd of men in flat caps hanging about on a corner outside the labour exchange started nudging one another and exchanging winks.

'Leave us alone,' Jenny snapped at Will, feeling embarrassed and humiliated by the attention they were attracting, 'just as you did when he was born.'

He looked at her for a moment as if she had physically slapped him in the face and then, without saying another word, walked away. His shoulders were bowed and he moved with that slouch peculiar to unemployed men looking for cigarette ends in the gutters. There was a trade in such things. Jenny watched him go with pity and with some pain, but no love. That was finally over.

Frank knew nothing of this encounter. But not long afterwards, as he was leaving school one afternoon, a shabby-looking, unshaven man accosted him at the gates. His clothes were ragged and patched and his shoes worn to the uppers and Frank's first impression was that he was a beggar, not uncommon even in Sydenham in those hard times.

He made to hurry past but the stranger blocked his way.

'Frank Cole, ain't it?' he asked, with a sorry attempt at heartiness.

'That's my name,' admitted Frank, eyeing the man uneasily. They were of similar height and build, although the man was stooped. 'How do you know?'

'You don't remember me then?'

Frank shook his head.

'Blackstaff,' the man prompted him. 'The Dawsons. Doesn't that ring a bell?'

The other boys, hurrying past with their satchels over their shoulders, turned their heads in curiosity.

'Go on, Cole,' one insensitive brute called out jovially, 'give him tuppence for a cup of tea. Don't be so stingy.'

The man flushed and shuffled his feet.

'Now I remember,' Frank blurted out. 'You're Stan's Uncle Will.'

'That's right,' replied Will, smiling for the first time. 'But I recognized you straight off even though you've grown so much and look such a toff.'

He indicated the blue and yellow striped blazer and cap and it was Frank's turn to blush.

'Oh, this bally schoolboy rigout,' he said. 'I hate it. You'd think they'd let us Sixth Form chaps off wearing it, but not they. It's compulsory.'

'Don't complain about it, son,' Will told him gently. 'You're very lucky to be going to college. I wish I'd had *your* chances when I was young.'

'I must be going,' said Frank. He found the intimacy of Will's manner more than a little embarrassing and he wondered why he was hanging about at the school gates waiting for him to come out. Remembering his manners though, he added: 'It's been very nice to meet you again.'

'Just a moment,' said Will, touching his arm. 'I want to give you something.'

He pulled a brown cardboard cigar case out of the pocket of his tattered jacket and shoved it into Frank's hands. Frank was even more discomforted to see that the man's eyes were brimming with tears, which Will brushed away with the back of his hand as he turned and walked off.

Inside the flat box, which consisted of two parts, one fitting snugly inside the other, Frank found a tarnished brass cap badge, a sergeant's chevrons and three 1914–18 campaign medals attached to multicoloured ribbons which bore an outsized safety-pin. When he showed them to Jenny and told her of the odd encounter at the school gates, her lips tightened but she made no remark on it.

That very evening she sent off a letter to Will Dawson couched in the strongest terms and warning him to stay away from the boy in future. In fact, Will made no further attempt at contact. It seems that having spoken to Frank and given him his pathetic souvenirs of the Great War he was satisfied. Frank put the cigar box away in a drawer and many years passed before he came to know its true significance.

At the time, Frank was much more interested in some news which arrived in a letter from his friend Jack Harris.

I've finally managed to land myself a job as a reporter. I got so wild about the editor constantly spiking the news items which I kept leaving on his desk that last week I just barged into his office . . . all up to my eyes in ink and grease, and told him I wanted a chance to prove myself. I thought I would probably get the sack for my cheek, but no, he said he'd had his eye on me and as it happened there was a vacancy for an improver in the district office at Penge. The money is not much (twenty-five bob a week) but I don't care about that. This is the chance I have been waiting for. How are things at St Wilfrid's?

Frank saw little of his friend in the next few months, so immersed was Jack in reporting 'fires, fatalities and fêtes' for the *Mercury*. The chief reporter spent most of his time in the Railway Arms, leaving Jack's initiation into the mysteries of journalism to his junior, who was only a year older than Jack but considered himself to be an old hand.

He was only too eager to pass on the routine round of local undertakers and vicars to the new recruit. Jack was an apt pupil. Within a couple of months he was writing to Frank on office letterhead:

You sound very depressed, my boy, judging from your letter but we all have our cross to bear. Mine is a balding old crab called Freddy Harbottle. (Better destroy this letter – I don't want any libel suits.) Believe me, that miserable old bugger is the bane of my life. He sits in the drab old *Mercury* office in Penge – when he's not in the pub that is – calls the woman reporter sweet names and continually barks at me: 'Ow much copy 'a you got, Jack?' Talking of copy, I really turn it out on this paper, AND you have to go and find it. Make no mistake, this district is teeming with really first-class human stories, old boy. Fortunately the subeditor at head office is all in favour of bright angles – and he gives me plenty of pats on the back to offset the droolings of Harbottle. I'm feeling a bit worried because they have persuaded me to sign this agreement. If I abide by it, it means three years in this hole. Sorry to load you with all my petty troubles. Here's wishing goodbye to your 'journalistic doldrums' – why not come over this way next Saturday? I'm covering Crystal Palace Reserves and might be able to give you some useful introductions in the Press Box.

The press box was literally that, a box with an open front and a corrugated iron roof, reached by a short flight of open stairs and commanding a good view of the football field. Frank paid less attention to the game than to the assembled gentlemen of the press. They were an oddly assorted crew. Apart from Jack, who seemed very self-assured, there was a young man in motorcycling leathers with thick black grease under his fingernails and a rosy-cheeked youth in a pinstriped suit who produced a notebook and a pencil box from an attaché case and arranged everything meticulously on the rough bench before the match started. At half time he sat reading a thick volume on economic theory, studiously ignoring everyone around him.

Next to him was a very old man in a tattered ulster coat who kept asking in a shrill, cracked voice: 'Who took the penalty? What's the score?' while scribbling furiously on a sheaf of flimsies.

'He was a reporter in the days when they wore top hats and took notes on their starched cuffs,' Jack remarked. 'He knows everyone and everyone knows him. He's as deaf as a post and when he turns up at the police court the magistrate has to stop every few moments while someone shouts in this old devil's ear and he writes it down. He works for about five weeklies and all the nationals for tuppence a line.'

Despite Jack's blasé manner, his life appeared to Frank to be verging on the glamorous. He wished that he was entitled to take his place on the press bench instead of being condemned to continue in the Sixth Form at St Wilfrid's. Jack Harris was working seven days a week for his 25s, on a never ending round of deaths and weddings, church fêtes and flower shows, golden weddings and retirements, dog shows and council meetings, yet oh, how Frank envied him.

From money earned by delivering newspapers in the morning before he went to school and sweeping up in Woolworth's on a Saturday, Frank bought a typewriter from a pawnshop in the Brixton Road. It was a German machine of obscure vintage, which employed an inked pad instead of a ribbon. The 'e' and 'o' appeared on the paper as indistinguishable black blobs and the machine had an infuriating habit of jumping a space in the middle of a word.

But it was a typewriter and Frank was convinced that if he typed his offerings they would be more acceptable to editors than pages written in a schoolboyish hand. It was an easy matter to learn how to operate it with two fingers, although Jenny found its continual clatter more than a little disturbing.

Her eccentric son was now writing a novel in a style strongly reminiscent of Ernest Hemingway, and although this lonely activity reminded her of her own youthful ambitions, she would have preferred him to concentrate on matriculating at St Wilfrid's.

The results of his examinations were abysmal and he was obliged to attend with his mother a painful interview at the college, during which Dr Pollen observed icily: 'I can hardly discuss with a tutor at Oxford the admission of a boy who shows no sign of applying himself to serious academic study.'

When she chided him on the way home in the tram he reacted heatedly: 'I hate study. I'm not a kid any more – I want to be out in the world. You know that I want to be a journalist like you were, and my grandfather, too. Jack's already got himself a job as a reporter and he's no older than me. Why won't you let me do the same?'

'And why won't *you* see reason,' she flung back at him, engaging the attention of the rest of the passengers on the upper deck. 'Get a place at Oxford. Get a degree. Journalism can come later – if you still want it. You'd be able to get into Fleet Street without having to go through all the drudgery of the *Mercury* or some other local rag.'

'You just don't understand, Mum,' he told her with all the superiority of his seventeen summers. 'Fleet Street won't look at a chap who's had no local-paper experience first. It doesn't matter how many bally Oxford degrees you've got.'

'But I do understand,' insisted Jenny. 'You may not think education matters now, but later you'll see it differently. The poise, the training of your mind, to say nothing of the social advantages of having been up at Oxford – they're all things that will help you in whatever career you take up.'

'Oh heavens, Mother,' replied Frank impatiently, 'times have changed. This is 1934 – all that sort of useless snobbery went out with the Edwardians.'

On politics at least the youthful Frank saw eye to eye with his mother. Jenny had not taken an active part in the Independent Labour Party since the war but she shared the idealism which had led it to break with the rest of the movement and live in what Aneurin Bevan described as impotent purity.

She voted for Ramsay MacDonald in 1924 and 1929 (had he not appointed the first woman Cabinet Minister?) but had become disillusioned with the party's performance in office. She had seen for herself the results of mass unemployment while attending to deprived mothers, and she still cherished the dream of old-style Socialists like her friends at the Woolwich Arsenal for world government and an end to war. She viewed with alarm the rise of Benito Mussolini in Italy and Adolf Hitler in Germany. Now Sir Oswald Mosley, a former white hope of the Labour Party, had formed the British Union of Fascists.

'Some of the chaps at school say he's equipping them with armoured vehicles and even aeroplanes,' Frank told his mother over tea. 'It sounds as if he wants to set up something like Hitler's Sturmabteilung or Mussolini's Squadristi. They got so mad when I called him Musso the Wop. They think he's marvellous, the saviour of Italy and all that. Mosley is just trying to copy Hitler and Mussolini. It really is a joke.'

'Oswald Mosley is no joke,' said Jenny. 'He is clever and he is rich, and like Churchill he's a man of vaulting ambition who switches from party to party as it suits him. When he came back from the trenches he was a Conservative, then Independent, then Labour and after all that he formed his own New Party. When *that* collapsed he went off to Italy to study Mussolini's methods. He would like to be a dictator, too, and he's got the backing of powerful people like Lords Rothermere and Nuffield.'

Frank adored his mother when she talked to him like this as an equal rather than as a schoolboy. Most of his attitudes had been moulded by her and he shared her pacifist ideals. When Dr Pollen belatedly organized a Sixth Form debate intended to repudiate the infamous Oxford Union motion 'That this house will in no circumstances fight for King and Country', Frank spoke vigorously in support of it, and Jack Harris was in the audience as the local reporter, trying hard not to throw aside his notebook and applaud.

In fact there were more boos than applause for Frank from the Old Boys who rallied from university or their respectable shipping offices and banks in the City to pack the school hall.

'War is anti-Christian,' he declaimed, with all the passionate conviction of his seventeen years. 'There is no such thing as a "just war" – that is the meaning of the . . . '

'Who's going to stop the Reds?' called out one of his schoolfellows.

'He's a Red himself,' shouted another. 'Red Cole.'

And the body of the hall took up the chant 'Red Cole, Red Cole . . . ' until the chairman called several times for order.

'Communism isn't the real threat to peace,' Frank continued, when he was able. 'Fascism is.'

'Rot! Rubbish!' was the answering cry. 'Sir Oswald Mosley believes in England for the English. He believes in strong government.'

'Well if you think Mosley's such a great man, why don't you join his Blackshirts?' Frank taunted them.

'Perhaps we will, eh chaps? Perhaps we'll show the . . . '

The rest of the cry was drowned in jeers and catcalls. The motion that Wilfridonians would 'gladly fight – aye, and die if necessary – for King and Country' was carried overwhelmingly. Thinking it over in bed that night, Frank was seized by a bold idea. The only way to find out what Fascism was really like was to join the movement.

That's what I'll do, I'll join the Blackshirts myself and expose their odious tactics from the inside. There's got to be a way out of that third-rate cramming machine, and this could be it. Fleet Street will jump at it. And won't Jack Harris squirm with envy when I've done it.

The very next morning, a Saturday, he cycled across Clapham Common and Chelsea Bridge to the Black House, the derelict former theological college off the King's Road, where Mosley's headquarters was located. He locked and chained his bicycle to some railings, took the clips from his trouser bottoms, straightened his tie and strolled up to the door.

A large Union Jack floated lazily in the breeze above the building and posters on the walls proclaimed: 'Fascism is Practical Patriotism' or demanded: 'Shall Jews Drag Britain Into War?'

Despite his outward show of sangfroid, his heart was hammering furiously. He half expected to find the place surrounded by armed guards with swastika armbands and fierce dogs, but there were just a few youths in black shirts leaning idly against the walls.

'Where do I join the BUF?' Frank asked one of them.

The youth gestured to a white painted door with a brass knob, just inside the entrance hall. A notice on it said: 'Please Enter.' Inside was a spacious, high-ceilinged room with a portrait of Sir Oswald Mosley above a marble fireplace and on the opposite wall a map of England dotted with little black buttons, each presumably denoting a Fascist cell or, as they were sometimes called, barracks.

A middle-aged man rose from the paper-littered desk in front of the window and greeted Frank with one arm raised stiffly forward. He was dressed totally in black, with shiny jackboots and breeches wired to make them seem even more voluminous than they were. His hair was dyed black and plastered flat against his skull, glistening with brilliantine, and his moustache was a thin black line which might have been drawn across his upper lip with a crayon. All in all, he looked like an actor made up to resemble the portrait of his leader.

When he spoke it was with a peculiarly clipped, nasal accent: 'What can Ai do for yeou?'

'I want to join,' replied Frank, struggling against an impulse to laugh at this absurd little man.

'Then you've come to the right man,' he said. 'I'm Redbarn, the recruiting officer. Do take a pew, old chap. First, I'd like you to fill in this little form.'

When Frank had supplied particulars of himself, Redbarn checked the form over, making delighted little clicking noises with his teeth and tongue.

'Capital, capital. Privately educated . . . OTC . . . trained to use the Lee Enfield rifle. We need more chaps of your calibre. Tell me, Cole, what are your politics?'

'I'm fairly apolitical really. I just can't stand the bloody Yids.'

Redbarn permitted himself a thin smile. 'Of course,' he said. 'We are not anti-Semitic. We are not anti-anyone, we're merely pro-British. We believe in discipline to keep our Empire great. As the Leader said after seeing Mussolini – Fascism is a new system of government which produces a new type of man. If the Jews or anyone else get in our way they will be dealt with. How many evenings a week can you attend for lectures and training?'

'As many as you want,' Frank told him.

'Capital fellow. And weekends, too?'

'I can't wait.'

'We'll have to check you out first, you understand,' said Redbarn. 'One can't be too careful. Reds everywhere.'

Frank's heart sank at this. If they checked with even a few of the boys who went to his school the game would be up. But either Redbarn's caution was just talk or the vetting procedures were simply not conscientiously carried out. In any event, Frank received his orders (under plain cover) within a week.

On his first evening he was issued with a black shirt and a truncheon. Lockers were provided and he travelled to and from the Black House in his everyday clothes, changing into uniform only when he was within its walls. He did not tell his mother or anyone else that he had joined the BUF.

His fellow recruits had been selected for their potential as strong-arm stewards at political meetings. They were mostly semiliterate working-class youths who had been on the dole since leaving school and were only too glad to find some outlet for their frustrations. The political lectures seemed to be completely over their heads and in any case they were under the voting age of twenty-one. Frank's questions at the lectures and his diligent note-taking quickly marked him out as a potential leader.

He discovered that of all the odd fish in the BUF (including William Joyce, later to become notorious as Lord Haw-Haw for his 'Gairmany calling' broadcasts) there was none odder than Redbarn. He had been a conscientious objector during the war and a member of the Independent Labour Party, several of whom had rallied to Mosley under the banner of Fascism.

He obviously swallowed Frank's story completely. Indeed, he took a great liking to him and after less than a month invited him to take part in 'an operational mission'. Neither Frank nor seventeen other Blackshirts who left the Black House late one Friday evening in an unmarked, closed van had any idea what their mission was. They loaded the van first with cooking and camping equipment under Redbarn's eye but he refused to tell them where they were going. He merely laid one finger along the side of his nose and looked sinister.

Frank had told his mother he was off on a weekend outing with the New Cross Wheelers. He reflected that she would have been horrified had she known what company he was, in fact, keeping. Redbarn, a trench coat covering his black shirt and breeches, sat up front with the driver as they rattled noisily and uncomfortably through the night in the windowless van, unable to look out for any landmarks or signposts.

When the vehicle came to a final halt, Redbarn came round to lower the flap and they tumbled out onto the dewy grass of a meadow.

'Get the tents pitched, chaps, and turn in for an heour or two,' he commanded.

They stumbled around in the dark, tripping over guy ropes and tent pegs and cursing, but eventually two bell tents were erected. Frank awoke to cocks crowing at first light and, leaving his fellow Blackshirts asleep, crawled out of the tent to reconnoitre. On the other side of a hawthorn hedge was a signpost reading 'Hunstanton 7 miles, King's Lynn 9', and in a cottage across the way a radio was playing 'I Want to Cling to Ivy'. Frank deduced that they were still in England and had not been spirited away in the night to Germany.

Redbarn emerged from his tent immaculate in black shirt and breeches and carrying a cane. He strutted towards Frank, cutting a ridiculous figure as he fastidiously avoided the cowpats.

'Up with the lark, what,' he called out. 'Tell the men to fall in *toot sweet*, as they say in France.'

It was difficult to prise the rest of the force out from their blankets but eventually they formed a ragged line, yawning and rubbing their eyes, while Redbarn strode up and down, whacking his breeches with the cane and yelling like a sergeant major. A more bizarre sight could hardly have been imagined but there were no spectators other than a few cows.

'We're here to protect the rights of a true-born Englishman against the victimization of a Jewish landlord,' Redbarn informed his stormtroopers.

He omitted to tell them that the doughty yeoman who was due to be evicted from his tied cottage that morning had not asked for the protection of the BUF, indeed he had never heard of it. But news of his plight had been passed to headquarters by a local cell, and there they were. No one was more astonished than he when a column of Blackshirts marched through his gate and posted themselves around his humble dwelling. A couple of hikers stopped and peered over the hedge.

When reporters arrived Redbarn went self-importantly from one to another demanding to know who they represented. One admitted to being there on behalf of the *News Chronicle*, which was outspokenly against Mosley.

'You'd better clear off while the geoing's good,' growled Redbarn through gritted teeth.

'What right have you got to . . .' the reporter began, but Redbarn cut him short.

'Unless you'd like to end up in the pigsties over there, where you belong.'

Some of his bullyboys moved forward menacingly, twirling their truncheons, and the reporter hastily withdrew a hundred yards or so to a telephone kiosk. Redbarn puffed out his chest and paced up and down until the bailiff arrived, accompanied by the village constable.

'What's a-going on 'ere?'

'We're here to protect the rights of true-born English . . .' Redbarn began, but now it was his turn to be interrupted.

'And who might you be, sorr?' inquired the policeman.

'We are members of the British Union of Fascists.'

'Look more like a concert party,' called out one of the hikers.

'Well now,' said the officer calmly, pulling out his notebook, 'I'm a member of the Norfolk Constabulary and *I'm* here to see that the bailiff is allowed to get on with his duty under the law of the land. I don't want to have to take no names if I can help it.'

The youths in black shirts looked uncertainly towards their leader. He glared ferociously at the constable but meeting an unwavering, almost placid, stare he suddenly went very red in the face and looked down at his mud-spattered jackboots.

'Fall in, men,' he muttered. 'Er – feollow me.'

As he led his ragged column off down the lane in his absurd pantomime pantaloons he turned and called out: 'Let this be a lesson to Jewboy landlords.'

Of course it was a propaganda exercise. They took their time on the return journey to London, camping overnight on Saturday just outside Colchester. Old ladies on their way to church to the sound of bells on Sunday morning were confronted by the Blackshirts marching past with hands stiffly raised, chanting 'Hail Mosley'.

Frank heard one Jewish grandmother with her wig all askew muttering in an alien tongue at the marchers. But the whole thing was a cheap deception. The van dropped them in quiet side streets in a number of small towns and picked them up out in the country again after they had strutted ostentatiously along the High Street. In this way Mosley hoped to convince the public that he had thousands of supporters all over the country.

5

The climactic experience of my father's brief 'service' with the Blackshirts was a rally at Olympia, the great stadium in Kensington. For thirty minutes the massed faithful chanted 'M-O-S-L-E-Y. We want Mosley' before a fanfare of trumpets signalled the arrival of 'the Leader'. The black figure moved slowly and deliberately towards the platform with one arm stiffly raised, his dramatic entrance emphasized by the blue glare of intersecting limelights.

As he proceeded down the gangway the ranks of Blackshirts rose, arms extended, and roared 'Hail Mosley!' Joining the chorus, Frank noted that Mosley had a gammy leg which he was obviously at pains to conceal. He stood feet apart on a dull pink drugget, thumbs tucked inside his broad leather belt, eyes glinting fiercely in the bright light focused upon him.

As soon as he started to speak ('rapidly without a pause for breath and without notes as if he was a robot with a magnetic tape inside,' wrote my father), interruptions came from the gallery and were brutally suppressed by the stewards.

'You can see how badly a Blackshirt force is needed to defend free speech in Britain!' shouted Sir Oswald, and a man who retorted: 'Does Hitler stand for free speech?' was promptly knocked to the floor and punched. All interrupters were frogmarched from the hall and scrimmages kept breaking out, but Mosley continued his harangue without pause until a shower of leaflets descended on the heads of his audience and a voice high above cried: 'Down with Mosley! Down with Fascism!' Every head turned upwards and every eye focused on a man perched on one of the iron girders spanning the auditorium.

He might well have had a gun or a bomb but Mosley showed no alarm. He simply fixed his gaze on the figure now spotlighted by lamps swung round from the platform and calmly pointed out the danger to him and those 150 feet below. The man began to edge to safety, pursued by several Blackshirts who had clambered up onto the girders. Every time the man stumbled there was a gasp from the crowd, but Sir Oswald simply continued with his speech: ' . . . in the lives of great nations comes the moment of decision, comes the moment of destiny . . . '

As he reached his crescendo, up jumped the front line of Blackshirts, shouting 'Hail Mosley!' As an impressionable youth of seventeen, Frank found it difficult not to be swayed by this handsome, dignified and articulate man and not to join wholeheartedly in the adulation of the crowd. There was so much that was sick and rotten in Britain – perhaps Mosley really was the man of the moment, the leader who would sweep aside convention and the little men who clung to office.

Then someone in the row behind Frank called out: 'Perish Judah. Down with the Jews.'

'Bleedin' Kikes,' shouted another, less educated, voice.

Cheers mingled with barracking from the young Communists and rowdies looking for trouble, and the nastiness of the racial hatreds which Mosley unleashed hit Frank in the guts. Later on fighting broke out in the gallery and, rushing to the stairs with the Blackshirt reinforcements, he was just in time to see a young man, stripped of his clothes and bleeding profusely, hurtling down the concrete steps. One of Frank's associates rushed towards him and started to kick him in the groin with the toe of his jackboot.

The fighting on the stairs was as vicious as any alley brawl. Another half-naked body hurtled down, almost bowling Frank over. It was a young girl, fourteen, or perhaps only thirteen. Her magnolia white skin was scored with long red stripes which could have been caused by an open razor or the nails of one of the girl followers of the Blackshirts. They deliberately grew their nails like talons.

Some of the combatants had pennies wedged between their fingers. Frank had already learned from his compatriots that pennies grasped like this and backed by a short pencil held in the closed fist made an efficient knuckleduster. Moreover, if questioned by the police, this crude weapon dissolved instantly into a handful of seemingly innocent objects.

'Come on, what are you waiting for?' yelled one of his squad, leaping into the fray with his truncheon. 'Let's get the Yids, bash the bloody Isaacs to hell.'

He started laying about him indiscriminately. A pale-faced youth staggered past, his hair matted with blood and more blood pouring from his nose, 'Take that, you Jewboy' ringing in his ears. Frank, feeling an urgent need of air, made for the exit. Outside the hall some of his friends were strapping the young girl that he had seen earlier to a hoarding, in an attitude of crucifixion. The police were just beginning to arrive in strength. Frank sought out a quiet corner to be sick in, and then he went home.

The brutality of his stewards at Olympia lost Sir Oswald Mosley the support of an influential body of opinion within the Conservative Party. Lord Rothermere, whose *Daily Mail* had shouted 'Hurrah for the Blackshirts' campaign', became cooler towards the BUF. Frank no longer attended drill at the Black House but spent long hours closeted in his room. As the frilled lampshade in the back parlour quivered from the unrhythmic clatter of the ancient German typewriter upstairs, Jenny wondered and worried.

Mysterious typewritten envelopes arrived by almost every post and one day Frank told her: 'If anyone calls for me who you don't know, tell them I've gone abroad and you don't know when I'll be back.'

'Frank, what *is* going on?' she asked anxiously. 'You've been behaving so strangely lately.'

'I'm sorry, mother. I can't tell you anything just now.'

The press lords of Fleet Street had just emerged from a circulation battle in which the time-honoured method used by Frank's grandfather to promote *Cole's Weekly* had been employed on a much grander scale to achieve a 'two million readers' figure. First, potential readers were offered free insurance, then all manner of gifts.

Door-to-door bribery was the name of the game, people being enticed to sign an undertaking to become a 'registered reader' with offers of fountain pens and silk stockings, teasets and ladies' underwear, mincing machines and mangles. The *Daily Mirror* promoted its 'Thirty-two Live Pages' with a youthful company of that number who toured the country by motor coach wearing brass-buttoned blue uniforms piped with yellow, handing out ten-guinea prizes.

But it was Lord Beaverbrook's *Daily Express* which reached the two million figure first (at a cost of 8s 3d per reader), shortly after moving into resplendent new offices in Fleet Street. Frank marched into the gleaming foyer of this black glass and chrome edifice and demanded to see the editor. A commissionaire with a full range of 1914–18 campaign medals on his chest looked him up and down before asking: 'Have you an appointment?'

'No, but he'll want to see me,' answered Frank confidently,

patting the large envelope he was carrying under his arm, 'when he knows what's in here.'

'Will he?' said the commissionaire sceptically. 'Wait over there.'

He lifted the phone and Frank heard him saying: 'Front lodge here. Someone wanting to see a reporter. Yes, that's right. Says he's got a story.'

Eventually a bored-looking young man in a bow tie came down and took a cursory glance at the contents of the envelope. It did not seem to interest him greatly. In that era of everything given away for cigarette coupons the pursuit of news had become a secondary activity.

'Try the *Daily Herald* – right up their street, old man,' he said at last. This was standard advice to the crackpots and fanatics who dropped in unannounced and uninvited at all hours of the day and night. The *Herald* was the *Express*'s closest rival at that time. After walking along the Strand and Kingsway, Frank located it in another new office block, a rather more restrained one in plain concrete, at the edge of Covent Garden fruit and vegetable market. The trade unions' own paper had become a part of Lord Southwood's magazine empire.

Frank's reception at the desk was virtually identical to that at the *Daily Express*, except that he had to wait even longer for someone to come down. This time it was a tall young man in a sleeveless red pullover, smoking a pipe.

'What is it then?' he asked. 'Your plan for reviving the League of Nations? A new craze to supplant the Yo-Yo? If it's a warning of invasion from another planet, we're not interested. The first Martian dropped in to see us this morning.'

'This isn't a joke,' snapped Frank. 'Just read this.'

'All right, old man, all right. No need to be touchy.'

Did all Fleet Street reporters call everyone 'old man' all the time?

This reporter, however, did take the trouble to read Frank's offering, flipping rapidly from page to page. Then he went back to the beginning and read it again, more slowly. Occasionally he whistled. His pipe went out and he made no attempt to relight it.

'How do I know you haven't made all this up?' he demanded at last.

'Does it look as if it's made up?' Frank retorted.

'Wait here.'

The reporter disappeared upstairs and Frank had to endure another long wait before he returned and said: 'Come with me. The news editor wants to see you.'

Silently exulting, Frank followed him up two flights of stairs, along a corridor with doors leading off, through an outer office occupied by a secretary and into a large room set at a corner of the building so that its windows looked out in two directions. A man in shirtsleeves at a desk motioned him to take a seat in a leather-covered armchair. He seemed quite young, no more than thirty, and spoke with a slight Welsh accent.

'Did you write this yourself?' he asked, holding up the sheaf of paper which Frank had delivered, and when he nodded, the editor went on: 'It's dynamite, do you realize that?'

He fired questions at Frank for half an hour, courteously but in a manner which suggested that he was not a man to be bluffed. Finally he stood up and asked: 'What's your price?'

'A job on the *Daily Herald*,' said Frank, amazed at the confident tone of his own voice. And that was how my father became a reporter on a national newspaper when he was barely past his eighteenth birthday. Of course, he pretended he was a couple of years older.

Dr Pollen took the news of Frank's departure from St Wilfrid's with commendable fortitude, remarking to the lad's house master: 'We might have guessed that young Cole would end up working for some rotten red rag. Good riddance to bad rubbish, eh?'

When, flushed with excitement, Frank told his mother how he had infiltrated the BUF and gained the confidence of the hated Fascists, only to expose them, she experienced mingled feelings of pride and dread.

'If this article is published they'll be baying for your blood,' she reminded him.

'They can't touch me,' replied Frank, 'not now I'm a journalist. This isn't Germany, you know.'

Jenny gave a sardonic little smile and said quietly: 'Perhaps. But these bullies could lie in wait for you and give you a beating.'

'I'm not frightened of *them*,' answered Frank. 'At heart they're all cowards.'

But Jenny remained deeply worried about the possibility of revenge. Without telling him, she telephoned the *Daily Herald* and spoke to Hannen Swaffer, the man who had been picture editor in her days on the *Daily Mirror* and was now one of the great characters of Fleet Street, equalling Beaverbrook himself in fame. She was reassured but her son was keenly disappointed when he learned that for his own protection his name would not appear on the series of whole-page articles which were being billed on London's buses and in the Underground as 'The Inside Story of Mosley's Private Army – Exclusive'.

Swaffer, an extraordinary figure with flowing white hair, a savant who watched the world go by from a seat at the Savoy Hotel, clapped him on the shoulder when they met and said: 'You will have plenty of by-lines in the future, mark my words, young man.'

A hardened hack in the news room put it more crudely: 'It'll end up wrapping tomorrow's fish and chips, just like all our deathless prose.'

There were those, however, who did not forget the headlines so easily, especially as the general outcry led to legislation banning the wearing of political uniforms and the holding of disgraceful rallies such as the one at Olympia. Soon after my father's series of articles appeared in print, two broad-shouldered young men in trench coats with trilby hats pulled over their eyes called at 35 Amen Road, demanding to see Frank.

'He's not here,' Jenny told them, quite truthfully as it happened.

'When will he be back?' asked one.

'I've no idea – what do you want with him?' she asked, thoroughly alarmed by their truculent manner and sinister appearance. 'Who are you?'

'Never mind who we are, lady,' answered the first man roughly. 'When you see him just tell him we're looking for him, that's all.'

When she passed the message on to Frank he went quite pale although he tried to make light of it. 'It's all bluster, Mum. They're cowards really – they won't do anything to me.'

'But shouldn't you go to the police, get protection or something?' she suggested. 'They really were the most awful people.'

'They don't frighten *me*,' he said boldly.

However, walking through the back streets of Covent Garden on his way home from the office a few nights later, he was grabbed from behind by two men who must have followed him from the *Herald* office, and dragged kicking and struggling into a dark alley.

He felt a sharp spasm in the head from a blow which must have been inflicted by a length of rubber hose because it left no mark, and fists pounding against his chest, ribs and face. He stumbled against a row of dustbins, knocking one of them over with a tremendous clatter, and sank to his knees amidst foul-smelling garbage spread over the cobbles.

Before he could attempt any retaliation, an excruciating pain in the groin doubled him up and the boot which had inflicted it went in again and again.

'Take that you Kike-lover,' hissed a voice in his ear. 'Write any more lies about us and we'll chop your bleeding fingers off.'

In the semidarkness his assailants were unidentifiable shadows. They might have given him a more prolonged going-over but for a sudden shrill whistle blast. A policeman on the beat in King Street heard the commotion and came to investigate. Writhing on the ground, Frank was aware of a lamp shining in his face.

'It's all right, son,' said a kindly voice. 'The buggers have scarpered. Don't try to move – I'll get help right away.'

An ambulance arrived within minutes and took him to the Middlesex Hospital. Only half-conscious, he lay back watching the street lamps flash before his eyes like a continuous chain and listened to the strident jangling of the bell warning other traffic to get out of the way. Although what had happened was scarcely unexpected, he found it difficult to take in.

The casualty officer who examined him was not unduly impressed with his injuries.

'No bones broken,' he remarked laconically, adding more cheerfully: 'Two lovely shiners though.'

Jenny, summoned by phone, arrived within the hour and took him home to Brixton in a taxi. For once he was glad to be fussed over and tucked up in bed. His head was throbbing and every other part of his body felt tender.

'I won't say I told you so,' said Jenny before she put out the light. 'I don't suppose it would make any difference if I did.'

'No, Mum,' answered Frank, trying to smile but wincing instead, 'it wouldn't. It'll take more than a couple of black eyes to keep me quiet.'

6

'That's how to write a story, old man,' said Frank in a loud voice as he ripped the sheet of copy paper from the typewriter and tossed it across the desk to the young man in the red pullover, the same which had greeted him on his first visit to the offices of the *Daily Herald*. His colleague glanced at it and then, without comment, went through it swiftly with a pencil. Then he threw back the piece of paper and went on with his own work, still without saying a word.

Frank retyped the few paragraphs as amended. He knew that if he had said: 'What do you think of this?' his colleague would have said: 'Very nice' and politely handed it back. Trevor Morley was a very nice man. This way Frank benefited from others' years of experience on this and lesser papers but unfortunately acquired at the same time a reputation for being a bumptious little upstart.

My father always said that after his dramatic debut in Fleet Street at such a tender age everything afterwards was bound to be an anticlimax. Certainly, even before the black eyes had faded, his young-hero status had begun to fade, too. Although hired at £10 a week, a fabulous salary for someone of his age, and at a time when a living wage for the father of a family was £3, he was still very much the tyro in a newsroom containing such characters as Swaffer, the pioneer science reporter Ritchie Calder, and the highly respected diplomatic correspondent W.N. 'Trilby' Ewer, who as a young man on Lansbury's strike sheet penned the memorable lines:

How Odd
Of God
To Choose
The Jews.

Small wonder that Frank sometimes felt, despite his inflated salary, more like an office boy than a reporter. In his premature efforts to become a man of the world, he took to shaving twice a week before it was really necessary, and smoking a briar pipe, which laid him open to a good deal of ragging from his older colleagues.

At least he was able to compensate for his lowly position in the *Herald* newsroom by lording it over Jack Harris, who was still tied to the parish pump and suffering cruelly at the hands of the almost permanently pickled Harbottle.

The *Mercury* office was in the High Street at Penge, sandwiched unbecomingly between a shoe repairer's and the Kozy Kafe. Frank found his friend in a small room at the top of a flight of uncarpeted stairs, tapping away at a battered Imperial typewriter among a farrago of papers, council minutes, clippings, wire trays, gluepots, dirty cups, spikes and scissors.

His eye, however, immediately lighted upon Jack's colleague, who had shingled blond curls and a boy-slim figure.

'This is Elaine,' said Jack, looking up from his typewriter and wryly noting the direction of Frank's gaze. 'She's our Bright Young Thing.'

He treated her as one of the lads, with good-humoured familiarity, but Frank took an altogether more flattering attitude towards her, in keeping with his man-of-the-world pose. And she was suitably impressed when she learned that he was on a national paper.

'How about a quick one across the road?' Frank asked Jack.

'I've got to finish these blasted flower show results first,' said Jack. 'Why don't you take Elaine? I'll join you as soon as I can.'

'Love to,' answered Frank, and Elaine agreed just as readily.

When Jack finally escaped to the Railway Arms he found them, heads close together at a corner table in the saloon bar, engaged in earnest conversation.

'Mine's a half,' he said to Frank, and to Elaine. 'What's that you're drinking?'

'Gin and It,' answered Elaine proudly.

'I wanted her to try a Pimm's,' said Frank, 'but of course they don't have it in this one-eyed hole.'

'A half of shandy's usually good enough for her,' retorted Jack, stung by his friend's criticism of his favourite watering hole.

'Frank says all his drinks are on exes anyway,' Elaine informed him in a crushing tone.

Frank returned from the bar with another round and then took out his pipe and a shiny new tobacco pouch. Elaine gazed at him with her chin in her hands and cooed: 'I simply *adore* men who smoke pipes.'

At this point Jack almost choked on his half of bitter. He never ceased to marvel at Elaine's ability to get any man, of whatever age, eating out of her hand. She had only to cross one shapely leg over another and hitch her skirt half an inch higher to have Harbottle at her mercy.

Jack returned from covering a minor league soccer match one Saturday evening to catch sight of Elaine, dressed to the nines, jumping into a little sports car which he immediately recognized as a GN two-cylinder motor. He had difficulty in recognizing the young man at the wheel as his friend Frank Cole, since Frank was wearing a check cap and jacket with a green silk scarf tied inside the open collar of his shirt, *à la* Ronald Colman, and fashionable plus-fours.

'Hello, old man,' he called out when he spotted Jack. 'What do you think of the beast?'

'Very nice,' replied Jack, dismounting from his bike. 'Is it yours?'

'Will be,' said Frank, 'when I've finished paying the instalments to the finance company.'

He vaulted lightly out, without bothering to open the door, ran his hand lovingly over the louvred bonnet. Jack saw with a further shock that he was wearing two-tone shoes.

'Fast piece of goods,' continued Frank with proprietorial conceit.

'You mean the car?' remarked Jack caustically.

Elaine attended to her make-up in her compact mirror and pretended not to hear. She had evidently forgotten about going to the second house at the Penge Empire with Jack, who was regularly given complimentary tickets by the manager.

'We're off up West for the evening,' she said haughtily.

'Care to make it a threesome?' Frank asked Jack without much enthusiasm. 'There's a dickey seat at the back.'

'No thanks, mate,' replied Jack in an exaggerated South London accent. 'It's the rich wot gets the pleasures – I've got work to do.'

'Well, cheer-ho then,' said Frank, jumping back into the driving seat, 'Have fun.'

'Bye-eeh,' called Elaine.

Jack watched the low-slung little red car roar off up the hill in the direction of the Crystal Palace.

'What do you think of the motor, old boy? Huh! And him working for a so-called Socialist paper.'

And with this bitter thought, Jack Harris let himself into the

Mercury office to start writing up his football report. Later he might permit himself a half of bitter in the Railway Arms, which was about as much luxury as the National Union of Journalists minimum wage for suburban office juniors afforded.

Frank Cole, on the other hand, as well as being paid a tenner a week, was allowed 'exes'. Trevor Morley had initiated him into the devious arts of filling in expenses forms, which called for much effort and not a little imagination as he was confined to making routine telephone calls, sorting copy on the news desk, doing the shifts that no one else wanted to do, sitting through the small hours in a silent newsroom after everyone but the late subeditor had gone home, waiting until the presses downstairs had disgorged the final edition. Outside the office one walked on a carpet of squashed tomatoes and cabbage leaves as the market awoke with the sparrows, and even at that hour it was possible to get a cup of tea or a pint of ale at the Nag's Head just across the way from the Royal Opera House.

Frank was fascinated by the nightlife of London and in a period of falling prices he could afford to spend freely on clothes, the latest gramophone record of Al Bowlly, who was Elaine's favourite crooner, dining out at the Metropole or fox-trotting until three at the Café de Paris in Coventry Street. Elaine was only too happy to encourage him in developing expensive tastes.

Jenny met her only once, when Frank brought her to tea on a Sunday afternoon, but that was enough to put her in the category of 'a bad influence'. Jenny immediately concluded that her cherished only son had fallen into the clutches of a gold-digger who wore too much make-up, smoked and drank to excess and was twenty-five if she was a day. She could also see that Frank was besotted by the woman and it would be foolish to antagonize him by criticizing her.

He often hinted that he would like a place of his own in town and Jenny did not want to give him an excuse to leave home by rowing with him over Elaine. When he arrived home with the milk and stayed in bed after noon, when the racket from his latest record of Count Basie or Joe Loss made her head ache, still she kept the peace. She could not bear the idea of losing him.

Secretly, Frank was ashamed of living in a poky little house on the wrong side of the river. Although he collected some smart and fashionable friends in his rounds of the clubs, he never brought them home to meet his mother. One of these acquaintances, the director of one of the many small airline companies competing with Imperial Airways, gave Frank a couple of plane tickets and an invitation to 'hop across the Channel for the weekend, old sport'. Elaine was thrilled at the prospect.

'Mother, could you look out my birth certificate? I have to produce it with my application for a passport – I'm going on a little trip to the Continent.'

This was the moment Jenny had dreaded. She went quietly upstairs and pretended to search through the drawers.

Tell him. Tell him now . . . he has to know some time.

Jenny had never lacked courage before. Indeed, her tiny frame concealed immense reserves, but on this occasion they failed her. Quite simply, she could not bring herself to tell her son the truth about his birth.

'I can't seem to find it anywhere,' she told him.

'Oh, what a nuisance,' said Frank. 'Still, never mind, I'll pop into Somerset House tomorrow and get a copy.'

She had to turn away so that he would not see the blood draining from her face, leaving it the colour of putty.

He came home late the next evening and hardly a word was spoken throughout dinner. Finally, Jenny could stand it no longer.

'Frank, what's the matter?' she asked.

'I think you know what's the matter,' he answered, so coldly that she almost flinched. 'I went to Somerset House today. Why didn't you tell me I'm a bastard?'

'Frank! Don't use that awful word. It's not nice.'

'*Nice*? What has being nice got to do with it? It's not nice to be a bastard – "My mind as generous and my shape as true, as honest madam's issue" – you see I know my Shakespeare, thanks to the good public school education you gave me. No, it's not nice, and it's not nice to be lied to. If you'd told me the truth I would have tried to understand.'

'I wanted to,' she cried, struggling to hold back the tears, 'but somehow I just couldn't.'

'Well, who was he?' demanded Frank, almost fiercely.

'He was already married to someone else, but we fell in love.'

'I want to meet him.'

'You can't.'

'Why not?'

'He was killed . . . in the war,' replied Jenny at last, but she knew as she said it that he would not believe her.

He grabbed her by the shoulders and started to shake her, shouting. 'Why won't you tell me the truth? God help me, if you won't tell me, I'll find him myself.'

She could hardly believe what was happening.

'Frank, stop it. Stop it.'

He suddenly released her and dashed upstairs. She followed, with tears streaming down her face, and found him in his room blindly throwing clothes into a suitcase. Socks, shirts, handkerchiefs, underwear – he jumbled them in together.

'I'm leaving,' he said.

'You can't leave like this, at this time of night,' she protested. 'Where will you go?'

'A hotel. Anywhere. It doesn't matter, just as long as I leave this place right now.'

She knew that he had been wanting to move out for some time, to have a place of his own in town, to avoid the embarrassment of having to admit to his smart friends that he lived in unfashionable Brixton. Perhaps, she thought, he was just using this discovery about his birth as an excuse to leave home.

'Wait,' she pleaded, forgetting her usual restraint and pride in herself. 'You can't just walk out like this. I'm your mother. You're all I have. Please Frank, just sit down and listen to me. I'll explain to you . . . you just don't understand how it happened.'

'It's no use, Mother,' he answered her coldly, continuing to pack his things. 'I'm going. I'm not going to let you ruin my life like you ruined your own.'

Suddenly, she was angry, and spat at him: 'You sound like an insufferable little prig. One day you'll realize how cruel you've been.'

She heard his footsteps heavy on the stairs and the slamming of the front door. For a moment she felt as if she was about to faint. Then she took a long, deep breath, straightened her hair in the mirror and walked calmly downstairs.

'Jenny,' she said to herself and to the silent, empty house as she poured herself a large whisky, 'you should have stayed a virgin.'

The silver-painted de Havilland bi-plane lifted slowly into the sky from the grass runway of Croydon aerodrome, the main centre of London's growing traffic by air. Elaine gazed down at the roofs and chimneys and suburban streets dropping away beneath their wheels and rapidly reducing to Meccano-model size. Beyond the built-up area the ground became a green, yellow and brown patchwork, occasionally obscured by a cotton wool puff of cloud.

'Isn't it exciting?' she shouted in Frank's ear above the roar of the engines driving three big propellors. 'Aren't you nervous?'

'Not a bit,' yelled Frank, a veteran of just one joy-ride at an Empire Day air display. He squeezed her hand. 'Flying's no more dangerous than motoring these days, what with all the traffic on the roads.'

All seven passenger seats were taken and everyone was well wrapped even though it was spring, having been forewarned that it might be chilly in the cabin at altitude. They continued to peer out of the windows at the white cliffs near Eastbourne as they headed out over the English Channel.

Elaine clutched nervously at Frank's hand as they came in to land at the fashionable French resort of Deauville nearly three hours later, bumping to a standstill in what appeared to be an unfenced meadow. The pilot cut the engines and, still wearing his leather helmet and goggles, shook hands with the passengers as they disembarked and were conducted to a wooden shed at the edge of the field.

For their first trip abroad they had chosen a resort whose name spelled sophistication, a place favoured for summer weekends by wealthy Parisians in fast windswept tourers and the sons of the even wealthier Vanderbilts and Rockefellers, sent to Paris to play. It was a place for polo and gambling and watching beautiful women.

After dinner at the Hotel Maurice, where Frank had booked separate rooms, they strolled along the Promenade des Planches, the boardwalk beside the beach. Elaine gazed at bathing suits, cubist sweaters and amusing scarves in Jean Patou's shop in what had once been a beach hut, and sighed like a child looking in the window of a sweet shop, pointing at a brightly striped bathing suit.

'Isn't that absolutely *divine*?'

'I'll buy you it tomorrow,' said Frank impulsively.

'But it probably costs a fortune,' protested Elaine, unconvincingly, as she took his arm and squeezed it.

'Who cares?' answered Frank nonchalantly, enjoying the role

of boulevardier.' I want to see you in it.'

'It's been such an exciting day,' said Elaine as they continued their walk. 'I don't want it to end. Tell you what – let's go to your room and tell them to send up a bottle of bubbly.'

She grabbed his hand and set off in the direction of the hotel, towing him in her wake. The receptionist gave them an appraising glance as Frank collected his key and ordered the wine, in passable French. His slightly impudent gaze drifted towards Elaine, waiting impatiently in the background, and his right eyebrow lifted just perceptibly. Frank scowled at him and headed for the lift.

As soon as they were in his room, Elaine disappeared into the bathroom. He heard the shower running. After what seemed hours she emerged, draped in a huge white towel, and sat in his lap. Her hair, slightly damp, brushed against his cheek like silk. As he kissed her she let the towel fall to the floor and she was naked in his arms.

'I love you,' he murmured, touching her small, fragrant breasts as if they were delicate flowers.

'Let's get ready,' she whispered. 'I can't wait a moment longer.'

'Get ready?' asked Frank.

She drew back sharply and looked at him as if she could not believe her ears.

'D'you mean to say you didn't come prepared for this?'

There was a rough Cockney edge to her voice, very unlike her usual refined tones. Frank stared back dumbly.

'What d'you take me for – a bloody fool?' she demanded angrily. 'D'you think I want to end up in the family way? Well you'd better do something about it quick or this whole weekend'll be a washout.'

She jumped up and wrapped the towel around herself again. Then she lit a cigarette and puffed testily at it while Frank hastily left the room. He knew what was required but he had absolutely no idea what French letters were called in French and he did not care to try to convey what he wanted in sign language to that impudent clerk at the desk.

After walking unhappily up and down outside the hotel for some time, he returned to his room to find that Elaine had departed, having drunk more than half of the bottle of champagne which stood on the table in a bucket of slowly melting ice. He drank the rest, without enjoyment, and went to bed.

First thing next morning he went out to the nearest coiffeur and had a shave, after which he tried to make his other requirements known in halting French. At first the barber was mystified but suddenly the penny dropped and he indicated with a graphic gesture of the forearm and clenched fist that he understood perfectly what Frank wanted.

He went to a drawer beside the till and produced a packet of contraceptives with a flourish, attracting the attention of all the other customers. Bright pink to the tips of his ears, Frank paid and left as quickly as possible. He imagined ribald laughter following him down the street, but nevertheless he was absurdly pleased with himself for successfully carrying out this delicate mission.

Elaine greeted him coolly at the breakfast table.

'Did you sleep well?' he asked.

'Like a top,' she answered. 'No thanks to you.'

'Look, I'm sorry about last night,' he went on, 'I mean, botching everything like that. But it'll be different tonight, I promise you.'

'It had bloody well better be,' she told him bluntly.

They spent the day on the sands. Still sulking about the previous night's fiasco, she eventually condescended to let him hold her hand. He thought she looked absolutely stunning in a costly Patou swimming suit which revealed all of her beautiful back, while she reflected that although his legs were rather skinny he had broad shoulders and a good chest in his black and white striped bathing costume with its white cotton belt.

That evening before dinner they had champagne in her room and he lay on the bed, enjoying the tickling sensation of bubbles in his nose, while Elaine, wearing only a brassiere and camiknickers, sat painting her toenails. Then she spent half an hour at the dressing-table mirror making her eyelashes navy blue while Frank admired her lovely back.

They dined on sole poached in a cider-laced *fumet*, *poulet vallée d'Auge* and ambrosial apple tart with cream and became slightly tiddly after the *trou Normand* pressed upon them by an attentive waiter. They floated on a cloud induced by the combined effects of champagne, fiery Calvados and the *vin du pays* into the casino, where Elaine ended up 100 francs better off from playing the tables.

At long last she glanced at her watch and said brightly: 'Half past two – time for bed.'

She stood up and with just the slightest unsteadiness of step led him towards the lift, pausing only to collect their keys at the desk, where the same receptionist (who appeared to be on duty twenty-four hours a day) followed their progress with the same quizzical expression.

'We'll go to *my* room this time,' said Elaine. 'Your room's got the wrong atmosphere somehow after . . . well, I mean, I hope you're prepared this time.'

'Oh, yes,' Frank assured her, putting his hand in his dinner jacket pocket just to reassure himself. His heart was hammering furiously.

She switched on the lights in her room to reveal a large bed with the covers drawn back and a pale blue silk nightdress laid elegantly across the pillow. She put her arms round his neck and kissed him lingeringly, Calvados fumes mingling in their fast breath.

'Undo me,' she commanded, turning her back towards him, and when he had done so, leaving her short taffeta frock in a crumpled heap on the carpet. Then she kicked off her shoes and sat on the edge of the bed unfastening her suspenders and stretching out one long, slender leg while she carefully peeled the sheer silk stocking from it.

Frank coughed, took off his jacket and moved towards the light switch.

'Don't do that,' she said softly. 'I like doing it with the light *on*.'

He grinned awkwardly, sitting down in a chair to take off his shoes and socks, undoing his bow tie. She had slipped out of her brassiere and camiknickers and came towards him, pressing his hot face against the soft, baby-smooth skin of her stomach just beneath her breasts.

'You're not shy are you?' she asked. 'Show me you're not shy. Kiss me. Kiss me, everywhere.'

Her fingers were in his hair, pressing his lips first against her navel then into the downy golden crown of pubic hair below. She swayed her hips, uttering little gasps of delight, her fingernails digging into his scalp. He struggled to his feet and kissed her fiercely on the lips, at the same time snatching his braces from his shoulders and fumbling with his fly buttons.

'Here, let me,' she said. 'You're such a clumsy boy. Give me the thingummy.'

He reached into the pocket of his jacket hung over the back of the chair and with obviously practised fingers she unwrapped a rubber sheath and slipped it into place, massaging his throbbing penis with both hands. This was an office performed until then only by himself in the dark in the privacy of his own sheets, but that excitement was crude and brief compared to this ecstasy, his masturbatory dreams come true.

Suddenly with another of those little cries, an almost animal expression of mingled pain and pleasure, she sank backwards onto the bed, her legs spreadeagled, drawing him down on top of her. Her voice was like the breaking of waves on the beach outside the window: 'Do it, darling. Do it, do it, do it.'

A solitary beam of bright sun penetrated the chink in the shutters. Frank lay for some time watching the motes dancing and swirling in the concentrated light, trying to remember where he was. A bare arm lay across his chest and silky blonde hair adorned the pillow beside him. From the promenade came the bells of the fiacres and the tinkle of china and glasses drifted up from the café terrace below. Someone, somewhere was crooning the French version of 'Love Is the Sweetest Thing'.

'Did you enjoy last night?' she asked, suddenly awake.

'Unforgettable,' he answered, propping himself up on one elbow and gazing down at her. 'But I can't marry you just yet.'

'I'm not trying to drag you to the altar, you dope,' she said. 'I just like doing it. Don't you?'

'Yes, of course I do, but . . .'

'No buts. Call room service, darling, and ask for coffee and croissants,' she told him.

'What, up here in your room?'

'Where else?' she replied, kissing him lightly on the cheek. 'The French are very broad-minded, you know.'

She got up to go to the bathroom, pausing on the way to bend down and pick up his jacket which had somehow fallen from the back of the chair and lay in a crumpled heap with his trousers. His passport fell from the inner pocket.

Picking that up, too, she opened it: 'I haven't seen your passport photograph. I wonder if it's as . . .'

She stopped suddenly, looking from the black-covered document to him and back again.

'My God, I don't believe it,' she muttered.

'What's wrong?' he asked.

'*You're* what's wrong,' she said, standing there in her nakedness staring at him. 'Eighteen years old. I thought you were a bit younger than me, but *eighteen*, that's ridiculous.'

And then she started to laugh.

'I'll be nineteen in September,' he said earnestly but that only made her laugh the louder.

'I just can't believe it,' she gasped. 'You've got a baby face but I thought that working in Fleet Street you must be twenty-one at least and now I find you're just a kid. Last night was your first time, wasn't it. My God, a virgin!'

'Well, what difference does it make?' he asked her. 'I'm the same person this morning that I was last night and I was man enough for you then. You said I was – remember?'

'It makes a difference to *me*,' said Elaine. 'If you can't see that, well I'm sorry, Frank. I admit I am fond of you but I don't want to be called a cradle snatcher. You'd better find a nice girl of your own age, Frank. We're finished.'

7

Frank and Elaine went their separate ways at Croydon Airport, she to her parents' house in Streatham, and he to his rented room in a large house in Tavistock Place, near London University. A fortnight later when he called at the *Mercury* office hoping to see her, Jack told him: 'She's gone – upped and gave a week's notice last Friday.'

'Gone?' Frank could scarcely believe it. 'Where to?'

'Search me,' said Jack. 'I think she said something to old Harbottle about a job on a paper at Slough, or was it Swindon? I only half heard what she was saying in his office. She didn't tell *me* anything – didn't even bother to say goodbye.'

Later in the saloon bar of the Railway Arms, Frank confided: 'I'm hopelessly in love with her, you know.'

'In love?' retorted Jack, looking at him as if he had just declared that he had typhoid. 'You must be battier than I thought. Elaine's not the sort of girl you fall in love with, anyone can see that. She's a tart, a bit of fluff for old fogies like Harbottle to salivate over.'

'Shut up,' said Frank sharply. 'You don't know what you're talking about. I don't suppose you've ever been in love.'

'I don't get any spare time for courting,' Jack told him. 'Harbottle sees to that. It's all right for you Fleet Street cads on fat expenses . . .'

He looked meaningfully at his empty glass but Frank, staring moodily into space, appeared not to notice.

'. . . mine's a pint of Young's Special. A bloke could die of thirst going for a drink with you. Thanks very much, old man, I thought you'd never ask.'

When Frank returned from the bar to their table in the corner with two brimming pint pots Jack said brightly: 'Cheers! Now take my advice and don't lose any sleep over Elaine. You've had a lucky escape, old man, if you did but know it.'

Frank knew it was good advice but had no little difficulty in taking it. In those days nice middle-class girls did not do *it*, as Elaine called it, until a gold band was securely in place on the proper finger of the left hand.

The fact that Elaine did it uninhibitedly, without charge and with every appearance of enjoyment made her worse than a prostitute; an easy woman, a tart. Of course Jack was right, but it made no difference.

That May, when Amen Road, like nearly every other street in London, put out flags and red, white and blue bunting for the Silver Jubilee of King George V, Jenny discovered quite by chance the death of Will Dawson. She was attending a case in the street where the Dawsons lived when she heard of it from gossiping neighbours. It was the talk of the road.

Will, it seemed, had staggered out of a pub in Bedford Hill directly into the path of an oncoming car and had been killed instantly. Jenny was more shocked by the news than she would have admitted.

'It's a blessing in disguise, if you ask me,' commented the woman who lived next door but two to the Dawsons. 'What that poor woman's had to put up with from him! All those kids to bring up and him boozing away every penny he could get his hands on.'

Jenny called on the Dawson family to express condolences and then attended the funeral at Camberwell Cemetery on the same day that King George and Queen Mary rode in procession through the streets of London. Will's interment, handled by the Co-op, was a plain but dignified affair. Ivy spent money she could ill afford because it was important not to lose face on occasions like this.

Jenny stood on the fringes of the little knot of people around that terminal hole in the ground, a little woman in a long black alpaca coat and a dark felt hat. Ivy was dabbing at her eyes with a handkerchief but the rest of the family, including the handsome grown-up son who had fetched Jenny to attend at the birth of his youngest brother, stood dry-eyed while the clergyman in his white surplice intoned the ritual words from his prayer book.

When he came to the phrase 'ashes to ashes, dust to dust', Jenny could stand it no longer. She turned away and stumbled along the path between the gravestones towards the gate, half-blinded by the tears which filled her eyes. She felt she was making an exhibition of herself by her lack of self-control but in fact her grief did not excite any particular notice.

She was a familiar figure in those parts and no one knew the real reason why she attended the funeral and why she was so upset by it.

As she left the cemetery Jenny found herself muttering the prayer which she had learned by rote at the Sacred Heart convent school: 'Oh God, creator and redeemer of all the Faithful, grant to the souls of thy Servants departed, the remission of all their sins, that through pious supplications they may obtain that pardon which they have always desired.'

No sooner were the words out of her mouth than she rejected them. There is no God, there is no Heaven – it's literally dust to dust when we die. Will loved me and I loved him – the only man I ever loved like that. Now he's dead, gone, buried. There are no angels playing harps for him. All that matters is to go on struggling against the evils of this world, fighting against fate. There is no hereafter.

Walking back to Amen Road, she saw that someone had chalked on a wall 'Flags today. Gasmasks tomorrow.' But the evening papers had forgotten about Hitler and Mussolini for the day. They were full of purple descriptions of the Jubilee parade.

Jenny's personal grief on that jubilant day was mingled with something like relief. She had heard nothing from her son since he stormed out of the house, not even a postcard from the

Continent, and she had been thinking of answering, despite her own misgivings, his demand to meet his father. Now Will's death made that painful introduction impossible and it was unnecessary to lie any more.

Sitting by the front window of number 35, looking out over the common, taking tea from her best china, Jenny thought sadly of Will showing her his wornout shoes, patched with cardboard. Not only had he lost everything he had gained materially, his pride had gone, too. Only fifty and nothing left to live for. Soon he'll be forgotten except by me. If only he had survived for a little while longer he probably would have found new hope. Unemployment's falling at last and there's more money about. The shops are looking brighter and people are better dressed, more optimistic looking.

But if things were getting better in London and the Southeast of England it was a very different picture 300 miles to the north in a little town on the River Tyne called Jarrow. Frank had been sent there by his paper to write a special article on the other England of the Depression, an industrial area which might have been occupying a different planet from the capital gaily celebrating the King's Silver Jubilee.

He travelled north in an express hauled by a streamlined steam locomotive which at times touched 100 miles per hour. He ate a three-course luncheon followed by coffee and cognac in the dining car and returned in a comfortable glow to his first-class compartment to settle his head back against the comfortable cushion, protected by a freshly laundered antimacassar, and watch moors and mill chimneys flashing past the window.

In this euphoric state he was unprepared for Jarrow. Unprepared for the shock of seeing children in the streets without shoes or stockings on their feet, unprepared for the boarded-up shops and grey-faced men and boys standing in groups at every street corner or wandering aimlessly up and down the street pouncing on any stray cigarette end they found in the gutter. Above all, he was unprepared for the ghastly silence hanging over the place and the almost total absence of motor traffic. Since the cruiser *York* was launched at Palmers in 1931 the shipyard gates had stayed locked and Palmers *was* Jarrow.

Frank wrote movingly of that northern town with threequarters of its people on the dole, an article that earned him a prominent by-line and a note of commendation from the editor. At around the same time he wrote an article about the German and Austrian Jewish refugees from the Hitler regime who were beginning to arrive in Britain and were a curiosity in a country where there were very few immigrants.

One of those he interviewed for the *Herald* was a young man of about his own age called Kurt. They met over tea and scones at Lyon's Corner House in the Strand but Kurt's story was far from being cosy. His father had been a high-ranking officer, with many decorations, in the Great War, but his mother was a Jewess and that meant trouble as soon as Hitler came to power.

Kurt described in his heavily accented English how he was arrested because of his opposition to the Nazis in local politics and taken to the Gestapo headquarters in Dortmund. He was asked about his German girlfriend, an association which had become illegal because he was half Jewish. They made all kinds of false accusations and threatened him with internment in one of the notorious concentration camps which the Nazis were already setting up.

But Kurt had been lucky. He had been released from Gestapo HQ with nothing worse than a shorn head and a yellow star on his jacket. They told him he could leave the country within forty-eight hours if he had somewhere to go.

So his parents bought him a train and boat ticket to London, where he was allowed to stay as a victim of Nazi oppression, working as a waiter. His only brother had fled to Holland but his parents remained in Germany, living in a constant shadow of fear. Kurt's story somehow conveyed the very smell of terror which the Nazis had brought to German life.

Generally, the *Herald* tried to look on the bright side. The Depression and talk of war were bad for advertising, and Lord Southwood, as much as the other press barons, was out to sell as many copies as possible. It was his custom to have all the dailies spread out on the floor of his room first thing in the morning so that he could 'see how they looked'.

The *Herald* was looking for 'human interest' stories to fit headlines like 'Little Ada Stops a Flood' or 'Girl Bride Saves Husband's Savings' – it agreed with the American news agency which cabled one of its correspondents: THINK-STUFF UNWANTED. In the next year Frank travelled thousands of miles up and down the country looking for this kind of story. Quite often he found himself on a wild goose chase, and if not the sub-editors usually rewrote everything he telephoned in so that he recognized hardly a phrase of his own in what appeared in print the following morning.

Unlike most of the other reporters, Frank did not complain about this treatment. On the contrary, his enthusiasm was legendary and his patent leather dancing pumps lay in the wardrobe at his Bloomsbury lodgings, gathering dust. Only by constant work could he forget for the while his wistful longing for Elaine, but his dreams were still haunted by her and the few blissful hours they spent together at Deauville before she dropped him. He never mentioned these feelings to Jack Harris when they met for a few beers. He made his life on the road sound like one long, exuberant lark. By contrast, the routine round of courts and councils at Penge seemed very dull.

'As soon as I've finished my indenture on the *Mercury* I'll be off,' Jack wrote to Frank. 'If I have to spend another year in this hole I'll end up strangling that old soak Harbottle. PS: He's had an invitation, by the way, to Elaine's wedding at the famous parish church of Bray. It seems that she's hooked the son of the proprietor of whatever newspaper group it is that she works for, and it is to be a stylish affair, all Brussels lace and orange blossom. Not bad going for a girl of adequate looks but negligible brains.'

8

'Have you got a pair of comfortable walking shoes, son?' asked the news editor benignly one morning. 'And a good mac?'

Frank wondered what was coming next. His recent assignments had included spending a night in the Chamber of Horrors at Madame Tussaud's and visiting a nudist camp. The news editor, a little man with a high-pitched voice that had been known to reduce strong men to tears, was not noted for his sense of humour, however.

Perhaps he's going to suggest that I take a walk to the nearest labour exchange, thought Frank, knowing that the news editor believed that no journalist who had not spent at least ten years on a provincial paper was worth employing on a national.

However, the querulous voice went on: 'Your friends in Jarrow are about to set off to London on foot. It seems that in their adversity they've still got a bit of spirit left. The town council and the mayor have given their official blessing. The editor wants you to go up there with Ritchie Calder and march with them, writing it up as you go.'

As Frank turned to go, he added: 'And I don't want to see any taxicabs on your expenses – shoe leather only.'

He and Ritchie Calder carried packs and groundsheets and slept rough on the bare boards of church halls along the way. The Labour Member of Parliament for Jarrow, Ellen Wilkinson, a fiery-looking little woman with red hair, marched with them.

It was almost three hundred miles to London and they averaged not much more than ten miles a day. The men reminisced cheerfully about wartime route marches and kept their spirits up by playing tunes like 'It's a Long Way to Tipperary' on mouth organs.

In every town and village people turned out to watch their pale, pinched faces, overshadowed by voluminous cloth caps, filing past. There was no begging or rattling of collecting boxes – every penny for the Jarrow Crusade, as it was called, had been raised in advance by public subscription.

While they were advancing slowly through Yorkshire down the Great North Road, in London Mosley's Blackshirts tried to march through the Jewish East End and were stopped in a bitter clash in Cable Street. Standing in line with Ritchie Calder and Ellen Wilkinson, waiting for a dish of porridge and a mug of tea from the enormous, blackened, steaming dixies from which the hunger marchers were fed, Frank saw the photographs of police chasing demonstrators and beating them with truncheons, slogans like 'Get rid of the Blackshirt thugs' scrawled on boarded-up shopfronts and blood running in the gutters.

The Battle of Cable Street was to become a part of the mythology of the British Left, as was the Jarrow March. It was just as well that my father was at the latter and not the former because if some of his former Blackshirt 'friends' had recognized him he would have almost certainly suffered another beating.

When the marchers finally reached London in a downpour after twenty-seven days on the road some of them called at the Ritz Hotel in Piccadilly. Frank wrote: 'They just stood there, dripping water from their oilskins onto the opulent carpets, staring at the silver tea services and the chandeliers, the fountain and the potted palms. The people having tea stared back, looking frightfully upper class. Nothing was said on either side and after a while the Jarrow men left quietly.'

He had no time to meditate on this sad little incident because no sooner had he set foot in the office than the whining voice of the news editor summoned him to the desk:

'The King's holding a small shooting party at Sandringham this week. Sir Samuel Hoare's there and Mrs Simpson is at Felixstowe' – pregnant pause – 'You do know about Mrs Simpson, I suppose?'

Frank had indeed heard of Mrs Simpson via the American papers which were full of her romance with the new King of England. One of them had trumpeted in a headline: 'Mrs Simpson all set to tour her Empire.' But so far the *Herald*'s two million readers, in common with the rest of Britain, had not been told about her.

'Felixstowe is quite handy for Sandringham, isn't it?' said Frank.

'Quite so, son,' replied the news editor, adding sarcastically: 'You know, you could be a journalist when you grow up.'

Despite his tone, Frank knew that the news editor would not be giving him a potential front-page story to handle unless his stock was high. To be sent chasing from one major assignment to another when reporters of twice his age and ten times his experience were kicking their heels around the racks of newspaper files (the forum of the newsroom) was the sincerest form of compliment on his success so far.

He was no stranger to Dersingham, the village at the gates of the royal estate at Sandringham. He had spent hours shivering in the snow-laden wind outside the gates the previous January while the wireless at the Feathers reiterated the mournful news that the life of King George V was 'moving peacefully towards its close'.

Now the leaves were falling again from the old trees in the park and Frank found himself waiting again for his turn to use the one telephone kiosk outside the creeper-covered post office and general store where a silver-haired spinster presided over an antiquated switchboard.

'The King still hasn't arrived,' he reported when he got through to London.

'He must have. The Court Circular says he's at Sandringham.'

'But he's not, I tell you,' insisted Frank. 'I've been watching the gate all day.'

'Listen, son,' said the news editor. 'The Court Circular cannot lie. If it says the King's at Sandringham then that's where he is. Go back and check again.'

This weary routine was repeated all evening and throughout the night. The news editor went home and was replaced by an equally intransigent night news editor, who told Frank: 'I've had my late reporter out in a car checking the route. He's searched every ditch and questioned every village constable between London and Norfolk. We've been in touch with Buckingham Palace. There's been no accident. The King must be there and that's that.'

At five in the morning, Frank crawled back to the cottage where he had rented a bed, as the Feathers was already full of press people. The last edition had gone to press and there was no point in staying up any longer. He was chilled to the bone and dog tired but when he opened the door to his room he found the bed already occupied by the man from the *Telegraph* on the right, Nicholls of the Press Association on the left and in the middle the representative of the *Amsterdam Telegraaf* with his beard sticking up like some medieval saint on a tomb.

He just lay down on the bare boards in his clothes and slept for four hours. After breakfast he went up to the butts – and there was the King, larger than life in plus-fours and a grey-green cloak with a Tyrolean hat, chatting to his guests. Other reporters saw the King showing off the roominess of his new Buick car by curling up inside the boot and drawing the lid down over himself, and they believed that was how he had slipped into Sandringham without being noticed.

Frank's news editor did not want to hear any theories. He merely clicked his teeth over the phone, a sign of extreme displeasure.

Later that day, still smarting from this failure, Frank chanced to get into conversation with a young man in the bar at the Feathers. After buying him a pint, he learned that he was a footman at Sandringham House.

'I dare say you know a thing or two,' remarked Frank.

'I do,' answered the man. 'I could tell you a few things about HM and Mrs Simpson.'

'Not here,' said Frank, glancing anxiously over his shoulder down the bar where several newspapermen were drinking and chatting. 'Let's go somewhere quieter.'

He drove his new acquaintance to a pub in the next village and after plying him with several more pints of ale and whisky chasers, and waving a crisp white £5 note under his nose, elicited the information that Edward had spent the night with Mrs Simpson at Felixstowe.

He could not get to a telephone fast enough. In a voice breathless with excitement he dictated this sensational tit-bit, embroidered with a few imaginative sentences.

'Good story,' commented that familiar high-pitched voice down the line, 'if true.'

To Frank's dismay not a line of it appeared in the next morning's *Herald*. When he ventured to ask why his copy had been spiked, he was told tersely: 'Too hot to handle, old boy.' When Mrs Simpson was granted her decree nisi the fact was briefly and circumspectly reported in the paper, without comment.

Frank drowned his disappointment at the bar and, in the way of all reporters, cursed those idiots in the office who would not recognize a story even if it was presented to them in ten-foot high neon lights.

A newsreel team arrived from Germany and striding arrogantly into the lounge of the Feathers gave the Nazi salute and said 'Heil Hitler!' A tall, balding reporter rose from the high-backed chair in which the King's grandfather used to take his ease on his visits to his 'local', raised a languid arm and responded: 'Bless Baldwin.'

On 2 December Mr Baldwin warned the country that a grave constitutional crisis was in the offing and on the following day he put his half-crown pipe in his pocket as he went into Buckingham Palace to tell the King that the Cabinet was opposed to his marrying Mrs Simpson. As the crowds gathered in Downing Street and at the gates of Buckingham Palace, Frank again found himself viewing the passing of great events from the tradesmen's entrance, as it were.

With no fewer than forty other reporters he took up temporary residence at the Wheatsheaf Hotel, Virginia Water, the nearest hostelry to Fort Belvedere where the King was staying.

A twenty-four hour rota covering all entrances was drawn up by H. de Winton Wigley of the *News Chronicle* and posted above the mantelpiece in the lounge. Outside it was snowing and as someone wisely observed: 'There's no point in dog eating dog in this weather, old man, and ending up frozen to death in a ditch.'

For extra comfort on this arduous assignment, the reporters took a leaf out of the night watchman's book and bought two buckets in Staines, drove holes through the bottoms and used them as braziers for warmth and for frying sausages and bacon. There was no lack of fuel from the royal woods. The ditches outside Fort Belvedere slowly filled with empty Gold Flake packets and Johnnie Walker bottles.

Frank bought himself a new overcoat and raincoat in the Aquascutum sales for little more than a fiver on his expenses and wore both at the same time on top of two pairs of flannel pyjamas, a sweater, a thick shirt and trousers, longjohns and several pairs of socks – and still felt cold.

They watched every car which passed through the automatically operated gates and noted the occupants: Mr Baldwin, Mr Walter Monckton KC, various members of the royal family (even on one occasion the film star Marlene Dietrich, who was refused admission). One wag declared that the latest 'inside' information was that Mr Baldwin had offered to give up Mrs Baldwin if Edward would give up Wallis. At the Wheatsheaf, a normally sedate establishment, bar takings broke new records.

Just a week after the nation was let into the secret of the King's love affair, the Speaker of the House of Commons read out his message renouncing the throne in favour of his younger brother, then Duke of York. The King was to broadcast his farewell to England and the Empire on the BBC the following evening, a Friday.

There was little or no information from official sources but Frank discovered from another servant plied with drinks in a public bar that the two kings would dine for the last time together with their closest relatives at Windsor Royal Lodge before the broadcast. He and the *Herald* photographer, a keen youngster of about his own age, worked out a plan to get exclusive pictures of the King on his way to this historic dinner party. They studied Ordnance Survey maps of the area carefully.

That evening Frank parked his GN on the main road just a

short distance from the point where the drive linking Fort Belvedere and Windsor Castle crossed it. The photographer hid in a ditch at the crossing. Frank sat in his blacked-out car with a peaked cap pulled over his eyes and the lower half of his face swathed in a woollen scarf.

At last he saw headlights approaching from the direction of Fort Belvedere. Normally the King's chauffeur would have been able to see the main road for hundreds of yards in either direction so that he could judge the moment to dash across without stopping, thus dodging any photographers who might be lurking there. At Sandringham the King had actually laid hands on a photographer he caught spying on him from a hedge.

This particular evening was foggy, which helped the plan laid by the *Herald* men. As the King's powerful Buick neared the junction, Frank's gloved thumb was poised on his light switch. The motor was thrumming under the louvred bonnet.

'*Now!*' he hissed to himself, pressing the switch so that the light beams suddenly lit up a hundred yards of the main road ahead of him. At the same time he released his foot gently from the clutch pedal and glided towards the crossing.

With a dramatic squeal of tyres on loose gravel, the King's car slowed almost to a halt at the junction, while a Sasha lamp lit up the foggy darkness and the shutter of a large PVN plate camera gave a loud click. Frank saw, in that split second frozen by the lens, King Edward wearing a light-coloured overcoat and muffler with a bowler hat tilted forward over his eyes, and with him in the back of the car King George and their brothers the Duke of Gloucester and the Duke of Kent.

Edward put his hands over his face and seemed to shrink back against the cushions. In a moment the Buick gathered speed again, crossed the main road and vanished in the direction of Windsor Royal Lodge. A chief inspector rapidly approached from a patrol car standing nearby and demanded furiously of Frank: 'What the devil d'you think you're up to?'

'Well, Superintendent,' answered Frank calmly – he had long since learned the value of currying favour with officers of the law by exaggerating their rank – 'well, Superintendent, I am on the major road so I assume I have right of way. I think you should question the driver of that Buick for approaching a major road without due care and attention.'

The police officer stared at him in astonishment, then tipped his cap forward and scratched the back of his head.

'You cheeky young bugger,' he said at last. 'Clear off, before I run you in for obstruction.'

In those days when royalty was spoken of with hushed reverence and royal persons were supposed to be different from ordinary mortals, it was unbelievably audacious behaviour. But it was a great picture.

The abdication was the main topic of conversation at Blackstaff Hall that Christmas, the only one in all those years which Jenny spent with her stepbrother, the retired general, and the Hallsburys, her sister Lucy and her husband and now middle-aged son, blinded in the Great War. It was a strained and stilted occasion with too many memories and the underlying feeling that they now had less in common with one another than they had ever had.

'How one does miss listening to the king on the wireless,' remarked Lucy as she sat with her sister in the drawing room after the traditional English Christmas luncheon of home-fed beef, Norfolk turkey and plum pudding. 'The old king I mean, of course. We always listened to him out in India. It meant so much to us - a suggestion of holly and mistletoe and robins, you know. The new king has a dreadful stutter. It will be difficult for him to broadcast, if not out of the question.'

Lucy always spoke of the royal family as if she was privy to the gossip of the Court, which of course she was not. It was one of her little pretensions which Jenny found irritating.

'I don't know that it matters whether the King speaks to us on the wireless or not,' she said.

'His wife is such a sweet thing,' Lucy prattled on, pretending not to have heard the remark. 'She will be a great support to him, I'm sure, and now that dreadful Mrs Simpson is out of the way we shall be able to have a splendid coronation.'

Over their port in the dining room, the gentlemen's conversation had taken a gloomy turn.

'India's no place for a white man any more, not since they started parleying with that four-eyed little fakir Gandhi,' Clarence Hallsbury was saying. He had returned to England for good with a CSI (Commander of the Most Exalted Order of the Star of India) and was settled in retirement at Bournemouth. 'Churchill's right when he says the Viceroy should have bound him up, laid him in the dust outside the gates of Delhi and had him trampled on by an elephant.'

'Winnie's right about a lot of things,' said the general. 'But they won't have him in the Government at any price. He's got people coming back and forth to Chartwell at all hours, it's more like Whitehall than a place in the country, and when he's not dictating to secretaries and superintending the building of swimming pools he's building brick walls with his own hands. He's got the energy and drive of twenty men.'

Churchill's country home was in the wooded hills on the far side of the broad valley of the Pilgrim's Way, less than two miles from Blackstaff Hall.

'One can't take tea with treason,' mumbled Clarence in his cups, still thinking about India. 'No wonder the old king said on his deathbed, how's the Empire?'

'Did he say that?' grunted the general, who found his brother-in-law a pompous bore sometimes. 'I read somewhere that what he really said was "What's on at the Empire?" Sounds more likely to me.'

No one laughed. Arthur Hallsbury, who was sitting near the window gazing out sightlessly at the afternoon mist settling on winter dormant lawns, suddenly asked: 'Is there going to be another world war, do you think?'

The question seemed especially poignant coming from one who as a young man twenty years before had lost his sight in a hail of mustard-gas shells near Camiers and had lived in darkness ever since.

'I don't believe we shall see another great war in our time,' replied the general. 'If there was it would begin and end with a single air raid. Look at Spain and Abyssinia – war today is nothing but blood and squalor and lying propaganda. There's no glory in it any more.'

'Are you a pacifist then, like General Crozier?' inquired Clarence mildly.

'You mean that loony who was drummed out of the Black and Tans and is going around with a bunch of parsons and lady novelists trying to get people to sign the peace pledge?' roared the general. 'Good lord, no. They're all cranks, devoted to vegetarianism, Morris dancing, knitting and Indian ahimsa.'

'I blame Gandhi,' said Clarence, 'and that slimy little agitator Jawaharlal Nehru.'

'Aunt Jenny was telling me that she attended a couple of pacifist meetings at which Canon Sheppard and General Crozier were speakers and Siegfried Sassoon read some of his war poems,' persisted Arthur. 'It seems there's something called non-violent resistance which they think would work.'

Clarence and the general exchanged glances and shook their heads sadly.

'Pay no attention to your aunt,' advised the general. 'She's never got over being a suffragette.'

'How is your boy?' Lucy was asking Jenny in the other room. 'He must be quite grown up, quite a man of the world.'

'Indeed,' replied Jenny, 'he is making a career for himself in journalism, following in the footsteps of our Papa, you might say.'

'Dear, dear Papa,' sighed Lucy. 'How far away it seems when we were all together in this house, growing up into young ladies. Which paper does Frank write for, I haven't seen his name?'

'The *Daily Herald*,' Jenny told her.

'Oh, my dear,' said Lucy, quite shocked. 'I couldn't possibly ask for *that* to be sent to the house. It's a Socialist rag.'

It was all Jenny could do to stop herself getting up and walking out. Nothing has changed, the same prejudices, the same snobbishness. But I won't say anything, I don't want to start another of those awful family arguments.

I loathe this place now, its big silent rooms and the musty smell of a museum. We are all like exhibits, old fogies mumbling over our brandy. How different it was when Papa was alive and we used to gather round the Christmas tree in this very room to get our presents, and the servants with us, a house full. Now there's only one shambling old butler and a housekeeper. The laughter, the singing, the dancing, and that kiss under the mistletoe which meant so little at the time, are distant music.

On the last night of a year which had brought him much excitement, some success and few major setbacks, Frank was at the Chelsea Arts Ball with his friend Jack.

Harris was riding high, too. While Frank had been involved in the Abdication story, Jack had covered himself in glory for his reporting of the fire which burned the Crystal Palace to the ground. Immediately afterwards he was offered a job on the *Nottingham Evening Post* and was able to escape from the hated Harbottle.

He told Frank: 'On my last day at the *Mercury* I said everything to his face that I always said behind his revolting back. I only wish Elaine could have been there to hear it.'

At the mention of Elaine's name, Frank experienced a pang. He thought he had got over her but even after eighteen months the wound was not completely healed.

However, he concealed his feelings from Jack by saying lightly: 'I don't think much of *yours*.'

The two girls they had picked up at the ball had gone to the powder room to repair make-up ravaged by two hours of fox-trotting and quick-stepping. They were typists, the sort of girls who believed magazine advertisements reading: ' "I love you," he whispered – this can happen to you, if you use Lux toilet soap for that "rich-girl" skin.'

'They live in some hostel at Earl's Court,' said Frank, 'and they've got to be in by two – tomorrow's a normal working day. I can take one in the car.'

'Which one?'

'Well, the little dark one – the other one seems to have taken quite a fancy to you.'

Phyllis, the 'little dark one' was much the prettier of the two. She was wearing a black-cat suit as fancy dress, which showed off her figure to advantage. Her friend, Ethel, had come as Little Bo-Beep in flounced gingham.

'And how am I supposed to get to Earl's Court?' asked Jack.

'You'll have to get a cab – there's only room for two in the car,' Frank told him. 'I'll pick you up afterwards.'

'I want to be happy,' sang a crooner, 'but I can't be happy . . .' Fanciful tableaux and floats got up by the students paraded through the Albert Hall among the milling crowds waving banners, blowing squeakers, throwing multicoloured streamers. Phyllis donned a cat mask, with long whiskers.

At the stroke of midnight hundreds of balloons floated down on their heads from the great domed roof and everyone started screaming 'Happy New Year! Happy New Year!' and kissing every member of the opposite sex in sight. Phyllis, flushed and giggly, snatched off her mask, flung her arms round Frank's neck, pressed her shiny red lips against his mouth and clung on for what seemed a long time. The band struck up 'Auld Lang Syne' and everyone was linking hands and singing 'Should auld acquaintance be forgot . . .' When that was done arms stayed linked for the latest crazes in communal dancing, the Palais Glide and the even more popular Lambeth Walk. The party was still in full swing at one o'clock when Frank and Phyllis left.

There was time to spare, almost an hour together in his car parked in a quiet side alley near the office girls' hostel with the lights out and the hood up. It was a dry night with a nip of frost in the air but neither of them seemed to notice it.

After several lingering kisses Frank's right hand started caressing her breasts. He could feel the nipples hardening under the black satin. Phyllis made no move to remove his hand, indeed her kisses became even warmer, until she felt his left hand unfastening the back of the cat suit.

'What are you up to?' she asked sharply, drawing her head back. Her eyes did not mirror the hostility in her voice and melted still further as his hand slid across the bare smooth skin of her back while the other cupped itself round one of her firm little breasts underneath the satin.

'Ooooh, stop it!' she exclaimed, but with a little shiver of delight. She made no attempt to break free and, after more sultry kisses, the hand wandered downward to the elastic barrier of her artificial-silk knickers and beyond into the erogenous zone between her warm thighs. This was going too far.

'That's enough of that,' she said, pushing him away. 'What do you take me for?'

She was clearly a good girl in the conventional sense, not one who did *it* as Elaine had, although in truth it would have been downright uncomfortable if not impossible in a two-seater G N. So Frank sighed and contented himself with some more impassioned fumbling under the cat suit.

'Ouch!' squeaked Phyllis, wriggling uncomfortably. The short, stubby gear lever had somehow intruded phallus-like between her legs. Pulling her cat suit back over her bare shoulders she grumbled: 'I'm freezing – there aren't even any proper windows in this thing.'

It was true that their breath hung as steam in the pale light from the gas lamp on the corner of the street. At the chimes of two from a nearby clock tower she sprang out of the car like a scalded cat and disappeared into the night. It was some time before Jack Harris appeared and climbed into the seat next to Frank, grumbling: 'Had to walk all the blinking way from the

Albert Hall – not a cab to be had for love nor money. And after all that, all I got was a quick kiss at the door. I suppose *you* were all right, tucked up in here.'

Frank started to laugh.

'What's so funny?' demanded Jack truculently.

'It's that . . . hat . . . you've got on.'

Jack was still wearing the miniature cardboard policeman's helmet, held under the chin by elastic, that he had worn at the ball.

As they drove through Piccadilly Circus and around Trafalgar Square, where policemen were dredging the last of the drunks from the fountains, Jack asked: 'Have you made a resolution for 1937?'

'Yes,' Frank told him, for once absolutely serious. 'I mean, somehow, to get to the war in Spain.'

9

Getting to the war in Spain proved to be more difficult than Frank anticipated. Unlike many of the editorial staff of the *Daily Herald*, and despite his customary affectation of a red tie, he was not a member of the Labour Party, much less a Communist, but he felt passionately that the Fascists must be stopped before the bombs started to fall on London as they had fallen on Madrid and Abyssinia. Cardinal Pacelli, blessing the Italian soldiers who were taking mustard gas to Abyssinia and telling them that they were doing the work of God in carrying the benefits of Christian civilization to the heathen, had finally destroyed any vestige of faith in the Roman Church in which he was brought up.

Had he got in touch with his mother, which he did not, she would certainly have tried to dissuade him from joining the fight. Her memories of 1914-18 were still uncomfortably vivid, the damage to young men's minds being, in her view, almost as appalling as the injuries to their bodies. Rupert Brooke's haunting lines

> If I should die, think only this of me:
> That there's some corner of a foreign field

would have been too hard to bear if she thought her own son was about to be sacrificed, however just the cause. In any case, she had come to believe with many others that there was no such thing as a just war and had joined Canon Dick Sheppard's Peace Pledge Union.

She had marched in poster parades with Sheppard, who was dying on this crusade although no one knew it, and George Lansbury, the grand old man of the Labour Party. The demonstrators wore bizarre paper gasmasks and the posters proclaimed DOWN WITH POVERTY, FASCISM AND WAR! and WOMEN OF BRITAIN! FIGHT FOR PEACE! Jenny went up to meetings at the P P U offices in Regent Street and around the streets of Balham, Clapham and Brixton, trying to get signatures to the declaration: 'I renounce war and will never sanction another.'

She felt the heady excitement of her days fighting for that other cause, so long ago, the cause of Votes for Women. She was almost absurdly pleased with herself when she managed to collect a dozen signatures in a week, in blissful ignorance of the fact that while she campaigned against war her son was desperately trying to join in one.

The *Herald* editor was of the opinion, however, that Cole was too green to be a war correspondent and not only rejected all the young man's lobbying but became more than a little irritated when Frank waylaid him verbally in the editorial floor lavatory.

'Get that bloody whippersnapper out of my hair,' he told the news editor testily, having given instructions that Trevor Morley was to be dispatched to the war zone on the Nationalist (that is to say, the Fascist) side.

The worm of envy entered Frank's soul. He chafed under the endless round of pettifogging human-interest stories with which the news editor sought to keep him out of the chief's hair.

'Nothing but cats up trees,' he wrote bitterly in a letter to Jack Harris, 'while Spain is in flames and Guernica in ruins. Last night I went to the People's Palace with some of the LSE undergrads from my digs. Isabel Brown was magnificent. You should have heard her, even a double-dyed Tory reactionary like you would have been impressed. She said that the International

Brigade is fighting not just against Franco but for world peace. I've half a mind to join.'

'Get down to Southampton, Mister.'

The peremptory tones of the news editor interrupted his private letter writing. 'The *Queen Mary*'s docking this afternoon and according to our shipping reporter Greta Garbo's on board. According to the tapes she's having an affair with Stokowski, the conductor. He's old enough to be her father but that doesn't seem to bother anyone. It could make a full-page special if you get it right.'

'Thanks,' retorted Frank. 'It's just the sort of opportunity I've been waiting for.'

But the news editor was already into his next conversation on the phone, as if Frank had already departed for Southampton.

Frank stomped out of the building into Endell Street, consigning Greta Garbo, Leopold Stokowski and the whole of Hollywood to perdition.

Any young reporter should have been excited by so glamorous an assignment, but not Frank Cole. He hailed a cab but instead of telling the driver to go to Waterloo Station, where boat trains departed at regular intervals for Southampton, he went to the International Brigade office, whose address he had scribbled on the back of an envelope the previous evening. There was a queue and after half an hour he gave up and resigned himself to going where he had been ordered.

The pride of the Cunard White Star fleet was lying resplendently alongside the quay when he got there. Despite himself, he was impressed by his first sight of the towering black hull and three huge red, black-topped funnels. But he had no time to stand and admire it for just as he arrived a chauffeur-driven Bentley purred past while a knot of men in raincoats and trilby hats dispersed hurriedly in all directions.

He had a fleeting glimpse of a woman swathed in furs in the back seat of the Bentley and that, I have to say, was the closest my father ever came to meeting the legendary Greta Garbo. The master-at-arms at the foot of the gangway appraised Frank with the air of a *very* superior butler and informed him: 'I believe Miss Garbo did have a few words up in the Observation Bar with those gentlemen of the press who was here.' Miss Garbo rarely said more than a few words, the most famous of which were 'I want to be alone.'

Without having been on board and meeting her Frank would have had some difficulty in contributing a full-page special on her to the *Herald*, even assuming that he could find a colleague friendly enough to supply the missing descriptive detail. He decided to make a clean breast of it.

'You *missed* her?' said that familiar nasal voice down the telephone line from London. Ferocious clicking of teeth. 'How in the name of God did you manage that?'

'My train was late,' lied Frank unhopefully.

'Boat trains are never late,' retorted the news editor. 'Roper managed to get there on time.'

Roper was the local stringer who regularly met the liners to interview the newsworthy who in those days before air travel became widespread arrived at Southampton almost every day of the week. There was an uncomfortable pause.

'Have you got a copy of *World's Press News* by any chance?' asked the news editor.

'No, sir,' replied Frank innocently. 'May I ask why?'

'Because you'll need it to look for another job,' was the unfriendly reply. 'You're fired, Mister.'

And with that the phone went dead. Frank was about to say he was going to resign anyway but the opportunity was denied him. As he walked glumly back into town he caught sight of an art deco poster advertising steamer services to St Malo. His knowledge of geography was sufficient to tell him that this Breton seaport was in the general direction of Spain and on the spur of the moment he stopped a cab and said: 'To the ferry docks, please.'

Later he admitted that it was probably the maddest and most impulsive act of his whole life.

The boat from Southampton crept towards St Malo with the dawn. Frank, stretching his aching legs on deck after a sleepless night in the second-class smoker, saw the granite bastions and ramparts looming out of the mist and leaned against the rail watching the activity of docking in one of the crowded basins. In his pockets he carried a one-way ticket, the passport that he had with him at all times in hope of an unexpected foreign assignment and a £5 note. The rest of his money, amounting to £10, he had already changed into francs. He had no idea what his next move was. I'll work that out when I get there, and somehow I'll get to Spain. Nothing else matters.

At the Restaurant de la Duchesse Anne, built almost into the ramparts inside the walled town, close to one of the gateways, he enjoyed a bowl of hot, milky coffee and crusty bread fresh from the oven and liberally spread with apricot jam. Outside they were putting up flags for a local festival. It was going to be a warm day. Frank stretched his legs and lit his pipe. The land beyond the Pyrenees where American planes flown by Russian pilots were machine-gunning Italian tanks, while Spaniard fought Spaniard with bayonet, rifle and grenade, seemed far, far away. This was more like a holiday than marching to war.

After a shave at a barber's shop in the Place Chateaubriand, he followed the signs to the *plage* on the western side of the ramparts facing the open sea, stretched himself on the sand with his jacket folded under his head as a pillow and was lulled to sleep by the murmur of the waves.

He was awakened by music, a band playing somewhere inside the walls, out of tune. His wristwatch had stopped at 10.30 and he had no idea how long he had been asleep. With his jacket over his shoulder he wandered back through the gate into the town. The steep, narrow streets were crammed with people, showers of flower petals and confetti descending on their heads from the upper windows of the tall granite houses. A small procession went by, headed by a man in traditional Breton costume, playing bagpipes.

The whole town was *en fête*. Frank made his way through the crowds to the square where the band was playing and people were dancing an energetic reel. Before he knew what was happening he found himself caught up in it, while an obliging bystander held his jacket. In the swirl of partners, a laughing girl with bobbed brown hair and warm brown eyes landed in his arms. Small and delicate of features, she wore a light summer frock and sandals, showing off the sort of suntan that was not acquired on an annual week's holiday at the seaside. Yet she was no Breton. As soon as she spoke he identified her as coming from the south west of England, Cornwall or Devon without a doubt.

After a while they left the dancers, the crowds and the noise and climbed up steps to the ramparts where statues of ancient *malouin* mariners such as Cortez stood sternly gazing out to sea. They walked and admired the views across the River Rance to Dinard on the opposite bank. When they came to the harbour the girl pointed out a rust-streaked cargo ship moored alongside one of the quays.

'My Dad's captain of that one,' she said proudly. Frank could see the words *Four Winds* on the stern and just make out Falmouth in smaller letters underneath. So I was right; she comes from Cornwall.

'Daddy takes me everywhere with him when I'm on holiday from school,' she was saying. 'My mother died when I was little so we're very close. During term I live with my aunt in Truro. My name's Jane, by the way. Jane Flippance.'

She held out her hand with almost comic formality and Frank shook it solemnly. The Red Duster hung limply from its staff while a faint plume rose vertically from the smokestack of the romantically named *Four Winds*. Bulging sacks were being loaded into holds by sweating men in berets and *bleu de travail* overalls. As if reading Frank's thoughts, Jane went on: 'It's not a luxury yacht exactly, but I love being with Daddy. I'm the only female on board, of course.'

'Don't the men find it a little . . . well, inhibiting?'

'Oh no, not at all. They watch their language when I'm around – Daddy's a bit old-fashioned that way – but even so I've picked up one or two useful words.'

'I can imagine,' said Frank. 'How old are you?'

'Sixteen,' she answered.' But I've travelled a lot.'

He could see that she was indeed a self-assured young lady, more than capable of handling a crew of hard-drinking deck-hands, firemen, greasers and donkeymen.

'At Easter, when I was convalescing from a pretty bad dose of pneumonia, we were supposed to go to the Med,' she told him, 'but just a few hours out of Falmouth, Daddy got a W/T message to say that the *Four Winds* had been bought by a French shipowner and we were to put into St Malo. They loaded us up with potatoes and sacks of flour and stuff and ordered us to Bilbao. Well, as you know, British ships are supposed to keep away from Spain and we'd read in the papers that Bilbao was surrounded by Franco's troops and the entrance to the port was mined.

'But the new owner told us that the people there were starving. They had only four days' food supplies left. So Daddy said we'd go, and anyway "orders is orders". Our owner lives over there, by the way . . .'

Jane crossed to the other side of the ramparts and pointed inland across the chimneys and rooftops to a substantial granite mansion.

'I haven't actually met him,' she went on. 'Daddy was called to the house. He says he's a little old man in a beret, all gnarled and incredibly tough like the oak trees that grow around here. He's a Basque and, of course, he *loathes* General Franco.'

'Surely your father didn't take you with him to Bilbao?' asked Frank.

'Oh yes he did,' said Jane, her eyes dancing. 'He wanted to ship me home, of course, because of the danger. But I wasn't going to miss out on such an adventure, oh dear me no. We had a terrific fight about it, but I won.'

Looking at her delicate features, Frank wondered what wiles she had used on her poor father to get her own way.

'Daddy said, "Your aunt'd have a fit if she knew". And she did when she read about it in the papers. "Girl on Health Cruise Defies General Franco's Blockade."'

Frank remembered now, a splash in the *Daily Mirror*.

'It was *jolly* exciting, I can tell you,' said Jane. 'We left here late at night with all the lights doused and when we arrived off Bilbao all the fishing boats started hooting to welcome us.

'Daddy kept glancing up at the sky and over the side, worried stiff about dive bombers and submarines, torpedoes and mines and whatnot, but he needn't have worried. We just steamed up the river to Bilbao – it's very narrow and there were crowds of people on both banks cheering and waving and making the sign of the cross. I couldn't help blubbing, I really couldn't, yet they were treating us like heroes. They even killed a bull in our honour. I *hated* that, but we had to watch or they'd have been dreadfully offended. They gave me an ear and Daddy one of the unmentionable parts – it's the custom apparently.'

When Frank burst out laughing she said sternly: 'It's not funny, you know. They took us to Guernica just after the raid.'

Frank stopped laughing.

'You went to Guernica?' The ruthless devastation of this village by German bombers had shocked the civilized world. While Frank had struggled in vain for months to get to Spain this schoolgirl had seen it all. He resented her. Even so he listened in fascination as she described the stream of refugees fleeing the village, laden donkeys, old men and women struggling along with what few possessions they had managed to save from the smouldering ruins, the dreadful silence hanging over a place that had been bustling with life and activity.

In that summer of 1937, neither of these young people in deep conversation, heads close together, on the ramparts of St Malo, realized that before long what had happened at Guernica would happen all over Europe.

They found it so easy to talk to one another, as if they were old friends rather than having met just a couple of hours ago in the most casual way. He found himself telling her about his mother, about his experiences in the Blackshirts and his brief newspaper career. She was the most attentive of listeners and time slipped away unnoticed. Dusk fell and lights came on around the harbour and on all the ships lying at the quaysides.

'I've got to get to Spain somehow,' he told her. 'I have to see if I can do anything.'

She smiled up at him and answered: 'You'd better come and have a word with my Dad.'

She took his hand and led the way down a steep flight of steps to the quay and up the gangway of the *Four Winds*. The captain was in his closet of a cabin, abaft the bridge. He looked up as Jane came in and said sternly: 'Where have you been, my girl? I was beginning to get worried.'

'It's all right,' she said, kissing him on the forehead. 'I've brought someone to see you. This is Frank Cole. He's a reporter from London and he's trying to get to Spain.'

'He is, is he?' grunted Captain Flippance, appraising the unexpected visitor with undisguised suspicion. His eyes, the same warm brown as his daughter's, hardened visibly. He was surprisingly youthful-looking with close-cropped dark hair.

'You're not a Franco spy are you?' he demanded bluntly.

Taken aback, Frank made no reply.

'If you are,' Flippance went on, 'you could well end up at the bottom of the Bay of Biscay feeding the fishes.'

'*Daddy*!' exclaimed Jane reprovingly in her finest high-school-for-girls manner.

'And you can get yourself off to bed, young lady,' he told her.

'But we haven't eaten,' said Jane. 'We're both *starving*.'

'Then get down to the galley and bring us some soup. It smells good. Vincent bought bream and whiting and vegetables for it in the market this morning. Mr Cole and I need to talk.'

Jane left the two men alone and Captain Flippance went over to a keg and poured two mugs of cider before gruffly inviting Frank to explain himself. When he had finished and shown the captain his National Union of Journalists membership card, Flippance remarked: 'You can't be too careful. France is full of people making a dirty living out of the war – forged papers, arms and God knows what else.'

He refilled their mugs from the keg and continued: 'We sail for Santander tonight on the tide and I'll take you there. I want you to understand, Mr Cole, that this ship is under charter to the Basque government – they've even given me a Basque passport. When we get to Santander, you're on your own.'

'I can't pay much,' said Frank. 'As I told you, I've left my paper. I really am on my own.'

For the first time, Captain Flippance smiled. He was not such a hard man, after all.

'Don't worry, m'dear,' he said. 'You can work your passage. If you really want to fight that bastard Franco, I'm on your side'.

At that point Jane came in with a large tray laden with steaming bowls of *cotriade*, a Breton version of bouillabaisse. It seemed to have everything in it as well as fish: potatoes, onions, tomatoes, celery, the whole thing flavoured with thyme, bay leaves, parsley, fennel and saffron, not to mention white wine and garlic. The bowls were topped with garlic-flavoured croutons and grated cheese. They fell upon them ravenously, while the captain poured more cider.

'This is good Devon scrumpy,' he told Frank, 'not that muck they call cider here.'

When they had finished eating, Frank signed some papers which the captain put in front of him 'just to make matters above board, like' and they drank a toast to a safe voyage. The combined effects of scrumpy and *cotriade* were beginning to overwhelm Frank. He had little or no recollection of moving from the captain's cabin to a stuffy forecastle reeking of oil fumes and bilge water. Somebody helped him to take off his shoes and get into a timber-framed bunk, which began to spin wildly like a carousel out of control.

When it stopped spinning, he was aware of an uneasy rocking motion and the rhythmic thump of an old steam-driven engine. The *Four Winds* was at sea.

Everything had taken on a dreamlike quality. Had he really

less than forty-eight hours ago set out for Southampton to interview Greta Garbo? Since then he had been given the sack, taken an unplanned ferry ride to St Malo, met an enchanting girl, danced in the streets and signed on as a hand in a merchant ship bound for Spain. Had it all really happened? If I really am on the way to Santander, it must be the hand of providence guiding me there, except that I no longer believe in providence.

10

Frank was lounging in the sun against a parapet of sandbags commanding a view down a steep slope of tangled unpruned vines and unharvested rotting maize to a thicket of barbed wire which marked the beginning of enemy ground. The country was too mountainous for a line of trenches; instead there were fortified positions zigzagging across the slopes, each marked with a red or a red and gold flag, depending whose side they were on.

'It's my birthday,' announced Graham Moody, who was sharing the lookout with him. 'I'm twenty.'

'Many happy returns,' replied Frank with a sardonic smile.

Graham, a stocky youth with a flat Midlands accent, looked older than his years, needing, unlike many of his contemporaries, to shave every day. At the moment there was a heavy growth of bristly black stubble around his red face. He looked like a farmhand, though he was, in fact, a Cambridge undergraduate, reading physics at Trinity College, before interrupting his studies to join the International Brigade.

They met at the barracks in Santander to which Frank was directed by the helpful Captain Flippance. They drove there through streets which bore evidence of Luftwaffe bombing: gaps in buildings, piles of rubble and the burned-out skeletons of vehicles. Most of the women queuing for bread and olive oil seemed to be wearing widow's weeds. The recently renamed Gran Avenida de Rusia was thronged with men in shabby uniforms and walls were covered with the initials of the various competing Leftist factions: POUM, CNT, FAI, JUU and others.

Passing a shop with '*No hay tobaco*' chalked on its shutters, Flippance gave Frank a carton of two-ounce tins of Three Nuns pipe tobacco with his best wishes. Frank had said goodbye to Jane on board the *Four Winds* just before he came ashore. They had spent little time together during the brief voyage from St Malo and the parting was made more poignant by her gift to him of a small snapshot of herself which he kept in his wallet. They promised to write to each other.

As the taxi pulled away from the dockside he looked back to see her waving from the rails on the upper deck. Am I here? Is this really me, or is it a film?

At the barracks in the old city near the Plaza Porticada, Frank was handed over to a *teniente* or second lieutenant wearing an exact copy of a British Army officer's uniform except that his boots were dirty. This officer signed him into the ranks with the minimum of formalities and passed him on to a *cabo* or corporal in the stores.

He was handed a blanket, some coarse brown overalls, a forage cap, a pair of rope-soled *alpargatas*, a goatskin water bottle, a mess tin, a rifle and a bandolier of 150 cartridges. The rifle was a German Mauser, at least forty years old. The corporal, with a droll smile, made a gesture of pulling the trigger and blowing his own head off.

In the barrack room Frank encountered a fellow Englishman, Graham Moody, sitting on his bunk removing rust from the stiff bolt of his rifle. 'Just like being back in the school OTC,' he said. 'Clean, bright and slightly oiled, what?'

On the way to the front in a convoy of trucks they were attacked by Italian planes zooming in low, machine guns chattering, and had to run for their lives into the pine woods. Later, entering a little town which had been taken and retaken, they saw bodies lying everywhere. Neither Frank nor Graham had seen a dead body before. These were grotesque inhuman shapes, skins turned black by the fierce sun.

From the church came a handful of Spanish militiamen dragging an effigy of Our Lord. They started shooting at it with their rifles until an officer called out to them to stop wasting ammunition, then some of them fetched an artillery limber and pushed it over the effigy so that one of the iron-shod wheels severed the plaster head.

'See how bitter they are against the Pope for supporting the

Caudillo,' said Graham as they rested by the dusty road.

He told Frank that Cambridge changed his life. The son of the works manager of a boot and shoe factory in Northampton, he went up to Trinity on a scholarship, having displayed a formidable aptitude for the physical sciences and mathematics at his local grammar school. Everything was different from anything he had experienced before at home or at school. The talk, the food, the ideas, all were new and fascinating, especially the ideas.

The Cavendish Laboratory at Cambridge was in the midst of one of the most exciting periods in the history of science following the discovery of the neutron and the existence of the positive electron. Graham Moody sat at the feet of Ernest Rutherford, the New Zealand physicist who had been created a baron and was the director of the Cavendish Laboratory. 'We are living,' said Lord Rutherford, 'in the heroic age of physics.'

And so it seemed to the young students bicycling through the streets in their flowing black gowns to listen to tutors such as C. P. Snow or Peter Kapitza who went regularly back and forth between Leningrad and Cambridge. Most of the lecturers took an active part in politics and Graham talked of the cell of Comrades at Trinity and proudly produced his green membership card. Graham felt they were patronizing him when they called him 'Comrade' in their self-admiring way. Yet despite their affected mannerisms and penetrating upper-class voices, he discovered that they were revolutionaries to a man, disgusted by their country's 'lack of leadership'.

Even so they remained part of the nation's establishment elite, nonchalantly involving themselves in the social round of other fellows' rooms, sherry parties and bumping races on the River Cam. In their society, Graham became a committed Communist who cared enough about the cause to come to Spain and fight.

In their dugout he and Frank swapped Left Book Club cheap editions and discussed the complications of Spanish politics, yet while the Communists, the Anarchists and the trade unionists squabbled among themselves, they, the poor bloody infantry, were left to hold off the superior weight of the Fascist forces without artillery, grenades or even tin hats. It could only be a matter of time before they were pushed back to the Bay of Biscay, but for the present exchanges with the enemy were limited to insults shouted through megaphones. *'Fascistas, maricones!'* brought the echoing response of *'Viva Franco!'* from the far side of the valley.

Their initial idealism faded in the fierce heat, with the torments of flies, mosquitoes, lice and fleas which were more their enemies than the Fascists dug in beyond the barbed wire. Dysentery had carried off more Republican troops than had enemy bullets. Water was brought up in canisters on the backs of mules and each man was allowed a quart a day for drinking only – the smell of unwashed bodies and excrement in the dugouts was indescribable.

'I tell you what,' said Moody, 'as it's my birthday, I'll open that packet of Army and Navy tea I got in the last parcel from home. I've been keeping it for a special occasion. Farewell to my teens and all that.'

As soon as they were relieved, water was boiled and the tea brewed. There was no milk or sugar to put in it, but even so it was ambrosial. Someone else found two small tins of anchovies and Frank opened his last tin of Three Nuns pipe tobacco and handed it round. He was known to the Spanish troops as the *'hombre con pipa'* – the man with the pipe – as most of the men were cigarette smokers. Nevertheless, they rubbed the moist curls of pipe tobacco to shreds which they allowed to dry in the sun for a while and then rolled in cigarette papers. It was luxury compared to imitation Lucky Strikes which spluttered and burned like firecrackers and cost a day's pay for a packet of ten.

Soon everyone was in a party mood and Frank and Graham Moody taught the foreigners some Walt Disney songs. The hillside resounded to 'Who's afraid of ze beeg bad wolf?' until a fusillade of bullets from the Nationalists brought it to an abrupt end.

This, as it turned out, was merely a prelude. As soon as darkness fell the artillery on the far side of the mountain opened up. They heard a roar like an approaching express train and the company commander yelled: 'Heads down boys – here comes a close one!'

The shell landed about fifty yards to their right, throwing a column of earth, rocks, debris and bits of bodies high into the air.

'Christ, Moody, they must have heard it's your birthday,' said the officer as they cowered like rats in their holes in the ground, the darkness repeatedly lit up by blue-white flashes of light from the exploding shells.

At dawn, the scream of Stuka dive bombers assailed their quivering eardrums, followed by the whistle and crump of bombs.

'Jesus!' shouted Moody, 'just look at that lot.'

The hillside in front of them was suddenly as alive with swarming figures as their blankets were with fleas.

'Fire!' bawled the company commander, standing up and blazing away at the advancing hordes with his Luger automatic. Before he had fired more than three rounds he fell back into the trench, his bearded face reduced to a jamlike pulp.

'I'm off,' yelled Frank. 'If we stay here they'll chop us to pieces.'

He and Graham Moody scrambled away up a hillside littered with discarded tin cans and empty cartridge cases, and managed to gain the brow without being hit by the hail of bullets at their heels. Within minutes the retreat became a rout.

For the first time in a month, Frank felt clean. He had just emerged from a long and heavenly wallow in the sea and was lying on the warm sand, slowly drying. There would be time later back at the barracks to run a candle flame down the seams of his overalls to incinerate the lice which lodged there like fat white grains of rice.

A few fat businessmen and their wives, taking the sun in deckchairs along the tree-shaded promenade of Sardinero, looked on with distaste at the bearded soldiery in its underpants plunging and splashing in the water.

The nearby city of Santander was without electricity since the Nationalist forces seized the hydraulic power station twenty miles away up in the hills. Santander's fate was sealed when the Navarrese brigades entered Torrelavega, thus completing their encirclement of the Republican armies. It could only be a matter of hours before they marched into the city in triumph.

The café-bordellos previously closed by workers' patrols were now open and doing a roaring trade on the biblical precept of let us eat and drink for tomorrow we die. Largely at Frank's insistence, he and Graham ventured into a smoky candlelit cellar where the waitresses wore nothing but a few spangles. The only drink available was Spanish champagne at 100 pesetas a bottle, ten days' pay for a soldier. They accepted eagerly enough a crumpled white note on which the Bank of England promised to pay the bearer £5, the one which Frank brought with him from Southampton.

'I am feeling reckless tonight, old boy,' he said to his companion, surveying the entirely nude cabaret on the tiny circular stage next to their table. 'What do you think of the girls?'

'Frankly, my dear, I prefer boys,' replied Moody in what he called his Noel Coward voice, contrasting so strangely with his rough exterior. 'I'll try that one over there.'

Frank laughed but he was not entirely sure that his friend was joking. He recalled the embarrassing attention which Graham had paid to the youngest member of the unit, a smooth-cheeked Basque boy referred to by his compatriots as *'el bambino'*. One night in the dugout he heard rustlings and whispers from the sleeping bag next to his, suggesting that Moody was not alone. After the noises had died away, someone crept out and, in the brief shaft of moonlight as the blanket covering the door was drawn aside, Frank recognized the same boy.

He said nothing at the time or since, being too embarrassed to mention it. In the circles he had moved in homosexuality did not exist, or at least was never openly acknowledged. Moody told him that it was the thing at Cambridge.

In sexual matters my father was abnormally normal and showed every sign of enjoying it when one of the scantily clad hostesses in that sleazy cellar planted herself in his lap. Poor Graham, however, treated similarly, went red to the tips of his ears and looked round as if for escape when the girl reached for his fly buttons. 'OK, baby, you like jig-a-jig?' she said.

Despite the close and affectionate attentions of *his* hostess, Frank noticed out of the corner of his eye the red-painted toenails of the girl who had entwined herself round Graham inching towards his jacket, which lay on the floor by his chair. As he watched, the toes worked like fingers extracting a notecase from the pocket. He leaned across and said: 'No payment in advance, darling.'

'*Que*?'

In answer he brought his heel down hard on her dishonest foot. She jumped up, screaming in pain. In the ruction all the girls ran about screaming, tables were overturned and glasses broken, *purons* of cheap red wine upset. Pausing only to pick up

Graham's wallet, Frank followed him up the stairs and out into the street.

Graham could not be persuaded to enter another bar after that and went off on his own in search of sleep. In no time Frank had made friends with a party of Russian airmen.

He left the café with them soon after midnight and they walked arm in arm through the deserted streets. Trams stood immobile on the rails. Café furniture was piled in heaps on the pavements. When a large brown rat scurried across their path one of the Russians drew a revolver from the leather holster at his hip and fired at it. The shots rang out alarmingly down the silent street, but nothing stirred and the rat disappeared into the shadows.

The only sign of life was at the Town Hall. As they passed they heard sounds of revelry and breaking glass and walking in uninvited, found the city fathers in the act of drinking the cellars dry, breaking open crate after crate of champagne. At 2 a.m. the members of the government left to take a boat to Gijon, but Frank and the Russian pilots, together with some of the stouter burghers, continued the party until dawn.

At 9 a.m. Santander officially surrendered and troops of the Legionary Division of the Twentieth of March entered the city behind a young general on a chestnut horse. They were followed by a detachment of Spanish cavalry and a long marching column partly formed by captured militiamen which added what *The Times* correspondent described in his cable to London from Bilbao as 'a Roman flavour' to the triumph. Further dramatic effect was provided by the motor cyclists of the Italian 'Black Flame' battalions roaring into the Plaza Porticada with their black plumes flying.

General Dávila, commander of the Nationalist Armies of the North, appeared on the balcony of the Town Hall while the band played the 'Marcha Reál' in the hot August sun. Many houses were already showing the red and gold Nationalist colours and car loads of political prisoners released from the gaols careered through the streets to cries of *'Tú arriba España, viva Franco!'*

The whole city, surrendered with hardly a fight, took on a carnival air. The guns of the tanks were garlanded with roses, carnations and fuchsias. Even the pack-carrying mules had vine leaves behind their ears.

Among the crowds, Frank watched the bearded, dusty infantrymen marching, or rather trudging, in the wake of the armoured columns – they seemed no different to his own comrades of the past few months, except that they were the masters now. Girls followed the flags, throwing flowers and kisses, as ready to shout Nationalist slogans as any others if only the tank crews would share some of their macaroni with them.

It was astonishing how quickly the conquerors took control. Electricity supplies were switched on and within an hour or two the trams were running and loudspeakers filled the air with Fascist propaganda interspersed with a brassy rendering of the 'Dance of the Cuckoos'. Frank thought it hilarious that Franco's forces should share the same theme tune as Laurel and Hardy.

But he barely had time to savour the joke before he found himself spreadeagled face towards a wall with some tough *requetés*, volunteer troops from the Navarre, frisking him. The only document he had on him was a National Union of Journalists membership card, which excited some earnest discussion in which the words *'estranjero'* and *'Communista'* occurred with ominous frequency.

He was roughly bundled into a closed van with half a dozen others who had been picked up in the streets and driven to Santander Gaol, where they were locked in a small cell already occupied by several other prisoners. It was so overcrowded that there was no room to lie down.

The only provision for sanitation was a large galvanized bucket in one corner of this stinking dungeon and the only food they received was a billycan of greasy fish soup and a few pieces of dry bread.

Soon after dawn the inmates of the cell heard the rattle of a machine gun in the courtyard outside their barred window and glanced fearfully at one another. A few minutes later the iron door of the cell opened and a red-bereted Spanish officer read out six names from a list, including Cole, which he pronounced Co-lay. Armed guards escorted them along a stone-floored corridor to a room draped with Nationalist flags and lined them up facing three high-ranking officers seated at a table.

Two of the officers were Spanish, but the chairman, seated in the centre, was an Italian colonel. Each of the prisoners was questioned in turn. When they came to Frank, the Italian colonel said in English: 'This is the foreign spy.'

'That's not true,' Frank protested. 'I was serving as a soldier with the International Brigade.'

'A soldier?' queried the colonel and then, holding up the union card which had been taken from Frank when he was arrested, added: 'Then why are you carrying this?'

'Because I am a journalist by profession. I enlisted with the International Brigade and I demand the protection of the Geneva Convention.'

'You will demand nothing,' snapped the colonel. 'You are lying. You are a Communist agent and this court martial finds you guilty of espionage. You will be shot.'

Frank could scarcely believe his ears. He started to protest further but was silenced with a jab from a rifle butt in his kidneys. The panel's attention had already moved to the next prisoner, a boy of no more than fifteen, and one of the Spanish officers was questioning him in the same rapid-fire fashion. In less than fifteen minutes this farcical tribunal tried all six prisoners, found them all guilty and sentenced them to death.

As they were taken out into the sunlit square and placed up against a sandstone wall pitted with bullet holes and stained with blood, Frank started to say to himself over and over again: 'Holy Mary, Mother of God, pray for us sinners, now and at the hour of our death . . .'

He thought he had renounced the faith which his grandmother had forced upon him in childhood but it was still there. The other condemned men were muttering prayers in Spanish and blessing themselves, while, facing them, a couple of bored-looking soldiers sat behind a machine gun, idly swatting flies. In a moment or two, when given the order, they would dispatch half a dozen human beings almost as casually.

Frank's shirt was wet with sweat and he felt sick. He closed his eyes tightly against the sun's glare. 'Holy Mary, Mother of God.'

11

Instead of the short, sharp, lethal rattle of the machine gun, Frank heard a sudden commotion of voices. English voices. He opened his eyes and, as if in a dream, saw Trevor Morley, his friend and mentor from the *Herald*, remonstrating with the officer in charge of the firing squad.

'This is monstrous,' he heard Trevor saying, and at the same time his own knees gave way and he collapsed in the dust.

Meanwhile Trevor had grabbed the lapels of the officer's tunic and seemed to be shaking him to emphasize the force of his protest.

The black-bloomered Italian colonel strutted across the square, demanding to know what was holding up the executions. Trevor abruptly released his grip on the officer and spoke in Spanish to the suave, red-bereted aristocrat who was in charge of the visiting party of correspondents accredited to the Delegación de Estada para Prensa y Propaganda. They had been brought along to the prison to dispel rumours of atrocities being committed against Republican prisoners.

'These men are all convicted spies,' screamed the Italian colonel. 'The penalty for spying is death.'

There was little love lost between the Spaniards and their Italian allies. The former considered that they had borne the brunt of the fighting for the important industrial and seaport sector of the north and now Mussolini's swaggering legions were trying to take all the credit for victory.

But, equally, both sides detested the Reds and were thirsty for vengeance. So a heated three-cornered discussion in a mixture of Italian, Spanish and English took place concerning Frank's fate, while he and the other condemned men looked on and the machine-gun crew continued to swat flies and yawn. Eventually the Spanish officer said brusquely to Frank: 'Come with me.'

As they left the courtyard, the staccato rattle of the machine gun echoed from the walls and, glancing back, Frank saw the five others, including the young boy who stood next to him at the 'trial', crumpling to the ground like rag dolls in a cloud of saffron dust.

At the headquarters of the propaganda unit in a five-star hotel with a foyer full of sandbags, Frank was grilled for several hours by a succession of officers. Trevor was called in to attest that Frank Cole was who he claimed to be and not a member of the Communist Party. Trevor Morley had toured most of the war fronts under the aegis of the Nationalist High Command and his standing was good, whereas Frank's story of how he enlisted for the Republicans was received with marked scepticism.

After the lengthy interrogation he was told: 'You entered our country illegally and you will be deported forthwith.' He left Santander in the back of a Ford truck, manacled to a *caribinero* and had no opportunity to thank Trevor Morley for saving his life. Ironically, only a few months later Morley himself was killed in a hail of machine-gun fire in Shanghai while reporting from another war, this time between the Chinese and the Japanese.

Frank was handed over to the French frontier guards at Hendaye. There was little love lost here and they often whiled away hot afternoons shouting insults at one another across the river. Frank was immensely relieved to see the back of those scowling, dark-jowled gentlemen in their black patent-leather hats.

As he had no money and no possessions other than the flimsy remnants of military uniform that he was wearing, they took him to the British vice-consul at Bayonne. The vice-consul sat in a dusty little office beneath a portrait of King George V and Queen Mary with the words 'Huntley & Palmer's Biscuits' printed at the bottom.

A dry, bald little man in shiny black alpaca, he regarded Frank over the top of his spectacles with severe disapproval. Britain was officially committed to non-intervention in the Spanish Civil War. He listened to Frank's story and wrote down the particulars in a thin, sloping hand.

'Let this be a lesson to you, young man,' he remarked, 'not to involve yourself in the wars of foreigners.'

He issued a paper document in place of Frank's passport (which he confiscated), together with a one-way third-class railway ticket to London and a few francs for minimum sustenance on the journey.

Frank arrived back at Victoria Station on a damp, murky autumn evening during the rush hour when homegoing London office workers were streaming out of the Underground and jostling their way through the barriers to the platforms. He struggled across the concourse against a tide of black bowler hats and umbrellas and stood beside the cab rank outside the station, shivering in his light khaki drill and rope-soled canvas sandals, uncertain where to go. He felt bewildered and a little frightened, a stranger in his native city.

A tram with 'Brixton' among the places displayed on the indicator made up his mind for him. He jumped onto the platform, climbed the stairs to the upper deck and from a seat at the front surveyed the streams of red buses and black taxis, the blazing shop windows and the multicoloured lights outside the Victoria Palace advertising the Crazy Gang, stalls selling sweets, fruit and flowers, the pubs and restaurants, the reassuring policemen and the newsvendors crying '*Star, News, Standard*' against the rumble and roar of the traffic.

'Did you MACLEAN your teeth today?' demanded a giant poster.

'Fares please! Any more fares please . . .' called the conductor.

Searching his pockets desperately, Frank discovered one silver sixpenny piece, a lone 'tanner' which he had carried with him from England and throughout his adventures in Spain. It was enough to get him home.

Jenny had just sat down at the table in the back parlour, or dining room as she preferred to call it, when the doorbell rang.

'Why is it that emergency calls always come when I am about to eat?' she asked herself as she hurried into the hall. At first she failed to recognize the figure at the door, a bearded young man with sunburned skin and hair cropped close to his head like a brush, but the eyes gave him away. 'Frank!'

She tried to make her voice calm and unemotional, but he was not so stiff-upper-lipped. He picked her up in his arms and swung her round and round, crying: 'Mother – you look wonderful . . . a sight for sore eyes.'

Jenny did indeed look little altered, unlike her son. If her hair was a shade or two greyer, her skin was smooth and unwrinkled, and those sloe-dark eyes sparkled as brightly as a young girl's at this unexpected surprise.

'It's so good to see you again after all this time,' she said as she took his arm and led him into the back room where coals blazed in the grate and the damask tablecloth was laid for dinner. 'You've no idea how much I missed you – I've been combing the *Herald* day after day looking for your articles and wondering what's become of you. Where have you been? What's happened to you? You're so painfully thin. Why didn't you tell me you were coming? I've nothing prepared.'

'Please, Mother,' he pleaded with a smile. 'Not so many questions all at once. I've only just got back to London from

Spain. It's good to be home.'

'From Spain? Oh, my goodness. I wish you had given me a call first.'

'I had no pennies for the phone,' he told her. 'I'm absolutely skint.'

'Oh dear, how dreadful. You must be tired – and hungry, too,' she said. 'I'll get you some food.'

A beef carbonnade was in the oven, giving off a mouth-watering smell as she brought the dish to the table and put out another plate. But when he started to eat he had to give up after a couple of mouthfuls and go to the lavatory which was outside the back door under the lean-to conservatory full of potted geraniums and other plants. It was the first decent meal he had tasted in weeks but his stomach was shrunk and could not take it.

'What on earth has happened to you?' asked Jenny, looking at him anxiously when he came back into the room. 'Here, sit down by the fire and I'll get you a cup of tea. I haven't anything stronger in the house, I'm afraid.'

'Tea will be fine, Mum,' he said, stretching himself full length in the chintz-covered easy chair. When she came back with the tea he was fast asleep. She sat on the hearthrug with her feet curled up under her, looking at him as he slept and trying to compare him with the angry and hurt adolescent who had stormed out of the house two and a half years before. In all that time she had received no word from him and had long since ceased to hope that the breach between them might be healed. Now, out of the blue, he was back. The change in him, she sensed, was more than merely external.

During the night, hours after she had gently wakened him from his doze by the fireside, and shown him upstairs to his old room where she had made up the bed with warm sheets from the airing cupboard, she heard him shouting and cursing.

Jenny got out of bed, slipped on her dressing gown and slippers, and went across the tiny landing to his room. He was sitting bolt upright in bed, sweat streaming down his face as he stared wildly at the window. Two brilliant white searchlights moving like groping fingers across the sky over South London cast enough of a glow to reveal the expression of terror contorting his features.

'We're being attacked!' he screamed. 'Take cover . . . we're being attacked . . .' With his close-cropped hair he looked uncannily like his father, lying in that ward at the military hospital in 1915 with shrapnel in his back. Will Dawson, too, had ranted in his sleep, she remembered, taking her son's hand in hers.

'There now,' she said gently. 'It's nothing to worry about – just the ARP, air-raid precautions, you know. They practise them all the time these days.'

He sank back against the pillow, still sweating profusely: 'Sorry I woke you, Mum. I was having a bad dream. It's all right now. Go back to bed.'

'Tell me about it,' she whispered.

So he told her about the war, but not all of it. He missed out some of the bloodier scenes, but described vividly how he was sentenced to be shot and escaped. It hardly seemed possible that all this had been crammed into just two months.

'The last week has been the longest of my life,' he told her when he had finished. 'You can't imagine how good it is to be home here in dear, safe old England.'

'Not so safe any more,' Jenny corrected him. 'Everyone is convinced that war is coming and that bombs will be crashing on London soon. There's talk of providing air-raid shelters for everyone and issuing gasmasks, even to babies. I sometimes wonder if I have any right to bring babies into such a mad world.'

They spent the rest of the night talking. In their new intimacy, Jenny felt able to tell him about his father, how she had first met him, how their paths had crossed during the war and how they had become lovers. She also explained the misfortunes which had hit Will after the war and how he died.

'I loved him so much,' she said, 'that I knew that I could never feel that way about anyone else – I don't know how to make you understand the intensity of that feeling.'

'Don't speak of it any more,' he answered her. 'I understand better than you think. Look, it's getting light now, and you've had hardly any sleep.'

The first grey tinge of dawn was lightening the sky and the sparrows in the eaves started chirping. For the first time in years Jenny felt at peace with herself; the burden of guilt had lifted from her shoulders.

'What's a few hours' sleep?' she asked, smiling. 'My sleep is often enough disturbed but I was much more disturbed at the way you left home, yes, and a bit angry, too. I was so unhappy and miserable at the way it came out but now that you're back, and we've talked, everything is fine again. It's going to be a wonderful day.'

When she had left the room he went to the dressing table and opened a drawer, looking for something. It was there, just where he had left it two years ago – the cardboard cigar box and its contents. He took out the medals and held them in his hands.

Less than a week after his arrival it was his twenty-first birthday and his coming of age was marked with an annuity of £350 from his late grandmother.

A call on the family solicitor in Chancery Lane and a visit to the bank manager was all that was required to complete the formalities for monthly payment. He celebrating by ordering a Marconiphone radiogram, a three-wave-band wireless and a gramophone in one handsome walnut cabinet, and paying the price of thirty-eight guineas in one go, by cheque. Jenny bought him a new Remington portable typewriter and they celebrated, just the two of them, with *filet d'agneau St James* and a bottle of Clos des Princes at the Ritz.

After the initial relief of being home had worn off, however, Frank felt unsettled and irritable. A coldly official letter from the Foreign Office informed him that his passport would not be returned until he had repaid the amount that had been expended on his repatriation.

'Dammit, I've been fighting against Fascism for all of us while that feeble Chamberlain lot sit on the fence and prattle about non-intervention,' he fulminated, waving the letter in the air. 'All they're interested in is the repayment of a few measly quid.'

Jenny listened patiently, but her own view that all war, even the Spanish war, was unjustified remained unchanged.

'I hope if we *are* involved in a war you will refuse to serve,' she told him. 'Better to be a conscientious objector than to murder innocent men, women and children for whatever cause.'

She was still very much involved with the work of the Peace Pledge Union. This meant that in addition to her midwifery work in the district, she was on any number of committees and, having learned to drive the previous summer at the age of fifty-six, had bought a new Morris Cowley. She was indeed the only owner of a motorcar in the whole of Amen Road.

Her busy life left her little time to spend at home with Frank and he mooned restlessly about the confines of the house, idly picking up a book or a newspaper for a moment or two, only to throw it down, exclaiming aloud to himself: 'It's all so disgusting. The newspapers are full of lies and the war itself has become nothing but a racket.' Now the Asturians were fighting with their backs to the sea and the French were still trying to cope with the flood of refugees after the fall of Santander – Frank had no idea what had become of Graham Moody and other comrades.

Doing anything seemed to call for disproportionate effort on his part. Every time he picked up the phone to dial the *Daily Herald* number, Temple Bar 7788, he never got any further than the initial TEM before putting the receiver back on the hook.

Leaving the house and going into London turned out to be an unnerving experience. The noise of the traffic and the crush in the tube reduced him to a state of panic. He intended to call at the *Daily Herald* office, but after walking up and down past the entrance and hovering undecidedly at the door of the Enterprise, a favoured haunt of the editorial staff, he abruptly strode away down Long Acre.

The thought of facing his old colleagues and answering the inevitable questions was just too much for him. He wondered what had happened to Jane Flippance and her father. Was the *Four Winds* carrying the Basque refugees to safety? He had the address of Jane's aunt in Truro and could have written. But at home he flopped into a chair and fell asleep listening to the new Marconiphone. A terrible lethargy seized him. He woke in the mornings feeling tired and uninterested in what the day might bring.

A letter from Jack Harris in Nottingham saying that he was coming to London for an interview with the editor of the *Evening Chronicle* and suggesting that they meet 'for a few beers' at the Cheshire Cheese seemed to cheer him. Frank waited for his friend in the dark little bar with sawdust on the bare-boarded floor and a window onto Wine Office Court.

Putting two brimming pints on the shelf above the fire, Jack announced triumphantly: 'They've hired me as a gallery reporter in the House of Commons.'

'Congratulations,' said Frank, raising his glass. 'That's what you said you wanted to be right from the start.'

'And that's not all,' Jack went on. 'I'm engaged to Ethel.'

Ethel was the girl in gingham, the plainer of the two they had met at the Chelsea Arts Ball.

'Congratulations again,' responded Frank, although this time with a slightly sardonic edge to his voice.

'Don't tell me,' said Jack. 'I should have my head examined, getting hitched at my age, but, well, the money's good at the *Chronicle* and we'll be able to get a nice little home together.'

'I didn't know you'd been seeing her,' said Frank. 'Her friend wrote to me, but somehow I never got around to answering. Pity really, she was quite hot stuff . . .'

'To tell you the truth,' Jack told him, 'I didn't really plan to get married. I only saw her on and off when I was down in London – we went to dances and the pictures, the usual stuff – and then she invited me down to Stoke Poges for the weekend to meet her family. Well, in the train coming back I just popped the question . . . it sort of seemed the thing to do.'

'Perhaps it was something her mother put in the walnut layer cake,' suggested Frank sarcastically.

Jack laughed ruefully.

'I don't know, old man,' he said, 'but all the way back to Nottingham I kept saying to myself "You've been and gone and done it now, Harris." And that was that.'

'Well, you didn't *have* to, did you?' asked Frank.

'Oh crikey, no, nothing like that,' Jack answered. 'Ethel's a nice respectable girl. She wouldn't allow anything like *that*, not till we're married.'

Jack did most of the talking during that meeting at the Cheshire Cheese, a most unusual state of affairs. Frank was not only taciturn about his exploits in Spain, but coughed repeatedly after lighting his pipe and soon laid it to one side.

Even more disturbing to Jack was the fact that after only two pints his friend said he had had enough and looked quite ill. Jack regarded him anxiously through his owl-like spectacles, but Frank insisted that he was perfectly all right. Yet it was obvious that both physically and mentally he was at a very low ebb.

He managed to rouse himself sufficiently to be best man at Jack Harris's wedding in October. It took place in a Methodist chapel at Stoke Poges, with a reception for about sixty guests in the church hall afterwards.

Jack's father did not attend, claiming that he could not afford to miss a shift at the Surrey Docks, where he had been employed for the past two years, as there were plenty of men in the pool of casual labour ready and anxious to take his place. After so many years out of work since the General Strike he was inclined to paranoia and, in any case, he feared his son's wedding would be a posh affair.

Mrs Harris went, dressed to the nines, accompanied by two other sons looking ill at ease in fifty-shilling suits bought for the occasion, with carnations in their buttonholes. Ethel's father, who managed a shaving-cream factory on the Great West Road, spoke at length at the wedding breakfast about what a treasure she was. Looking at her down the table, poised to attack a three-tiered wedding cake, Frank found her even less alluring in bridal white than she had been as Bo-Peep at the Chelsea Arts Ball.

There was nothing stronger to toast the happy couple with than a rather watery claret cup, and Frank was so irritated by the social airs put on by Ethel's family to the discomfiture of the Harrises that he made an inappropriately satirical speech. It was received in silence except by one of the bridesmaids who started to giggle, then stopped when she saw everyone else glaring at her.

All in all, it was an uncomfortable and embarrassing affair, and Frank arrived home late that night after a tedious journey by train looking like death. Jenny dosed him with syrup of figs and the next morning sent for a doctor.

'His temperature is not wildly abnormal but there are symptoms of a virus infection, Mrs Cole,' he told her after he had completed his examination. 'He has been in Spain, you say? Well now, I'm not quite sure what to make of it – I'd like a second opinion. The best thing would be to get him into King's for observation.'

So Frank went into the private patients' wing at King's College Hospital where he lay, between X-rays, in a comfortable room reading Cronin's new novel *The Citadel*, exposing the methods of certain so-called 'society doctors'. He was in the middle of it when a young registrar came in and stood fiddling with the sounding fitment of his stethoscope, staring out of the window at the traffic on Denmark Hill. He looked as if he would rather be somewhere else.

'About your X-rays,' he said at last, then stopped and played with his stethescope again.

Frank stared at him impatiently: 'Well? What about them?'

'You've got tuberculosis, I'm afraid,' the registrar blurted out.

'Badly?'

'Well, pretty badly, yes. It's both lungs,' he answered, then added reassuringly, 'The right one's worse than the left.'

After the doctor had gone, Frank lay quietly for a time with *The Citadel*'s shiny new jacket spread open on the counterpane beside him. On the bedside cabinet was a picture postcard of palm trees at Torquay where Jack and Ethel were spending their honeymoon. They were 'having a lovely time', it said.

Frank was not feeling sorry for himself. If he felt anything, it was relief. For weeks he had wondered what was wrong with him, why he felt so low and wretched. Now he knew.

So that's that, he told himself. It's TB, the scourge of modern man. Now they can do the worrying. And with that thought, he turned over on to his side and fell fast asleep.

12

A couple of weeks before Christmas the taxi from the station drove through the wrought-iron gates of Downshall Sanatorium, past the croquet lawn and the rockery, the banks of rhododendrons and the ornamental lake and fountain to the red-brick Edwardian mansion. Seated in the back with his mother, and wrapped in a plaid travelling rug, Frank was reminded of his first day at Chelwood Abbey school, which, as it happened, was not many miles away across the green, undulating Sussex countryside.

He had spent the intervening weeks since he learned he had TB in a grim old institution in one of the sootiest and foggiest areas of the East End – the home, paradoxically, of the London Chest Hospital. He was now the possessor of an artificial pneumothorax, or AP, which meant that his right lung had been collapsed by a technique which at that time was in the van of chest surgery. He had come to Downshall ('A sanatorium for patients over 18 of good education and background. Terms 4 guineas per week, inclusive') to learn how to live with it.

A uniformed porter hurried down the steps as the taxi drew up, opened the door for them and picked up Frank's suitcase. In a hall furnished with Lloyd Loom chairs and low glass-topped tables, a pretty nurse was putting up paper chains and tinsel with the eager assistance of some young men, who took no notice whatever of Frank's arrival, so absorbed were they. They looked extraordinarily fit and only the fact that they were wearing dressing gowns and slippers indicated that they were patients.

The porter showed them upstairs to a bright, airy room with wide french windows and green shutters, leading onto a tiled balcony with planters' chairs overlooking the lake, lawns and shrubberies.

'It's so peaceful and pleasant here,' said Jenny, looking round. 'I'm sure you'll find it easy to rest and relax.'

'Dr Shendham said I'll be back at work in six months,' replied Frank.

'You must be patient,' Jenny reminded him gently, 'and do exactly as you're told – I know that's not easy for you. Don't try to hurry things. It will take time.'

The past month or two had not been easy for her. On top of the shock of Frank's health breaking down came the news of Canon Dick Sheppard's death. She had worked closely with him in the Peace Pledge Union, which had enjoyed popular success beyond their wildest dreams, so much so that it was becoming almost a new party.

On the sideboard at 35 Amen Road was a photograph of this lovable priest carrying a sandwichboard announcing a mass protest in Hyde Park against £500,000,000 being spent on rearmament: WAR – WE SAY NO! Speakers at the rally included George Lansbury and Vera Brittain, whose world war memoirs, *Testament of Youth*, had been a best-seller. Jenny, it must be admitted, savoured being on the fringes of the political literary world which had surrounded her father and the country house at Westerham where she grew up.

Like Jenny's former suitor, the Marquess of Broucester, who was killed in the war, Sheppard had lived and worked among the poor in the East End and organized boys' clubs when he came down from university. From the moment he became vicar of St Martin-in-the-Fields, overlooking Trafalgar Square, in 1914, Dick Sheppard made it the church of the soldiers and at the same time the church of the down-and-outs. He became the best known and most popular parson in England.

He unashamedly enjoyed his regular visits to Broadcasting House, that gleaming new white building which looked like a great ocean liner incongruously washed up in Portland Place, meekly accepting a ban on what the B B C regarded as his peace propaganda. He had a page in the *Sunday Express* every week and his populist books flowed from the presses: *Sheppard's Pie, Some of My Religion, We Say No, More Sheppard's Pie*.

He was, however, a complex man, in some ways a Jekyll and Hyde. Everyone's friend, he could on occasion become quite haughty and grand; a lover of the poor and deprived, he was none the less a bit of a snob, who bought his suits in Savile Row and had his hair cut in Bond Street; a man full of fun who could sink into despair. 'I'm bedridden again,' he wrote in one letter, 'and blub a lot when no one sees me – any little courage I once had is beginning to ebb.'

He ended up as a canon at St Paul's Cathedral, hating the quarrels in Chapter, the ill will and jealousy and what he called 'those cold, cold stones' – they had finally worn him out and placed him in the ground. Just because he preached peace not war, Jenny Cole was his disciple in the unfashionable cultural wilderness south of the river. She would carry on the fight, trying not to break her heart and her health in the process as he had done. With Frank in a sanatorium, her burden was heavy, but she was used to that, wasn't she?

Every Monday after lunch the patients at Downshall lined up for what was irreverently known as 'Archibald McNee's Picture Show'. Dr McNee, the superintendent, sat flanked by subordinates facing a screen. One by one the patients took their turns to stand behind the screen while their chests were briefly illuminated for the scrutiny of the medical staff. Occasionally Dr McNee would make a comment, but in too low a voice for the victim to hear what he said.

The men stripped to the waist for this ordeal while the women, who went in first, wore shapeless white linen blouses. Most of them were young, but one in particular immediately attracted Frank – a fair-skinned girl of about eighteen with short light-brown hair. Even in that unbecoming garment she managed to look like a mannequin. He noticed her again at dinner in the refectory where the men occupied one set of tables and the women another.

'Who is that stunning girl over there?' he asked his neighbour, an extrovert young New Zealander who greeted him on the first night with a cheery: 'Hello, I'm Ralph Greedie – Greedie by name, greedy by nature.'

Ralph glanced across the room and answered Frank's question: 'Oh, *her* . . . snooty Sheila.'

'Is that her name? Sheila?'

'No mate,' said Ralph laughing so uproariously that the entire room turned to stare at them. 'Sheila's my word for all judies . . . you know, girls.'

It did not take Frank long to discover that she was called Dorothy Plumley-Greene and that she was a Roedean girl, the daughter of an army officer. His first opportunity to talk to her was at tea, when male and female patients were allowed to sit together and guests were admitted for tea at sixpence a head. She was sitting alone, however, in the corridor sun lounge reading *Esquire*.

'May I join you?' he asked.

'If you wish,' she answered, glancing up briefly, and continuing her reading. He did not let this put him off.

'I'm Frank Cole,' he said. 'I'm new here.'

Dorothy put down her magazine and looked at him for a moment before asking: 'Have you been visited by the ghouls yet?'

'The ghouls?'

'Yes,' she went on, 'they usually try to get at new patients in their first week. They were onto me the moment I arrived, absolutely *oozing* friendliness and sympathy, yet once they got on to details of treatment and surgery their lurid descriptions were enough to frighten one out of one's wits. One of these harpies solemnly warned me not under any circumstances to submit to gold treatment – it seems that in some cases they actually inject gold into patients. According to her, this not only plays havoc with one's kidneys but has the effect of turning one's face blue in bright sunshine!'

They both laughed, bringing a suspicious glance in their direction from one of the sisters in navy blue uniform who was passing with a tray of cucumber sandwiches.

'Look out,' whispered Dorothy. 'One of the "blue jobs" is watching us.'

She made him smile again with her description of the institutional snobberies of Downshall: 'Thoracoplastic cases look down on extra-pleurals, who in turn consider themselves to be a cut above simple APs. APs, however, can scarcely bring themselves to acknowledge the existence of phrenics.'

'Phrenics?' asked Frank. 'What on earth are they?'

'People who've had the phrenic nerve crushed to paralyse for the time being the lower lung,' explained Dorothy. 'But right at the very bottom of the pecking order are people like me, humble LTDs – allowed up for lunch, tea and dinner.'

After sipping her tea, she went on: 'Actually, I shouldn't be in here at all – I haven't even got TB, I'm merely convalescing from a particularly nasty attack of pleurisy. Poppa knows McNee frightfully well so he pulled some strings to get me in here for complete and absolute rest. I must say that compared to school it's heaven – divine food, glorious idleness and lots of lovely men to talk to.'

Frank found her captivating, delightful to look at in her smartly tailored play suit with trousers or 'slacks', and witty in conversation. The attraction was mutual. Dorothy noted their first meeting in her diary with the initials SA, which stood for 'sex appeal'. Most of the other male patients had been listed as CIBP, 'comb in back pocket', PITP, 'pen in top pocket', or most damning of all, NQOCD, 'not quite our class, darling'. A few, including Ralph Greedie, were catalogued as WHT, wandering hand trouble, or MTF, 'must touch flesh', not that there were many opportunities for *that* at Downshall when the sexes were kept so strictly segregated. Doctors and nurses were aware that TB patients generally were highly sexed, and sex in those days was looked upon as the greatest of all the snares laid on the pathway to heaven.

Christmas, apart from the seasonal fare and decorations and the fact that everyone pulled crackers and wore paper hats at lunch, was like any other day, regulated by bells. There were bells to get up, bells to lie down, bells for mealtimes. In his first few weeks at Downshall, Frank was allowed up only from the 1 p.m. bell and the one at 5.30 in the evening signalled his bedtime.

Every few days he was required to visit the 'light room' to have a needle stuck in his chest, and lay listening to the air bubbling from the AP box. The air pressure which kept his right lung collapsed was gradually absorbed by surrounding tissues, hence the necessity for regular refills.

It was Ralph Greedie, who occupied the room next to his, who more than anyone kept his spirits up. He was dark-jowled, with twinkling blue eyes. He was seventeen when he ran away from home in a prosperous Auckland suburb to join Slattery's Flying Circus, which toured fairs and race meetings with a couple of worn-out Sopwiths giving death-defying displays. Ralph specialized in wing-walking.

His father, who owned a chain of department stores, became so alarmed that he sent his son to the Royal Air Force College in England under the Dominion training scheme so that he would be 'taught to fly *inside* an aeroplane – it's safer that way'.

'The last thing I wanted to do was get dressed up in a blue uniform and perform all that garbage of drill and saluting,' said Ralph. 'I just wanted to fly.'

His habit of addressing everyone as 'mate' struck rather jarringly in the officers' mess at Cranwell, but Ralph was a natural aviator and at the end of the course stepped up proudly to have the coveted 'wings' pinned to his breast. Unfortunately, during a passing-out aerobatic display he suffered an inexplicable blackout and was picked out of the wreckage of his Gypsy Moth with two broken legs.

There was worse to come. The X-rays showed not only broken bones, but ominous spots on one of his lungs. That was how Pilot Officer Greedie found himself at Downshall Sanatorium long after his broken legs had mended. Yet he refused to take his condition seriously.

'I'll be flying at Hendon this year,' he kept saying, but the last RAF display there came and went, and Ralph was still at Downshall.

He *was* getting better though. Long after he was tucked up in bed in the evening, Frank heard through the party wall a scratchy gramophone rendering of 'Hotcha Momma from Alabama', accompanied by a frantic rat-tatting. This was Ralph learning to tapdance. He loved playing practical jokes on Sister, or taking potshots at the gardener from the balcony with his peashooter. Most of the staff found him irresistible.

Jenny, meeting him on her regular weekend visits to Downshall, took an immediate liking to him, and he to her. He called her 'the Duchess'. Jenny was not so impressed by Dorothy Plumley-Greene.

'That young lady is too superior by half,' she remarked, but she could see at once that Frank was smitten by her, and felt a little pang of jealousy for which she soundly rebuked herself on the way home.

The coming of spring brought a golden-yellow sheen of daffodils to the lawn leading down to the lake, and house martins returned from south of the Sahara to their old nesting places in the eaves of Downshall. Frank and Ralph lounged in the sun on the balcony, watching them diving, swooping, wheeling, banking, as they patiently built up their nests, layer after layer, from mud carried in their beaks.

'Mate, if only I could fly like that,' remarked Ralph. 'Those little buggers could dive-bomb a sixpence from two thousand feet.'

From an open window came the sound of Bob Hope singing 'Thanks for the Memory'. By this time both Frank and Ralph were potty over Dorothy Plumley-Greene and she was enjoying the game of playing one off against the other.

One afternoon she shared her very expensive brand of chocolate biscuits with Frank, the next afternoon she was tête-à-tête with Ralph. These biscuits came in a hamper delivered to the door by a chauffeur in a straight-twelve Minerva.

'Did you see his gorgeous new livery?' Dorothy asked Ralph. 'Momsy bought it in Gorringes – isn't it a simply *lovely* shade of grey?'

Ralph winced at such affectation and dropped crumbs on his grey flannels. The biscuits, like other patients' 'special treats', were kept on the sideboard in a tin with Dorothy's signature pencilled on the lid. He felt that she looked down her nose at people who went in for Kunzle Cakes or Lyons' swiss rolls.

Neither Frank nor Ralph played bridge, so they could not join the after dinner 'fours' in the corridor lounge as Dorothy invariably did. Despite her youth, she was in the Portland Club class. These evenings at Downshall were somehow reminiscent of first class in the *Queen Mary*, except that it was lights-out at ten and the patients were allowed no alcohol. Downshall boasted a newfangled television set in the lounge, but the programmes, detailed on a single page of the *Radio Times*, were limited to half an hour of cabaret from Alexandra Palace, a British Movietone newsreel or perhaps a film. The main source of entertainment was the wireless – plays, talks, news, outside broadcasts, hour after hour of concerts, and dance music from Henry Hall, Geraldo and the Savoy Hotel Orpheans. There was even an enthusiastic audience for 'Toytown' on Children's Hour. On Sundays, though, a Reithian piety filled the airwaves with hymns and prayers and organ music. The sporadic clatter of Frank's Remington portable rivalled Greedie's tapdancing in nuisance to other patients. Because of his poor health, he found it difficult to concentrate and most of his writing ended up in crumpled balls of paper in the wastepaper basket. In any case, everyone was writing about the war and when George Orwell came out with *Homage to Catalonia* that year there seemed little left to say.

Dorothy liked to hear Frank talk about his writing and told her parents about him. To Colonel Plumley-Greene, a member of the fashionable bow-and-arrow brigade who still regarded Captain Liddell Hart as a dangerous lunatic, Frank became 'that Fabian writer chap' – a description which my father took as a compliment. As for Greedie, he was a common colonial, quite beyond the pale – he even went in for bets on the pools and laughed at Charlie Chester's jokes – yet Dorothy found him amusing company.

Frank the intellectual she summoned after breakfast to help her with *The Times* crossword. Ralph was later dispatched to the little room under the stairs smelling of leather and blacking to fetch the croquet mallets. Both danced attention on her, and she loved it.

One scented May evening Frank managed to escape alone with her into the shrubberies. She looked her best in a summery frock with sunburn silk stockings and he brought with him a Murphy portable radio and a car rug to sit on. They were getting on famously together ('He put his arm around my waist,' she noted in her diary that evening), listening to Carroll Gibbons and the Savoy Hotel Orpheans, when Dr McNee himself suddenly appeared round a purple-flowered bush, taking his dog for its usual evening stroll.

'Damp grass isna going to do your lungs much good,' he remarked tersely in passing.

'It's my fault, Doctor,' said Frank, jumping up. 'I asked Miss Plumley-Greene to join me for a breath of air.'

But the great man strode on, an incongruous figure in plus-fours and carpet slippers, without looking back. From then on his eyes always narrowed whenever they lighted on Mr Cole. He had labelled him as a ladies' man, which to Dr McNee's Calvinistic bachelor mind was no compliment.

Soon after this incident Miss Plumley-Greene left the sanatorium. Whether it was because she was restored to health, or because Dr McNee considered it would be detrimental for her health to stay, is open to question.

In any event, Downshall was not the same without her. In the eyes of Frank and Ralph she had become more desirable than Jessie Matthews, Vivien Leigh, Lilli Palmer or any other film star of the day. However, they became even closer companions now that the only source of rivalry between them had disappeared.

Frank was now allowed to walk a mile a day and when the Sanatorium XI played the local village cricket team he joined Ralph and a group of other patients in the shade of the yew trees which bordered the green.

'We look like an outing from the loony bin,' said Ralph, gesturing towards the uniformed sister and two nurses who were there to keep an eye on them. The afternoon passed lazily, watching the clumsy performance on the field while listening to the commentary by Howard Marshall on the cricket at Lord's coming over the wireless. Bradman was busy knocking up 278 for Australia against the MCC.

Ralph lay on his back, gazing up at the white vapour trails drawn across the blue sky by unseen high-flying aeroplanes and listening to the distant drone of their engines.

'Churchill's right, you know,' said Ralph. 'We should be building up fighter squadrons as fast as the factories can turn them out like Hitler's doing. Those chaps up in London are only playing at it.'

It was a subject which he and Jenny argued heatedly on her

visits to the sanatorium. Her attitude towards Churchill was coloured by bitter memories of his treatment of the suffragettes when he was a member of a Liberal government before the Great War. For long years now he had been excluded from the National Government, which he railed against from his country home at Chartwell in between laying bricks and making vast sums of money from his writings.

'Winston is rattling his sabre because he can't bear to be out of office,' said Jenny. 'He is living in the past – he still can't imagine that the days when everyone trembled at the might of the British Raj are over.'

'Excuse me for saying it, Duchess, but you're talking through the top of your tiara,' retorted Ralph. 'Winnie is the only British politician that Herr Hitler is scared of – because he's the one who's rumbled him. It's a flaming disgrace that Churchill isn't in the Cabinet.'

Despite their disagreement over rearmament, Ralph and 'the Duchess' remained the best of friends. On one of her visits she persuaded Sister to let them go out for tea in the garden of the Royal Oak pub nearby. Sitting among the rosebeds under a sunshade emblazoned with the word 'Tizer', Frank and Ralph enjoyed a few pints of something a little stronger.

Sister looked at them with narrowed eyes when they returned to the sanatorium flushed and overtalkative. They slept until the bell went for dinner. Jenny did not shop them.

Oddly enough, although alcohol was forbidden to patients, they were allowed to smoke almost without restriction. Frank bought two ounces of Three Nuns flake with his *Picture Post* from the hospital shop every week and Ralph got through two packets of Greys cigarettes, 'a tanner for ten', every day.

Their doctors and nurses never objected to this. It never occurred to anyone in those days that smoking might give them a disease even more deadly than the one they already had. Tobacco was the most commonly used method of relieving the boredom of waking hours at Downshall. One of their fellow patients resorted to another drug – an eastern root with an Arabic name which sounded remarkably like 'Uncle Arthur' – which he firmly believed did him more good than the extra-pleural which Dr McNee had performed on him. He had this quack potion sent to him under plain cover, to keep it secret, or so he imagined.

'Another consignment of Uncle Arthur for you, mate,' said Ralph in a voice which everyone could hear when he volunteered to take round the mail one morning.

The guilty recipient went red, while Frank stuffed his handkerchief into his mouth to stifle an explosive fit of the giggles. At the same time he felt a lunging pain in the ribs and collapsed in a heap on the floor.

13

'It's such a pity,' Dr McNee was saying, 'when the boy seemed to be making such excellent progress. We shall have to operate.'

'Is it serious, Doctor?' asked Jenny. She had driven down to the sanatorium in her speedy black Morris as soon as she heard of her son's collapse.

'Och no, my dear,' said McNee reassuringly. 'The job is done with a local anaesthetic, just a wee snipping of the lesions between his right lung and the pleural wall – the blighters that are interfering with his AP.'

She caught a glimpse of Frank on a trolley, wrapped up like a mummy in flannel bandages, as they wheeled him into the operating theatre. He waved at her cheerfully, having just been injected with omnopon and hyoscine, but looking up a moment later at a circle of faces in masks and little white caps he experienced some doubts. The doubts grew when they squeezed him into a contraption like an oversized trouser press and began sticking needles into him.

The surgeon inserted a thoracoscope through the chest wall and suddenly ordered: 'Lights out!' After a moment or two he gave a low whistle and said to McNee, who was standing beside him: 'Have a look at this, old boy.'

Frank wondered what it was they found so interesting, but they ignored him completely while they carried on poking around inside his chest. He heard and felt the lesions snapping like elastic bands as they got to work with their instruments. He gritted his teeth and clung to the theatre sister's hand, trying hard not to scream. The nurse at the far end of the table began stroking his bare feet. It helped.

After half an hour of this they took out the instruments and stitched him up. Frank had a raging thirst and when they gave him a drink of lemon squash from a thing like a baby's bottle he emptied it at a gulp, then remarked: 'What I could really do with, Sister, is a pint of best.'

She smiled at him and told the porters to wheel him back to his room. Although it was a warm summer's night they packed him in hot-water bottles.

Jenny came in and said to him: 'Don't worry, you're going to be all right.'

But her encouraging smile and optimistic words masked what she felt inside, unease and foreboding for the future. Her son's health had been broken in a cause worth fighting for, she told herself, but she did not really believe it. In her heart she was against all war, even just wars. She had known war and had seen the horrors it inflicted on human flesh and minds.

This time it would be worse, with bombs raining down on innocent women and children. Photographs and newsreels of families huddled together for shelter in the underground of Madrid had made a vivid impression on her. As she went on her daily rounds, checking on 'her babies' and delivering new ones into the world, she tried not to imagine their fragile little bodies crushed beneath the masonry of bombed buildings. The fear was so intense that she had nightmares about it: a devastated city in which there were no survivors.

Everywhere she went she produced peace pledge forms from her bag and tried to get people to sign. But most people were fatalistic, believing that war was inevitable and no amount of 'peace pledges' would avert it.

Jenny saw, with a feeling of helpless horror, preparations for war proceeding apace. On Clapham Common and Tooting Bec, volunteers were digging trenches and painting tree trunks white so that they would stand out in a blackout.

'ARP' badges were issued, searchlights and sound locators demonstrated as a defence against the bombers. The Cement and Concrete Association put forward the absurd idea of overhead roads through the capital 'to make evacuation easier.' There was talk of secret food storage centres and fleets of emergency ambulances.

Jenny felt like rushing through the streets shouting: 'Stop it! You've all gone completely mad.'

'People are very worried and concerned about the prospect of war,' she wrote to Frank during that anxious summer in which the Spanish War was all but won for General Franco and Adolf Hitler, having gobbled up Austria, prepared to make a meal of Czechoslovakia.' 'If it does come they won't be out in the streets cheering and throwing their hats in the air like they did in 1914. Young wives and mothers with sons of military age are sick with apprehension – I pray to God that you and Ralph and young Jack will be kept out of it.'

Even before this letter arrived, Ralph Greedie was pronounced fit to leave Downshall Sanatorium and had been to say goodbye, wearing his pilot officer's 'best blue' with the brilliant white wings on the breast.

'I have to go before a board to determine whether I can resume flying duties,' he explained. 'Wish me luck, mate.'

'Good luck,' said Frank, shaking him by the hand. 'Don't go breaking any more aeroplanes will you?'

'Just let me get at one of those new Spitfires, that's all,' retorted Ralph.

Frank knew that he would miss him, they had been such friends. Now he felt alone at Downshall and confined within the four walls of his room. A visit from Jack Harris, who came down one Sunday with Jenny in the car, did not make him feel more cheerful. Jack was wrapped up in his job and his marriage. They had moved into a five-roomed flat in a newly built block with gardens and hard tennis courts at Beulah Hill, and Ethel had just given birth to their first child, a girl.

'You, a daddy,' said Frank. 'I just can't imagine it.'

'Well it's real enough,' retorted Jack, 'and keeps us up half the night to prove it. Still we're lucky to have such a nice home for £135 a year including central heating and constant hot water. It's only seventeen minutes from Victoria to Crystal Palace or West Norwood and the buses stop at the door. You'll have to come and stay with us when you get out of here – Ethel would love to have you.'

'What about the war jitters?' asked Frank.

'Ethel's got a bit jumpy about it,' Jack told him. 'She went out shopping the other day for some shoes and bought stout, flat-heeled ones instead of high heels – "More suitable in case of air raids," she said. And she made me cancel an order for a bedroom suite until things settle down. Personally, I don't think there'll be a war – Chamberlain's determined to do a deal with Hitler.'

After Jack had gone, Frank felt depressed. Since their earliest days at school their lives had run parallel courses and now, it seemed to him, Jack had forged ahead.

Married, set up in his own home, with a child . . . doing the job he always said he wanted, he thought, while I'm lying here like a wreck, everything ruined, no job to go back to.

Through the open window he could see the black and white martins diving and soaring at incredible speed, swooping to their nests under the eaves to feed their young with insects snapped up in flight. The brood kept up a continual chirping chorus from dawn to dusk.

'Oh, shut up!' yelled Frank, burying his head under the sheets.

On August Bank Holiday he was allowed to get up and watch Downshall's annual sports day from the balcony outside his room. Only nurses and doctors were permitted to take part in the games, which included sack, and egg and spoon races, nailing a tail on a donkey while blindfolded, shove ha'penny and a mock Derby with wooden horses. The patients looked on and cheered their favourite members of staff. The atmosphere was somewhere between a school sports day and a vicarage garden party. It was difficult to believe that outside the walls of this little community the war clouds were gathering.

On the first day of October, the house martins abruptly decamped from the eaves, heading south to Africa for the winter. One of the gardener's assistants was busy demolishing their nests with a brush attached to chimney sweep's rods. The dried mud disintegrated easily and came tumbling down in a shower of dust and feathers.

'A right old mess they make,' he grumbled, looking up at Frank watching him from the balcony. 'Blessed droppings all over the terrace and the windowsills. They'll be back next Spring to do it all over again – like night and the Jesuits, they always return.'

Frank went inside, smiling. Where will I be next spring? That's anybody's guess.

His bag was packed ready for the taxi which was coming to take him to the station. He had arrived at Downshall ten months ago weighing less than nine stone, haggard and constantly tired. Now he was around eleven stone, bronzed and bright-eyed, looking as if he had just returned from a Mediterranean cruise.

'You've got a perfect AP,' Dr McNee told him after his final check, 'and your other lung has cleared up completely – your sputum has been TB-negative for three months. There's no reason why you should have any recurrence of this disease – provided that you behave yourself *and don't try to burn your candle at both ends.*'

The superintendent was looking at him with those narrowed eyes as he uttered the last few words, obviously harking back to that business in the shrubbery.

He was not among the little group gathered on the steps to wave goodbye as Frank was driven off to the station. Waving back, he experienced something like panic and an almost overwhelming desire to stop the cab, jump out and run back into their sheltering arms.

At the station the billboards at the newspaper stand proclaimed in large letters: 'IT IS PEACE FOR OUR TIME! CHAMBERLAIN.' Everyone had gathered round the wireless at the sanatorium the previous evening to hear the Prime Minister, just returned from Munich by aeroplane with a foolscap piece of paper 'which bears Hitler's name upon it as well as mine'.

The relief was palpable, last night and again that morning. There were smiles on every face. Frank bought a penny copy of the *Daily Herald* to read on the train, feeling that his return to the world was well timed. The photographs showed Mr Chamberlain acknowledging the cheers of the crowd from an upstairs window at number 10 Downing Street, surrounded by smiling members of the Cabinet, reading his scrap of paper in front of the BBC microphones at Heston Aerodrome, waving it triumphantly, accepting more plaudits on the balcony of Buckingham Palace with the King and Queen.

Reading between the lines, Frank could see that his older and wiser colleagues on the *Herald* did not wholeheartedly share the general mood of euphoria. Adolf Hitler had scored a personal triumph with the sacrifice of Czech independence. Hannen Swaffer reported from among crowds singing 'Land of Hope and Glory' in Downing Street that, using newspapers as a shelter, they actually kept off the rain with the peace terms Czechoslovakia had been forced to sign.

He ended his report: 'This was the supreme irony of an evening in which you would think, when you heard the cheering, that

Britain had really gained a great victory over the forces of Might.'

But Jenny, too, was smiling as she waited for him at the barrier at Clapham Junction.

'Isn't it wonderful, wonderful news?' she said, hugging him so fiercely that the pain was almost enough to make him cry out. 'No more war. Think of it!'

She rushed to take his case away from him, leading him to the car. Over Tooting Bec a large silver barrage balloon – 'Blimps', the people called them – floated lazily.

'Thank heavens *they* won't be needed,' said Jenny, noticing Frank's curious stare upwards. 'People can start talking about next year's summer holidays instead of ARP drills. And I'll be able to think about getting some new winter curtains instead of blackout material.'

The South London streets were thronged with Saturday shoppers, women bustling in and out of department stores buying fashionable suits and hats for autumn wear, gossiping about colour schemes, besieging the jewellery counters, swapping jokes with smiling shop assistants.

Jack Harris, too, was bubbling with good humour when he called round that evening to see how Frank was getting on.

'Hasn't it been a lovely day?' he said. 'I don't remember ever enjoying a sunny day so much. I'd cancelled some white paint that I'd ordered because Ethel and the baby went off to Stoke Poges for safety in case the air raids started. Well today I went and reordered it – I'll get the bathroom done before they come home.'

They stayed up until midnight listening to American dance music from Shep Fields and his Rippling Rhythm Orchestra on the BBC National programme.

Despite the Munich agreement, trench digging in London parks went on, as did the equipping of sand-bagged shelters with first-aid equipment, the distribution of gasmasks and the recruiting of air raid wardens. The strains of Bob Hope crooning 'Thanks for the Memory' with Shirley Ross from *The Big Broadcast of 1938* made Frank think of the delectable Dorothy and May evenings in the shrubberies at Downshall.

Dorothy's diaries do not show that she gave any thought to either Downshall or Frank. It was evidently a closed chapter of her life and the world that she inhabited, the upper-class Home Counties society, which had survived virtually unchanged since Queen

Victoria's reign, was far removed from the lower middle-class suburban existence of Jenny Cole and her son. Although Oak House, the Plumley-Greenes' Edwardian mansion on the borders of Surrey and Sussex, was less than twenty miles south of Amen Road, it might have been on another planet.

Neither Frank Cole nor Ralph Greedie were invited to spend weekends at Oak House since the social fence surrounding it was as impenetrable as the thickest hedgerows surmounted by the East Surrey Hunt.

Foxhunting was a way of life for the Plumley-Greenes and their friends. Dorothy's mother hunted side-saddle and was Master of the Hunt for ten years. Dorothy's first sight of a fox was on a walk with her nurse when they came upon one nibbling blackberries on a slope of the North Downs, unaware of their approach until they were almost on him.

'Nice doggie,' said Dorothy, stretching out her hand as the startled fox scurried into the brambles but the nurse corrected her: 'Horrid little beasts. They get my dad's chickens no matter how much wire he puts up.'

Shortly afterwards, at the age of four, Dorothy followed the hunt on a little pony called Sugar and at nine she was ritually 'blooded', her face daubed with the blood of a freshly killed fox.

'I can remember riding home at a furious pace, praying that the rain wouldn't wash all the blood off my face before I could show my father,' she said.

But in the summer following Munich her mind was more on the pursuit of young men than foxes as she took part in the unchanged ritual of the Season for the first time and was seen at Henley and Cowes, at Ascot and Goodwood, at the Cambridge May Ball and the Fourth of June at Eton. Almost every night there was a private dance at someone's house.

'Rattled home at dawn from the Hardings,' says her diary for 18 July. 'Poppa's chauffeur waited outside in the car until I was ready to come home. Filled up from numbers 5 to 10 in my programme with H. but saved the supper dance for William, who is definitely in the wayside pleasure category. Heavenly tune 'All of me, why not take all of me?' and afterwards we sat and talked for simply hours. H. frightfully cut up about it . . .'

Dorothy, who was slim with very nice legs and bobbed light brown hair, had enough clothes to make the most of her natural good looks. She had cotton frocks for day wear and a silk frock for the races or cocktail parties, which had only just come in, and she had six evening dresses.

Like the other debutantes she was going about to see and be seen by eligible young men. She was no longer a schoolgirl but a young lady of marriageable age, and marriage was still the only objective in life of most young ladies, preferably to a lord.

'Perfectly awful picture of me in the *Tatler* at Queen Charlotte's Birthday Ball . . .' her record of the relentless round continues. 'T. asked me to dance No. 7 but I refused. Momsy says he's NSIT ('Not Safe in Taxis') and anyway he has dreadful acne.'

'H. took me to Lady Diane's dance in his little Morgan two-seater – very dashing . . .' and a week or so later: 'Climbed out of my bedroom window, down the conservatory roof, to go up to town with H. in his car *to a night club*. Dark and grubby with some girls in a cabaret. One could almost see through the tops of their dresses and H. was quite lascivious about it.'

She was invited to stay with the Astors at Cliveden, one of a house party of young people who played tennis in the mornings and danced the nights away. They dressed in their smartest clothes for the races at Ascot, the boys in top hats, and gardenias and carnations for them to wear were laid out on silver trays in the hall. In her diary Dorothy agonized over how much to tip the servants when she left.

Naturally, the Plumley-Greenes gave a coming-out ball for their daughter at the Oak House.

The gardens were floodlit, although it was hardly necessary as there was a full moon that night. The guests started to arrive before dusk in a fleet of chauffeur-driven Daimlers, Bentleys and Rolls-Royces. Young men in white ties and tails stood around sipping sherry and nervously eyeing the young ladies.

'Truly *awful* band,' wrote Dorothy afterwards, 'played things like "Valencia" and "Good Night Vienna" until I insisted on "Happy Days Are Here Again". Walked with William in the rose garden and heard the nightingales singing, with the sound of the band coming from the house. *He held my hand*. Breakfast served at 3.30 a.m. – bacon, eggs, sausages and kedgeree and then (utter bliss) strawberries from the kitchen garden with lashings of cream. Absolutely ravenous. Got to bed at five after everyone had gone home.'

The climax of all this ritual gadding-about was the Presentation itself. Dorothy wore white brocade with a train and long white gloves, just as a bride might wear. She carried a spray of white carnations, and fastened to her hair with Kirbygrips and bits of elastic the three Prince of Wales feathers.

She sat with her parents in the back of the Minerva, nose to tail in the Mall with all the other expensive cars waiting to enter the courtyard of Buckingham Palace.

'The lights were switched on inside the cars so that the crowds waiting outside the Palace could see us,' wrote Dorothy. 'They just stared through the windows. Momsy had on her tiara and was simply dripping with pearls and diamonds but of course we girls wore no jewellery, not even a pair of earrings. There were soldiers lining the red carpet all the way up the stairs to the ante-room where we sat on gold chairs for what seemed hours.'

When at last they were called into the Throne Room they saw King George and Queen Elizabeth seated on two chairs on a dais. Mothers and daughters came forward in turn to curtsey as their names were called: 'Lady Plumley-Greene. To be presented, Miss Dorothy Plumley-Greene.'

No one at the time realized that this would be the last time this ceremony would take place for several years and that even then, after a brief flowering, the custom of Presentation at Court would wither and die. Yet underlying the sweetness of that last summer was a feeling that something awful was about to happen. Amidst all the dinners and balls in Dorothy's diary is the repeated note: 'Red Cross. First-aid class.'

While Dorothy Plumley-Greene lived dangerously through her first London Season, my father stoically endured a nine-to-five routine commuting between Fleet Street and Balham.

They did not write to one another and, as I said, in the buttery dance of society, she did not give him a thought. He, of course, saw her photograph in society columns, reminding him of their brief time together at the sanatorium.

Through the good offices of Jack Harris, Frank had been taken on the staff of the *Evening Chronicle* to read copy on the news desk. It was something of a comedown for a young man who had reached the pinnacle of being a special correspondent at the beginning of his career, but Frank was glad to take it. The hours were regular, the duties sedentary and his colleagues treated him with great consideration.

He had to take things easily, climbing stairs slowly, remaining seated in buses and the tube despite disapproving stares from people who considered him a lout for not giving his place to women who were standing. He was especially nervous of hearty bar-room gladiators who slapped him vigorously on the back. This was agony. Gradually, he recovered his strength and confidence.

He kept in touch with Ralph Greedie, who spent that summer waging a personal war against the Air Ministry who repeatedly refused on medical grounds to return him to operational flying. In between attending boards, Ralph kept his hand in by training pilots for the RAF in readiness for war at No. 19 E & RFTS (Elementary and Reserve Flying Training School) at Gatwick Aerodrome.

'I've logged a hundred hours in Tiger Moths, Hawker Harts and Miles Magisters,' he wrote to Frank, 'but my fingers are itching for the joystick of a Spitfire or a Hurricane.'

Frank saw little of Jack, who worked late hours at the House of Commons, but occasionally he visited the Harrises in their flat at Beulah Hill at the weekends or met his friend on the Southern Electric train into Victoria.

'Is there going to be a war, do you think?' Frank asked him one Monday as they rattled over the points at Battersea among all those people hiding their faces behind their newspapers.

'I'm afraid so,' said Jack, 'and when it comes we're all going to be in it. There's all kind of legislation coming up – conscription, suspension of habeas corpus, powers to commandeer private property and lock up people allegedly in sympathy with the enemy, without the formality of a trial. It'll be worse than Hitler, I tell you.'

'Will you join up, or wait to be conscripted?'

'I don't know,' Jack answered, staring out at the strings of barges as they clattered over the bridge across the Thames. 'I've got Ethel and the child to consider . . . and anyway, I'm a natural coward. But if I have to go I'd rather go in the RAF than the Army or the Navy.

'So would I,' said Frank.

The *Daily Express* that morning was congratulating itself for having predicted that 1939 would be a year of peace and plenty, and assured its readers that 'peace was secure'.

14

Frank Cole and Ralph Greedie were hiking on the South Downs on that Sunday morning in September when the bells of St Andrew's, so soon to be silenced except in case of enemy invasion, rang out on the still air from the village in the Cuckmere Valley below them. A group of men and girls in shorts, with knapsacks on their backs, passed them in the opposite direction, climbing up towards Firle Beacon.

'Chamberlain's on the wireless at a quarter past eleven,' one of the older men called out, 'so make the most of this glorious sunny day before the balloon goes up.'

It was indeed a fine morning after violent thunderstorms the night before, when rain lashing against the windows and teeming down on the tiles made them thankful that they had decided to put up at comfortable inns along the way rather than making it a camping weekend.

'I'd better go back up to town today,' said Ralph, untypically anxious. 'I want to be on the doorstep of the Air Ministry first thing tomorrow morning. They'll *have* to post me to a squadron now.'

In the public bar of the medieval Star Inn in Alfriston, opened early for the occasion, they heard the trembling voice of the Prime Minister: 'I am speaking to you from the Cabinet Room at 10 Downing Street. This morning the British Ambassador in Berlin handed the German government a formal note stating that unless we heard from them by 11 o'clock that they were prepared at once to withdraw their troops from Poland . . .'

There was absolute silence in the bar. Everyone was staring fixedly at the rising sun fretwork front and bakelite knobs of the radio set on the shelf.

'. . . I have to tell you now that no such undertaking has been received and that consequently this country is at war with Germany.'

His words seemed to hang in the air for several moments after he had finished speaking. Then one of the regular customers who had been playing darts when the broadcast started picked up his darts and walked over to the board.

'What was that I wanted, Bert?' he asked.

'Double top, weren't it,' said Bert.

And they carried on with their game as if nothing had happened.

Up and down the country the news rang out like a knell, none the less dreadful for having been expected for months.

The Hallsburys heard it in their drawing room at Bournemouth just after they got back from church.

'Oh, dear,' sighed Lucy, as she rang for the maid to bring in the sherry, 'I suppose it will soon be impossible to find servants, just as it was last time.'

Dorothy Plumley-Greene and her father did not hear of the announcement until they returned home for luncheon after a morning spent in pursuit of a fox across the sun-dappled slopes of the North Downs. The fox escaped, and for once Dorothy was unable after a long chase with the hounds to keep her make-up looking as if she was not made up at all.

'Damn!' said the colonel, when his wife broke the news. 'I suppose this means the brigade will be posted to France and I'll miss the October point-to-point.'

After fighting a long rearguard action, his cavalry squadrons had been forced at last to accept tanks and armoured cars, but he much preferred horses.

A few miles away at Blackstaff Hall, where Jenny grew up, her ageing stepbrother, the general, received the message broadcast by the BBC with barely disguised jubilation. Stomping around the bottom meadow with his dog at his heels, inspecting the concrete pill boxes and iron anti-tank traps which had been recently and hastily constructed to foil any attempted advance by the German Panzers, he was looking forward to some 'hand-to-hand combat with the Hun'. In his one remaining hand he carried a stout blackthorn stick; his other arm had been lost long ago in the last cavalry charge of the British Army. Occasionally, he glanced up as if expecting even now to see parachutists descending from the clear blue skies.

At Beulah Hill Jack Harris was sitting in his silent flat surrounded by copies of every Sunday paper. As before, at the time of the Munich crisis, Ethel and the child had gone to Stoke Poges to stay with her mother. He reckoned they would be safe from Hitler's bombs there.

When he saw them off at Paddington the station was packed with evacuees, carrying their gasmasks in cardboard cases along with their satchels, shepherded by harassed and anxious teachers. Now he was listening to Chamberlain's voice.

'Bloody wars,' said Jack savagely in unconscious imitation of his late senior, Harbottle. 'Bloody, bloody wars.'

At twenty past eleven, the rising and falling note of air-raid sirens wailed out over London.

Jack's father, putting on his cap, with his Sunday best choker tucked inside his collarless shirt, said to the third of his five sons: 'Come on, son, let's git dahn the boozer before the bleedin' bombs start fallin' on our 'eads.'

The Harris boy had already enlisted at the Royal Artillery depot at Woolwich and had arrived home on his first thirty-six-hour pass with his buttons gleamingly Brasso'd and his boots mirrorlike from hours of 'bull'.

Harris Senior's anxiety to sink a few pints before the holocaust turned out to be unnecessary – the alert was a false one. Even so, Jenny looked up anxiously at the sky as she hung out sheets and pillowcases to dry in her tiny back garden at 35 Amen Road.

Her next door neighbour Mr Glover appeared at his back door wearing a tin hat and shouted at her over the fence: 'For Gawd's sake, Mrs Cole, don't show anything white – it makes a perfect target for enemy planes.'

'Really, Mr Glover?' said Jenny politely while continuing to hang out her washing. 'I should have though the Luftwaffe was more interested in bombing the Maginot Line than my washing line.'

Mr Glover retreated indoors, slamming the door behind him. He had recently enrolled as an ARP warden and had been going up and down Amen Road handing out stirrup pumps and buckets of sand for fighting incendiary-bomb fires and officiously inspecting everyone's blackout arrangements.

In the event no German bombers appeared in the skies over London that Sunday or in the weeks to come. While England waited for the first blow to fall, everyday life went on, but not quite as normal.

As in hundreds of other streets, workmen arrived with lorries in Amen Road and started cutting down and carting away the wrought-iron railings and gates which fronted the terraces of Edwardian houses. The metal was needed, so the residents were informed, to make bombs and shells.

In the rows of neatly tended back gardens, Anderson shelters

– curved sections of corrugated iron bolted together – were embedded in concrete-lined tanks in the ground and covered with earth. One of these giant molehills appeared in place of Jenny's little patch of lawn and the rockery on which she, and Mr Barratt before her, had lavished so much care.

As the phoney war continued into 1940, Colonel Plumley-Greene's armour and the field guns manned by volunteers like young Harris were ferried across to France with the rest of the British Expeditionary Force.

Frank tried to join the RAF but got no farther than the doctor in the first cubicle at the reception centre in Kingsway. As soon as he put his stethescope on his chest, the doctor demanded: 'What's up with you, man?'

'I have an AP,' Frank admitted.

'Then why are you wasting our time? Get out of here.'

In the next cubicle another doctor was asking an unseen youth: 'Have you ever had VD?'

'What's VD?' asked the lad.

The two medical referees at the end of the line gave Frank a slip of paper saying he was Grade IV, in other words 'unfit for National Service'.

Ralph Greedie wrote jubilantly from 'somewhere in England' with the news that he had joined a fighter squadron at last, and after much agonizing Jack Harris had joined the RAF, too. He was now AC2 Harris, J., with his 'last three' numbers stamped or stencilled on every item of his kit, pounding a barrack square in Lancashire and enduring the daily sarcasm of a semiliterate corporal drill instructor.

'We call him Holy Joe,' he said in a letter to Frank, 'since he was heard at a compulsory church parade to growl to one of us erks: "Look to the front, ****, and take yer 'at orf in the House of the Lord.' He reserves his vilest obscenities though for the lads who've volunteered for aircrew. I would *like* to myself, but what with my eyesight they won't even look at me (much to Ethel's relief). I will probably end up as a ground Wop (wireless operator, to you) or even worse, as a clerk, although I am trying to keep quiet about my shorthand. The cookhouse food is unbelievable, so most of our pay goes on bangers and mash and Heinz beans in the NAAFI. Yet the Pongos (sorry – Army chaps) think we're in clover and call us the Brylcreem Boys.'

In Jack's absence, Frank found himself trying to do his job at the House of Commons. He took over Jack's desk in the Long Room, just along the corridor from the Black Room, feeling at first like a new boy at a public school. Like the rest of the House, the press gallery was steeped in tradition. Every member had his own hat peg and woe betide any other man who inadvertently used it. Typewriters were a fairly recent innovation and most of the older reporters still preferred to write up their copy by hand.

When Frank first took his place in the gallery, looking down on the green leather benches facing one another on either side of the Speaker's chair, he saw a David Low cartoon come to life. All the men of power were there on the front benches – Chamberlain, Churchill, Attlee, Eden, Bevin and Lloyd George in the late evening of his political career.

It was like being in a theatre but in that lonely, unreal year of 1940, when battle commenced, the players were real enough. Chamberlain, the failed man of peace, made his exit as Prime Minister with Cromwell's words to the Long Parliament, quoted by Leo Amery, ringing in his ears: 'For the love of God, go!' Churchill bowed on to the stage with Shakespearean drama: 'I have nothing to offer but blood, toil, tears and sweat.'

Never in the history of the Parliamentary press gallery was so much vivid oratory heard by so few reporters. And never was there so little newsprint to accommodate it – editions were sometimes down to four pages. It was doubly difficult for Frank, struggling to take down the speeches in improvised shorthand among relays of reporters who covered waxed 'flimsies' in impeccable shorthand at breathtaking speed.

The awful acoustics of the place made it difficult at times to hear what was being said. A leading news agency reported Churchill's ringing 'This was their finest hour' as 'their finest flower' and its reporter continued to swear by his note even after his employers had disowned it and put out a corrected version.

After the fall of France and the mass evacuation of British troops from the beaches of Dunkirk in an armada of *Saucy Sues* and *Skylarks*, debates were constantly interrupted by the crump of bombs falling, the sharp crackle of ack-ack fire, the wailing of the sirens and the unmistakable slow thrumming of Dornier bomber engines. Again and again the Palace of Westminster was shaken to its Victorian foundations.

On more than one occasion Frank walked ankle deep in glass

splinters up Victoria Street on his way to work. Yet even Armageddon had its humour in Cockney eyes. A newsvendor on the corner of Francis Street chalked on a board under Latest War News: 'Biggest raid yet. Score 78 to 26. England still batting.' When the windows had been boarded up it was 'Business as usual.'

Jenny was helping out at the Clapham Maternity Hospital whose windows had been protected from the outside by sandbags piled from the ground to within two feet of the top by workmen from Lambeth Borough Council. The protection proved to be necessary as the hot summer mellowed into autumn with days and nights of constant warnings and alerts and high explosive bombs and incendiaries damaging houses in Paradise Road, Studley Road and Clapham Road.

The Battle of Britain had become the Battle of London, with aerial dogfights going on over the capital and blazing aircraft as well as bombs crashing down onto the rooftops. On Wednesday 18 September a landmine fell in Bromfield Road at the junction of Union Road, causing considerable damage to the maternity clinics at 41 and 43 Jeffreys Road and, despite the sandbags, blowing in all the windows at the nearby hospital where there were twenty-five women and babies.

'We found the babies all asleep and covered with leaves,' Jenny wrote to Lucy at Bournemouth. 'By some miracle not one was hurt. Indeed, two more babies were added to their numbers during the night.'

She did not mention in this letter how she and the sisters and nurses worked through the night in the dark in their wards, keeping the mothers cheerful. Nor did she mention that the following day she drove sixteen mothers and babies to a maternity hospital in the safer area of Redhill in an ambulance converted from a Green Line coach.

That evening a man in a pinstripe suit and a tin hat knocked at the Coles' door. Frank answered it.

'Does Mrs Cole live here?' asked the man, checking a list on a clipboard attached to his canvas respirator case.

'Why do you ask?' replied Frank, taking an immediate dislike to the stranger and his poor imitation of Clark Gable's moustache.

'It's my job to ask the questions,' the man went on. 'Ministry of Information.' He flashed a card.

'So that's it,' said Frank. 'You're one of Cooper's Snoopers.'

Alfred Duff Cooper was the Minister of Information with power to detain any 'suspect' indefinitely without appeal under the emergency regulations. Informers were invited to denounce so-called chatterbugs and defeatists, neighbour to spy on neighbour. The man from the Ministry reddened when Frank used the derisive nickname coined by the public to describe official busybodies.

'I'd like to see your identity card,' he demanded aggressively.

'You're not in uniform and I'm not obliged to produce it,' retorted Frank.

'Your uncooperative attitude will not go unrecorded.'

'Neither will your arrogance. Perhaps you'd be so good as to tell me why you want to see my mother.'

'It's the job of my department to check on people whose affiliations might be suspect,' the official explained.

'What the hell are you driving at?' said Frank, his voice rising.

At this point Jenny appeared in the hall behind him, wearing a drab green uniform (for the first time in her life she was in trousers), her eyes red-rimmed from lack of sleep over the past twenty-four hours. The grey streaks in her hair were accentuated by the dust of falling masonry.

'What is it?' she said. 'Is something wrong?'

'Mrs Jenny Cole?' asked the man, and when she nodded he continued: 'According to our records you are a supporter of the Peace Pledge Union, which has been the subject of a Parliamentary question by Sir Henry Page Croft. I would like to ask you a few questions about your . . .'

Jenny drew herself up to her full one inch over five foot and said coldly: 'Young man, I have just got home after being on duty at a maternity hospital all night and driving an ambulance all day and I am in no mood to discuss my views on war and peace with you.'

Frank put it more bluntly. 'Now push off you little twerp – before I forget which side *I'm* on.'

And with that he slammed the door on the official and his clipboard. They heard no more from him or his department.

My father's contacts with Whitehall were on the whole rather cordial. Journalists soon learned to live with censorship and defence notices prohibiting the mention of certain facts, recognizing that in wartime some things, like ration books and identity cards, the blackout and queues for everything, were unavoidable.

The more absurd activities of the Ministry of Information, whose employees were known in Fleet Street as 'the cousins' because so many of them were related to one another and the peerage, were regarded with amused tolerance.

At the end of October, when the onset of winter obliged Hitler to abandon his plans for invading England, the Luftwaffe began to bomb provincial cities. Frank was taken away from parliamentary reporting for the time being and, armed with a Ministry of Information permit, sent on a tour of the bombed areas – Coventry, Southampton, Bristol, Birmingham and Sheffield. His reports from these places concentrated on stories of individual heroism and the pluckiness of the people at large. He trailed in the footsteps of the King and Churchill, rallying the people.

Because train services were overcrowded and unpredictable owing to the air raids, he was allowed to travel by car, resurrecting his mother's Morris from the lock-up garage where it had been interred for 'the duration' as it was called, in the absence of any certain knowledge as to how long the war might last. Petrol was hard to come by and there were very few private cars on the roads. Daddy's was one of the few.

One spring weekend in 1941 Frank illicitly used part of his petrol ration to take his mother on an outing into the country. Jenny had a nostalgic desire to see the daffodils in bloom in Kent and they drove down along quiet roads where all the signposts had been uprooted to confuse any invading army. It had certainly done a great deal to confuse Britain's own army lorry drivers.

The golden trumpets were pushing up bravely in the grounds of Blackstaff Hall, between wireless vans and cables snaking in all directions on churned-up lawns. Anti-aircraft guns, searchlights and listening devices were hidden away in shrubberies and beneath camouflage nets covered with budding boughs. Mysterious aerials sprouted everywhere.

'God knows what they get up to in there,' said the general cheerfully when they ran him to ground in one of the flint farm cottages which used to accommodate the Dawson family. 'It's all so frightfully hush-hush that they won't even tell *me* and I'm CO of the local Home Guard. They just commandeered the place and that was that. Now it's dispatch riders coming and going at all hours of the day and night, plus regular visits from Jerry. Never a dull moment.'

When the Local Defence Volunteers formed, they had armbands and gasmasks but little else. The general added his old cavalry sabre and a couple of fowling pieces to an assortment of armaments which included more than a few weapons captured from German troops in the 1914–18 War. Now, a year later, they had proper battledress and tin hats, Lee Enfield rifles, mortars, grenades and flares.

'Why aren't you in uniform, young man?' rasped Uncle Patrick after glaring at Frank for some moments. 'You're not one of these damned 'conchies' are you?'

'He was turned down on medical grounds,' interjected Jenny hastily.

'You were in Spain, weren't you?' said the general suspiciously. 'The Reds had a hand in that one.'

'So did the Fascists,' Frank reminded him.

'Maybe they did. Never could understand politics myself. I suppose you write that awful tripe in the press.'

Frank tried to look noncommittal but the general rambled on: 'Saw a copy of the *Mirror* the other day . . . one of the chaps in the unit had it. Dreadful rot about brass-buttoned boneheads, implying that the Army's run by a lot of Blimps. I can't understand why Winnie doesn't suppress it just as he's done with the *Daily Worker*.'

Jenny caught Frank's eye and smiled. They let the old boy go on. He was equally irritated by the Morris car they had arrived in.

'. . . people joyridin' when seamen are risking their lives bringing petrol to these shores. I go everywhere by bicycle. If I can learn at my age, why can't everyone else?'

He gesticulated with his one arm, with which he had managed for forty years.

Jenny got up to make tea, noticing as she did so how neat and tidy everything was in the little back kitchen.

'Who looks after you?' she asked her stepbrother.

'Oh, my batman comes in from time to time when he's not too busy with his ARP duties,' said Patrick nonchalantly. 'I've learned to do for myself – washing the dishes and so on. Broke quite a few at first but I've got the hang of it now. I can't think why you women make such a fuss about a few simple chores.'

At two o'clock that afternoon Leading Aircraftwoman Plumley-Greene came off-duty in the Operations Room at Blackstaff Hall which covered the nearby RAF station at Biggin Hill and the one at Kenley and was linked to Bentley Priory, from which Lord Dowding directed the whole of Fighter Command. Walking up the lane, with her respirator case and tin hat slung from her shoulder, she was surprised to see a familiar face coming towards her. So was Frank.

'Dorothy,' he exclaimed as she rushed up and threw her arms round his neck.' 'I hardly recognized you in uniform.'

'I know, isn't it ghastly,' she said, smoothing the light blue tunic over her hips and adjusting the soft-topped peak cap. 'It's such a bore polishing these silly brass buttons and I hate wearing flat heels and these *awful* lisle stockings.'

'You remember Dorothy, Mother,' said Frank. 'She was in the sanatorium at the same time as me.'

'Yes, I remember,' replied Jenny, without enthusiasm. 'You were recovering from an attack of pleurisy, I recall.'

'How clever of you to remember, Mrs Cole. I'm A1 now though. What a coincidence, bumping into you like this. I'm sorry, I must dash, I've got a date.'

She started to walk away, then stopped and called over her shoulder: 'Would you care to join us for a drink later, Frank?'

'That would be nice.'

'I'll see you at the White Hart at Brasted then, about eight o'clock. TTFN.'

TTFN meant 'ta-ta for now' and was one of the catchphrases from Tommy Handley's 'ITMA' programme on the wireless. Jenny, watching Dorothy's jaunty progress, experienced a feeling of angst, remembering, as if it was yesterday, how daringly she had worn short skirts as she bicycled up this very lane forty years ago.

'She's a very attractive young woman,' she remarked, giving her son a sidelong glance.

'Is she?' answered Frank casually. 'I suppose so. But she's a bit too cut-glass for my taste.'

Jenny kept her own thoughts to herself as they walked on arm in arm between hedgerows just beginning to slip into their summer dress of green.

* * *

Frank spent a somewhat strained evening at the White Hart in the company of Dorothy and a group of boisterous young fighter pilots from Biggin Hill. They were very polite to 'Dot's friend from London', but he felt out of it, an interloper. He was of their generation but they were in another world, with its own language, the language of 'ops' and 'prangs' and 'Roger this', and 'Roger that'.

Their conversation, like their lives, was fast and brittle. They did not dwell on the hot summer gone when they sat in their deckchairs with the smell of new-mown hay in the air waiting for the word 'Scramble!' over the loudspeakers. He felt like a filing clerk in the company of glamorous actors.

During that summer they were up in the morning at half past four, flying five or six missions a day until half past nine at night. Now it was all night work and the dishes of grated raw carrot on the mess tables (carrots were supposed to give a pilot cat's eyes, or the ability to see in the dark) were really only a spoof. It was radar which enabled them to stalk the enemy at night, but they were not allowed to talk about that – 'Careless Talk Costs Lives' as the posters said.

Nor did they talk of the summer to come and whether they could go on defending an island standing alone off the shores of a Nazi-occupied Continent. Their minds were concentrated on the present moment, this drink, this evening's girl.

They were different people from the junior clerks and undergraduates and upper-sixth formers they had been only a year before. The war had changed them, just as it had changed Dorothy from a brainless deb thinking of little else but what she would wear at the next ball into a rather nice, broad-minded young woman, determined to make the best of the dramatically changed circumstances.

Dorothy's date, a twenty-year-old pilot officer wearing a silk-lined flying jacket over his best blue, obviously resented the amount of attention Frank was getting from her. He spent most of the evening sulking in a corner seat. Frank left the party quite early, muttering an excuse about 'having to get back up to town'. As he climbed into the Morris, parked among the pilots' sports cars, he heard their high-pitched laughter and loud confident voices from behind the blackout curtains of the White Hart.

15

Less than a week after the visit to Blackstaff Frank received a phone call at the House of Commons: 'It's Dorothy – I've got a pass and I'm up in town for the day. May I come round?'

'By all means,' said Frank. 'We'll have tea.'

'That would be splendid.'

He left word with the police sergeant at St Stephen's entrance and felt very proud to be connected with the vision that was ushered in – Dorothy in a smartly tailored suit, a fashionable hat, high heels *and* silk stockings. Frank showed her the library and the bar with its 'Spy' cartoons of politicians and journalists of the past and a silver-mounted snuff horn behind the glasses.

'It's one of the traditions of the House,' he explained, like a guide. 'Churchill always takes snuff from the attendant before he enters the chamber.'

'As well as smoking all those big cigars?' commented Dorothy. 'It's no wonder he has such a gravelly voice.'

They reached the lobby in time to see the Speaker in his full-bottomed wig and knee breeches proceeding solemnly with other functionaries towards the chamber.

When they were seated in the tea-room she asked Frank: 'Do you think me fast?'

'What do you mean?'

'Well, ringing you up and inviting myself here. Propositioning a man is terribly bad form for a lady.'

'Are you propositioning me?'

'Of course, darling,' she said, laughing. 'What time do you finish here?'

'It's difficult to say. The House sometimes sits into the next day.'

She looked at him archly: 'Can't you slip away for a few hours?'

'Where to?' he asked.

She took a card from her handbag and pushed it across the table. On it was an address in Welbeck Street and a telephone number, Langham 2603.

'It's Poppa's *pied-à-terre*,' she explained. 'But there's no one there at the moment – we'd be all by ourselves. Won't you come?'

Frank took a taxi to Welbeck Street soon after eight that evening, planning to return before the House rose later. He found the flat on the third floor of a tall, thin red-brick Victorian town house which stood on a corner. There was no porter at the door and no lift.

Dorothy answered his ring at the bell. The apartment was well lit and sumptuously decorated in Regency style; she mixed him a drink at the cocktail cabinet while he made himself comfortable on a candy-striped sofa. 'A Nightingale sang in Berkeley Square,' crooned a female voice on the wireless.

Dorothy put the drinks on a table and snuggled beside him on the sofa, resting her head on his shoulder.

'Do you remember that afternoon at Downshall when Dr McNee caught us in the shrubbery?' she asked. 'It seems so long, long ago.'

'Of course I remember,' said Frank. 'What a pity he had to come along.'

'A pity?' she said, looking up at him with wide, innocent eyes. He noticed for the first time their exact shade, the brilliant blue of lapis lazuli. 'Why was it such a pity?'

'Well – er – I just meant that . . .'

'I know what you meant, you clot,' she said, taking his hand and placing it on one of her breasts, firm and round beneath the silk of her blouse.

'This is the BBC Home Service,' said a perfectly modulated male voice from the radio. 'Here is the nine o'clock news and this is Alvar Liddell reading it.'

For once he paid no attention to the nine o'clock news. He was too preoccupied with undoing the pearl buttons down the front of Dorothy's blouse and kissing her at the same time.

'No,' she said faintly, 'you mustn't. What if Poppa were to come in?'

'You said we'd be alone,' he reminded her.

'Yes, I know, but . . .'

Her voice trailed away to nothing as he peeled the blouse from her shoulders and started to fumble clumsily with the clasp at the back of her brassiere.

'Here, let me do it,' she whispered at last.

The brassiere fell to the carpet just as the Alert sounded, a dismal wailing in the night.

'Oh, blast,' said Frank. 'Do you want to go down to the shelters?'

By way of an answer she took him by the hand and led him into the bedroom where she unzipped her skirt and removed it. Then sitting on the edge of an enormous canopied bed with primrose silk covers and drapes, she unfastened her suspenders and peeled off her silk stockings, carefully so as not to ladder them. Frank hastily undressed, too.

Nude, save for a pair of lacy black camiknickers, she held out her hands towards Frank. They scarcely noticed the shrill whistle of the bombs falling around, or the violent shaking of the house as they made love. A particularly heavy thud nearby was followed by a blast wave which shattered the windows, although the blackout curtain and the heavy satin drapes stopped most of the splinters flying into the room.

Still coupled, they rolled off the bed onto the carpet on the side farthest from the window.

'Please, please don't stop now, darling!' she hissed into his ear, while her nails dug into the flesh on his shoulder-blades.

'I feel so delightfully wicked,' she remarked, when it was over. 'This is Momsy's and Poppa's bedroom, you know. Am I not a totally shameless baggage?'

'You are, indeed,' he said, kissing her again.

It was, of course outrageous behaviour for a Roedean girl who, only eighteen months before, had thought that holding a man's hand in a rose garden was exciting enough to put in her diary. But then, when air raids, sirens, blackouts, unexpected meetings and partings were part of everyday life (or death), conventional morality seemed to matter less and less.

After the All Clear had sounded, Dorothy put on a silk wrap and went into the kitchen. Frank pulled aside the torn curtains and looked out at a half moon sailing in a clear sky tinged with red from the blazing West End. He was wearing his socks and nothing else, but it seemed perfectly natural to wander into the kitchen in Dorothy's footsteps.

She had lit a candle and had her back to him at the sink, where she was trying in vain to fill a kettle.

'There's nothing coming from the tap,' she said.

'Who needs tea anyway?' replied Frank, slipping his arms round her from behind. They made love again and again, in the kitchen, in the sitting room and back in the bedroom, their bodies luminously pale in the moonlight filtering through the chinks in the blackout curtains, until the grey tints of dawn crept in.

'It wasn't the first time for you, was it,' she said as he got dressed to leave.

'No,' he admitted at once. 'There have been others.'

'Were they as good as me?' she asked, propping herself up on one elbow and looking at his back and his image in the dressing-table mirror, frowning as he fixed his collar stud.

'No,' he answered without looking round. 'It's never been as good as that.'

'I'm so glad,' she said, lying back with a smile. 'We must do it again soon.'

Unfortunately there was no opportunity for them to do it over the next few weeks because of Hitler's continuing efforts to reduce London to ruins. Their lives consisted of nothing but spells of unremitting duty with snatches of restless sleep in between.

During the Easter recess Frank was asked by the editor to help get the paper out. Throughout the Blitz Geoffrey Elms appeared every morning wearing jacket and striped trousers, with a freshly starched wing collar, immaculate spats, a bowler hat and carrying a tightly rolled umbrella. He went home to his Victorian villa in Beckenham every night. He was that sort of man. But the strain of air raids and paper shortages, rota problems caused by a severely depleted staff, had undermined his normally robust health.

'There are so few young men of ability available,' he told Frank over a drink at the Press Club in Salisbury Court. 'You've been holding the fort at Westminster extremely well and I would like you to become involved in the production of the paper and perhaps write some of the leaders as well. You'll be my assistant editor and I'll pay you another fiver a week.'

He omitted to mention that Frank's new duties would include fire-fighting, first aid and gas drill. The *Chronicle*'s rackety offices in Fetter Lane had suffered several near misses from 'heavies' and more than one incendiary bomb had pierced the roof, which was now draped with tarpaulins to keep the rain out, but not a single edition had been missed since the Blitz started.

When the presses on the ground floor rolled, churning out 100,000 copies an hour, it was like being in the engine room of a battleship. Outside was a public eager for every copy they printed and for the war news which dominated the contents. Sensational murders merited only a paragraph or two and advertisers were begging for space.

Frank, in his shirtsleeves, unlike the stiffly formal editor, was everywhere in the news room and composing room – reading news flashes as they clicked from the tape machines, 'spiking' unwanted material, reading proofs of leaders which he had written himself, correcting errors on the stone where the pages were made up in type. And often his nights were spent in a tin hat taking his turn with one of the copy boys or commissionaires, or someone from the library or the foundry, fire-spotting on the roof.

He did not go home to Amen Road for days at a time, but slept on an iron bunk down in the basement. There was so much to do, and so little time to do it in, that he completely forgot about his collapsed lung.

The climax of the Blitz came on a weekend in May, the night of a bombers' moon, but the air traffic was not one way only. Jack Harris spent the Saturday hoisting bombs into the bellies of Wellingtons from lines of trolleys. The black cigar-shaped casings were chalked with puerile messages like 'To Adolf with Love from Winnie'. In Hamburg or Berlin, whichever was the target for tonight, innocent women and children would be killed and maimed, or trapped in living tombs beneath the rubble of demolished buildings. Jack could not forget a spell of leave in the previous autumn when he was at his parents' home in Walworth during a mighty Luftwaffe raid on London docks. They spent the night in one of the street shelters, singing 'Roll Out the Barrel' and 'I've Got Sixpence' to keep their spirits up while the bombs whistled down and ack-ack guns blazed away. In the morning they found their little terraced house full of broken glass and fallen plaster but they were lucky. At least, unlike some of their neighbours, they had a house to go back to.

Jack Harris was thinking of this as he watched the Wellingtons heaving their full fuel tanks and loaded bomb racks into the darkening sky, before setting off in formation towards the North Sea. He waited until the roar of their engines had faded away in the distance, then mounted his bike and set off round the perimeter track to the NAAFI canteen.

A hundred and fifty miles to the south, Frank was settling down for another night of fire-watching on the roof of the *Evening Chronicle* with a copy boy called Syd. Frank would rather have been with Dorothy at the Globe watching Rex Harrison and Lilli Palmer in *No Time for Comedy*, but duty called. The roof was never without spotters, two to a shift.

Wave after wave of German bombers were approaching from the east following the sinuous silver ribbon of the Thames. At 11.40 the sirens sounded and they heard the crackle of anti-aircraft guns approaching like a brush fire. Then the Dorniers and Heinkels were directly overhead and stick after stick of high explosives and incendiaries came shrieking down on their heads.

At one point he and Syd counted fifteen fires blazing around their building and from the street below he heard one of the Auxiliary Fire Service officers yelling in desperation: 'The pressure's dropping again.'

Frank and the lad from Bethnal Green dashed frantically hither and thither with stirrup pump and buckets of sand and water, smothering incendiaries and dousing fires before they could spread.

The raid did not end until half past five on the Sunday morning. Frank decided to drive home by way of Westminster Bridge to get some idea of the damage which had been caused. Everywhere he looked were burnt-out buildings, smouldering and smoking. Big Ben's face was blackened but almost unbelievably it was telling the correct time – ten minutes past six.

Frank parked his car in Bridge Street and splashed through the water from a fractured main flooding across Palace Yard. The policeman at the side gate recognized him and let him through with only a cursory glance at his pass.

The chaos inside the House was appalling. The debating chamber was gutted and it was impossible to get through the Members' lobby for the wreckage of twisted girders. He climbed the stairs to the ladies' gallery and found himself looking at the open sky. While he was standing there several tons of masonry crashed down within a few yards of his feet.

Frank had had enough. He drove home and let himself into the empty house. Jenny had been out all night, too, driving an ambulance for the Women's Voluntary Service and had still not returned. After what seemed only a few minutes he was awakened from a drugged sleep by the ringing of the telephone in the hall below.

It was Dorothy ringing from Biggin Hill: 'It's Ralph. He was shot down last night in the big raid.' She was sobbing into the telephone. Frank passed a weary hand over his eyes. He felt nothing. He could think of nothing to say.

'Are you still there?' asked Dorothy. 'Are you all right?'

'Perhaps he's OK,' he managed to say at last. 'He probably baled out.'

'Oh God, I hope so,' said Dorothy. 'Foxtrot leader saw his kite going down over the Thames Estuary trailing smoke. He didn't see any parachute.'

'He'll be all right. You'll see. He'll be all right.'

After he had put the phone down Frank sat for a long time in the kitchen on a bentwood chair, smoking his pipe and staring at the gas cooker. There was no point in going back to bed. He knew he would not sleep.

Somehow his brain refused to focus on the fact of Ralph being shot down. When he did force himself to consider it, the only emotion he felt was jealousy that Dorothy was so upset.

I wonder if she's slept with him, too?

Frank immediately castigated himself for this thought as Jenny came in looking dog-tired, her face blackened and her unbecoming green uniform made even drabber by a thick coating of dust. 'Balham High Road got it, a big one. They're still looking for bodies in the ruins . . . what's wrong?' she broke off her account, noticing his bleak expression. When he told her she sighed: 'Oh, this awful war. How much longer can it go on? Such a dreadful waste . . .'

But shortly afterwards the phone rang again and Dorothy, laughing and crying at the same time, gave them the news that Ralph was alive and well and enjoying a belated breakfast in the officers' mess at Hornchurch.

'You were right, Frank, he did bale out. He rang me himself a few minutes ago. God, I'm so relieved. The Navy fished him out of the water and landed him on what he thought at first was a battleship but turned out to be Southend Pier in a coat of grey paint.'

'You're very fond of him,' said Frank quietly.

'Of course I'm fond of him – so are you, aren't you?' she responded, a bit testily.

'You know what I mean,' Frank went on.

'Oh, for heaven's sake, what are you getting at? Really, sometimes you are just too possessive,' she snapped, and then, repenting immediately. 'I'm sorry, Frank. I do love you. And, yes, I *adore* Ralph because he's absolutely priceless. He bagged two Dorniers before they got him but he's *furious* because the first thing that happened when he got back to base was the equipment officer telling him he owed the RAF 2s 6d for failing to bring back the release handle with his parachute.'

Laughing with Dorothy over the phone, Frank forgot his fit of jealousy.

Dorothy was on night duty and that Sunday night she found it hard to concentrate on the little counters and discs which she was supposed to move around the plotting table with a long pointer.

'Top Hat Control – hostiles twenty miles east of you. Vector one two zero. Trade for you building up over Gravesend . . . Starlight Control to Dogtail . . . Roger, Starlight.'

She was hardly listening to the jargon which came from the loudspeaker until the greying wing commander at the control desk suddenly snapped: 'Plumley-Greene, what the hell do you think you're doing? You've just put bandits on vector nine zero. It's one two zero, you clot.'

'Sorry, sir,' said Dorothy. 'I didn't get much sleep . . . a friend of mine went down and I was worried about him.'

The wing commander tutted and reflected bitterly that while these young flying types were enjoying themselves screwing every WAAF in sight, he had to contend with them when they turned up for duty looking as if they had been dragged through a hedge backwards.

Dorothy left the table for a moment to consult a coded chart on the reinforced concrete wall which had replaced the kitchen range where in days long since gone Mrs Beegan used to make her plum puddings for the Cole family. Dorothy's mind was not really on her work because she had missed a period and was worried about it.

Oh, God, supposing I'm preggers. I should have taken some precautions – what a brainless little twerp I am. If I am preggers, Momsy will give me such a rocket, and Poppa, what about Poppa?

At that precise moment the bomb-aimer in a Dornier 17 pressed the button and cried: *'Los, los!'* into the intercom. A squat black object tumbled through the open doors in the belly of the aircraft, turning slowly in the starry sky until a green silk parachute billowed out. It floated gently downwards onto the tall ornamented brick chimneys and lichened tiles of Blackstaff Hall. Neither Dorothy nor anyone else in the basement Operations Room heard it coming.

16

There was one horrendous crash and the roof of the Operations Room caved in in a storm of bricks and stones, masonry and mortar, splintered timber and jagged steel. The plotting table collapsed like matchwood under the weight of it and the girls who were standing round it were instantly buried.

By some freak of blast effect, the corner by the door where Dorothy was standing looking at the chart escaped the shock waves although the door itself was torn from its hinges. She was temporarily deafened by the explosion and blinded by the shower of dust from the mortar and plasterwork, but as the dust settled, the moonlight, streaming through a great jagged hole where the roof of the cellar had been, illuminated a terrifying scene of desolation.

There were moans and cries coming from beneath the heap of rubble and she started to claw frantically at the bricks and stones with her bare hands but it was a hopeless task.

'Joyce! Sylvia!' She called out the names of two of her friends who had been on shift with her, but there was no answer. The desk where the wing commander sat, and the wall to wall map behind it, had simply vanished.

She was anxious to be out of the cellar now, reckoning that it would be safer to be out in the open in case there were further collapses. She crawled out on her hands and knees, her stockings torn, her face blackened and her hair full of dust. Once outside she realized for the first time that one of her shoes was missing and she wandered about in a daze, blood trickling down her forehead from a slight scalp wound, mumbling: 'I've lost my shoe. I've lost my shoe.'

An AC2 in a brand new 'sprog's' uniform took her by the arm: 'Here, Miss, get in here.'

He looked about sixteen but he propelled her gently but firmly towards a bus parked by the gates.

People were running around everywhere on the drive and the debris-strewn terrace, shouting conflicting orders. One of the WAAFs was screaming hysterically. Here and there among the wreckage of Blackstaff Hall flames were licking the baulks of timber and a column of smoke drifted upwards against the stars. Dorothy noticed part of an anti-aircraft gun hanging incongruously from the branches of an apple tree.

Major-General Brogan saw the red glow in the sky as he cycled up the lane towards Blackstaff, returning from a night exercise with the Home Guard. As he tried to increase his speed, his control of the machine with his one hand became erratic and he veered from one side to the other.

Little moonlight filtered through the thick beech boughs overhanging the lane and the headlamp on his bicycle was masked to comply with blackout regulations. So were the lights on the bus which came suddenly round the bend, travelling at speed in the opposite direction.

The young recruit at the wheel caught a fleeting glimpse of a shadowy figure but had no chance to avoid it. There was a dull thud against the off-side mudguard but he did not stop – it was more important to get his busload of wounded to the sick bay up at the camp than to stop for one road casualty. Dorothy heard that sickening bump, too, but in her dazed condition attached no particular significance to it.

Later, when she learned that it was Frank's Uncle Patrick who was found lying dead in the ditch beside the crumpled remains of his bicycle, she was conscience-stricken to think that she had made no attempt to get the driver to stop.

A week after the bombing, none the worse for her dreadful experience, physically at least, she attended the funeral as part of a small contingent of airmen and airwomen from Biggin Hill, paying their last respects to the nice old gentleman who used to bid them a hearty good morning when they passed him in the lane.

The local Home Guard provided the pallbearers and fired a salute as the Union Jack-draped coffin was lowered into the grave after requiem mass at the chapel of St John the Baptist. A bugler from the town's Boys' Brigade sounded the Last Post. The whole of Westerham, it seemed, had turned out for the general's funeral on a warm May afternoon and a wreath from Mr Churchill lay among the spring flowers on the fresh greensward between the gravestones. 'Died on Active Service in his 82nd Year' read the inscription on the headstone placed there later.

Frank drove his mother down to Westerham from South London while her sister Lucy and her husband came up from Bournemouth, bitter about the trains being full of troops and the unpredictability of Southern Electric's wartime timetables. Looking at Jenny and Lucy standing side by side at the graveside, Frank found it incredible that they were sisters who had shared their childhood together and had an identical upbringing. His matronly aunt in her fox furs and dramatic black veil attracted attention to herself with her penetrating voice and haughty expression, while his mother in her plain black coat and beret exuded an air of quiet dignity.

Their lives were in their appearance: Lucy's years as a memsahib out in India, surrounded by menials, nothing to occupy her but the spending of her husband's money and overweening ambition for him and their offspring; Jenny's days of self-effacing service and devotion to lost causes.

Jenny's thoughts were in the past as they drove up the hill to Blackstaff Hall after saccharined tea and spam sandwiches at the Grasshopper Hotel. She thought of the carriages proceeding along this road after Lucy's wedding and Lucy in her gown of cream-coloured Indian muslin. She thought of her own dress of 'London smoke' nun's veiling trimmed with lace and embroidery on that day when she first put up her hair and how dashing Patrick looked in the full dress uniform of a major of horse.

They were not allowed beyond the gate where an RAF policeman in white webbing stood guard: 'It's a high security area this,' he explained. In any case there was little to see but the blackened shell of the family home beyond the clouds of pink and white blossom on the apple trees and the carpet of bluebells at the edge of the wood.

'There's nothing to be salvaged,' said Lucy dolefully. 'All Mama's beautiful things gone.'

'Patrick took some of them with him into the cottage,' said Jenny, trying to cheer her up although she felt the same nostalgic sense of loss herself. 'And I believe the more valuable stuff was sent into store at Sevenoaks.'

'But it's so sad,' wailed Lucy, dabbing at her eyes with a scrap of lace handkerchief. 'It's one's youth destroyed.'

'Hmmm-m,' mused her husband, stroking his chin. Thirty years in the Indian Civil Service, a dried-up little man in a Homburg hat and double-breasted black overcoat. 'There'll have to be reparation for this. I'll telephone the permanent under-secretary at the Air Ministry as soon as we get back up to town, my dear.'

Frank drove them up to Waterloo Station for a train back to Bournemouth. He had had no opportunity to exchange more than a few words with Dorothy as they filed from the graveyard.

'When will I see you again?' he asked her under his breath.

'Heaven alone knows,' she whispered back. 'Since the bombing we've been on duty round the clock, trying to get it all together again in a bunker at Biggin. I'm being posted to Tangmere next week. I'll write from there.'

A warm Saturday in June found Frank and Dorothy together, walking barefoot on the shores of Chichester Harbour at low tide. Dorothy had a weekend pass out of Tangmere RAF Station nearby and had managed to borrow a thatched cottage in the village of Bosham from some wealthy friends.

They were raking cockles out of the sandbanks with sticks and popping them into a basket which Frank was carrying. The air was filled with the cries of gulls and oystercatchers wheeling above the barbed wire barricades and the gun emplacements.

In the midst of their search they came across another ugly reminder of the war – the remnants of a bright yellow rubber dinghy overprinted with instructions in black German script.

'Whoever used this wasn't as lucky as Ralph Greedie,' said Frank, pointing to the bullet holes with a grim expression.

'Come on,' said Dorothy, taking his hand and leading the way back towards the closely packed cottages lining the quayside with the church spire rising above them. 'It's too gorgeous a day to be morbid.'

They walked across Quay Meadow and along an avenue of evergreen oaks and holly trees to Bosham Lane and the cottage. A poster advertising 'War Weapons Week' was prominently displayed on the stone wall of the Saxon church but otherwise it looked much as it must have when King Harold prayed there in 1064.

It was such an attractive village, so close to the sea that the houses along the jetty had doors halfway up the wall, approached by flights of steps to keep them beyond the reach of the high tide.

They drove into Chichester on Saturday evening to see a film and sat holding hands in the back row. The film was *Boom Town* starring Spencer Tracy, Claudette Colbert, Hedi Lamarr *and* Clark Gable, who had been Dorothy's screen idol since she saw him four times in *Gone With the Wind* with Vivien Leigh.

Back at the cottage, they went early to bed under the thatch. Through the open dormer window came the clear liquid sound of a blackbird as the shadows lengthened.

'Shouldn't we be taking some precautions?' asked Frank, 'against your getting pregnant, I mean.'

'I usually wear a diaphragm,' Dorothy told him. 'All the girls do. But I've forgotten to bring the beastly thing.'

'Forgotten?' said Frank, raising himself on one elbow and staring down at her. 'It's a hell of a risk to take, isn't it?'

'Actually,' confided Dorothy, 'I was quite worried after the night we spent at the flat. I thought I'd had it – my next period was awfully late.'

'Why didn't you tell me?'

'There was no point in both of us getting in a flap about it. Anyway it was a false alarm. My next period's due in a day or two so there's no need to worry.'

'But aren't *you* worried?' he asked, amazed at her casualness. 'I mean, what would your parents say if you got pregnant?'

'They'd be furious, simply furious, but I don't care,' she answered. 'I want you and I want you right now.'

She pulled his head down towards her and kissed him almost fiercely. It was useless to protest, and anyway Frank was not that strong. Later, as they lay quietly together, her naked body snuggled up against his and her head resting on his chest, he suddenly asked: 'Have you been to bed with Ralph, too?'

'Christ! Not *that* again,' she cried, pulling away from him abruptly. 'Why, when we're together for the first time in ages, do you keep going on about Ralph?'

'It's just that I can't help feeling there's something between you two,' explained Frank. 'When you came on the phone that time, when he was shot down, you were distraught. I couldn't help wondering if it was because . . .'

'Shhh . .' she whispered, placing her soft, cool hand over his mouth. 'Make love to me again.'

'But I must know,' he insisted, looking more miserable than ever.

'I love you, I love, love, love you,' she answered lightly, rumpling his hair. 'What else do you need to know?'

On Sunday, one of the hottest June days ever, they sat under an awning in the garden among lupins and roses bursting from the bud in premature profusion, and heard the urbane tones of a BBC announcer giving the news of Hitler's forces marching against Russia at dawn along a thousand-mile front.

The significance of this development failed to register in Frank's mind, he was so preoccupied with more personal events at the time. All day hardly a word had been spoken until he said: 'There's something about me that you don't know, Dorothy, and when I tell you what it is I doubt if you'll want to marry me.'

'Darling, don't be a clot,' she said. 'Marriage hasn't been discussed.'

'Don't you love me enough to want to marry me?' he demanded.

'Of course I do,' she replied. 'But I don't want to think that you're doing the honourable thing just because we've slept together.'

'That's not it at all,' he assured her. 'I love you and I want to spend the rest of my life with you.'

'So you're really serious,' she said, looking at him speculatively. 'What's this guilty secret you're dying to tell me?'

'Simply, that I'm illegitimate,' he replied, 'one of the war babies I think they were called, from the last little lot.'

She started to giggle.

'I don't see anything funny about it,' he snapped. 'Can't you be serious about *anything*?'

'It's just that you look so funny sitting there with such a long face calling yourself a war baby,' she said, still smiling. 'Is that why you've been trying so hard to make another "war baby" with me?'

He laughed, too, at that but only for a moment before he became serious again and went on: 'You've got to face facts, Dot. Your mother and father aren't all that keen on me as it is.

They'd be even less keen on having a bastard for a son-in-law.'

'Don't use that awful word about yourself,' she told him, again putting her hand over his mouth. 'It's not your fault that your father and mother never married, you silly boy. It's the sort of person one *is* that counts. You're an adorable amusing man when you're not being pompous and I'm head over heels in love with you. I'll be twenty-one in August and I can marry whom I choose.'

There was a small silence during which nothing broke the soporific peace of a lazy summer's afternoon but the drone of the bees.

'So you'll marry me?' he said at last.

'Yes, you clot,' she said, putting her arms round his neck and kissing him, 'I'll marry you.'

And that was how Mummy accepted Daddy's proposal of marriage.

BOOK TWO

Winners, Losers and Survivors

September 1941

On 18 September at Caxton Hall, Westminster, Frank Cole of George Street, W1, to Dorothy Elizabeth Plumley-Greene of the Oak House, Limpsfield, Surrey.

From the marriage announcements
in *The Times*.

17

The wedding took place on the Saturday before Frank's twenty-fifth birthday, with the bridegroom in a lounge suit and the bride in her WAAF best blue. As a concession to matrimonial tradition, he had a carnation in his buttonhole.

Colonel Plumley-Greene strongly disapproved of his only daughter marrying the man he referred to as 'that Fabian conchie writer chap' (a description which Frank found flattering rather than insulting) but there was nothing he could do about it as he was in Cairo. He had fled there with the remnants of his regiment from the island of Crete after the airborne invasion by the Germans.

Like her husband, Lady Plumley-Greene disapproved of the match, having dreamed of a smart wedding in the Guards' Chapel at Windsor. Nevertheless, she attended the brief, austere little ceremony at Caxton Hall looking strikingly elegant in a smartly tailored Glenurquhart suit and fashionable hat with a veil. She looked askance at the bridegroom's mother in her crumpled tweed suit and somewhat battered felt hat.

Ralph Greedie, now a squadron leader leading a comparatively relaxed life since the might of the Luftwaffe was switched to the Russian front, was there and so was Leading Aircraftman Harris, on embarkation leave, wondering whether to shake hands or salute when they were introduced outside the register office. Ralph immediately put him at his ease with a warm handshake.

After the wedding the total party of six crammed itself somewhat inelegantly into Daddy's Morris and drove to the Savoy for lunch.

Dorothy had to report back for duty to Tangmere less than twenty-four hours later, but before the month was out the medical officer, having carried out certain tests with the help of a small frog, was able to confirm that she was pregnant. She was granted a 'compassionate discharge', something that happened all the time in the women's services.

Frank had no difficulty finding them a suitable place to live in town – a flat in Nell Gwynn House, a block built just before the war in a fashionable district near Sloane Square. The exodus from London during the Blitz had made even such desirable properties with their lifts and porters and cocktail bars a drug on the market and Frank secured a two-bedroomed apartment with all modern conveniences for a very modest rent.

Visiting the newlyweds on the day before he sailed from Southampton in a troopship, Jack Harris was frankly envious.

'You're a jammy bastard to be out of this lot,' he said indicating the rough blue cloth of his tunic. Two of his brothers were in the Royal Navy, another was somewhere at sea in a cargo ship having survived two sinkings by torpedo, while the fourth, a survivor of Dunkirk, had spent a year patrolling the beach at Winchelsea, waiting for the invasion which never came. By contrast Jack's war had been blissfully unheroic so far. 'To think I used to complain about life being boring up at Syerston – no air raids, all the chocolates, sweets and cigarettes you want off the ration and petrol so easy to come by that some of the blokes clean their working-blue in it. I thought with all these big bomber raids coming up I was there for the duration – I was even thinking of finding a place in Newark for Ethel so that we could be together after the new baby is born.'

Ethel, heavily pregnant, was still living with her parents at Stoke Poges and complaining how they spoiled little Brenda, now three years old and into all sorts of mischief.

'It's bad luck getting an overseas posting now,' Frank commiserated with his old friend. 'Where are they sending you?'

'Probably to Archangel, as we've been kitted out for the tropics,' answered Jack with a wry smile. 'Seriously though, my bet is North Africa. Things aren't going too well out there, are they?'

'Cheer up,' Frank told him. 'Look on it as an opportunity to see the world while there's still some of it left. Anyway, let's pop down to the local and have a couple of pints.'

'Don't be late,' said Dorothy. 'I'm preparing something rather special for dinner.'

A high-ranking army friend of her father's who was stationed in Yorkshire had presented her with a brace of grouse which he had bagged on the moors while ostensibly on anti-tank manoeuvres. Jenny was taking tea with Dorothy when the gift was delivered and inspected the birds with expert fingers, feeling the pliability of their feet and beaks.

'They're young,' she pronounced, 'and fairly small, but quite plump. You must hang them for at least a week by their beaks before you cook them.'

'I know perfectly well how to prepare game for the table,' replied Dorothy haughtily, feeling that her mother-in-law took her for a fool. 'I've seen Cook do it millions of times.'

This was a slight exaggeration, but Dorothy was determined to play the good little wife and become competent in the domestic arts. She hid the birds in the airing cupboard, from which emanated after a few days an overpowering aroma of decay. She was not, however, worried by this as she vaguely remembered her mother's cook saying that pheasant and grouse was not fit to eat until it was 'high'.

Now, with Frank and Jack safely out of the way, she took the birds out of the cupboard and started to pluck them. The feathers came out easily but there were more of them than she would have believed possible. Her kitchenette was knee-deep in them when she had finished and they danced in the air as she tried to stuff them into a pillow case.

That done, she stood regarding the naked carcasses with distaste, carving knife poised. It was only by closing her eyes that she managed to sever the heads and draw the horrid little things, then truss them and lard them ready for the oven.

Then she uncorked a precious bottle of Nuits St George, set it down among the crystal tumblers which Ralph had bought them as a wedding gift, and settled back on the sofa to await the men's return.

Their return was announced by singing in the hall outside and a good deal of fumbling with the lock before Frank stumbled into the room with his arm round Jack's shoulders.

'Hello, darling,' he called out. 'We're home.'

He paused for a moment, noisily sniffing the air.

'Wha's that smell?' he asked Jack. 'Something's burning.'

Jack stood swaying gently from side to side, saying nothing.

'Close your eyes,' commanded Dorothy brightly from the kitchen. 'This is a surprise.'

When they opened their eyes they saw a large serving dish on the table with two wizened dark brown carcases nestling side by side on burned toast in a bed of yellowing sprouts and overdone game chips.

'What is it?' said Frank, moving in for a closer look. 'Pigeon?'

Jack giggled but had the presence of mind to turn it into a hiccough. Dorothy glared at him.

'It's grouse,' she said. 'Uncle Bertie's compliments.'

'Good old Uncle Bertie,' said Frank, filling the glasses with wine, and raising his: 'Here's to Uncle Bertie.'

'Frank!' snapped Dorothy.

'Just a sip to prepare the palate for the feast, dearest,' he mumbled, hastily putting down the glass and picking up a knife and fork.

The flesh was dry and stringy, tasting not unlike a reheated kipper, but they chomped away with beaming smiles fixed on their faces. Suddenly Jack put his fingers to his mouth and said: 'I think I've found the thruppeny bit.'

He placed a shiny metallic pellet on the edge of his plate while Frank hooted: 'That's a whiff of Uncle Bertie's grapeshot, by Jove, sir.'

Dorothy jumped to her feet, throwing her napkin down on the table.

'I'm not going to sit here being insulted,' she said, her eyes brimming with tears.

The two young men stared at her in astonishment.

'Who's insulted you?' asked Frank.

'You have,' she insisted. 'You're always making sarcastic remarks about my cooking. No matter how hard I try, you always find fault.'

'But it's delicious,' said Frank, getting up and trying to put his arms round her. 'It's delicious isn't it, Jack?'

'Mmmm-mmm,' answered Harris, chewing on another dry mouthful.

'You're just saying that,' she said. 'It's all gone wrong because you were so late back. It's all your fault . . .' And turning on her husband she yelled: 'I hate you, you brute,' burst into a flood of tears and ran into the bedroom, slamming the door behind her.

'Women,' said Frank, looking at Jack with a helpless shrug of the shoulders. 'What was all that about?'

'Shouldn't you try to talk her round?' asked Jack, embarrassed at being caught in the middle of a matrimonial quarrel.

'I'm damned if I'm going to run after her and beg her pardon,' retorted Frank. 'She can turn on the tears like a tap. Well, let her . . .'

'I'd better be going,' muttered Jack, getting up from the table. 'I've got to report at Waterloo at the crack of dawn. Take my advice, old man, never sleep on a quarrel with the Missis.'

But Dorothy refused to open the bedroom door, which she had locked from the inside, and Frank was obliged to spend the night alone in the spare room.

The fact was that dining out in Mayfair was more Dorothy's style than learning how to make carrot flans or eggless cakes from 'Kitchen Front' on the wireless or wrestling with the sordid restrictions imposed by ration books with their dreary little pages of coupons for 1 oz of cheese, 4 oz of bacon or 2 oz of tea, which the shopkeeper had to tear out when he served these meagre quantities. Shell eggs were strictly controlled and the allowance of dried egg was one packet per month. In the circumstances it was too much to expect her to be glitteringly successful in the culinary department.

Frank was more often out than in and she spent hours alone in the flat, reading, smoking and listening to the radio. The news she heard was not of a kind to relieve the depression she felt as her pregnancy reached an advanced stage.

The troopship in which Jack Harris and several hundred others sweated away long days and even longer nights eventually ended up in Singapore as two British battleships, the *Prince of Wales* and the *Repulse*, were sunk. Now the Japanese were surging into Malaya and the bombs were falling on Rangoon and Singapore.

Such was the start of 1942. In late January Churchill returned from conferring with President Roosevelt, the new ally, to face a censure motion in the House of Commons with the defiant words: 'I offer no apologies, I offer no excuses, I make no promises . . .'

'The old man's losing his grip,' said Frank pessimistically after listening with Dorothy to the nine o'clock news on the BBC. 'Hong Kong gone, Penang gone, Singapore going. Poor old Jack – he's right in the thick of it. A ringside seat at the farewell performance of the British Empire.'

A couple of weeks later two German battleships, the

Scharnhorst and the *Gneisenau*, sailed unchallenged from Brest through the Straits of Dover and three days after that Singapore fell.

For Dorothy, although she sympathized with Jack Harris's wife waiting for some word of his fate, the fall of Singapore meant more shortages and longer queues everywhere. Soap rationing was announced and the weather was bitterly cold.

She took long solitary walks while Frank was at the office, along Chelsea Embankment and across the bridge into Battersea Park where the trees were white with frost. Chunks of ice floated in the river.

Fuel shortages meant that the central heating in Nell Gwynn House was turned off for hours at a time and because of the Japanese conquest of Malaya's rubber plantations hot-water bottles were unobtainable. Rubber-soled shoes vanished from the shops at the same time.

Dorothy sat huddled in a siren suit, mittens and a pixie hood, feeling desperately unattractive. The baby was now high in her belly and she imagined herself resembling a barrage balloon. She longed for silk stockings and make-up, things which had become luxuries obtainable only on the black market.

One day she could stand it no longer and jumped into a cab to Debenam and Freebody's in Wigmore Street where she splurged ten guineas and her total allowance of clothing coupons on a gorgeous maternity frock. She then went to her hairdressers in Brook Street and had her blonde hair 'permed' in tight waves.

When Frank arrived home, instead of being pleased and complimenting her on the transformation, he said: 'My God, don't you realize there's a war on?'

He was at the time conducting a vigorous campaign in the pages of the *Evening Chronicle* against waste and extravagance but Dorothy was in no mood to be lectured.

'I hate to be told "there's a war on" – as if that excused the abandonment of all one's standards,' she told him, 'Damn the war. I'm sick of the bloody war, and I'm sick of you going on and on about it. You're a selfish bastard.'

She had forgotten in her anger how that last adjective would sting. Frank went very white and stormed out of the flat, to spend the rest of the night in the company of the night owls at the Press Club, getting horribly drunk. He did not return home until the small hours, pallid and unshaven, and was greeted at the door of the flat by the unsympathetic gaze of the local doctor.

'I was called out by your wife, Mr Cole,' said the doctor, whose steady grey eyes seemed to bore straight through him, 'just a short while ago. She's in considerable pain. I've sent for an ambulance.'

18

Frank went to St Stephen's Hospital, Fulham, with Dorothy and was left waiting on a hard chair in a bare, brown-tiled little anteroom after they had carried her on a stretcher through a pair of swinging doors. Despite the cold and his desperate anxiety for her, his eyes kept closing and his head nodding forward. He was awakened from one of these fitful dozes by a light tap on the shoulder and started up to see a man in a white coat looking down at him.

'Mr Cole? I'm the registrar,' he said. He looked very young, no older indeed than Frank himself. Frank wondered how recently he had qualified, as the man went on: 'Mr Biggerstaff the gynaecologist has examined your wife and decided to operate immediately. He's reasonably certain that the problem is a ruptured ovarian cyst but we'll do a laparotomy to make sure.'

'May I see her?' asked Frank.

'I don't think that would be advisable at the moment,' said the registrar, stepping back as he caught a whiff of Frank's alcohol-laden breath. 'Your wife is in no condition to see visitors.'

He hurried back through the swing doors and in a moment or two the night sister came out and said to Frank: 'I suggest you go home and get some rest, Mr Cole. There's nothing you can do here.'

'She won't . . .?' asked Frank, his voice shaking. 'I mean, Sister, there isn't any chance is there that she might . . .'

'Might die, you mean?' said the nurse. She was in her late thirties, with a crisp and efficient look about her, but she had kindly brown eyes. She put a hand softly on his shoulder before she went on. 'There's always an element of risk in any surgery, Mr Cole, but Mr Biggerstaff is one of our most respected consultants. A very experienced man. She's in good hands, Mr Cole, so go home. I will telephone you as soon as I have some news.'

On his way to the exit, Frank heard loud female screams coming from behind the swinging doors through which Dorothy had disappeared on a stretcher and the sound echoed in his ears all the way back to Nell Gwynn House. Alone in the flat, waiting for the telephone to ring, he prayed that she would pull through safely and that their unborn child would live. He was frightened and conscience-stricken.

When he married Dorothy he was not sure whether he was in love with her, or whether she really loved him. They were physically attracted to one another but initially had no intention whatever of getting married. Frank, if he had thought of it at all, would probably have reckoned on settling down when he was about thirty. Dorothy, for her part, with her social background and upbringing, might have been expected to find a husband among the upper crust with good family connections and probably inherited wealth.

Now what had begun as a lark was suddenly in deadly earnest. To love and to cherish, in sickness and in health – the awesome responsibility of the marriage contract, even though theirs was not solemnized in church, dawned on Frank for the first time.

The urgent peal of the telephone penetrated his consciousness. The flat was in darkness as he groped for the instrument at the bedside and switched on the lamp, mumbling into the receiver: 'Sloane 3440.'

'St Stephen's here,' said a gentle female voice. 'Sister Evans. Your wife has just come round from the anaesthetic, Mr Cole.'

'How is she?' asked Frank.

'Comfortable.'

'And the child?'

There was a pause before the voice answered: 'Mr Biggerstaff will see you at nine o'clock if you come down to the hospital and you may visit your wife afterwards.'

Mr Biggerstaff received him in his office with a benign smile and an invitation to 'take a seat, my boy'. Without unnecessary preliminaries he told him: 'Your wife has lost the child I'm afraid. The operation was a good one, that is to say the excision of the cyst was carried out without complications, but unfortunately was followed by a miscarriage. There was nothing we could do to save it.'

Frank looked at the consultant, saying nothing, until Mr Biggerstaff continued: 'Don't reproach yourself, Mr Cole, these things are not that uncommon. Your wife is a healthy young woman. You will be able to have babies if you want them – Nature thoughtfully provides many of our accessories in pairs, and one ovary's as good as two.'

Lady Plumley-Greene did not take such a sanguine view of her daughter's misfortune when she heard of it and was horrified to find Dorothy in a public ward when she hurried up from Limpsfield to visit her.

'Who is Biggerstaff, anyway?' she demanded. 'He probably botched it. Heaven knows what damage he might have done, darling. If only Frank had had the presence of mind to telephone me at once I would have made arrangements with our man in Harley Street. I shall insist on him seeing you now so that he can give you a check-up, but it's rather like locking the stable door after the horse has bolted. Poppa will be frightfully upset.'

Dorothy allowed her mother to move her into a private room, although the care and attention she received there was no better than in the ward. Indeed, left on her own without the distraction of other women's voices all round, depression descended on her like a fog. When Frank, trying to cheer her, said something about trying again she snapped at him: 'I'm not going through *that* again. And anyway what's the point of bringing children into this miserable world?'

Dorothy came home from hospital a week later and Jenny moved into the flat temporarily to look after her. There were no consolations of grapes or peaches during the convalescence as the people's diet was fruitless.

Pursuing his campaign against 'black marketeers and greedy guts', Frank fearlessly exposed war criminals like the woman who was fined £10 for throwing breadcrumbs to the birds in her garden. Attacking those who tried to evade Lord Woolton's imposition of a maximum price of 5s for a meal in a restaurant, he wrote in the *Chronicle*:

In certain smart restaurants in Soho people who should know better can be observed at luncheon every day guzzling fine cuts of meat and rich sauces and puddings. The 5s limit is evaded by charging up to 30s a bottle for wine, of which there appears to be an inexhaustible supply despite Hitler's occupation of France. Fine Camembert cheese is available for those 'in the know' and crêpes suzette – less than five bob for the pancakes but a fiver for the liqueurs in which they are flamed.

'Do you have to be so *holy* about it?' demanded Dorothy when she saw this article. 'What's wrong with having a little fun? I wish somebody would take me to Prunier's or the Ecu de France for lunch, and blow Lord Woolton, and that gloomy Stafford Cripps, too.'

Those who dared (as Dorothy dared) to exceed the official limit of five inches of hot water in their bathtubs could feel the chilly eyes of Sir Stafford glinting through steel-rimmed spectacles at them.

'There never was a more melancholy time,' complained my mother from the depths of post-operative depression.

The tonic that Dorothy needed arrived one afternoon in the form of Ralph Greedie carrying a bunch of daffodils, a welcome sign of the healing spring which had come at last after one of the longest and coldest winters of this century. When Frank turned his key in the door of the flat that evening he heard Dorothy laughing, the first time he had heard that sound since she came home.

His delight was tinged with jealousy when he saw that Ralph was the cause. They were sitting side by side on the sofa, their heads close together, enjoying some private joke. Frank never put it into words, but he was probably rather envious of his friend, the handsome young air ace.

'I can't believe that you could possibly want me, a Grade IV crock with one lung,' he once wrote to Dorothy before they were married, 'when you've got the cream of No. 74 Squadron to choose from.'

He remained sensitive throughout the war (and after it) about being in civilian clothes when most men of his age were in uniform. Perhaps it was to compensate for not being in the fighting services that he took such a vitriolic line against what he described in print as 'the superannuated war horses and Colonel Blimps who are running the war from Whitehall.'

Under the editorship of Geoffrey Elms, the *Chronicle* candidly mirrored the nation's resentment against continued defeats and supported pressure from Russia for the Allies to open a new front in the West, a demand that was being discussed in factory canteens and bus queues. 'Second Front Now' was scrawled across walls and the sides of those ubiquitous tanks where emergency supplies of water for fire-fighting were stored.

When the whole of Cyrenaica fell to Rommel's Afrika Korps in June, the *Chronicle* cartoonist, Hackett, portrayed two Tommies in conversation against a background of camels and the Pyramids.

'Good news at last,' one was saying to the other. 'Two of our generals were captured at Tobruk.'

This was the last straw for authorities already groaning under the weight of press criticism. Elms and the proprietor, Viscount Edgbaston, whose fortunes and peerage were founded on the manufacture of nuts and bolts in Birmingham, received a peremptory summons to wait upon Mr Herbert Morrison in Whitehall.

What went on inside the large green and gold room whose long windows overlooked St James's Park was never published but Elms looked ashen, tired and very, very old when he returned to Fetter Lane and sent for his young assistant, Frank Cole.

'I've just been to see our 'Erb,' he said, with a wan smile. Mr Home Secretary Herbert Morrison retained the accent of the Brixton back streets where he was born and Elms went on to give a passable imitation of it. 'He told us that if we "continued to take the Mickey aht of the Harmed Forces" he would 'ave the lor on us.'

Frank could not help smiling but Elms continued: 'It's really no laughing matter, Frank. It was a real block-buster. He had a dossier on us, including a lot of your stuff and finally Hackett's Tobruk cartoon. " 'Ow can you expect Tommies to fight for generals you keep telling 'em are no good?" That was his line, and I felt like reminding him that he was a conscientious objector in the last war. But I didn't. He implied that we were working for the Fifth Column and reminded us that he closed the *Worker* down under Regulation 2D and would do the same to us if we weren't careful. It was a repeat of the warning he gave the *Mirror* in April.'

'How did His Lordship take it?' asked Frank.

'Like a lamb in the Secretary of State's room,' replied Elms. '. . . "I can assure you of this, Mr Home Secretary" and "I can assure you of that". It was only after we got outside that he started ranting about "that bloody, one-eyed little Cockney upstart trying to tell me how to run my paper . . . to think that he has powers to hang or reprieve murderers . . .", etcetera. Edgbaston has the contempt of the *nouveau riche* for others who have bettered themselves.'

'So what do we do now?' Frank asked his editor. 'Suppress the facts? Bury our heads in the sand?'

'I just don't know,' said Elms, passing a hand wearily over his eyes. 'I've had enough of it. The Blitz, paper shortages, decimated staff – and now censorship. I don't think I can take any more. I think I'll retire and concentrate on Digging for Victory in my garden.'

Geoffrey Elms had had a long and distinguished career in Fleet Street. He had been one of Northcliffe's bright young men and had stayed with him to the end when 'the Chief' finally went off his rocker and made the head porter at Carmelite House head of the advertisement department. There was no more respected editor and Frank thought that he must be joking about going into retirement. As it turned out, he was not.

On that damp summer's evening when Frank hurried home to the flat in Chelsea, bursting with some personal news, Dorothy was not there. He poured himself a Scotch, switched on the wireless and sank down in an armchair, feeling deflated.

Half an hour later he heard laughter and the sound of the key in the door and Dorothy came in with Ralph.

'Darling!' she said to Frank. 'What brings you home at this unaccustomed early hour?'

Then without waiting for an answer, she rattled on: 'I've had an absolutely super afternoon. Guess where we've been?'

Again before he could open his mouth she continued: 'The Zoo! And Madame Tussaud's – can you imagine it, darling? Ralph had never been and neither had I, so we decided to give one another a treat. We got caught in the rain and had to take shelter in this awful teashop where the chair simply collapsed under poor Ralphie and the waitress accused him of breaking it deliberately . . .'

She was flushed with excitement and looking her prettiest in a light summer frock but so like a child, thought Frank, trying to stifle a feeling of irritation.

'I have some news,' he managed to get in at last.

'Naturally,' said Dorothy, giggling. 'You're a newspaperman aren't you?'

'Not just a newspaperman,' retorted Frank. 'A newspaper editor. Editor of the *London Evening Chronicle*, if you must know.'

Dorothy threw her arms round his neck and kissed him. 'Darling,' she cried, 'how clever of you! But what have you done with the old one?'

'Geoffrey's retired,' said Frank. 'He's had enough. Lord Edgbaston sent for me this afternoon and asked me to take over – it was Geoffrey's recommendation.'

'How much?' asked Dorothy.

'We didn't talk about *money*,' replied Frank, as if the subject were indelicate. 'He offered me the job and of course I jumped at it. Who wouldn't? The salary will match the job, naturally. It's not necessary to dot the "i's" and cross the "t's" in a situation like this.'

'Congratulations,' said Ralph, slapping him on the back. 'It couldn't have happened to a nicer joker. Let's celebrate.'

'I've already booked a table at the Hungaria for dinner tonight,' said Frank, having forgotten for once his Crippsian scruples.

'Great,' whooped Ralph. 'What are we waiting for?'

It seemed unfriendly to point out that the table at the Hungaria was for two. Ralph was not in the least abashed when he discovered it and had no difficulty in persuading the waiter to lay another place and discover a bottle of champagne hidden somewhere in the cellar.

'I hope Sir Stafford Cripps doesn't get to hear about this,' Dorothy chaffed her husband as the cork popped, attracting envious glances from the other diners in the restaurant.

'Here's to you, Mr Editor,' said Ralph raising his glass.

When they had drunk the toast he put his arm round Dorothy, kissed her and said in a stage whisper: 'Remember, doll, if he doesn't treat you right, old Ralph will be standing by, ready to scramble.'

Late that night, after they had gone to bed and turned out the light, with Ralph asleep in the next room, Frank suddenly asked: 'Are you having an affair with him?'

Dorothy laughed. 'What a preposterous suggestion,' she said.

'Well, you're seeing a lot of him when I'm not around,' he grunted.

'Ralph's good for me,' she answered. 'He makes me laugh.'

As editor, Frank's salary was raised to £2,000 a year, only half what Lord Beaverbrook paid the thirty-year-old Michael Foot when he hired him as editor of the *Evening Standard* in the following year, but a substantial salary for all that. Despite income tax at 10s in the pound, my father was able to afford a mortgage on a Regency lodge in Albany Street overlooking Regent's Park, which mother furnished expensively with fine carpets and period pieces from antique shops and auction rooms and some generous gifts from Lady Plumley-Greene.

The Government that summer called on manufacturers to produce basic articles to approved standards, using specified materials, to be sold at controlled prices, but 'Utility' furniture was not for Dorothy. Nor were 'Make Do and Mend' jumble sales. She expected the best and was prepared to spend every penny of Frank's salary and his inherited annuity in pursuit of it. Eagerly, she scanned the 'For Sale' columns in *The Lady*.

Frank, however, maintained his patriotic spirit. Lord Edgbaston presented him with a Wolseley Hornet motor car but rather than use petrol which seamen were risking their lives to bring to Britain he left it in the coach house beside his imposing house and cycled to the office.

When Ralph was posted to North Africa that autumn, Dorothy felt lonelier than ever. They exchanged regular letters written on pale blue aerogramme forms, Ralph graphically describing the discomforts of sand and flies from a tent in the Western Desert, Dorothy saying how much she enjoyed *Blithe Spirit* at the theatre.

After a wet summer, the lawns in the gardens behind Albany Street had the richness of velvet while the trees in the park showed scarcely a sign of autumn tinting. Yet London wore a drab wartime coat.

'How I detest those posters everywhere,' she wrote in one of her letters to Ralph. 'Coughs and sneezes spread diseases. Is your journey really necessary? Even poor old Eros in Piccadilly is hidden behind National Savings posters. Lyttleton, the Minister of Production, came up with a brilliant new slogan the other day – "TNT", "Today Not Tomorrow". Sunday is the only day that Frank spends at home and then his mother comes to tea and they sit for hours going on and on about "Bomber Harris" and the wickedness of bombing German civilians – as if they didn't bomb us just as much! How I wish you were here to make me laugh and forget that there is a wretched war on.'

She cheered up a few weeks later when the Russians defeated the Nazi invaders at Stalingrad and General Montgomery's tanks rolled over Rommel's forces at El Alamein, writing: 'Church bells ringing for the first time since the war started. Good old Monty! Good old Desert Rats! If you happen to meet Poppa at Shepheard's or the Turf Club do crack a bottle of bubbly with him for me. He's so despondent, poor man, without his hounds.'

There was however, no reply from Ralph. Christmas came and went without one of his flimsy aerogrammes covered with his untidy scrawl dropping through the letter box at Albany Street, and a blessedly mild winter was followed by the riotous blossom of spring.

19

Sitting at breakfast on a sunlit morning, picking her leisurely way through the post, Dorothy came across a typewritten envelope with an unfamiliar postmark. Inside was a single sheet of notepaper headed, Queen Victoria Cottage Hospital, East Grinstead, Sussex, Dorothy felt the blood draining from her face as she read:

Squadron Leader R.J. Greedie has been admitted as a patient at the Plastic Surgery and Jaw Injuries Unit here. As you know, he has no relatives in this country and a visit from you would work wonders for his morale. I write to you without his knowledge, but please come if you can. He is in Ward Three. If you wish to contact me first, please ring East Grinstead 987.

An illegible signature was scribbled above the words 'Welfare Officer'. Dorothy sat very still for what seemed a long time, staring out of the french windows open onto the terrace. Birds were singing over the distant rumble of traffic and a Painted Lady butterfly settled on the rim of the water butt. She noticed that its black, orange and white markings were faded and its wings tattered after a long journey from the Mediterranean. Even a war like this could not halt the migrations of nature, though it had swept away their friends like twigs in a brook.

Jack Harris, they knew, was a prisoner of the Japanese and beyond the reach of normal civilized communications. They had heard nothing of Ralph for more than six months until this letter from a stranger. As she got up to go to the telephone to tell Frank, who left for the office before the postman came, Dorothy was amazed at her own calmness, although her hand shook slightly as she lifted the receiver.

They drove down to East Grinstead in the Hornet on the following afternoon, a Saturday. The dreary wastelands of London south of Waterloo Bridge were brightened by purple masses of rosebay willowherb flowering amidst the bombed ruins.

Once clear of the suburbs beyond Purley, bowling down the Eastbourne road through bright green woods and lush meadows, there were no visible signs of war at all. They reached the homely country town of East Grinstead in about an hour and had no difficulty in locating what had been before the war a quiet cottage hospital and was now one of the busiest surgical units in Britain.

Ward Three was one of a group of huts just inside the main gate, to the left of the main brick building surmounted by a green serpent and staff of Aesculapius, the Greek god of medicine. The interior of the hut was painted in regulation Ministry of Works dark green and cream, with an unlit black coke stove in the centre. At the far end was a grand piano and a barrel of beer.

A radio was blaring out the *Warsaw Concerto* at full volume while patients in dressing gowns and portions of service uniform sat around laughing, chatting and smoking. Some were playing cards, others were reading Penguin paperbacks. It might have been an ordinary mess hut but for the mummified appearance of the occupants.

One of them detached itself from a group and came towards them. A squadron leader's tunic with the ribbon of the Distinguished Flying Cross on the breast hung from this figure's shoulders, with the sleeves pinned to the pockets. The head was swathed in crepe bandages but from the middle of it sprouted a strange, pink sausage-like object, a sort of embryo elephant's trunk.

Frank involuntarily recoiled from this apparition as the familiar antipodean twang of Ralph Greedie muttered from beneath the bandages: 'Christ, mate, you look a fright.'

Dorothy's fingernails dug into Frank's arm as Ralph laughed and went on: 'You'll have to excuse me, I can't shake hands.'

He held up two bulky dressings like oversized boxing gloves.

A pretty nurse with a long white headdress but wearing open sandals said to them: 'You must be Mr and Mrs Cole – I'm Jean Fuggle. Thank you for coming.' Then, turning to Ralph, she suggested: 'Why don't you take your friends for a walk? You can't hear yourselves speak in here, they're such a noisy lot.'

Together they walked into the town up a road like a green tunnel through a wood above banks of weathered sandstone and past the gates of a mansion with views across a landscape resembling folds of emerald velvet.

'Out in the desert I dreamed of views like that,' said Ralph, 'just like it was at Downshall. It was a relief to get to Malta just when the spring flowers were out – masses of them, all scarlet and gold. And that unbelievable blue sea, bluer even than it is at home in Auckland Harbour. Mind you, though, Malta's all rock – I thought to myself when I flew in there for the first time, Ralph my boy, don't get engine failure on take-off, those rocks'll rip you to shreds. Not a bit like the nice soft green fields around here. Jerry's been pounding hell out of that little lump of rock in the middle of the Med for the past couple of years but it's still there. More like a bloody aircraft carrier now that Desert Air Force is going for Italy, with twenty squadrons of Spitfires at Luqa and Safi, not to mention the Wellingtons and Baltimores, Beauforts and Mosquitoes, all packed like sardines. Grand Harbour at Valletta – what a sight that is from the air, crammed with warships inside those big stone battlements from the Great Siege. Down on the ground it's not quite so pretty – pongs, dust everywhere and damn flies, no better than El Hamma really. And I was in dock with a touch of Malta dog after my first dinner in the officers' mess in Sliema but I couldn't get a wink of sleep for sirens going and bells ringing all the time.'

And so he chattered on as they walked over the bridge crossing the railway, and on past a Jacobean almshouse and St Swithun's church, built soon after the Norman invasion. The

High Street was crowded with Saturday afternoon shoppers. No one stared at Ralph, despite his bizarre appearance. It was obvious that local people were quite used to the sight of Archibald McIndoe's 'guinea pigs' strolling about the place. McIndoe was already famous for his remodelling of badly burned faces and bodies and he had made a bonfire of military regulations, including the traditional hospital walking-out uniform of bright blue suits and red ties. This was now used only as a punishment. Normally the patients wore their military uniforms or civilian clothes.

'Social life in Malta's pretty basic,' Ralph was saying. 'There's the Union Club, Charlie's Bar and the Chocolate King, pink gins and the local plonk, but I kept longing for a good old English pub' – one of his mummified hands gestured towards the Tudor buildings lining the High Street – 'and a pint of draught bitter.'

Outside the Crown Hotel a Spitfire was on display as part of the 'Wings for Victory' drive.

'A Mark V,' remarked Ralph as they passed it, 'just like the one I was flying when I copped it.'

It was the first mention he had made of the dreadful thing that had happened to him and for the moment he said no more. They were aching to question him further but were too embarrassed to do so. All Ralph said was: 'Let's have tea at the Whitehall.'

The Whitehall in London Road was a brash concrete and glass addition to the centuries old stone, brick, tile, clapboard and half-timbered architecture which made up most of the town centre. It included a cinema and a dance hall as well as the restaurant which they now entered.

'Hello Mabel,' said Ralph to one of the waitresses. 'Pot of tea for three, please, and your best cakes.'

The restaurant was packed with people taking a break from shopping or waiting for the 'second house' at the cinema and *they* waited for some time in awkward silence until Mabel arrived with the tea, smiling at Ralph.

'Will you be Mummy, or shall I – after all, I look the part,' said Ralph with a laugh at his own grisly joke. 'Would you mind lifting my cup for me – I've learned how to pick things up with my teeth but I haven't quite got the hang of holding a teacup in my teeth and drinking at the same time.'

Dorothy obliged while Frank, looking round, was intrigued

to see that here as in the High Street there were no curious stares.

'I got my first saline bath in the Med,' Ralph was saying, 'so fortunately the temperature was about right. They took me to the naval hospital in Valetta, but there wasn't a lot they could do for me there. I was wearing flying helmet and goggles, so I wasn't blinded, thank God, but I'd no gloves on and I was in KD shirt and shorts so I was pretty well roasted from my nose to my toes . . . a classic case of airmen's burn. They told me McIndoe was the only man who could give me a new face and hands and that's why I'm here, special delivery by Dakota via Gilbraltar.'

Another laugh emanated from beneath the crêpe bandages and Frank smiled, feeling his face crease with the effort. He could not equate the grotesque figure in front of him with the debonair dark-haired young man who used to tapdance to 'Hotcha Mamma from Alabama.'

'It's a holiday camp at the Queen Vic compared to Downshall,' said Ralph, as if reading his thoughts. 'The barrel of beer never runs dry and the Boss sometimes comes down to give us a tune on the piano. You know, he's a Kiwi like me – comes from Dunedin – and we hit it off right from the start. His only unbreakable rules are, one, don't touch the nurses and, two, don't touch his daughters. I've already broken both.'

Another unnatural guffaw was followed by an uncomfortable silence, while Frank looked at the ceiling, at the floor, anywhere but at that grinning mummy across the table.

'How long will it take, Ralph dear?' said Dorothy at last.

'McIndoe says maybe two years,' answered Ralph, and raising one of his bandaged hands to his face, went on: 'This funny old sausage believe it or not is the beginning of a new nose – a pedicle, the medicos call it – being transplanted from my forehead, one of the few bits of me that wasn't fried. I've been under the knife half a dozen times already. Hunter, the Gas Man, is as much of a card as the Boss himself. "Just a little prick, if you'll pardon the expression," he says when he gives you a jab.'

Once again, Frank and Dorothy found themselves forcing a laugh, trying to pretend, as Ralph was, that it was all a great joke. They had to keep reminding themselves that underneath the bandages was the same old irrepressible Ralph.

The horror of the war seemed far away as they took tea in that very normal-looking English country town, yet just one week later, on a busy Saturday afternoon just like this one, a lone Messerschmitt swooped low, spraying bullets and dropping bombs on the defenceless population. People were destined to die or suffer terrible injuries over their teacups at the Whitehall and bodies would be dug out of the rubble and shattered glass. It would seem like the hand of fate to Mummy and Daddy and Ralph Greedie that their reunion took place when it did.

Dorothy visited the hospital regularly in the coming months, usually going down to East Grinstead by train from Victoria. Ralph would meet her at the station and walk with her. She never asked him about his prang, as he called it, but one afternoon when they were discussing the hit and run Messerschmitt he said: 'Funny, isn't it, how things work out? On the morning I bought it I should have been standing in for my wing co at the Wing Leaders' conference with the AOC – "father's prayers", we called it – and he took a dim view if you didn't turn up. But the duty controller tipped me off that morning that Badger Stokes from my squadron had gone down in the drink coming back from a night op over Sicily and they were sending a clapped-out old Walrus amphibian from Kalafrana to look for him.

'Well, you know how it is, Dot. Badger was an oppo of mine and a thoroughly nice bloke and I hate meetings anyway, so I hurried off down to "the ditch" – that's the ops room buried away in some impregnable rock face – to see if I could be of any help. In no time I was airborne with a couple of sprog pilots, Brookie and Dicky Davis, to act as escort for the Walrus and search for old Stokesie. "It'll be a piece of cake," I told my chap over the R/T. "We'll fish him out of the drink and I'll be back in time for father's prayers." It was a lovely clear morning and the coast of Sicily was in view when Brookie spotted a yellow speck against the deep blue in the area of Badger's last reported position. I went in with wingtip just a few feet above the sea and waved at the bod in the dinghy. He waved back. It took ten minutes for the slow old Walrus to catch us up and put down with difficulty on the swell. In the meantime we circled low, probably almost deafening Badger (I had no doubt that it *was* him) with the roar of our Merlins.

'We were so preoccupied with what was going on below that we committed the basic fighter pilot error of not keeping our eyes peeled for what was *above* us. The other two were green but there was no excuse for me getting caught with my pants down.

'The Me109s came down on us out of the sun. We were a gift to them, like wood pigeons feeding on a lawn. Brookie was on my starboard beam and I saw large pieces suddenly flying off his wing and a puff of smoke from his engine before four cannon shells went into me, thud, thud, thud, thud, one after the other. Flames licked past my cockpit and when I opened the hood and released the door I got the full blast of engine oil in my face, like hot black tar. It covered my goggles so I couldn't see a thing but escape is instinctive, part of the training: pull the split pin out of your sub-harness, unplug your oxygen tube and R/T lead . . . the bloody harness wouldn't come undone and I realized by the rush of air that I was diving fast. The heat of the flames was unbearable. I was *frying*.'

Dorothy shuddered at the brutality of his description but continued to listen. She realized his need to talk about it.

'At last I got the harness undone,' Ralph went on after a moment, 'heaved myself onto the seat, got one leg over the side and kicked at the stick with my other foot. The kite went over on its back and I tumbled clear, groping for the ripcord of my parachute. A few seconds, and then a terrific thump which knocked all the breath out of my body. I tore off my goggles – God knows how, because my hands were almost charcoal – and saw my open parachute above and that dark, dark blue sea below. I saw a Spitfire hitting the water and exploding, sending up a huge white fountain of spray, but I didn't know whether it was mine or somebody else's. The sky seemed to be full of Me109s – the din was fantastic. One of them flew right past me, so close that I could see the black-helmeted head in the cockpit. I thought he was going to open fire on me but it didn't seem to matter, anyway. He just gave me a V-sign, then went into a tight climbing turn, streaking back towards Sicily.

'I could see the old Walrus, wallowing in the sea below but no sign of the other Spits or of poor old Badger. I was swinging gently from side to side, still hanging on to my ripcord ring. And do you know what I was thinking? They're not going to get half a crown off me for this bugger this time . . .'

Despite her horror at the tale, Dorothy had to smile at the memory of Ralph being asked for 2s 6d by the equipment officer at Hornchurch for failing to bring back the release handle with his parachute after ditching in the Thames Estuary.

'I still hadn't realized what had happened to me.' Ralph said. 'Until I smelt something very much like roast pork, and then it dawned on me and I thought, Christ, *I'm* the meat. I'd taken off in such a hurry from Luqa that I'd not changed into flying clothes. Shorts and a short-sleeved shirt had left plenty of flesh exposed to the flames.

'I'd no time to dwell on it though before I hit the sea, released my parachute and disappeared for a while underneath the surface. Jean Fuggle says it was the best first aid I could possibly have had. When I came up bobbing like a cork, I pulled the parachute pack towards me by the shroud lines and reached for the rubber dinghy which should have been attached to it. But it wasn't. Somehow or other it had come adrift. I inflated my charred Mae West and swam around in circles for ages looking for the missing dinghy. No sign. Now I was *really* worried. I didn't mind nearly roasting to death but I drew the line at being drowned. The sun was blazing down on me out of a clear blue sky and I was in agony. Also I had swallowed a lot of sea water.'

'Where was the Walrus?' asked Dorothy.

'That was the problem,' said Ralph. 'It seemed to have vanished. I thought perhaps Jerry had blasted it out of the water, leaving me up the creek without a paddle. I could see the outline of Cape Passero on the distant horizon but my chances of swimming there were zero, especially as the current seemed to be carrying me farther out to sea. Although the sun was still high in the sky, I felt cold and my teeth started to chatter. What happens when it gets dark? Better to give up the unequal struggle, I thought, just lying on my back, not caring which way the current took me. Then I heard the shug-shug shug-shug of an old aero engine, very faint at first but getting louder. The skies were empty, but twisting round I saw the outline of the Walrus no more than a hundred yards away. I struggled to get one of the small rescue rockets out from under the retaining flaps on my Mae West but my fingers were too badly burned to manage it.

'In sheer desperation I thrashed at the water, kicking up all the foam I could, and bawled, yelled and shouted at the top of my voice. As I lay back, exhausted and gasping for breath, the flying boat taxied towards me across the swell.

'A rope was thrown and somehow I managed to hang on to it.

Hands dragged me on board and a sergeant W/Op tried to rub me down with a coarse towel until I screamed at him to lay off. Then he forced some brandy between my chattering teeth and I felt better. The Walrus was in a shocking state, with six inches of water swilling about inside from a cannon shell hole below the waterline and petrol leaking from one of her wing tanks. It was a wonder the Me109s hadn't finished her off as they could easily have done. Brookie and Davis, only twenty and just out of FTS, both got the chop and Badger, poor sod, had disappeared without trace just as help was at hand after being six hours in the sea.

'We were lucky to be alive – that's if we could make it back to Kalafrana, as the captain of the Walrus remarked on take-off. But he made a brilliant landing in his shot-up old crate, which never flew again. They whisked me off to hospital in my bare feet (I'd lost my shoes and socks in the sea) before I even had a chance to say thank you. For weeks I had shocking nightmares of Brookie and Davis and Badger screaming for help while they drowned and I burned.'

Back at Ward Three, Dorothy was introduced for the first time to the Boss, a stocky man in horn-rimmed glasses; she noticed how short and stubby were the fingers which had performed miracles on the burned body of Ralph and scores, if not hundreds, of others. Privately, she mentioned to Nurse Fuggle that Ralph had talked about his trauma and was told: 'That's the first time. You can't imagine what it does for these men's morale to see familiar faces and get out for a change. Do come again soon.'

The next time Dorothy brought Jenny with her. Ralph was overwhelmed with joy at seeing his beloved Duchess again. As for Jenny, the visit brought back painful memories of that other war, of the young man who had loved her and died flying over the trenches of Flanders, and of all the other young men, including her beloved Will, who passed through the wards of the Endell Street military hospital. Nevertheless, she became a regular visitor with her daughter-in-law to Ward Three.

One afternoon in late summer they arrived to find Ralph lying immersed in a saline solution in a large old-fashioned tub standing on four legs and surrounded by a paraphernalia of pipes, lamps, buckets, thermometers and bells.

'Come on in, the water's lovely,' he called out as they

appeared in the doorway. 'It's not often I get the chance of entertaining beautiful ladies in my bathroom – excepting you, of course, Nurse.'

After he came out of the bath, they strolled together on the shaven lawns among the shrubberies and sat in deckchairs eating ice cream.

'Which flavour do you prefer,' asked Ralph, playing waiter, 'strawberry or vanilla?'

Ice cream was unobtainable in the shops but as it was the only solid food that some of the badly burned patients could take there were lashings of it at the Queen Victoria Hospital. Drums of it in powdered form were shipped across the Atlantic following the addition of a Canadian Wing to the hospital.

'Suddenly everything seems so much more summery,' said Dorothy, kicking off her high-heeled sandals to wiggle her toes and stretch her bare legs in the sun.

Frank was not with them. He usually managed to find an excuse for not going to East Grinstead – an important meeting to attend, a backlog of work at the office, anything to avoid having to look at that face, those hands, when the bandages came off. It was horrific to shake one of the wizened claws. Ralph's blue eyes twinkled as mischievously as ever from the outline of pilot's goggles etched into his face by the flames. Inside this scar line his skin was unblemished but the rest of his face was a grinning mask of white and salmon pink.

'I just can't bear to look at him,' Frank admitted to Dorothy that evening when she returned from what had seemed to her a delightful picnic. 'It makes me feel physically sick.'

'And what about Ralph?' she demanded. 'How do you think he feels? Apart from his appalling injuries, he blames himself for getting shot down and losing two of his pilots.'

'I'm sorry, I just can't pretend that nothing has changed,' he explained. 'I'm terrified that the nausea which I feel when I look at him will show on my face.'

'Do you think he doesn't know what he looks like?' she said angrily. 'He's looked at himself in the mirror and he can even joke about it, but not you, oh no, you can't face it. God, you make me sick! All your lofty editorials on the Beveridge Report and the new world we're going to have when the war's over that you're always going on about to your mother. All that *New Statesman* idealism, yet when it comes down to it you can't bring yourself to comfort a friend who needs it.'

Frank turned away without replying to these hurtful words, all the more hurtful perhaps because he acknowledged their truth.

'What about you?' he said after a while. 'What are *your* motives? Lady Bountiful visiting the war-wounded? It can hardly be physical attraction any more, considering the mess he's in.'

'That's unforgivable,' she snapped back. 'But I wouldn't expect you to understand my feelings, or Ralph's. Yes, he's very badly burned, but he's still the same lovable man inside. He needs love more than anything. I kissed him this afternoon as I was leaving and there were tears in his eyes.'

Dorothy herself was now crying, but when Frank tried to comfort her she shook him off. He felt a deep disgust at his own apparent callousness and lack of compassion for a friend in trouble but could find no words to explain or excuse it. Perhaps his own experience of war in Spain had killed something in his psyche, or did it spring from guilt at his lack of direct involvement in the present conflict? Could it have been jealousy of that object in Ward Three, so repulsive yet capable of arousing in his cool, beautiful wife emotions that were beyond his reach? Whatever it was, he could not bring himself to revisit the Queen Victoria Cottage Hospital.

20

On the 8 May 1945 Winston Churchill stepped into a limousine outside 10 Downing Street to be driven the few hundred yards to the House of Commons to announce victory in Europe. He raised his bowler hat to the ecstatic crowds pressing around his car and puffed at the inevitable cigar, a hero to his people.

Five days earlier and hundreds of miles away on Lüneburg Heath, Colonel Plumley-Greene was among the privileged group which had witnessed the surrender of the Germans in Montgomery's tent. All over London at dusk on that sultry May evening bonfires blazed in celebration of VE-Day and the lights shone out at last from a thousand streets, north and south of the river, as blackout curtains came down from windows.

Looking up and down Amen Road, bomb-scarred and shabbier than ever, Jenny saw young women (and not so young women) throwing their arms round everyone who came by, kissing and shrieking with joy, dancing on the pavements. Union Jacks were flying everywhere.

Life was so drab that everyone craved a little colour and excitement. Even the officious Mr Glover next door, carried away by the mood of the moment, seized a paint brush and daubed red and blue stripes on the white gauze which replaced the glass in his front windows after one of the last V-2 missiles, Hitler's final secret weapon, descended without warning on Amen Road, killing the occupants of two houses and injuring many more.

Jenny had been asleep in bed when the V-2 went off and she woke up to find her eiderdown covered with fragments of glass and plaster from the ceiling above. But she was unhurt and got up, threw on a coat and shoes and dashed down the road to do what she could to help the rescue operation.

Like most of her neighbours she had long since stopped using her Anderson shelter which was half full of stagnant water and had become the home of frogs. Amen Road had been spared any direct hit from the eight thousand V-1 flying bombs – ironically called Doodlebugs – which roared over England plunging to earth and exploding when their fuel ran out. The V-2s were even worse because they could not be heard coming, travelling faster than the speed of sound.

Jenny received a sad letter from her sister Lucy down at Bournemouth:

I am sorry to have to tell you that dear Clarence has passed away. I wish I could say he died peacefully but I cannot. These past two years have been a nightmare, residing as we do in a defence area, we were kept awake all night long by heavy tanks and lorries lumbering past on the main road to Southampton during the preparations for the D-Day landings in Normandy and Clarence had an attack of angina. He needed complete rest but of course that was impossible and those dreadful Doodlebugs roaring overhead spurting out smoke and flames and then suddenly cutting out and crashing down kept him in a constant state of agitation. Now these awful rockets. I think it a merciful release for Clarence that he will be troubled no more. The Funeral is on Tuesday but it will be a very quiet affair and I shall not expect you to attend as travelling these days is extremely difficult and there are thousands of Americans everywhere . . .

As Jenny looked out of her window on that May evening two heavily made-up girls in garish Utility print frocks, their hair in turbans, click-clicked by on impossibly high heels, arm in arm with American soldiers. A chorus of 'Got any gum, chum?' from small boys followed them down Amen Road. Everywhere the Yanks went they left a trail of Wrigley's chewing gum, Lucky Strike cigarettes and nylon stockings.

Jenny smiled. The atmosphere reminded her of Mafeking Night but so much had changed since that distant war. The Great War, apart from all the loss and suffering, had changed their lives completely.

And now this latest and greatest war was over, in Europe at least, though fighting continued in the Far East. Women and children had been involved in it almost as much as the fighting men, dying in their hundreds of thousands.

Perhaps better times are coming at last.

Ever the optimist, Jenny, at sixty-five, was getting too old to be a practising midwife, although she was still ready and willing to answer a knock at her door at any hour of the day or night.

In his office in Fetter Lane, Frank was scanning the front page of the late night final edition, still damp from the press and smelling of ink. It was dominated by a large picture of 'Winnie' beaming from a balcony in Whitehall, his fingers held aloft in the familiar 'V' for victory. There had not been an election in Britain for ten years – now he would have to go to the polls.

'I think he'll call an election sooner rather than later,' remarked Frank at the editorial conference. 'He'll want to cash in on all this euphoria.'

'What's our line?' asked Benson, the leader writer.

'We're independent, of course,' Frank told him with a devious grin. 'We'll advise our readers to vote for the party which is most likely to implement Beveridge. Need I say more?'

'In other words,' muttered some wag down the table, echoing an old joke about the Beveridge Report from the 'ITMA' radio show, 'we're backing that best-selling number "Gone with the Want".'

The young editor pretended not to hear. He had already made

up his mind to back Labour without consulting his proprietor. It was Edgbaston's contributions to Liberal Party funds which had earned him his peerage, but the Liberals were a spent force. It would be a straight fight between Conservative and Labour.

Before the month was out Churchill resigned and three weeks later the battle for political power was joined. Blue posters appeared all over the country appealing to the electorate to 'Help Him Finish the Job!' They were countered by pictures of a tin-hatted private soldier captioned: 'This is your chance to *Labour* for him. Vote Labour and win the peace.'

Churchill's clumsy attempt to portray his opponents as a potential Gestapo in Britain had little appeal to a mass audience with bitter memories of the 1930s. In July, barely two months after the crowds had cheered him to the echo in Whitehall, they voted decisively against his party.

On 26 July a banner headline in the *London Evening Chronicle* proclaimed: BRITAIN GOES LEFT. SOCIALISTS WIN LANDSLIDE VICTORY OVER TORIES.

Jenny was among the jubilant when the poll was declared. On the two occasions Labour had been in office before it had lacked a working majority. Now when nearly four hundred victorious Labour MPs sang 'The Red Flag' in the House of Commons it looked as if the New Jerusalem had arrived at last and my grandmother saw it as a vindication of everything that she had fought for.

My father, deprived of his first opportunity to vote for so many years by the longest of Long Parliaments, also derived immense satisfaction from the election result, unlike his parents-in-law. The colonel regarded it as 'rank ingratitude' while Lady Plumley-Greene doubted whether it was possible to take an illiterate former day labourer, Ernest Bevin, seriously as His Britannic Majesty's Foreign Secretary.

Dorothy was merely bored by the whole business and hoped that rationing and Utility clothes would speedily pass into history. Her hopes were soon dashed. Shortages and controls on virtually everything continued into what was to be a long and dreary period of postwar austerity when even bread had to be rationed for the first time.

Nor was there any immediate sign of Jenny's New Jerusalem; indeed, an even greater beastliness was about to take place in

August when the Americans dropped a new kind of bomb on Hiroshima and Nagasaki, forcing the Japanese to surrender.

In a letter to the *Chronicle*, which Frank published, she wrote:

> Celebration of VJ Day should be tempered by the reflection that victory was achieved by far worse genocide than that perpetrated by the so-called 'saturation' bombing of Hamburg, Berlin or Dresden. This action not only carries the barbarism of total war to its logical conclusion but threatens an unborn generation of children with the effects of atomic radiation. What right have we to try the Nazis as 'war criminals' when we have this monstrous act on our consciences?

Frank wrote more than one leader on the subject, pointing out that the atomic bomb made armies and navies, tanks and battleships, and even the concept of war itself, as obsolete as the bow and arrow. 'For the survival of the human race, President Truman must keep it under strict lock and key,' he declared innocently, unaware, like most other people at the time, that British scientists had been involved in the Tube Alloys project, as atomic bomb development was code-named.

Generally, he adopted a restrained tone in his editorials following the Labour landslide. As he explained to Jenny during one of their weekly tête-à-têtes in his office over tea and toasted buns: 'I'm keeping my head down in the long grass for the time being. His Lordship is on the warpath.'

Lord Edgbaston had taken a poor view of Frank's championing of the Labour cause during the election campaign and he had no intention of being made the scapegoat for the fact that only twelve Liberal MPs had been returned to Westminster. He accused Frank openly of disloyalty and even, during one heated interview, suggested bluntly that he should resign.

He was further enraged by Frank's nonchalant reply: 'My Mummy told me, never resign.'

'I'm warning you, Cole,' he growled, 'you've made an important enemy.'

But following his initial success in the editor's chair, when he had briefly flowered as one of Fleet Street's wonder boys, Frank had engaged a clever lawyer to draw up a new contract and Edgbaston knew it would cost a lot to sack him. As a self-made millionaire he hated spending money if he could avoid it.

* * *

On a drizzling December afternoon two liners passed each other on Southampton Water with a wailing exchange of siren calls. Among the passengers on the outward bound ship, bearing the flag of the Shaw Savill line, was Ralph Greedie. After weeks of waiting he had obtained passage home to New Zealand where he would greet his parents with something resembling a human face, the result of twenty-six painstaking operations.

Pricked by conscience and trying to make amends for earlier neglect, Frank Cole had driven him and his luggage down to the port to save him the trouble of catching the boat train, and stood with Dorothy on the quay waving as the liner slowly pulled away. Ralph, conscious of the sympathetic stares of the other passengers at the rail, went below to his cabin as soon as his friends were out of sight. He did not want sympathy and also he needed a good cry. Tears, of course, were unmanly and could not be shown in public, but in the privacy of his cabin they splashed down the front of his new blazer with the squadron badge on it.

His friends, just as emotional at the farewell, although Frank refrained from tears, were already on their way back to London, unaware that among the repatriated prisoners of war in the incoming ship, the *Nineveh*, arriving from Singapore via Cape Town, was another old friend.

Jack Harris's war scars, though not visible to the eye as Ralph's were, remained with him for the rest of his life. After years spent in the steaming heat of the Far East, the chill dampness of the English winter made his teeth chatter as he stood watching the other ship pass.

There was no one to greet him at the docks, other than a series of impersonal faces behind plain deal tables, glancing at documents to the rhythmic thud of rubber stamps. On the way to the dispersal centre in a coach and still wearing brown and green camouflage, he looked out at weed-grown bomb sites under a leaden sky.

After the usual wait in a queue he was handed one large flat cardboard box containing a grey chalk-stripe suit, a shirt, two collars, two pairs of socks, one pair of black lace-up shoes, a nondescript tie and a trilby hat. A bored clerk handed him a book on resettlement and another a second-class rail warrant.

He was a civilian again, but in the train up to London he hardly recognized the image that he saw in the rain-speckled window. After three years in Changi Prison he was a walking skeleton, from which the ill-cut demob suit hung in limp folds. Throughout the long days and weeks, running imperceptibly into months and years, he had dreamed of this moment. Going home. But now it was happening he felt like someone else, a stranger in his own country.

He had sent a telegram to Ethel and she was waiting for him at the barrier at Waterloo with the two children, Brenda, who had grown so he could hardly believe that she was his daughter, and a son almost four years old that he had never set eyes on before. They hung back and peeped at him around Ethel's skirts almost as if they were frightened of him.

Homecoming, instead of being a relief, turned out to be a series of rude shocks: his parents dead and their home gone, Ethel still living with her parents at Stoke Poges, little prospect of getting a home of their own. Rented accommodation was scarce and prohibitively expensive. He thought of applying for a 'prefab', one of the emergency prefabricated buildings with built-in cupboards and fittings which the Government was putting up on bomb sites, but Ethel would not hear of it.

'I'm not going to live in one of those glorified shoeboxes,' she said. 'We're going to stay where we are until you can find us something better. This is my home. And anyway Brenda is doing so well in school she shouldn't be uprooted just now.'

They had long, whispered discussions about it in their room at night, with her mother in the next room straining to hear every word. The walls were so thin that Ethel kept hushing even when they were making love.

'First of all, I've got to get my old job on the *Chronicle* back,' said Jack. 'Then we'll see about getting a place of our own – I can't stand it here.'

He had to steel himself to walk into the *Chronicle* newsroom amidst all the bustle of getting the closing prices edition to bed, with typewriters and teleprinters clattering, people shouting to one another, telephones ringing and boys charging around with bits of paper.

From out of this bedlam a voice yelled: 'Harris!'

Stung by the condescending use of surname only, Jack rapped back: '*Leading Aircraftman* Harris to you' and then saw that the greeting came from Frank Cole. He was standing in waistcoat and shirtsleeves at the back bench behind the chief subeditor and he beckoned his old friend over in a peremptory way.

Jack had no idea that Frank had become the editor of the paper in his absence, although it soon dawned on him when, after a hearty slap on the back, he was propelled down the corridor by his elbow into the office that was formerly occupied by Geoffrey Elms. In his day there had still been a brass bellpush marked 'Ring for Hansom' on the desk. Now there was a battery of multi-coloured telephones and a cocktail cabinet gleaming with chromium plating.

Frank motioned towards the black hide Chesterfield and stood looking at his old friend as he took a seat.

'My God, you're a sight for sore eyes,' he said, then turning towards the cocktail cabinet, asked: 'What'll it be – Scotch?'

Jack nodded, and looking round the room, remarked: 'You've done well, Frank, and you haven't aged a bit – not like some of us.'

'Nonsense,' replied Frank, handing him his drink. 'You look fine considering what you've been through. Ethel will soon fatten you up.'

'Oh, yes,' answered Jack. 'It's easy enough to put back a few lost pounds – some other things aren't so easy to put back. Three lost years, for instance.'

He sounded bitter and Frank hastily changed the subject.

'I daresay you'd like to get back to the gallery,' he said. 'That was always your province. When can you start?'

'Right away,' Jack told him. 'My shorthand's a bit rusty but it'll improve rapidly with a bit of practice.'

'Hang on though,' said Frank. 'I don't want you in the gallery.'

Jack's face fell.

'No,' Frank went on, lighting his pipe and puffing out a dense cloud of blue smoke. 'I want you in the lobby. The chap I've got there is about as much use as a one-legged man at an arse-kicking contest. He never gets to hear about anything until it's in the *News* or the *Standard*.' He crossed over to the cocktail cabinet and poured himself another generous measure of Scotch. Jack, only halfway through his first, declined.

'I swear to God,' Frank continued, 'that man couldn't tell Aneurin Bevan from Ernie Bevin. He's as pissed as a newt most of the time. As of now, Jack my lad, consider yourself to be the *Evening Chronicle's* political correspondent. I shall enjoy telling that incompetent old hack to go to hell.'

Frank's dark eyes sparkled and his cheeks were flushed. He looked no older than his twenty-nine years but an inward change had taken place. The iron had entered his soul and he clearly had a taste for management, and blood.

'I don't know that I want to pinch another man's job,' Jack began, but Frank cut him short.

'Don't be a fool, man,' he snapped. 'There are only three kinds of people in this world – winners, losers and survivors. What are you?'

'A survivor, I suppose,' answered Jack. 'I survived Changi, didn't I?'

'Well, that fellow's a born loser,' said Frank. 'He would never have got the job in the first place if you hadn't been away fighting for your King and country. You're the man for the job and that's an end of it.'

Would you be editor, if the rest of us hadn't been away in the Forces, wondered Jack, and it was on the tip of his tongue to say it, but he thought better of it and simply said: 'OK, I need the money to get a mortgage. I've got a wife and kids to consider.'

Frank clinked his glass against Jack's and said: 'Here's to friendship and mutual interest, old man.'

Jack swigged the remains of his Scotch and grinned.

'Well there's no doubt which category you're in, Frank,' he said with just a trace of mockery. 'You're one of life's winners.'

Jack and Ethel paid just one uncomfortable visit to the Coles' home in Albany Street. Dorothy considered them to be NQOCD ('Not quite our class, darling') and made little attempt to hide it. For his part, Jack considered her to be a snobbish bitch and insisted on praising Clement Attlee and his creation of a new order, much to her irritation.

'How anyone could prefer that insignificant little man with the pipe to a giant like Churchill is quite beyond me,' she commented.

'I heard an amusing story about Bevin and Churchill the other day,' said Frank. 'The old man was horrified to discover when they went on one of their foreign conferences that Ernie always polishes his own boots instead of having some valet do it for him. But Bevin wasn't in the least abashed when he mentioned it, he just said: "I get some very good ideas when I'm doing my boots." Apparently, he advised Molotov to do the same.'

Ethel smiled politely without really seeing the joke, and Jack merely grunted: 'I suppose it's difficult for some people to accept that others who used to be servants are the masters now.'

'Let me show you round the place,' interjected Frank, taking his friend by the arm and leaving the hapless Ethel alone with a bored-looking Dorothy.

Jack dutifully admired the terrace with its marble statuary, the walled garden at the back and the view across Regent's Park from the front of the house, the highly polished Hornet in the coach house alongside, the gravelled drive and the handsome wrought-iron gates (not sacrificed to the war effort as so many had been).

Oh, yes, it's easy to be a Socialist, living here. He's done very nicely indeed out of the war while ex-bloody Leading Aircraftman Harris, J., is struggling to get together enough for a deposit on a semidetached in Orpington.

Frank wanted to confide in his old friend, pour out his troubles, but he was discouraged by a certain barrier that existed between them as editor and correspondent. A mutual wariness had entered the relationship. Frank needed a friend because he felt isolated and vulnerable. His political disagreements with Lord Edgbaston had left him sitting out on a limb.

It was only a matter of time before the noble lord took a saw to that limb and within two weeks Jack Harris and everyone else learned that Frank Cole and the proprietor of the *Chronicle* were parting company 'amicably'. The rumour was that Edgbaston had to pay well into five figures to get rid of his troublesome editor.

'Have you heard of this new species of rosebush?' Jack asked the barman over his mid-evening half of bitter in an out-of-the-way House of Commons watering hole.

'No, what's that, Mr Harris?' asked Ronnie, who was known for his horticultural interests.

'Well,' said Jack, 'no matter how much of the smelly stuff you throw on it, this rose always comes up smelling of Frank Cole.'

'He must know something that the rest of us don't,' said Ronnie, laughing. 'Either that, or he went to the right school.'

'Albion Hill Elementary, Deptford,' replied Jack. 'We used to play marbles and swap cigarette cards in the playground there.'

'Get away,' exclaimed the barman. 'I thought he was one of those public-school Socialist intellectuals. His wife's a Plumley-Greene, isn't she?'

'Exactly,' said Jack, sipping his warm beer, 'that's just what I mean, Ronnie. Roses, nothing but roses all the way for Frank Cole.'

It was widely believed that Frank had been responsible for the eye-catching posters which had helped Labour win the election. This was not so, but he had acted as an unofficial publicity adviser in those innocent days when public relations, advertising hype and news management were in embryo. No sooner had he left the *Evening Chronicle* than he was taken on the payroll at Transport House as a full-time consultant.

The pay was but a fraction of his Fleet Street salary but he had his golden handshake to sustain him and he was content to beaver away in the back room for a while, waiting for his chance to launch himself into a new career in politics. It came when the Member of Parliament for a marginal constituency in South London suffered a heart attack and announced that he would not be able to stand at the next election. In the winter of 1948, Daddy was adopted as the prospective parliamentary candidate.

The constituency was West Wickham.

21

West Wickham was a green suburb on the farthest southern fringe of Greater London. It was here in the 1920s that my unacknowledged paternal grandfather Will Dawson found temporary prosperity as clerk of works for Holmes' Sweet Homes until the racket of building sub-standard mock-Tudor and pebbledash semidetached went sour. Walking the tree-lined avenues of houses which his father had superintended as building sites, Frank saw the H-aerials of newfangled television sprouting from the rooftops, the newest of status symbols and a sign that more prosperous times were just around the corner.

Up to the war, West Wickham had always voted Tory. In 1945, swept along by the tide of enthusiasm for social change, it had returned a Labour man to Westminster for the first time, albeit by a majority of little more than a thousand. Now after four years of continued rationing and shortages, of power cuts and financial crises, West Wickham was inclined to think that the experiment had been a ghastly mistake. The long awaited peace had turned out to be no better than wartime in civilian clothing.

The commuters who caught the 8.25 up to town were singularly unimpressed by the launching of a National Health Service as the cornerstone of the new welfare state. They saw it broadly in terms of a lot of scroungers getting free teeth and spectacles. West Wickham was undergoing a marked swing back to the values of the prewar parvenu middle class when Frank Cole arrived on the scene. He quickly realized that he would have his work cut out to retain the seat for Labour with such a narrow majority.

Somewhat to his surprise, Dorothy devoted herself to the cause of getting him elected. 'After all, my place is at your side, darling, even if you do happen to be fighting on the wrong side.'

She welcomed the opportunity of being, for the first time since they married, a part of his everyday life, of having a positive role to play. Not yet thirty, Dorothy still possessed a quite stunning figure which she had no wish to spoil by joining the rush to add to the postwar baby boom. Advertisements extolled the virtues of women resuming their proper place in the kitchen but my mother wasn't really cut out for the role of happy housewife. So, despite her arch-Conservative upbringing, she revelled in being the beautiful young wife of the handsome young Labour candidate at West Wickham.

My maternal grandfather had had a good war after that little bit of unpleasantness in Crete, riding on Monty's bandwagon from the triumph of El Alamein through to victory in Europe, and emerging from it all with red tabs as a brigadier on the Imperial General Staff in London.

Brigadier Plumley-Greene was based at the War Office, as it was still called in those franker days before *defence* was the euphemism for military activities, and for a time became a bowler-hatted, first-class commuter between Oxted and Victoria Station in London. Owing to the shortage of suitable nutty slack, the unreliability of the steam train service soon obliged the brigadier to spend the working week at his *pied-à-terre* in Welbeck Street, that comfortable flat where Frank and Dorothy once made love during an air raid, leaving early for the country on a Friday afternoon and returning to town late on Monday morning.

It was a gentlemanly life in the time-honoured way. Every day at a quarter to one Plumley-Greene took lunch at his club, the In and Out in Piccadilly, but it was not what it had been. The menu was frankly uninspired and occasionally meatless and the price of a good bottle of claret was exorbitant. The brigadier found, too, that the use of his staff car for a run out say to Ascot was restricted by petrol rationing.

Plumley-Greene was accustomed to a privileged position near the top of the middle class, a place to which he considered himself entitled by virtue of the fact that he had been to the right schools and was a member of a good regiment. Although he never pondered on such matters, he was in his own small way part of the landed gentry.

In the eyes of the Plumley-Greenes the two world wars had been uncomfortable interruptions in the English way of life; once they were over everything should have returned to normal. Alas, things had not returned to normal. There was rationing, strikes and shortages, but even more disturbing a mood of 'We're the masters now' among grubby little Labour politicians, and some who should have known better were encouraging this egalitarianism.

Clement Attlee's a decent enough chap in his own way, from a good background and all that, but he got all these romantic ideas about the great unwashed when he was running boys' clubs in the East End and now he's trying to act as nursemaid to the whole country. Of course, he's an able chairman of committee but he's a colourless little fellow, a dry stick. He's given away India and made a botch of Palestine and here at home he's handing over everything – the mines, the railways – to the bureaucrats. No wonder the trains aren't running properly and we keep getting power cuts. Now if Winnie and Monty were in charge . . .

This was Brigadier Plumley-Greene's view of the New Jerusalem in the shaping of which his son-in-law was now to play some small part. Nevertheless, as a good soldier Plumley-Greene took his orders from the political masters of the moment and as a careerist he looked forward at the age of fifty, if not to a field marshal's baton, at least to becoming a major general.

His masters at that time were Manny Shinwell, a streetwise self-educated politician from the slums who was Secretary of State for War, and A.V. Alexander, a leading light of the Co-operative movement, who was Minister of Defence. So, despite his personal dislike of my father and his conviction that Dorothy had made a great mistake in marrying that Fabian conchie writer, Plumley-Greene invited them both down to the Oak House for the weekend.

It began inauspiciously on the Friday evening with Frank's refusal to dress for dinner.

'Momsy and Poppa *always* dress for dinner,' said Dorothy.

'Well I'm not going to imitate a bloody penguin for anyone,' replied Frank ungraciously. 'And anyway I haven't packed a dinner suit and a black tie.'

'How can you be so pig-headed?' complained Dorothy.

'A matter of principle,' said Frank, knotting the red tie that he insisted on wearing with his grey lounge suit.

'Principle be damned,' yelled Dorothy. 'You're just being as awkward as you can be. I do think you might be reasonable just this once, for my sake. You can borrow Poppa's spare.'

But Frank was adamant and descended to the dining room dressed as he was. Over sherry, the Plumley-Greenes steadfastly refused even to notice, much less comment upon, his lack of manners. And Frank, of course, was resolutely determined not to be embarrassed by their haughty civility as he was introduced to the two other couples, middle-aged and formally attired neighbours, who had been invited to dinner.

'Mr and Mrs Tilsley, Mr and Mrs Walter, this is my son-in-law Frank Cole,' Lady Plumley-Greene was saying, adding 'He's standing for Parliament' as if that explained his obvious eccentricity. Tilsley was a stockbroker, Walter something at the Ministry of Fuel and Power. They were by no means intimates of the Plumley-Greenes (beyond the fringe, in fact, of what would have been considered 'county' in prewar days) but acceptable makeweight guests for minor social occasions such as this small dinner party. Frank noted with contempt that they clearly considered it an honour to be invited to the Oak House.

Dinner was announced with due formality by Plumley-Greene's batman, Brownlee, who was dressed not in military uniform but in a black suit of antiquated style which seemed to have been handed down from some departed butler.

'Entertaining is almost impossible these days,' remarked Lady Plumley-Greene as they took their places around the long table in the dining room. 'One can't get the staff any more. My mother had a staff of fourteen before the Great War, don't you know, and considered herself hard done by. At least after that war *some* of the gels came back from the factories. Today it seems they all want to be shorthand typists or comptometer operators or whatever they call themselves. They're simply not interested in domestic service. If one wants to keep staff one has to allow them all kinds of privileges and pay inflated salaries. I pay Mr and Mrs Arrowsmith £3 a week as well as their keep and their own staff flat . . .'

Mrs Arrowsmith, wearing a green overall but no cap, was helping Brownlee to serve the soup.

Since the hostess and her guests studiously ignored the subject of their dinner conversation, Frank made a point of smiling at her and saying thank you as she filled his dish from a silver tureen but she studiously ignored *him*. Servants were still servants even under a Labour government, reflected Frank remembering the humiliations of his boyhood at that big house on Blackheath where his mother was cook.

Lady Plumley-Greene was still going on '. . . they expect wireless concerts every evening and afternoons off to go to the cinema. Of course Lionel has Brownlee and a groom provided by the regiment who can help Mr Arrowsmith do the lawns and the rose garden but one wonders how long even that will last under Mr Attlee's rule.'

She shot a meaningful glance in Frank's direction while sucking noisily at a spoonful of soup. Mesdames Tilsley and Walter, who had no living-in servants and were hard put to find dailies to come in, made sympathetic cooing noises none the less.

'Should be a fine day for the hunt tomorrow,' said the brigadier cheerily, hoping to change the subject and realizing too late that this was another potential minefield. He was a tall good-looking man with silver sideburns and an apparently permanent tan from his service in the Western Desert. His one mild affectation of sand-coloured chukka boots worn with his Whitehall pinstripe and bowler hat was the subject of some comment at the In and Out.

'Nothing better than a good hunt,' brayed Lady Plumley-Greene while Mrs Arrowsmith deftly removed the empty soup plates and Brownlee brought on the roast grouse, 'orf the ration' as the brigadier put it.

'Socialists don't approve of hunting, do they?' asked Tilsley the stockbroker.

'The unspeakable chasing the inedible,' chipped in the man from the Ministry, not to be left out. 'Wasn't that Oscar Wilde's phrase?'

'The unspeakable in full pursuit of the uneatable,' murmured Frank, somewhat condescendingly.

'Baaah!' exclaimed Lady Plumley-Greene, or something very like it, spraying the company with a half-masticated mouthful of grouse. 'Oscar Wilde was a nancy boy.'

'There was no hunting in Cairo,' said the brigadier, 'so I took up polo instead. I did hear of a very good pack of hounds at Yalta.'

'Uncle Joe Stalin doesn't approve of blood sports unless the prey is human,' growled Tilsley. 'At least we kill Reynard fair and square, according to the rules. There's nothing cruel about it.'

'I wonder if the fox would agree?' asked Frank.

'That's just sentimental tosh,' retorted his mother-in-law brusquely. 'Brownlee, do ask Mrs Arrowsmith if the lemon sorbet is ready to be served.'

'Christ, what a boring evening,' groaned Frank when he and Dorothy at last got to bed. 'The English upper middle class at home. What people! Two world wars and a social revolution and they're still with us, still behaving as if nothing had changed, still thinking they've got some divine right to run the country, arrogant as ever.'

'Oh, darling,' said Dorothy, slipping a smooth bare arm round his neck and kissing him. 'You're such a pompous snob.'

'Me? A snob?' Frank was highly indignant. 'I'm the one who wants to get rid of all this class nonsense, but *your* lot are dedicated to . . .'

'Oh, phooey,' whispered Dorothy, blotting out his protests with her delicious mouth. She was wearing a most expensive off-the-shoulder cerise silk nightdress and an even more expensive Parisian perfume.

'Dinner with the Tilsleys and the Walters isn't exactly a riot for anyone,' she said, brushing a bare foot against his under the sheets. 'I need some excitement.'

'You're such a well-bred bitch,' he said, taking her in his arms. 'I hate you.'

* * *

Dorothy was up as soon as the woodpigeons started cooing and sparrows chirruping. Frank lay with the sheets up to his chin, watching with one eye as she wriggled into skintight white breeches and feeling immensely privileged.

But as she went out he could not resist calling after her: 'I hope the poor little fox gives you all the slip.'

When he himself rose much later to wash and shave at the basin in the room, and dress, he could not find his shoes. He looked in the cupboards and under the bed but they were nowhere to be found. Eventually he padded downstairs in stockinged feet. The house seemed deserted yet on the sideboard in the dining room there was an appetizing array of bacon and kidneys, kedgeree and scrambled eggs, kept warm by little spirit burners under silver lids.

Brownlee came in so softly that he made Frank jump. 'Tea or coffee, sir?'

'Tea, please. Strong and sweet,' said Frank. 'And have you any idea who's pinched my shoes?'

'I've been cleaning them, sir,' said Brownlee apologetically. 'I'll fetch them at once.'

He was actually wearing a green baize apron, but, as Mrs Beeton once said, we need not dwell on the boot cleaning process. Frank helped himself to eggs and bacon. No sign of ration books cramping the style at Oak House, despite her ladyship's moaning.

When Brownlee returned with the shoes, gleamingly polished, and a shoe horn to help him put them on, Frank tried to engage him in conversation.

It was not easy but he discovered that Brownlee was a Cumbrian who had enlisted in the cavalry in the summer of 1939 just before war broke out, having been in the Territorial Army, and had been Plumley-Greene's batman ever since.

'You'll be voting for us of course in the next election,' said Frank, smiling.

'Labour, you mean?' replied Brownlee, looking uneasy. He glanced over his shoulder and lowered his voice before continuing. 'I've thought about it, sir. Oh, yes, I've thought of it. I would have voted for Mr Attlee in 1945 but I reckoned they'd find out and I'd be out of a comfortable billet. I've signed on for twelve, you see.'

'They?' asked Frank. 'Who are they? You're in the Army,

aren't you? You're an employee of the Government and the Government is Labour.'

'Ah, well, I don't know a lot about politics,' said Brownlee, 'But I do know the regiment. They've got their own way of doing things and I didn't fancy going back to tending sheep up out on the fells in all weathers. So I voted Conservative, just to be on the safe side like, sir.'

At that moment a youth in khaki denims and a black beret passed the window, whistling as he pushed a wooden barrow laden with horse manure in the direction of the rose garden.

'That's Trooper Lovelace,' said Brownlee, '*he's* a Red, if you'll pardon me for saying so, sir. It's all right for the likes of him. He's a National Serviceman, just eighteen months and he's back to Civvy Street. He's always going on about capitalists and that. I can't be doing with it myself, sir.'

Frank ate his solitary breakfast and drank several cups of Brownleee's regimental dark brown tea before venturing out for a breath of country air. In general, he disliked the country in winter, with its soggy fields and dripping bare trees, but he set out regardless, out through a side entrance and past the stable yard.

The cheerful voice of Trooper Lovelace drifted over a high brick wall:

> 'My tin roof leaks and my chimney leans
> There's a hole in the seat of my ol' blue jeans
> And I've finished the last of my pork and beans
> Life gets tedious don't it?'

Frank smiled at the words of this popular American record coming from the lips of an impudent Cockney who had never been trained to know his place. Servants should be neither seen nor heard. When he comes of age, may he vote Labour.

Beyond the outbuildings, to the rear of the Oak House, a rough cart track led down a gentle grassy slope to a brook. Frank's black leather shoes were not designed for this and although he trod carefully, trying to avoid the puddles and the deepest ruts, he was soon spattered with mud up to his knees. Why didn't I ask Brownlee to find me a pair of wellies?

The track crossed the stream over a red-brick bridge, lichened with age. He carefully descended the bank to the water's edge and was idly casting a twig on the current when he suddenly noticed two sharp, bright amber beads glinting from the shadows beneath the bridge. His townsman's blood froze as he made out a long, pointed muzzle, and erect ears.

Do foxes attack humans, when cornered?

He stayed very still and so did the fox, up to his chest in the water which he had entered downstream to throw his pursuers off the scent. Frank was acutely aware of the animal's strong, musty smell, as he heard the hounds and huntsmen approaching and the urgent peal of the horn. A horse loomed on the bridge above Frank's head, its flanks lathered and steaming, and from an even greater height a red face topped by a black hat peered down at him.

'Ah, Cole. Playing at mudlarks, I see. You haven't seen our friend Reynard by any chance?'

Frank recognized him with difficulty as Tilsley the stockbroker. The fox stayed where he was, not moving a muscle, while the foxhounds lolloped around, sniffing at the ground and baying their silly heads off.

'As a matter of fact, I spotted one a couple of minutes ago,' said Frank. He pointed across the fields on the far side of the bridge. 'He went off over there towards that copse, going like the clappers.'

'Thanks, awfully,' said Tilsley, and digging his heels into the flanks of his hunter, called out: 'Tally-ho! After him, before he goes to ground.'

Off they went in full cry, the clamour of their hooves and the baying of the dogs rapidly fading in the wintry mist. The fox slid like a red-brown shadow up the bank just a couple of feet away from Frank.

His white-tipped brush, fully sixteen inches long, quickly vanished into the undergrowth.

Ungrateful beast. Not a word of thanks for saving your life. You're like me, though, a survivor.

BOOK THREE

Clouded Hills

December 1949
On 3 December at the
Queen Charlotte Hospital,
to Frank Cole and Dorothy
(*née* Plumley-Greene) a
daughter.

From the birth notices in
The Times.

22

My arrival was unconventional enough to bring a smug smile to the faces of my father and his agent, Stan Taylor. Mummy was sitting on a flag-draped platform in a draughty British Legion hall that Saturday evening listening to, or rather pretending to listen to, a speech of Daddy's which she had heard fifty times before.

'. . . It's all very well for Mr Bascombe to say that the Tories will end rationing and sweep away all controls but how are we to know that in five more years they won't be spending more of our taxes on guns than on butter . . .?'

Dorothy imagined another flag-draped platform in another equally draughty hall not a million miles away, and Mr Bascombe declaring vehemently: 'How are we to know that in five more years there'll be any more coal in our bunkers, any more good red meat in our larders? Can our Socialist friend Cole deliver the *coal* that we need?'

She was just reflecting how puerile politics was when the contractions began and she clutched at Frank's arm, halting him in mid-sentence. Amidst scenes of great drama among the dozen or so people who had bothered to attend the meeting, she was helped to the exit while Mr Taylor telephoned for an ambulance.

I was not in fact due for another two weeks, but displaying the impatience which was to be characteristic, I was now clamouring lustily for a premature entrance on stage. By the time the ambulance reached the Elephant and Castle, its bell clanging shrilly, poor Mummy had reached the second stage of labour and it was obvious that we would not reach Queen Charlotte's Hospital in time for the third and final stage of delivery.

The driver pulled off the road on to that large bombed and derelict site on the South Bank beside Waterloo Bridge on which was soon to rise the Dome of Discovery, the Skylon and other futuristic shapes of the Festival of Britain which Herbert

Morrison announced as 'the people giving themselves a pat on the back'.

Frank and the driver looked on nervously while the male attendant dealt with delivering the baby. Poor Daddy almost fainted at the sight of so much blood. When it was over, the journey to hospital was resumed.

So, despite what the birth announcement in *The Times* said, I was actually born not in Hampstead but on the South Bank, and christened just before Christmas at the parish church of St Marylebone, wearing the same cotton and lace gown decorated with a delicate pattern of ears of wheat that my great-grandfather was christened in at Rotherhithe 120 years earlier.

My grandmother had worn it, when she was baptized at birth into the Roman Catholic faith and kept it through all her tribulations after her father gave it to her on her coming of age, just before he died. Now after all these eventful years in the Cole family, the robe returned with my baptism (at Dorothy's insistence) to the Anglican church, the denomination in which my great-grandfather was reared.

I suppose I was the result of the new togetherness, as the advertisements called it, which Frank and Dorothy had discovered, not over the kitchen sink but in working together to cultivate West Wickham. Although the general election was not due until 1950 the campaign began in the constituency at the beginning of the previous year. Unlike the candidate's mother, who joined in enthusiastically, Dorothy could not avoid a slight air of condescension as she took part in the fund-raising efforts and feigned interest in whether there was to be a new pedestrian crossing outside the infants' school. It was all so suburban.

On the other hand, she enjoyed the knowledge that every eye was on her when she accompanied her husband on the ingratiating round of mothers' meetings and jumble sales, local balls and dinners, elegantly turned out in the latest fashion, with nipped-in waist and tight skirts, long gloves and, of course, pearls, always pearls.

Clothes and shoes were derationed at last but materials, like everything else, were still in short supply. Dorothy, however, knew her way around the salons of the West End and had clever copies of Dior's New Look made up for her by black market dressmakers. Frank never quibbled at the exorbitant bills. He wanted Dorothy to dazzle, not to say overawe, the local party hacks and their dowdy head-scarved wives.

Shrewdly sensing West Wickham's mood, Frank went out of his way to impress on the electorate that modern Socialism did not necessarily mean austerity. Dorothy helped to spell out the message as she wafted among the hoi polloi, being awfully charming.

Hello, Ron. Hello Reg. How are the children?

Nothing could have been less helpful to Frank's efforts to create a new face for Socialism than the headquarters of the local party in the High Street. It was housed in what had once been a newsagent's shop and the sign of the previous occupant – 'F. Coleman, Newsagent & Tobacconist' – could still be faintly discerned under a thin coat of bilious yellow paint over which was inscribed in black: WEST WICKHAM LABOUR PARTY.

Just a few doors down the street, in a similar decayed Edwardian shop, was the office of the local weekly *Gazette*. Its window was full of photographs of fêtes and baby shows, as many faces as possible, all looking the camera straight in the lens.

Soon after his adoption by the party, Frank marched in with a copy of *Tribune*, the badge of the new Socialist thinking, tucked under his arm. (During the war it had always been the *New Statesman*, and before it, the *Daily Worker*.)

A short, round, middle-aged woman with bright yellow hair sat behind the counter filing her crimson nails.

'I'm the parliamentary candidate for the Labour Party,' Frank informed her. 'I'd like to see the editor.'

She sniffed and said: 'I'll see if Captain Barker-Harding is in. He may be in the booz – out seeing someone.'

She turned to a little wooden box with an array of plugs, wires and switches at the front and a black metal handle at the side, which she twirled with immense vigour. Frank watched, fascinated, her ample breasts bouncing up and down beneath the lacy trimmings of her blouse.

'Halleo, halleo!' She was screaming in what he took to be her *telephone* voice. 'Halleo, Arthur. Yeoung man heah to see you, sez he's the Leabour cendidate. Oh, quaite. Yes, indeed. Very good . . . I'll tell him.'

She turned back to Frank and announced: 'Straight up the

stairs. First door on the right, ducky. 'E'll see you right away.'

It was exactly as he remembered the *Mercury* office in Penge in the days when he and Jack Harris were starting out on their careers. He knocked at the door with a little card saying EDITOR stuck on it with a drawing pin and a hearty voice called out: 'Come!'

Inside was a room scarcely larger than a broom closet, filled by a large, old-fashioned roll-top desk just like Harbottle's.

The man seated at the desk sported a luxuriant handlebar moustache and wore a loud check hacking jacket with a silk scarf tucked inside the open neck of his shirt.

'Good morning, Mr Barker-Harding.'

'*Captain* Barker-Harding,' responded the other man, shaking hands gingerly as if the visitor might be suffering from some contagious disease, then resuming his seat and placing a pair of sand-coloured suede boots on the edge of his desk. 'How do you do?'

'Quite well,' answered Frank. 'But better still, I hope, with your support.'

'Support?'

'Yes, indeed,' Frank continued confidently despite the faint note of alarm in Barker-Harding's voice. 'This week's edition of your paper is somewhat heavily weighted on the side of the Conservative candidate.'

'My newspaper is independent,' retorted the editor, huffily. 'It reports all sides without fear or favour.'

'A splendid slogan,' said Frank, 'although hardly original. To be precise, you've given no less than twelve column inches to the speeches of Mr Bascombe and less than six to mine.'

'Speeches are reported on their news value and local interest,' snapped Barker-Harding.

'In that case,' demanded Frank, 'why are Mr Bascombe's views on the dollar gap considered to be more newsworthy and of greater "local interest" than my speech on Wednesday evening deploring the pro-American and anti-Russian attitudes of . . .'

'I'm not going to argue about it,' said Barker-Harding defensively.

'I have a list here of my forthcoming engagements,' Frank went on, waving a piece of paper. 'I trust you will give me a fairer crack of the whip in future.'

'My subeditor looks after the diary,' muttered Barker-Harding, diving for the door and calling into the next room: 'Les, have you a minute?'

After a curt introduction to Les Tooley, a freckled young man with a stub of pencil behind his right ear, the editor left them alone together.

'Care for a pint?' asked Frank.

Young Tooley glanced at the clock, pulled his jacket on and answered: 'Don't mind if I do.'

They strolled down the High Street to the Swan and over not one, but three pints, Frank discovered that Barker-Harding had started the *Gazette* with his gratuity from the Army Pay Corps, in which he had served at Devizes throughout the war, attaining the dizzy rank to which he still clung. It was printed on the premises on an ancient flatbed machine and ten thousand copies distributed around the district every Friday by Tooley himself and the lady with the yellow hair.

'Our Arthur's a member of the Urban District Council, on the Tory side, of course,' said Les, lighting a Woodbine from the stub of its predecessor, 'and he's on the committee of the Country Club. His next step is to get himself on the Bench, as a justice of the peace, and that's why it's yes, Mr Bascombe, no, Mr Bascombe, three bags full, Mr Bascombe . . .'

Tooley took a long swig from his pot as if to wash a nasty taste from his mouth and Frank knew that he had found an ally inside the *West Wickham Gazette*. Sure enough, in the coming months his doings and speeches began to receive more space.

My premature and dramatic arrival gave my father just the sort of propaganda he needed. The *West Wickham Gazette* reported it on the front page under a somewhat fanciful Tooley headline: 'Labour Man Midwife at Own Daughter's Birth'. Frank Cole was shown to be not only human but verging on the super-human.

Mr Bascombe, the Conservative candidate, appeared in the *Gazette* office angrily brandishing a copy of the paper and demanding of its editor: 'Are you supporting me, Barker-Harding, or are you behind this Socialist chap?'

'The *Gazette* is independent,' mumbled Arthur Barker-Harding, turning rather pink above his pale, sprouting whiskers.

'Poppycock!' snorted Bascombe. 'You're giving young Cole all the publicity he could want. It's Mr Cole this, and Mrs Cole that, all over the front page. I have to search among the odds and sods at the bottom of the page inside to find a mention of *my* activities. I won't damn well stand for it.'

'It's all a matter of n-news value,' stammered Arthur. 'When a candidate's wife gives birth on the way to . . .'

'I don't want to hear another word about his blasted publicity stunts,' snarled Bascombe, and stomped out of the office before the cringing Barker-Harding could point out that the premature birth of a baby was hardly a stunt.

When he had gone, Barker-Harding vented his irritation on his young colleague. 'Do we have to have this cheap sensationalism?' he complained, pointing at the famous 'Labour Man Midwife' headline. 'We're not catering for the sort of people whose lips move when they read, you know. Do try to be a bit more mature, Les.'

No sooner were the Christmas and New Year festivities over (my father and mother were obliged to spend the last moments of the 1940s dancing the Gay Gordons in a school hall as the guests of honour of West Wickham and District Scottish Association) than Mr Attlee proclaimed the date of the general election.

It was to be in February, and with little more than a month to go, the campaign in the constituency took on a note of urgency. 'Let Us Win Through Together' pleaded the new posters in the window.

At the back of the Labour offices was a wooden shed in which the previous occupant, F. Coleman, Esq., used to sort his morning papers for delivery. Now it was stacked high with bundles of election handbills and leaflets, with an evil-smelling paraffin stove to provide warmth for the helpers.

Jenny Cole, determined not be left out of the battle, was there in her balaclava helmet and mittens, licking envelopes. She also did her share of knocking at doors.

Walking along those tree-lined avenues of neat little semi-detached houses which his father built, Frank saw mostly blue posters peeping from the lace curtains. Only here and there did he find 'Vote Labour, Vote Cole' blazing out defiantly in black letters on a yellow background.

'The Reds will stop at nothing to cling to power,' Bascombe told Barker-Harding over the phone. 'They'll resort to any cheap election trick they can think of. Well, I've got a trick or two up my sleeve. If it's copy you want, you shall have it. I'm doing a whistle-stop tour of the entire district on Tuesday evening. Send your chap along – he can have a place in one of the cars leaving my office at six sharp. I'll give him something to put in his notebook.'

Barker-Harding put down the phone and hurried through to the room next door where his assistant was sitting with his feet on the desk reading the *Daily Mirror*. He remained in this relaxed position as Barker-Harding issued instructions to him for covering the Tory election caravan.

As he went out of the room Les Tooley made a derisive gesture with two fingers at his back and resumed reading an editorial which said: 'We believe the ideas of social justice which Labour-led Britain has shown the world are the only effective answer to Communism.'

'Amen to that,' said Tooley, lighting another Woodbine.

Bascombe had laid on a convoy of Bentleys and Daimlers for his whistle-stop tour, a rare sight in those days of petrol coupons, and Tooley travelled in one of them. He conscientiously took a verbatim note of an extremely long and boring speech by the Conservative candidate, which he ended by saying: 'Ladies and gentlemen, I have just noticed in the audience a man who is not a native of these parts but whose name is as well-known to you as it is to me – Wing Commander Sammy Wilmslow. Goodness knows how many times he took off from Biggin Hill to perform deeds of valour in the skies above this very hall. He will not tell us how many Nazi raiders he shot down – he's too modest. But "never in the field of human conflict was so much owed by so many to so few" – the words of our great leader, so unfairly rejected in 1945, and now once again awaiting his destiny in the wings. Let's ask one of The Few what he considers to be the right thing for this great country of ours in her latest hour of need. Like all brave men, Wing Commander, I know you are a shy and retiring man, shirking the limelight, but would you do us the honour of stepping up on to the platform for a moment . . .'

A tall, craggy-faced man rose from his seat three rows back and came diffidently forward, to a spattering of applause, to tell the audience why, in his opinion, they should vote Conservative. Appropriately enough, his words were few, and he returned to his seat to loud clapping.

It seemed like a spontaneous, unrehearsed demonstration of support for Bascombe, and Les Tooley was surprised, when the cavalcade moved on to the next hall, to see Wing Commander Wilmslow climbing into the Bentley ahead of him. He was less surprised when Bascombe said at the end of his next speech: 'Ladies and gentlemen, I see we have in the audience a man whose name will be as familiar to you as it is to me – Wing Commander Sammy Wilmslow . . .'

Once again, amidst applause, the reluctant hero mounted the platform and said his piece. The performance was repeated at the Scout hut, the Women's Institute and the grammar school hall. On each occasion Mr Bascombe 'just happened' to notice among the good people who had turned out to hear him Wing Commander Wilmslow.

When the *Gazette* appeared on Friday, a full report of Mr Bascombe's whistle-stop tour was spread across the front page. Dull stuff was it indeed, but right in the centre was a large photograph of Sammy Wilmslow headed: 'The Bashful Wing Commander' and underneath it a description in bold black type of how he happened to turn up at every one of Bascombe's meetings.

The effects of that one satirical caption were many and widespread. Frank Cole and his supporters howled with laughter. Mr Bascombe danced with rage. Wing Commander Wilmslow threatened to sue. Captain Barker-Harding had not been present when Tooley finally made up the front page on Thursday night and put the paper to bed. He was white with rage when he discovered what Tooley had done, and fired him for it on the spot.

All the parties were present at the council offices on a chilly February night when the returning officer read out the results of the count, concluding with the words: 'I declare Frank Cole duly elected representative of the said constituency.' The majority was 680 votes, somewhat less than in 1945 but enough.

Dorothy and Jenny hugged and kissed him and he made a short speech and shook hands with Barker-Harding and Bascombe, who said there were 'no hard feelings'.

They scowled nevertheless when he gave a particularly warm

handshake to young Les Tooley. The redrawing of constituency boundaries before the election to include a large London County Council estate housing families from dockland probably contributed more to Frank's success than any other factor. Bascombe had made some scathing remarks about endless labour troubles at London docks and the effect on food supplies.

Captain Barker-Harding remained convinced that the subversive role of Tooley, the viper he had nursed to his bosom, had prevented the Tories from regaining the seat, cut the advertising revenue he received from local businessmen and robbed him of whatever chance he might have had of becoming a justice of the peace.

Tooley took refuge on the subs' desk at the Press Association. As it turned out the move was timely because within the year the *Gazette* folded and Captain Barker-Harding departed in the night with the lady with yellow hair, leaving behind his former ATS sergeant wife and a large number of unpaid bills.

On his first day as a Member of Parliament, after visiting a small office in the House of Lords where the Clerk of the Crown formally acknowledged receipt of a writ from the returning officer for West Wickham, Frank Cole strode jauntily across Star Chamber Court, under the black canopy leading to the Members' cloakroom in the Old Cloisters. His name was neatly printed under one of the rows of pegs from which hung loops of red tape (originally meant for members' swords, now holding their umbrellas).

Along with the other members of the Commons, he shuffled into 'the other place' (the Lords) for the State Opening of Parliament and the King's speech, which of course was written for him by the Government. As a sympathizer with the dissidents shortly to produce their own policy in a pamphlet called *Keeping Left*, Frank disagreed with most of the speech from the Throne. Nevertheless, back in the Commons chamber, when called upon to take the oath of allegiance he swore by Almighty God that he would be 'faithful and bear true allegiance to His Majesty King George, his heirs and successors, according to the law', so help him, God.

My father's first speech in the House, like most maiden speeches, created not so much as a flutter in the dovecotes of Westminster. When he succeeded in 'catching the Speaker's eye' and heard his name echoing round the half-empty chamber, he stood up in his seat three rows up just below the gangway and launched dry-mouthed into his well-rehearsed memorial lecture deploring the pro-American and anti-Russian policy of the Government and demanding that 'the Right Honourable gentleman in front of me should do more to restrain the Americans and deter the Russians to avoid the terrifying possibility of a third world war.'

Ernest Bevin did not so much as bother to turn his head to glance at him while he was speaking, and Eden and Butler, lolling on the Front Bench opposite, with their feet on the table of the House, ankles crossed, and their heads leaned back against the green cushions, looked as if they were asleep. The retired brigadiers on the other side might be inwardly fuming at this Bolshie but there was no waving of order papers, no rowdy shouts and catcalls to bring the familiar cry 'Order! Order!' from the Speaker.

He sat down at the end of his oration in total silence, broken a moment or two later by a journalist MP on the Tory back benches rising to deliver 'the polite remark', the traditional congratulations to a maiden speaker. He had enough experience of the House as an observer from the press gallery not to be surprised that the only report of his remarks was in *Hansard*, the official proceedings.

He was not abashed, indeed he was probably less overawed by the pomp and circumstance of the best club in Europe than most new boys, and quickly familiarized himself with its labyrinthine passages and discovered just where the lavatories were.

That summer the Korean war broke out and certain classes of British Army reservists were called up, while every young man approaching eighteen felt the finger of Mr Shinwell's sergeant majors on his collar for National Service and had at the front of his mind the idea that he might be called upon to fight for King and country in another 'faraway place of which most people knew nothing'.

My grandfather, the brigadier, felt the draught when Trooper Lovelace was peremptorily removed by the regiment from the care of horses and shipped out East to fight. As for my father, at first he supported the war as a genuine attempt to establish through the United Nations an effective international resistance to aggression. He soon realized his mistake and spoke out vigorously against the use of napalm bombs and General MacArthur's threat to drop an atomic bomb beyond the Yalu River.

At Westminster, with its overall majority slashed to a mere seven members, the Attlee government quietly forgot about the social revolution and concentrated on survival. Frank Cole found himself to be a Member of Parliament of the Long Nights.

23

The army of Whitehall charladies was arriving for its daily mopping-up operation in a stream of buses across Westminster Bridge as Frank emerged, blinking in the cold grey light, into New Palace Yard. The policeman on duty at the side gate saluted and gave him a cheery 'Good morning' as the bell rang out over Parliament Square and the light flashed from the railings at the end of Bridge Street to summon any cab for hire which might be passing.

Frank turned up the collar of his Crombie overcoat and shivered in the raw, misty February morning. A year had passed since he first entered the House, and in that year he felt he had accomplished nothing of practical value either to his constituents or mankind at large.

He arrived home in Albany Street to find Dorothy still in bed and he took her a cup of tea and *The Times*. She blinked sleepily as he drew the curtains.

'Another all-night sitting?' she asked.

He nodded.

'What was the outcome?'

'Three votes in our favour with the help of a convoy of wheelchairs and a few crutches,' he answered. 'God, it was pathetic, so was the debate – Manny Shinwell demanding billions for armaments, for Christ's sake, and the Old Man on about waste and bungling and making his usual demand for a secret session at which he would make further revelations, etcetera, etcetera. I felt like filing into the No lobby myself, just for a change.'

'That wouldn't be very astute would it, darling?' commented Dorothy, sipping her tea.

'I get so sick of being lobby fodder, toeing the party line, obeying the Whips,' he complained. 'Dammit, someone needs to speak out about the drift away from Socialism.'

'Really, darling, you're talking like an undergraduate,' she admonished him. 'And please do stop whining. It's not at all attractive.'

'Dick Crossman buttonholed me in the Smoking Room last night,' Frank went on. 'He says there's a buzz that Gaitskell intends putting a charge on National Health prescriptions to pay for all those Canberra bombers and tanks and jet engines. Four thousand seven hundred *million* pounds over the next three years! The mind boggles. It wouldn't surprise me if Nye and Harold walked out. The old gang are prepared to sell out on everything and the little man himself seems to have lost his grip.'

Frank sighed and started to undress. From across the landing came the sound of my screeching greeting to another day and the gentle murmur of Helga, the nanny, trying to silence it. Helga, a sensitive fraulein who had eaten rats in the ruins of her native Cologne just to stay alive, was pathetically grateful to Dorothy for providing her with employment and a home. She was a domesticated girl who willingly took over all the chores of looking after me while Mummy concentrated on keeping her looks and buying new clothes.

The only problem with Helga was that she sometimes woke up in the middle of the night screaming.

Hugh Gaitskell had succeeded Sir Stafford Cripps as Chancellor of the Exchequer when that incorruptible Christian Socialist was forced through ill health to resign. In his first budget he did indeed commit the heresy of placing a charge of one shilling (5p) on prescriptions under the National Health Service. He also decreed that half the cost of false teeth and spectacles would have to be met by the patient.

As predicted, Aneurin Bevan and Harold Wilson, both leading members of the Government, resigned in protest, and John Freeman, then a junior Minister, went with them.

Quite a lot was happening elsewhere in the world that spring. General Douglas MacArthur was sacked as Commander-in-Chief of the American forces in the Far East by President Truman, and in Korea the Glorious Gloucesters made their gallant stand on Hill 235. But at Westminster they were preoccupied with the spine-tingling excitement of a Cabinet split.

In the ensuing Left-wing furore my father allied himself with the Bevanite dissidents who produced a pamphlet claiming that the arms programme had nothing to do with what arms were required or what they would cost: 'The Government fixed a money figure as a result of calculating what would satisfy American desires, and then, only after they were committed to that figure, did they start to evaluate the money figure into terms of guns and tanks and aircraft.'

The pamphlet, written by Michael Foot and Bevan's wife Jennie Lee, was called *One Way Only* and Frank Cole had little difficulty in deciding that it was his only way, too.

As summer passed into autumn, Clement Attlee, having lost Cripps and then the redoubtable Ernest Bevin through ill health, and feeling under considerable strain himself, was forced to go to the country again. Dorothy showed little enthusiasm for fighting a general election campaign at West Wickham so soon after the last one.

'It's such a bore, dear,' she told Frank. 'All those dreary speeches about Britain acting as a mediator between the Russians and the Americans and all that snivelling about the meat ration being reduced to 8d-worth because the Argentinians are being beastly to us, and isn't it ghastly that income tax is up to 9s 6d in the pound and because of devaluation the Americans only give us $2.80 for one anyway. Really, darling, I can't stand it.'

Dorothy had a better excuse than boredom for keeping away from the election campaign because, despite Frank's frequent all-night absences at the House of Commons, she had become pregnant. In view of her medical history, there was every reason to avoid overstraining herself and risking another premature birth, or worse a miscarriage. How like my mother to pretend that she had decided to stay out of the political kitchen through sheer ennui. Thus it fell to Jenny, past seventy but still bursting with radical zeal, to go hammering on the doors of West Wickham. She kept her bicycle in the shed behind the Labour Party headquarters, while Frank drove her from and to Amen Road.

'It reminds me of my days with the suffragettes,' she told her fellow volunteers as they stamped and addressed election literature, 'except that we used chalk to spread our message – on the walls and the pavements.'

They laughed at her and took up the nickname which Ralph Greedie had given her, the Duchess. She took it in good part and was so easy to talk to in contrast to the Member's wife, who always gave the impression of looking down her nose at them. Lady Muck, they called *her*.

They had to work that much harder because with the *Gazette* defunct, they had to rely on the district edition of the *Croydon Advertiser* for publicity and there was obviously less space available.

When Frank cut the ribbon to declare open Bevan Way, a new section of the LCC housing estate within his constituency boundaries, Jenny posed proudly alongside him for the press photographer. In the background bulldozers and tippers carried on clearing the ground and laying sewers for still more roads – Attlee Avenue, Cripps Close and so on. Each new house that went up represented two or more votes for the Labour Party and Frank was truly grateful.

This, more than Grandma's energetic electioneering, accounted for Frank's return to Westminster while many hard-won Labour seats went over to the Tories. More people actually voted Labour than Conservative, but Churchill ended up with more seats and at the age of seventy-seven became Prime Minister again.

Dorothy insisted on celebrating Frank's victory with champagne, even though Labour had lost the election (down at West Wickham they had toasted him with mugs of cocoa).

'You won't be out for more than four years,' she said, 'and anyway, that's the time for making an impression on the right people.'

'Who are the Right People?' he asked.

'People who can further your career, of course,' she exclaimed, with a hint of exasperation in her voice.

'I hate dining with people I hate,' was his infuriatingly flip reaction.

'Politics isn't about mixing with people you like,' Dorothy went on, as if talking to a child. 'It's about getting power and hanging on to it. Do you suppose that Gaitskell or Morrison or Bevan got where they are by being *nice*?'

Frank returned to Westminster like an old campaigner returning from the wars, in a mood to view the passing show with a jaundiced eye.

In the smoking room and the tea-room the Members gathered in groups, chatting and gossiping like schoolboys back from the hols, garrulous from sheer relief at having not lost their seats. In the Chamber, the Old Man flanked by his newly appointed Cabinet, failed to remember the constituencies of Members he had to refer to during the proceedings and was too deaf to be prompted.

Spurred on by Dorothy, Frank began to scheme for Ministerial office when Labour returned to power, dreaming of a Ministerial car, a Ministerial chauffeur and a retinue of civil servants following him around with red dispatch boxes.

To pave the way, she gave regular dinner parties at Albany Street or they dined out with those she deemed to be the Right People, or in this case the Left People. Although she winced at Hugh Delargy singing Irish rebel songs and the Fabian jokes of Ian Mikardo and his daughter made her cringe, she relished the role of political hostess.

Although she entertained film people and Left-wing publishers, at the same time she stayed in touch with the more traditional Establishment circle into which she was born and with whom she shared a set of unshakable attitudes, convictions and opinions about who had the right to rule whom.

Early in February, Frank telephoned from the House to tell her: 'I've just come from a Party meeting. The little man slipped out for a few minutes, then came back to tell us the King is dead. Had you heard?'

'No. I read in the paper that he was out shooting at Sandringham yesterday,' said Dorothy.

'It seems he passed peacefully away in his sleep,' Frank went on. 'Sydney Silverman was in full flood on the errors of a bipartisan foreign policy when Clem Attlee interrupted the meeting – as someone said, it takes a king's death to silence Sydney.'

'Frank!' protested Dorothy, shocked at his flippancy.

'I'm sorry darling, but really only Clem Attlee had personal contact,' he said. 'I must say the little man looked very cut up about it. "He was always very nice to me," he said.'

'You will have to get a top hat and a coat from Moss Bros. and a new pair of black shoes,' Dorothy told him.

'Why? I don't wear a top hat.'

'But you will at the funeral,' said Dorothy in a voice that

brooked no argument, and hung up. She immediately picked up the telephone again and rang her mother for a long conversation which ended with their discussing the possibility of getting tickets for the Coronation.

There was a good deal of discussion about top hats, both in the Whips' office and at Albany Street, over the next week. In the event, my father did not get one and did not march in the funeral procession, although he was among the MPs and peers lining a chilly Westminster Hall when the King's coffin was carried in by eight stalwart Grenadiers followed by the new Queen Elizabeth in deep black mourning, her face hidden behind a thick veil.

Mummy was proud of her prewar acquaintance with one or two of the smart set who were bridesmaids at the royal wedding five years before, titled young ladies who had since married farmers or bankers, had children of their own and lived quietly in Devon or Scotland, after working in publishing or opening twee little teashops with their mothers. She absorbed every morsel of gossip she read about the royals and had paid especially close attention to the births of Prince Charles and Princess Anne.

Now, in the midst of mourning for the king, Dorothy gave birth to a son. No sooner had he been delivered, on time and in good order, than the Plumley-Greenes snatched him to their collective bosom, as if protecting him from his unfortunate parentage and trying at the same time to obliterate the painful memory of that shabby little wartime wedding in a register office.

At the in-laws' insistence, the baby was christened not as I had been in decent local obscurity at Marylebone, but in the Guards' Chapel at Windsor with the brigadier reading the lesson in his fine resonant soldier's voice. His second name was conferred on the baby: Nigel Peregrine Cole. A fine resonant name. Even Lady Plumley-Greene showed emotion as the little chap was baptized.

Jenny was there, but rather elbowed to the rear of the elegant little crowd gathered around the font. She was regarded by the Plumley-Greenes as being something of an embarrassment, eccentric to the point of being a crank. Her offer of the Cole christening robe was spurned in favour of a less yellowed, and also less ancient, garment handed down by the Plumley-

Greenes. If Jenny was affronted, she showed no sign of it.

Even while Dorothy was still suckling young Nigel Peregrine, the brigadier put the boy's name down for Harrow, his old school. This was anathema to Frank. However, Dorothy and her family ganged up against him and at the time he was preoccupied with rebellion against Churchill's defence estimates. Indeed, he defied a three-line whip in order to vote against his own side in the House of Commons.

The truth was that my father was in love with the idea of being a red rebel. He was determined, despite all the pressures brought to bear on him by the Plumley-Greenes, not to become a Ramsay MacDonald, a drawing room Socialist preening himself in Court dress. Nevertheless, Mummy forced him into a morning suit and grey topper for the Coronation.

On a grey, windy day in May 1953 they took their seats inside Westminster Abbey among the chosen few. Frank was disdainful of the splendours of the occasion, which he considered to be an anachronism in a modern democracy, and made it plain to his friends in the House that he was going only to please his wife.

All the Commonwealth Prime Ministers were there, among the peers and commoners, the heralds and pursuivants, to see Queen Victoria's great-granddaughter crowned by the Archbishop of Canterbury, to hear the fanfares and '*Vivat! Vivat!*' ringing out. So, too, was the television camera, hidden in the floor of the Abbey choir.

Jenny, visiting her sister Lucy in a nursing home just outside Bournemouth that day, said they had a better view on the screen in the sitting room than the most exalted participant.

'Of course, one missed the colours of the costumes and the flags and heraldry,' she told Frank afterwards, 'but one saw the whole thing and Richard Dimbleby described it so movingly that I almost cried.'

Lucy, although frail and only a year away from a peaceful end, observed the liturgy so closely that when the Archbishop proclaimed Elizabeth 'of the United Kingdom of Great Britain and Northern Ireland and of her other Realms and Territories, Queen, Head of the Commonwealth, Defender of the Faith', she muttered: 'But not Empress of India, you see. I'm glad Clarence isn't here to see this – it would have broken his heart.'

Catching a glimpse of Nehru in a silken jacket she muttered:

'Slimy little agitator, that's what Clarence thought of *him*.'

Not all the symbols of imperial splendour, the bearskins and the battle honours, nor the news that Mount Everest had been conquered at last by a British expedition, nor all the highflown talk of a new Elizabethan age, could console this ageing memsahib for the fact that India had been handed over to the natives.

When Jenny tried to hush her, Lucy said, with an older sister edge to her voice: 'Jenny, don't interrupt, *please*, when I'm speaking.'

The other old ladies sitting around the television nodded and smiled. They had no idea what was going on. Jenny found it unbearably sad to look at her sister and these other shipwrecks of old age cast up in this awful seaside establishment where faded gentility bore the aroma of stale urine.

24

It was borne in on me early in life that Daddy was an important person. We did not see a great deal of him. Whenever he was at home he seemed scarcely aware of his children's existence, with his nose buried in books or piles of papers, looking up to pat us on the head and give us an absent-minded kiss as Helga propelled us firmly towards bed.

That is how I remember him.

The fact was that he was away from home more often than he was in it. Apart from attendance at the House of Commons five days a week when it was in session, he had to go down to West Wickham at weekends when he was not lecturing or making speeches up and down the country.

He also travelled abroad a good deal. Mother never went with him on these trips and he always returned laden with gifts for us. The shelves in my room were lined with ranks of dolls in saris and kimonos, beads, furs and feathers, each representing one or other of the countries he had visited.

Daddy went to Moscow for the first time in 1954 as a guest of the Soviet Peace Committee. By that time the world was clearly divided into opposing camps separated by an Iron Curtain and the

Berlin Wall and the very word 'peace' had been devalued. 'Peace' had come to mean supporting your side's preparations for total annihilation.

In March of that year the *Daily Herald* first alerted Britain to H-bomb tests in the Pacific with a banner headline 'Call off that Bomb!' Frank Cole resumed his association with his old paper, writing impassioned articles about the folly of pouring vast sums which should have been spent on new hospitals, schools and welfare services into armaments for no better reason than to maintain the illusion that we were still a Great Power.

He was present at a meeting at the House of Commons, sponsored and chaired by the veteran pacifist Fenner Brockway, following the Government's announcement that Britain intended to manufacture its own independent H-bomb. Something like two hundred people attended, including a number of Labour MPs and delegates from church and pacifist groups. Out of it came the Hydrogen Bomb National Campaign with Dr Donald Soper as chairman and a mass meeting at the Albert Hall calling for a disarmament conference. My father was there, too, with his mother, but not Dorothy, who took the Establishment view that it was right for Britain to go ahead with the manufacture and testing of its own nuclear weapons.

The Hydrogen Bomb National Campaign was premature and it flopped. But the seeds of dissent had been sown and were taking root when in 1956 Britain's *folie de grandeur* was exposed by the Suez fiasco.

My father achieved instant fame with his trenchant attacks on a Government which had sent a hastily assembled task force limping from Malta towards Egypt, hoisting sails to help it on its way when steam power faltered. He was on the box almost every evening and if he was aware of lanced remarks at his back, while some members of the Front Bench regarded him through slightly narrowed eyes, he did not let it worry him. He was riding high and the *Manchester Guardian* at least was on his side.

The Opposition, too, had a new leader in Hugh Gaitskell, the type of dry, intellectual, upper-middle-class Socialist for whom Frank had little time. Gaitskell was slow to realize that Eden had botched everything and must pay with his head, the demand brayed out by the mob in Trafalgar Square after Daddy's hero Aneurin Bevan bellowed through the loudspeakers: 'There is only one way in which they could try to restore their tarnished reputation and that is to get out . . . get out . . . get out!'

I remember watching it all on television on that Sunday evening in November when the cameras showed mounted police charging the crowds in London and Russian tanks lumbering in firing shells to suppress the Hungarian dissidents in Budapest. Daddy was at home that evening, sitting in a worn leather armchair in his study, where he had had an extra television set installed. It was a rare privilege for me to be allowed in that room but I felt neglected with father just sitting there giving all his attention to that small flickering screen.

'You care more about that old Colonel Nasty than you do about me,' I said petulantly.

He smiled and sat me on his lap, replying: 'Not so, milady. It's just that Colonel Nasser has been very, very naughty and getting all the attention while you're being very, very good.'

'What's he done then?' I demanded.

'He's bunged up the Suez Canal, that's what he's done,' explained Daddy patiently, 'and the Suez Canal, if you believe the Conservatives, is the jolly old imperial jugular.'

'What's the Suez Canal?' was my next question.

He put me down while he went over to the bookshelves and fetched an atlas to show me how the canal linked the two blue splodges of the Mediterranean and the Red Sea and how its closure mean that our ships had to voyage all the way round the Cape of Good Hope, adding many thousands of miles to their voyages between east and west.

Daddy's instruction in Middle East geography was interrupted by the sudden appearance of his face on the television, being interviewed at the demo in Trafalgar Square.

He was talking excitedly about matters which I did not really comprehend and looking much sterner than he usually did in real life.

'The microphone wasn't working properly and we had to do it all again a second time,' he remarked while watching himself.

Then the programme moved on to Hungary and all those menacing tanks arrayed against people in the streets.

'Daddy,' I asked. 'What will the world be like when I'm as old as you and Mummy?'

'I don't know, sweetheart. A better one than it is today, I

hope,' he said, putting his arms round me.

'I don't think it will be,' I went on, with all the confidence of my six, almost seven, years. 'It'll all have been blown up by then, I expect.'

It was, as far as I can recall, my first geography lesson. I was just about to be transferred from a dame school in genteel St John's Wood to a Church of England school in Marylebone High Street.

I had to feign a Cockney patois to avoid getting constantly beaten up by my fellow pupils and to pretend that Mrs Battie, our cleaning lady, was my mother. Father seemed to think that it would be good for me to be educated among what he called the ordinary people, just as he firmly believed that Albion Hill Elementary had done more for him than Chelwood Abbey and St Wilfrid's put together.

'But we're not *ordinary* people,' Mummy protested in vain.

She wanted to send me away to school in the country, in preparation for a place at Roedean, *her* old school. Frank, still smarting over his son's name being put down for Harrow, stubbornly refused to budge on the question of my education. Their tense late-night conversations on the subject could be heard through the closed bedroom door, always ending with both of them shouting and Mother sometimes sobbing. Then to my relief they started sleeping in separate rooms.

My father believed that the question of whether we continued to engage in the nuclear arms race was probably the supreme moral issue of the day. On Good Friday, 4 April 1958, he was again among the speakers at the foot of Nelson's Column in Trafalgar Square, a stone's throw from Dick Sheppard's former ministry of St Martin-in-the-Fields, where several thousand people had gathered instead of the few hundred expected. The plan of the Direct Action Committee against Nuclear Weapons was to march to the Atomic Weapons Research Establishment at Aldermaston, fifty-two miles away in Berkshire, and Frank Cole was among those MPs who had pledged their support.

Ritchie Calder, my father's comrade from the *Daily Herald* on the Jarrow Hunger March, turned up with his wife and children and several of his grandchildren, determined to walk all the way to Aldermaston. Frank greeted him with joy bordering on tears.

It was there in Trafalgar Square on Good Friday that he first met the newly elected leader of the Campaign for Nuclear Disarmament, Canon John Collins, an earnest-looking bespectacled Anglican prebendary in an ankle-length black cassock. Frank wondered how such an evident member of the ecclesiastical establishment, living on a stipend at Amen Court in the shadow of St Paul's Cathedral, had come to be the leader of such a potentially subversive movement and he discovered that Collins had in a sense taken on the mantle of his predecessor at St Paul's, Dick Sheppard.

The good canon, however, was off to church with his wife and young sons after the preliminary rally – 'A lifetime's training,' he murmured by way of excuse as the march set off with banners flying and trumpets playing.

Dorothy was down at Limpsfield with Nigel and me for the Easter weekend, while Daddy slogged along the road to Reading with the Ban the Bombers, sleeping in a tent overnight and trying to ignore the inevitable blisters. The weather was dreadful, it even snowed, and by Sunday evening only about three hundred of those who had left Trafalgar Square were still on the march.

Frank attended the reception given by the constituency Labour Party at Reading Town Hall and then accepted a lift back to town from a fellow MP who had just driven out for the evening.

'I don't think Ian* was too happy with the element that wants civil disobedience,' remarked Frank's benefactor, opening up his new Ford Consul on the A4 highway between Maidenhead and Slough.

'Actions speak louder than words, old boy,' replied Frank, all too aware of his throbbing feet. 'The natural reaction of the Establishment is to sweep dissent under the carpet. You've got to make 'em sit up and take notice.'

'Yes, but once you get started along the road of confronting the law, where do you call a halt?' his friend reminded him. It was curious how two educated and intelligent men fell into the habit of conversing in clichés when they were talking political shop, but the point they were discussing was fundamental to the future of CND.

But the movement would soon fall victim to the need to stay

* Ian Mikardo, then Labour MP for Reading.

in the headlines by ever more extreme forms of protest. The dilemma was borne in on Frank in those early days through his mother, always ready despite her advancing years to embrace a cause. 'I may be too old to go in for route marches,' she told him, 'but I can sit down as well as anyone else.'

Just before Christmas 1958 she caught a train to Norwich and a country bus to Swaffham, where a hundred supporters of Pat Arrowsmith's Direct Action Committee against Nuclear War had gathered together. The marchers were divided into two groups – those who were prepared to be arrested and a second group of supporters only. Jenny was all for joining the first group but was gently dissuaded on account of her white hairs.

One of the last to arrive was a Scotsman in a kilt who asked: 'Where do I go if I want to be arrested?' With him he brought 'the gospel of selfless action – the *Gita* according to Gandhi'. The demonstrators left Swaffham under a hail of ripe tomatoes and trudged through the empty Norfolk lanes under the eye of the county constabulary.

Superintendent Canham, in charge of Downham Market district, met them at the gates of the airfield and informed them politely that if they entered they would be breaking the law. Needless to say, they marched through the gate making for a concrete mixer behind the barbed wire, and sat down. They were lifted out again by the police.

They stood there in a knot, quietly discussing their next move, while someone called for a prayer: 'Quiet time, Quakers!' Then they moved towards the wire again and an RAF policeman in a white cap said into his walkie-talkie: 'Demonstrators going in. Over.'

Despite her instructions to the contrary, Jenny went with them, squatting on the muddy concrete.

'Thank you, young man,' she said to the constable lifting her up, 'you are much more gentle and considerate than the policemen in my day.'

'If I get much more of this, you'll wear me out,' he retorted.

In fact he carried her as easily as a child. The whole thing was as polite and formal as a minuet. Along with the others, she was taken to Swaffham police station and charged with wilfully obstructing the police.

Frank was shocked when he heard what had happened, jumped into his two-litre Rover car and rushed up to Norfolk early on a Sunday morning, breaking the speed limit throughout the journey. He found his mother calm and unrepentant in the cell where she had spent the night.

'Mother, we all want to abolish nuclear war,' he scolded, 'but breaking the law is not the way to go about it.'

'That's how we got the vote,' retorted Jenny. 'By direct action led by attractive and spirited young women, just like Miss Arrowsmith. Our demonstration was a completely peaceful one in the Gandhi tradition, there was no force or violence whatever. No policeman was hurt.'

Unlike many of the other demonstrators, Jenny was given bail and did not spend Christmas in jail. Instead she sat with us under the Christmas tree at Albany Street helping to unwrap our presents. The festivities were overshadowed by the knowledge that after it Grandma would be up before Colonel Boag, the chairman of the Bench at Swaffham.

In the event she was ordered to enter into a recognizance in the sum of £10 to be of good behaviour and keep the peace for a year, but it was the publicity which really angered my mother.

'Forget about banning the bomb and just concentrate on winning the next election,' she told Frank. 'Let your mother go on marches and demonstrations with all those unwashed, long-haired Beatniks if it makes her feel young again. I think it's simply ridiculous at her age and there is absolutely no need for you to join her. You must concentrate your mind on getting into Government.'

25

Frank glanced at the message board in the Members' lobby. Nothing for him there. The clerk at the desk in the post office did not need to be told his name but immediately called 'Mr Cole' into the speaker and a fat bundle of letters came tumbling down the chute from the sorting room above. Frank removed the rubber band, expertly riffled through them, tossing the obvious circulars, unnecessary bumph and those written in capitals with a leaky ballpoint pen into one of the large oak waste-paper bins.

Then he went to the tea-room, joined the queue at the coffee urn and took the cup and saucer over to one of the large armchairs near the door, where he settled down to read his mail. A famous Tory Minister nodded cordially in his direction as he swept by like some battleship with a fussy parliamentary private secretary and a flotilla of minions bobbing in his wake. Frank nodded back.

Earlier in the week Frank had crossed swords with him verbally across the strip of carpet which divided the two sides of the House, but there were no hard feelings. This was how the game was played, with public hostility and private chumminess. It was a Friday, and Frank was hoping that the House would rise promptly at 4.30 p.m. so that he could get down to West Wickham. His appearances there had become even more erratic since his party had suffered another election defeat.

He opened a foolscap envelope and took out some glossy photographs. He only glanced at the top one before hastily pushing them back into the envelope, getting to his feet and hurrying out of the room, leaving his coffee half finished.

He literally bumped into a fellow back bencher coming the other way, who asked anxiously: 'Are you all right, old man? You look as if you've seen a ghost.'

Frank brushed past him and hurried across the central lobby and down the steps past St Stephen's Hall. People queuing for places in the Strangers' Gallery stared at him curiously.

Frank blundered on, looking neither left nor right, making for the exit. He felt in need of fresh air because of what that innocent-looking brown envelope contained.

It began, innocuously enough, over the morning mail, what was it, three years ago? Esther Rutley, the secretary whose quiet, efficient services he shared with two other MPs, was at her desk in a poky office down some remote corridor and he was saying: 'Decline with regrets the invitation to open the Royal and Ancient Order of Buffaloes' smoker and the Methodist bazaar, accept the nurses' prize-giving and the Rotary whist drive,' when he noticed what extraordinarily fine eyes she had.

He started putting letters on the desk one by one: 'Send the stock answer to that one . . . housing case . . . and that's another housing case. Then there's this, a sticky war pensions problem, I'd better have a word with Johnson's PPS before I answer that one.'

'You didn't answer Mrs Hopwood's letter about the parking in Greentree Close,' said Esther.

'Great balls of fire!' he shouted, clapping his palm against his brow. 'The parking in Greentree Close. Oh, calamity!'

'She says she sent a stamped, addressed envelope,' continued Esther accusingly, but smiling just the same. Lovely eyes, brown and tender.

'The trouble with answering Mrs Hopwood's letters,' he remarked, 'is that she immediately writes another one. You know, Esther, I think I could do with a break from the debate on the National Insurance Bill this evening. Do you ever go to the pictures?'

'Frequently,' said Esther. 'It's my favourite pastime.'

'Have you seen *Room at the Top*?'

'No, not yet.'

'Then why don't we go and see it this evening?' he suggested. 'I'll pick you up at the gate at half past five.'

He bounded up the staircase leading to the committee corridor and sat through the proceedings doodling on the blotter in front of him and gazing at the shafts of wintry sunlight streaming through the mullioned windows, for all the world like a schoolboy day-dreaming through maths or history rather than a supposedly serious-minded middle-aged Member of Parliament.

At lunchtime he met Jack Harris and one of the other lobby correspondents in the Strangers' Bar.

'Hullo, Frank, how are you?'

'Never ask a politician that question,' responded Frank, obviously feeling on form. 'As Macmillan says, a politician is always feeling well, whatever he's feeling.'

'All right,' said Jack. 'How's Gaitskell feeling?'

'I've no idea – he doesn't confide in me,' answered Frank. 'As Rab Butler put it, in another context, he's the best Prime Minister we haven't got, but God, isn't he dreary? Always holding his finger up to test the wind. He and Nye are working together to win the election but really they hate one another's guts. Hugh distrusts men of ideas like Nye and Dick Crossman . . .'

'Ah, "Double Crossman", the king-maker,' said Jack and a few heads turned in their direction as they all laughed.

After several large Scotches and nothing to eat, he walked somewhat unsteadily along the Members' corridor in the wake of the little procession of bewigged functionaries headed by the Speaker moving into the Chamber for prayers which opened the day's business. Halfway through the afternoon Frank was given a message to ring Broadcasting House and went to the row of telephones at the top of the staircase to the Members' cloakroom.

A duty producer asked him if he would like to come in to the studio to comment on a report by Chapman Pincher in the *Express* that the Government intended to cancel the Blue Streak missile project, but Frank told him: 'I'm sorry, I've no information. And in any case I've got a prior appointment. Some other time perhaps.'

Esther was waiting for him by the railings, looking even younger than she did at her desk, without make-up and wearing a black plastic mac. Pinned to it was a familiar round black disc with a drooping white cross, the semaphore symbols for N and D and the badge of the Campaign for Nuclear Disarmament.

'I didn't know you were a member of the CND,' he said.

'Oh, yes,' she replied. 'I was on the Aldermaston March and I'm going again this Easter.'

They made for Westminster Underground and stood wedged tightly together among a press of home-going commuters to the next stop, where they changed for Leicester Square. In the queue outside the Odeon, Frank lit his pipe and said: 'I'd almost forgotten there was a world outside the House of Commons.' The renowned 'Egyptian' buskers cavorted up and down the pavement and he gave them a shilling.

'I hope you're not going to make a habit of playing hookey from debates,' said Esther, slipping her arm through his. Just then the queue started to move and soon they were seated in the velvety darkness of the auditorium watching young Joe Lampton's cynical acquisition of an Aston Martin, a three-guinea linen shirt and a rich man's daughter.

Halfway through he ventured to take Esther's hand in his and during the intermission he bought her a choc-ice from the usherette who came round with a lighted tray. He felt about twenty again, remembering Deauville and the sticky excitement of sex for the first time with Elaine. He hadn't given her a thought in years, until now. After the film they went to a pub in St Martin's Lane, where Esther insisted on paying.

Watching her bring the brimming glass to the table, with both hands round it so as not to spill any, he suddenly asked: 'How old are you, Esther?'

'Eighteen,' she said, adding quickly, 'and please don't remind me that you are old enough to be my father.'

'I wasn't going to,' he replied. 'But it's true, all the same. I'm approaching that dangerous age where a man is apt to fall head over heels in love with the first young woman who doesn't treat him like her father. It's the male equivalent of the menopause.'

She laughed and told him: 'Actually, you're not a bit like my father. He's bald and he drives a London Transport bus and he thinks that all CND supporters are Commies who should be deported to Russia.'

They laughed again and sipped their beer (she had a half) and discussed the film.

'It captures the spirit of the age,' she said. 'Materialist, acquisitive, I'm all right, Jack, Supermac's in the chair and all's right with the world. Never mind if we blow the whole bloody lot up tomorrow.'

'I found it nauseating,' he admitted. 'How to work your way up from the borough treasurer's department in six easy lessons.'

She then told him that she had read *Her Majesty's Bomb* in paperback and thought it 'terrific, an absolute blockbuster of the pretence that Britain can be a nuclear power'.

'It's a bit of a potboiler,' he said modestly. 'I wrote it in haste, inevitably, between debates, doing most of the research in the Members' library. The academics and the posh Sundays dismissed it as trivial and sensational.'

'That's because you wrote it in a way that people can understand,' said Esther. 'It's not obscure enough for academic taste.'

'Well, it's made me some money,' commented Frank. 'Joe Lampton would approve of *that*.'

After a reflective silence, he went on: 'We've never really talked before. I see you every day and dictate letters, yet I know nothing about you. Tell me.'

'There's not much to tell,' she answered, blushing slightly. 'I went to an Ursuline convent school and from there to Clark's College to learn shorthand and typing. I live with my parents and younger sister at Newbury Park and commute every day on the Central Line. Actually, I hate it. I'm always having rows at home, especially with Dad. I'm thinking of getting a bed-sitter in town.'

* * *

It was almost 10 p.m. before Frank got back to the House after saying goodnight to Esther at Leicester Square Underground. The division bell rang out as he walked into the Chamber and shortly afterwards the cry 'Who Goes Home?' signalled the end of another parliamentary day.

Dorothy was still up when he got home.

'Drink, dear?' he asked, and she said no thanks. It occurred to him as he poured himself a large Scotch that he had eaten absolutely nothing since breakfast.

'What are you reading, dear?'

She held up the book to show him the cover: *No Love for Johnnie*, by Wilfred Fienburgh.

'Interesting day at the House, darling?' she asked as she went back to her book, without looking up as she spoke.

'Oh, very,' he said.

Dorothy was no longer beautiful. As she approached her fortieth birthday her figure thickened to an extent that even her fashionable, flowered trapeze-line dresses could not conceal, and her chins multiplied alarmingly. She was an English rose overblown.

Part of her problem was that she took little or no exercise, preferring to sit down with the latest novel and a box of handmade chocolates from her favourite confectioner in Mount Street. The physical attraction between her and Frank had long since died a natural death and there had never been any other kind of bond between them.

While she was writing long, wistful letters to Ralph Greedie, with whom she was having an affair by airmail, she might well have noticed the spring in Frank's step, a new erectness in his bearing, the even greater care than usual he took with his grooming. But if she noticed these things, she never mentioned it to him.

If Esther was in love with my father, who could blame her? He was in the prime of life, good-looking in the distinguished manner with his dark hair turning silver grey, witty, if slightly bitchy at times, intelligent and seen regularly on 'Tonight' and 'This Week' on the box. Moreover, she shared his political ideals. Whether he was in love with her from the first, or merely flattered by the adoration of a young and attractive girl, is another matter.

Shortly before I went away to Bridgelands, a 'progressive' boarding school for girls on the south coast near Littlehampton, I had tea on the terrace at the House of Commons with Daddy and his secretary.

I vividly recall that afternoon on the terrace, eating strawberries and cream and looking out over the stone balustrade and boxes of blood-red geraniums at the barges and pleasure boats with their striped awnings. I was ten at the time. I had met Esther for the first time during the Easter recess when Daddy took us and my grandmother Cole on the Aldermaston March, which looked like becoming as much of an annual event as the Grand National. Of course, Mummy, as one might have expected, wanted nothing to do with it.

After the first march, at the suggestion of Jacquetta Hawkes, it was switched to the opposite direction, starting at Aldermaston and ending up in London, the seat of political power. We drove out in a hired limousine to meet what seemed like a never ending column just beyond Heathrow Airport and joined in.

It was the greatest of these rallies ever held, with a hundred thousand people taking part, sixth-form students and young people pushing prams or carrying infants on their shoulders. Famous faces like that of Frank Cousins, the trade union leader, could be seen in the crowd. Canon Collins, in his inevitable black cassock, carried a rucksack on his back. Michael Foot brought his dog. Quakers and Catholics, Communists and Atheists, Pacifists and Anarchists and Rationalists all marched along together singing 'Ban, ban, ban, the bloody H-bomb' to the tune of 'John Brown's Body'. The Red Flag was carried alongside the Cross of Christ.

DISARM OR PERISH, said the homemade banners. NO H-BOMBS FOR BRITAIN. I carried a large white card bearing the inscription MANKIND IS ONE FAMILY suspended in front of me by a piece of string around my neck.

The four of us walked side by side holding hands: Grandma on one side, helping herself along with a stick (at eighty she had at last admitted to a touch of rheumatism now and again, although she had never had a serious illness in her life), then me, then Daddy, with Esther on the other side of him.

My mother was furious when she saw a picture of us in the paper and accused Frank of making a political pawn of his own child.

'You will not get your hands on Nigel for your propaganda,'

she told him. 'I shall take great care to keep him away from your precious Ban the Bomb marches.' In this she was echoing the sentiments of her father. Brigadier Plumley-Greene was already teaching young Nigel to ride and looking forward to the day when his grandson would join the regiment.

A couple of months later as I took tea with Daddy and Esther on the terrace, I remember thinking how much younger he looked than when he was at home with Mummy, and how much they smiled at each other as they talked, and how pretty Esther was in a summer dress with her dark brown hair worn in a pony tail. I remember, too, a pang of guilt at thinking such disloyal thoughts.

'Shall I accept this or say no?' asked Esther, holding up a white card, edged with gold, requesting the honour of the company of, et cetera.

The invitation was to a reception at the Soviet Embassy in Kensington Palace Gardens.

'Would you like to go?' he asked her.

'Perhaps you should take *Mrs* Cole?'

'Mrs Cole hates diplomatic parties,' he replied, 'and in any case wouldn't be seen dead at the Soviet Embassy.'

So they went. Inside the portals which always seemed so sinister in those days of the Cold War when Russian and American tanks were face to face in a divided Berlin, an unsmiling attendant took their coats and they were greeted at the entrance to a large, richly carpeted room by their host General Surkov, the senior military attaché. The room was already full of people and the surf-like roar of cocktail-party conversation.

Frank steered Esther through the throng to a relatively quiet alcove, expertly lifting two glasses of vodka and cornets of smoked salmon filled with caviare from passing trays.

'You look particularly charming tonight,' he told her, and indeed she did in a simple black dress – the 'Sack' look, abolishing the waist – with her dark hair pinned up in a bun. She wore little make-up and no jewellery.

'Aren't we supposed to circulate?' she asked.

'Heavens no,' answered Frank, snatching another vodka, 'these dos aren't for meeting people. Nobody knows anybody else – they're all here for the beer.'

She giggled and he went on: 'The last time I saw General

Surkov we were watching a Marine Commando staging a mock landing on the coast of Pembrokeshire. A frightfully pukka British brigadier came up to him and brayed: "D'you see that ship, General, not sheep – *baaa-baaa* – but ship . . ." Well Surkov's face turned to stone and he replied in perfect English: "In Russia there would be a fleet of ships, not just one. And what about tanks. Where are the tanks? I've seen enough of this piffling exercise." And with that he marched off with this twit of a brigadier trotting after him, pleading.'

Just at this point, the general himself in his bemedalled Red Army uniform, approached their corner and bowing slightly towards Esther said: 'You are enjoying the party, no?'

Arrested in mid-giggle she made some polite reply and Surkov moved on.

'Actually he's head of the KGB in London,' hissed Frank when he was out of earshot.

'I find it so strange, drinking here on such friendly terms,' said Esther. 'I would feel more at home in a CND demonstration outside demanding that they call off their wretched fifty-megaton bomb test.'

Nevertheless, she enjoyed the party, the more so when they were joined by an exceedingly handsome blond young man who presented his card introducing himself as Oleg Rostov from the Soviet trade mission. He, too, spoke good English but was so drunk that when a toast was proposed to Yuri Gagarin, who had just completed the first manned flight in space, he said in a loud voice which made every head turn: 'To our glorious Union of Soviet Sophocles Reepboles.'

In the midst of unprecedented affluence (for as Harold Macmillan had told the people in the last general election, they 'had never had it so good'), my father sensed an atmosphere of effete decay.

'While the Russians and the Americans put men into orbit round the earth,' he wrote, 'we offer our defunct rocket (Blue Streak) to Europe as a gift. Europe doesn't want it, and as General de Gaulle has bluntly told Mr Macmillan it does not want him and his Front Bench of Old Etonians in the councils of the Six. Our Prime Minister must now go cap in hand to Washington to see if they will help him maintain the illusion that Britain is an independent nuclear power, when he has turned it into a land of bingo halls and betting shops.'

Watching the octogenarian Sir Winston Churchill shuffle to his place on ritual visits to the House of Commons, a totem figure representing vanished greatness, Frank looked wistfully towards America, even when the young President John F. Kennedy's attempt to put down the Cuban revolutionaries ended embarrassingly in the bungled landing at the Bay of Pigs.

On the day that the news came through, Frank was invited to join the celebrations at the Cuban Embassy in Mayfair. At three in the afternoon he was pacing up and down on the corner of South Audley Street where he had arranged to meet Esther. He now had no doubts whatever that he was in love with her. When they were apart his thoughts constantly turned to her and their moments together had a glow that he had experienced before only with Elaine in the summer of his youth. Here he was now, a middle-aged Member of Parliament, waiting anxiously on a street corner for the loved one to appear.

She arrived in a red Morris Mini, apologizing for being late and at the same time appealing for sixpences for the parking meter. Together they went into the embassy and up two flights of stairs to the reception, where Bacardi rum had been flowing since the message stuttered from the teleprinter machine at 11.30 a.m.: 'Everything is finished in Cuba with victory to Castro.'

A young man in shirtsleeves staggered towards them waving two paper cups: 'We have-a run out of glasses. Help yourselves.' He looked about nineteen, but turned out to be the chargé d'affaires. Unlike Fidel Castro and the guerrillas in the mountains, he could boast no beard. 'I am berry, berry happy,' he kept saying. 'Berry, berry happy.'

In one corner stood a group of Venezuelan students planning a revolution of their own, in another a group of Oxford undergraduates who had just come from an anti-American demonstration outside the US Embassy in Grosvenor Square. The Bacardi continued to flow like water.

As afternoon passed into evening, songs of the revolution drifted from the second floor embassy in Mayfair, interspersed with loud, and largely incoherent, speeches. Delegations arrived from the Soviet and Red Chinese embassies and were handed paper cups full of rum. The speeches became more noisy still.

A fat, and bald middle-aged man in a well-cut grey flannel

suit lurched out of the tobacco haze and said: 'Frank Cole, isn't it? Young and handsome as ever. You've hardly changed.'

Frank stepped back a pace, defensively. He hated being confronted by strangers, which happened quite often since he started appearing on television.

'I bet you don't remember *me*, you old scrounger,' said this stranger.

Frank stared back, blankly.

'Spain, summer of '37,' the man went on. 'My birthday, outside Santander, when the bloody Fascists came down on us like the hordes of Gengis Khan.'

Christ, it's Graham Moody, this fat stranger who is now embracing me and planting a slobbering kiss on my cheek.

An ageing queen with dyed black hair, bags under his eyes and rouge on his cheeks, he could not have been more unlike the youth who fought alongside Frank in the Republican trenches in that long forgotten war. Totally ignoring Esther, he was prattling about '37, three years before she was born, for God's sake.

'What are you up to these days, my dear, or rather *who* are you up?' nattered Moody, plunging on without waiting for a reply. 'I'm in electronics. Wonderful stuff. Fabulous contacts with the Eastern Bloc, you know.'

Frank was only half listening. He resented Moody's making him feel his age. Esther had drifted away and he could see her across the room in conversation with Oleg Rostov, the good-looking young Russian they had met at the Soviet Embassy. Silently, he cursed Moody, still rabbiting on.

Most people don't actually improve with keeping, do they?

He glanced at his watch. A quarter past eight. We have been on our feet, drinking for five hours, with nothing to eat but peanuts and olives and that incredible beardless chargé d'affaires is still on his feet, filling paper cups with Bacardi.

Now Frank was taking out his wallet, extracting a creased and yellowing snapshot of a young woman taken on the deck of a ship. Thirty-seven, 'member that. Jane Flipping . . . Flippance. That was her name. Wonder where she is now, eh. Wonder where?

A blank. Where am I now? I'm in bed, or rather *on* a bed and there's someone sitting astride me. Esther, actually. Naked. Over her bare shoulder he could see another image of her back and buttocks reflected in a brightly lit mirror. The mirror was circular and split into segments like an orange and it was set into the ceiling of the room above where they lay on soft satin cushions. The carpet he recognized as 'Skater's Trails', the epitome of what was called 'Contemporary', as were the spindly-legged moulded chairs and little Formica-topped tables and the studio couch in the alcove beyond, up two steps.

Esther's hair, released from the Kirbygrips which held it in place around a kind of fibrous doughnut, fell straight below her shoulders, which were bronzed in marked contrast to the startling white of her breasts where a bikini top had covered them. He reached out to touch them and she leaned her head back, sighing and swaying her hips from side to side as he entered her.

He had no idea where he was, how he came to be there or how he had parted company with his clothes, but none of it seemed to matter compared to the exquisite pleasure, a pleasure heightened by the reflected view in the mirror.

He was amazed at her voluptuousness and even more at his own sudden rush of virility. No sooner had they reached a climax than they made love again in a different position, three or four times before he lay back on the cushions, pleasurably spent.

'Don't fall in love with me,' she said. 'Whatever happens, don't say you love me.'

She said nothing more, just smiled, planted a kiss on his lips and got up to go into the kitchen. She returned a few moments later with two beakers of coffee and they sat cross-legged and naked on the cushions drinking it.

'The MP and the secretary,' she said with a grin. 'If only your colleagues on the Back Bench could see you now.'

She was so relaxed, so natural, as if she had not been brought up to believe that nice girls didn't. She did, and she did it like no woman he had known.

'Is this your flat?' he asked at last.

'I live here,' she said.

At that moment a telephone on a low table rang and she leaned over to answer it while he lay back on the cushions and admired her gorgeous body.

'Hello, yes . . . I will . . . OK. It's all right, don't worry. I'll see you soon.'

She hung up.

'Who was that?' he asked.

'Time you went home to your dear lady wife,' she answered, handing him his shirt. She knelt at his feet while he put it on and suddenly throwing her arms around his legs pressed her lips against the soft hairs, caressingly at first but becoming fiercer as she moved upwards.

He bent down to kiss her and she drew him down on top of her on that carpet of mad, multi-coloured squiggles to reach another unbelievable climax.

'Now you really must go,' she said, helping him on with his trousers and his socks. 'I'll ring for a taxi.'

Sitting in the back of the red Renault mini-cab as it sped towards Regent's Park, he literally hugged himself at the sensuous recollection of the night; despite all he had drunk, he felt totally sober and clear-headed.

Dorothy heard the cab door slamming, his key in the lock, footsteps on the stairs, the opening and closing of his bedroom door just down the hall. She glanced at the luminous dial of the little brass clock at her bedside – it was ten minutes to three in the morning.

He's been in his latest pick-up's bed, I suppose, or boozing at clubs, only he'd blame it on another late sitting if I bothered to ask him, which of course I shan't.

Whereupon she rolled over and went back to sleep.

Esther was in her tiny office when Frank poked his head round the door just before noon the next day.

'Good morning, Mr Cole,' she said circumspectly.

She is the very soul of discretion. What a woman. He handed her the day's letters, briskly rapping out instructions.

'Have you seen the papers?' she asked, and when he shook his head handed him a clipping pasted to a piece of foolscap. It was from the Henry Fielding diary column in the *Daily Herald* and was headed: 'A Very Rum Day at the Embassy'. Skimming through a colourful description of the previous day's party, he read: 'Among those present, the Left-wing Labour MP and television pundit, Mr Frank Cole.'

'Blast,' he said. 'That'll go down well in the constituency – giving the impression that I spend my days boozing with Cuban revolutionaries. At least your name's not mentioned, that's something to be thankful for.'

Lowering his voice, he went on: 'I must see you. Can you

meet me in the Dive at one?'

Over drinks in the basement of the tavern opposite the House in Bridge Street he said: 'I owe you an apology for last night. I was very drunk and I . . .'

'Are you saying that you only made love to me because you were plastered?' she demanded, staring at him in disbelief.

'No, of course not,' he said. 'It was the most wonderful thing. Absolutely fabulous. But I mean, it's so risky.'

'Risky? Not at all,' she told him. 'Haven't you heard of the Pill?'

Looking at her, he was struck by the enormous change in her over the past three years, from a wide-eyed idealist taking part in Ban the Bomb marches to a cool young sophisticate who took what she wanted when she wanted it. Her taste in drinks had changed, too. She now asked for a Pimm's No.1 rather than a glass of ale.

'I wasn't talking about the risk of your getting pregnant,' he went on. 'I'm talking about the whole set-up – I mean whose flat was it?'

'You sound like my father,' she retorted impatiently, probably not realizing how unkind the observation was. 'I left home to get away from constant questions. I *am* over twenty-one you know, a free agent. You didn't ask any questions last night, I noticed. Stop being a hypocrite.'

'I'm just curious to know about the flat,' he insisted. 'I mean, I don't even know where it was.'

She sipped her Pimm's No. 1 and regarded him coolly over the rim of the glass for a moment or two before she answered: 'It's in Holland Park – 32A Addison Mews. Oleg Rostov lives there and I live with him. The landlord is a little Polish Jew in dark glasses. He's stinking rich, drives around in Rolls-Royces and Jaguars and owns property all over Notting Hill and Paddington.'

Two days later, on a Friday, when the photographs arrived in the mail, Esther had already left for a holiday on the Costa Brava.

On the following Thursday, when Frank was in the Chamber during Question Time, one of the badged messengers brought in a green card from the lobby. On it was written: 'G.B. Moody, BSc(Econ.), 93 Westbourne Grove, W2. Purpose of visit: Foreign relations.'

He hurried out to the central lobby where Moody rose beaming to greet him.

'I can't spare more than a moment,' said Frank, looking at his watch as they sat down side by side on one of the dark green overstuffed benches. 'I've got a private notice question down for the PM.'

'This won't take more than a moment, dear,' replied Moody camply. 'It's just that we can do business.'

'What business?' asked Frank, beginning to feel distinctly uneasy.

'Just business,' said Moody, opening his briefcase and taking out a foolscap envelope. 'We can talk about that later. In the meantime, I'd like you to study what's in here. I won't detain you any longer, Comrade, I know what busy people you MPs are.'

Back in his place in the Chamber, Frank opened the envelope. One furtive glance was enough to tell him that it contained a similar set of photographs to the one he had already received through the mail. He tugged at his collar, which seemed to be choking him, and the rows of green benches swam in front of his eyes.

Then he was aware of a nudging in the ribs by the MP sitting next to him, and faces turned towards him.

'Frank Cole', called the Speaker, for the second time.

Frank got to his feet shakily and blurted out his question: 'Will the Prime Minister make a statement on recent developments in Cyprus?' He sat down again heavily and heard not a word of what the Prime Minister said in answer to his question.

As soon as Question Time was over he left the Chamber just as the wigged and gowned clerk rose to announce Orders of the Day. The cry 'Orders of the Day!', taken up by the policemen in the lobby, echoed down the corridor after him.

Frank Cole was waiting in the arrivals lounge at Heathrow Airport when the British European Airways Viscount turbo-prop airliner touched down after its flight from Barcelona. He sat, puffing furiously at his pipe, for a further period as the homecoming holidaymakers queued at the immigration desk, collected their baggage and ran the gauntlet of the customs, duty-free bottles chinking guiltily in plastic bags.

He caught sight of her at once among all those tacky stuffed donkeys and straw hats, a girl to turn heads – tall, willowy and bronzed from the Mediterranean sun. She was wearing a sleeveless black sweater, a flowing tan skirt and open sandals, carrying a BEA bag over her shoulder and taking long, purposeful strides towards the exit where the buses picked up for West London.

'Esther!' he called after her, relieved to see that she was alone. He had half expected that the handsome Oleg might be with her. She swung round and held out her bare brown arms to him.

'Frank, what a lovely surprise,' she said. 'How clever of you to find out what flight I was on.'

He did not care if anybody saw them. Let them. He had intended to be icy, but the sight of her melted his heart at once. Although she had been away for only two weeks he had missed her dreadfully.

But he forced himself to say sternly: 'Something's happened while you've been away. I need to talk to you about it – somewhere more private than this.'

'What is it?' she said. 'Your wife?'

He did not answer but led the way out of the terminal and across to the car park where he had left his Rover. When they were inside it he did not start the engine but unlocked the glove compartment and produced two brown foolscap envelopes, watching her closely as she examined the contents briefly while he explained how they came into his possession. She stared at him in utter astonishment.

'You don't know anything about these, how they were taken?' he asked.

'Frank, I'm horrified . . . I've no idea . . .'

'Well, I've got a pretty shrewd idea,' he said harshly. 'That's a two-way mirror in the ceiling of your flat and judging from the angle of these charming pictures there was someone in the room above with a Rolleiflex, snapping away merrily. There are hidden microphones, too, I shouldn't wonder, and they'll have our love talk on tape.'

'The bastard,' she said, and started to cry.

'Rostov?'

'It was he who rang the night you were there, do you remember?' she said. 'He said that he was at the Le Condor Club and going on to the 150 Club in Earl's Court Road – he often stays out all night gambling. But he must have been in the flat upstairs taking pictures of us.'

'And you didn't know he was doing it?' he asked.

'Christ,' she said through her tears, 'what do you take me for?'

He lit her a cigarette and she took it with a trembling hand before going on to tell him how Rostov telephoned her at the House of Commons after they first met him at General Surkov's reception at the Soviet Embassy and invited her out to the theatre. They saw the witty new Oxbridge revue *Beyond the Fringe* and she found Oleg a lively and amusing companion. When they got to that line about Britain's four-minute warning of nuclear attack ('I would have you know that some people in this great country of ours can run a mile in four minutes'), he had laughed louder than anyone sitting around them.

After that they went out regularly, with Oleg prepared to spend freely. He took her to La Discotheque in Wardour Street, Soho, where the rock and roll beat of Bill Haley, Elvis Presley or Marty Wilde (real name, Reg Smith) swept away the sedate foxtrots of the traditional Palais de Danse and introduced the word 'disco' into the language.

'I stayed out all night one Saturday,' she told Frank. 'That's when he took me to a house by the Thames at Maidenhead. He said they had fantastic parties there where they filled the pool with champagne and every girl who dived in naked was rewarded with a mink stole. I didn't know whether to believe him – he is always name-dropping about the people he meets in the clubs: the Duke of Kent, lords and Cabinet Ministers, or gangsters like the Kray brothers. There was no champagne in the pool *that* night, but Oleg's landlord, Rachman was there with a blonde called Mandy, dripping with diamonds and rubies, who apparently came down from Birmingham as Miss Austin for last year's Motor Show. The living room was absolutely vast and there was a secret room behind a concealed door at the back of the bar – just large enough for a bed and not much more but with an enormous mirror. We went into this little room and made love, well it was rather more like rape and it was my first time. I didn't much enjoy it and when I put my dress back on and came out they were all sniggering and nudging one another. It was a two-way mirror and they'd been watching us and listening to us, too, on concealed loudspeakers. It seemed very kinky to me and I couldn't really join in the jokes about it. I was just disgusted, even though I was pretty drunk, and I asked Oleg to drive me home. My dad made a terrible scene and threatened to throw me out, but I said I was going anyway and packed my case there and then on that Sunday morning just as they were going out to mass. I moved in with Oleg the same day.'

Sitting in the car at London Airport, with the windows opaque from tobacco smoke, he listened to her story with a growing sense of horrified disbelief.

'But why?' he asked. 'Why?'

'Because I love him, that's why,' she almost snarled.

'What about me?'

'Frank, I don't love you. I'm fond of you, I enjoy your company, but I don't love you.'

'And he's madly in love with you, I suppose,' he suggested in a bitter tone.

'He doesn't love me,' said Esther, 'but he loves the good life – women, dancing, drinking, gambling, especially gambling. He's known in all of Rachman's clubs and thinks nothing of winning or losing hundreds of pounds in a single night.'

'Where does he get the money?' asked Frank.

'I don't know,' said Esther, 'but he is never short of it, however much he loses. He never talks about his work at the embassy, it has something to do with shipping.'

'All their trade people are agents of the KGB and no doubt Graham Moody's electronics business is no more than a front for his spying activities,' said Frank. 'Don't you see? They've used you to trap *me*.'

'What do they want?' she asked.

'Inside information, probably,' he answered. 'Reports on the personal and political activities of my friends and colleagues in the House, material for blackmail. If they can recruit me and I attain a ministerial position in the next Government, all Oleg Rostov's expenditure will be more than justified. They haven't told me yet what they want, but whatever it is I shall have to give it to them. If those photographs got out, I'd be finished.'

26

Early in the New Year Oleg Rostov was recalled to Moscow, probably because he appeared to be enjoying Western decadence too much, and Esther Rutley moved into a bed-sitter in a Victorian mansion in Lambeth, just a few minutes' walk from the House of Commons across Westminster Bridge. She was still my father's secretary and, despite all that had happened, he was still seeing her outside the office.

When he took her to the opening of a new club called The Establishment in Greek Street, Soho, the *Daily Herald* published a photograph of Frank Cole MP and 'his constant companion' over their scallops in wine sauce and a diary paragraph in which he was quoted: 'I think we need this sort of political satire, cabaret dedicated to poking fun at authority.'

Dorothy, however, was not amused. She did not read the *Daily Herald*, but the telephone was soon ringing with friends anxious to draw her attention to it, and she confronted Frank that evening: 'So you *are* having an affair with that pinko Liberal slut . . .'

'For God's sake, Dorothy,' he answered. 'Esther's been working for me for years.'

'Are you trying to tell me that you're not sleeping with her?' she demanded angrily.

'I don't sleep with you, do I?' he threw back at her, 'so what difference does it make?'

'It makes a difference to me,' she said, 'when you flaunt your mistress in public and provide gossip for the gutter press.'

'Well, you can have a divorce if you like,' he told her. 'I'm the guilty party.'

'There will be no divorce,' she answered, adding very quietly and firmly: 'I haven't worked for all these years to get you office in the next Government just to see it all smashed by a sordid scandal in the papers.'

'People's attitude to divorce has changed,' he said. 'Anthony Eden thought his divorce might preclude him from succeeding the Old Man as PM but he was wrong, and Selwyn Lloyd worried unnecessarily about what people might say about the break-up of his marriage when he was at the Foreign Office. It's time all that Victorian hypocrisy was buried and forgotten.'

'Of course, it suits you to take that line,' Dorothy remarked, and repeated: 'There will be no divorce. In future you will be seen in public with me and not with your fancy woman.'

Dorothy was definitely not in tune with the new mood of permissiveness, having apparently forgotten her own period of wild abandon during the hectic days of the Blitz. She did not approve of the current fad for mocking Establishment values, as these were the mores she had grown up with. She approved of Mr Anthony Armstrong-Jones being given an earldom after marrying Princess Margaret, just as she believed it right for her to renounce Group Captain Peter Townsend, an earlier suitor, because he was divorced. Frank regarded this as further proof, if it was needed, of the stuffiness of the English Establishment, still doggedly entrenched behind the barricades of old prejudices and decaying snobberies.

Now, however, he was obliged at Dorothy's insistence to confine his extramural social activities to occasional candle-lit dinners in out-of-the-way Chelsea restaurants, which cost not much more than £2 each with wine, and furtive visits to the bed-sitter in Lambeth.

Publicly, he endured the social whirl at Dorothy's side. She enjoyed dressing up for Ascot and Henley in large hats, with long gloves and tent-like flowered frocks which hopefully disguised her ample proportions. Her one regret was that 'Coming out' was not what it had been in her day.

'What a pity we can't look forward to your being presented at Court when you're eighteen,' she told me wistfully.

As the Che Guevara of the Lower Third at Bridgelands School, I remained uninterested in these discarded upper-class rituals. That summer of 1962 my parents rented a house beside the sea on the Isle of Wight for the holidays, which included Cowes Week. My grandfather had taken up yachting and I remember the little brass cannon outside the Royal Yacht Squadron signalling the start of the Admiral's Cup races, wave after wave of multi-hued spinnakers passing the line.

Daddy and I escaped alone together as often as we could through the iron gate leading from the large overgrown garden of our rented house directly onto the sands. I was not too old, though, to enjoy exploring rock pools or making sandcastles with Nigel and decorating them with shells we found on the beach.

One day the *Queen Mary* came sailing by, outward bound from Southampton to New York with plumes of smoke drifting from her funnels, and Daddy told us about the time he was sent to interview Greta Garbo.

'Greta *who*?' I asked, with the intolerance of youngsters for the stars of their parents' youth.

'She's a Hollywood film star,' explained my father patiently. 'In those days the famous crossed the Atlantic by sea. Now everyone goes by air.'

'I shall fly to America and become a star,' said I.

'What as – Dracula's bride?' scoffed my horrid little brother.

The weather was glorious and in a week or so we were all as brown as berries. Grandma Cole came down to stay with us and sat in a deckchair beside the ornamental lily pond watching Daddy and Nigel and me play tennis on a grass court speckled with daisies.

Her conversation was lively and I much preferred her to my other grandmother, who was constantly criticizing the way I behaved and talking to mother about me over my head as if I were deaf or stupid. Grandma Cole entertained me with colourful descriptions of her neighbourhood. Grandma Plumley-Greene strongly disapproved of these lowlife stories, as she called them, but Mummy told her that Jenny only did it to be irritating. Nothing could stop her.

In Emanuel Road, she said, 'there's a dozen assorted singles and couples from Trinidad and Tobago who've come to London to work on the buses. They are very nice people, always smiling and joking, but they *are* rather noisy. They tend to play their wireless sets out in the garden when they are having open-air parties, and they are always having parties. Their landlord is a Nigerian gentleman, a Mr Adulyi. He is very tall and coal black and he drives a large white motor car. He doesn't actually live there but he calls once a week to collect the rents.'

'Perhaps you should move, Mother,' suggested Frank, 'to somewhere a bit more peaceful.'

'Oh, dear me, no,' replied Jenny. 'I should find too much peace rather boring. I like a little life about me at my age, and anyway I like my home, modest though it may be, and I do not intend to leave it.'

'Sometimes I worry about you, living there alone,' said Frank.

'I am not alone,' she said, patting his hand and smiling at him. 'I have my cats for company.'

'You're not getting any younger,' he reminded her gently.

'None of us is,' she retorted. 'I am perfectly able to look after my own needs, which are few, and do my own bit of shopping. Fortunately the shops are near at hand, because I can't walk very far or very fast, I find. However, as long as I have my health and strength I shall be all right. You mustn't worry about me.'

Nevertheless, Father did worry about her. The Tory Rent Act which became law in 1957 gave landlords the right to charge as much as they could get for accommodation, provided they could get the sitting tenants out, and this had led to extortion, evictions and profiteering. Frank had read and heard stories of intimidation by teams of strong-arm men. Although Jenny was the owner of her own house, not a tenant, she might become a target of harassment designed to make her sell at a low price and move out.

He discussed the situation with a fellow Labour MP, Ben Parkin, who had a dossier on rapacious landlords operating in his Paddington constituency, to which scouts directed thousands of Blacks who jammed the platforms at Waterloo and Victoria when they arrived from the West Indies with nowhere to go. The most powerful of the landlords, owning a thousand overcrowded slum homes through dozens of nominee companies, extending from Paddington through Notting Hill (where race riots had broken out) to Earl's Court, Shepherd's Bush, Maida Vale and Battersea, was Perec Rachman.

Frank sensed the rottenness at the heart of the affluent society which the Tories had built. Like maggots, the new Nazis were feeding off this decay, trying to achieve what they failed to achieve in the 1930s, only now their cry was 'Get out you black bastards' as well as 'Down with the fucking Jews.'

One of the delights of my holidays was being allowed to sit up late with Daddy in his study watching 'That Was the Week That Was' on television. We were allowed to watch only a few carefully selected programmes at Bridgelands, despite its progressive reputation, and these did not include 'TWTWTW' in which David Frost and a team of young Oxbridge trendies cracked jokes about homosexuality, sent up Maigret and Dixon of Dock Green alike, mocked British technology and the accents of Tories before an invited audience on a stark bare set with the camera dolleys in view.

There had been nothing like it before on television and Daddy loved to watch it with a bottle of Scotch at his elbow. It went out late on a Saturday night. On the last night of 1962, aged twelve, I sat at my father's feet watching a special edition of the show called 'That Was The Year That Was'. Most of it went completely over my head but I enjoyed Millicent Martin singing the headlines and thought Willie Rushton doing Dixon of Dock Green in French hilarious.

Daddy howled when they said 'Mr Gaitskell was impaled on the fence for so long you could have torn him in half along the perforations.' Looking at the early editions of the Sunday papers they ridiculed the Crossbencher column of the *Sunday Express* for its record of incorrect predictions, the latest being that Gaitskell had no reason to worry about his health.

'Sorry, Hugh!' wisecracked Frost, but a few days later the joke proved horribly apt when Gaitskell died in the Middlesex Hospital from a renal complaint.

Even before the body was interred in the snow at the parish church in Hampstead, the struggle for the leadership of the Labour Party was joined. Inevitably, the lobbies and bars at the House of Commons sweated with gossip and intrigue. George Brown, a contender for the leadership, did much of the talking himself while his rival, Harold Wilson, kept a low profile, determined to avoid starting any rumours of deals over jobs in his Shadow Cabinet if he was elected.

It was at this delicate moment that a story appeared on the front page of the *Evening Chronicle* claiming that if he won, Wilson would offer Charles Pannell, who was running the Brownite campaign, a job and put his own kingmaker, Dick Crossman, in charge of his private 'Brains Trust'. 'SECRET WILSON DEAL' was the headline on the story by the *Chronicle*'s political editor, Jack Harris.

My father always denied that he gave his friend inside information and Jack Harris, good newspaperman that he was, never disclosed his sources of information, but the story was too well-informed by half for some people's comfort.

For weeks conversation at Westminster was dominated by speculation over who would be the new leader of the Labour Party and the atmosphere of suspense heightened as the election drew near. Frank telephoned Dorothy as soon as the result was known, before going off to appear on a television programme:

'It's Harold,' he told her. 'He got 144 to George Brown's 103.'

'That's splendid news for you, darling,' she replied. 'At last, the light at the end of the long tunnel.'

'I hope so,' he said. 'Certainly I couldn't have expected any favours from Hugh and his Hampstead clique, whereas Harold's one of us.'

But even as he said it, he felt a qualm about his future instead of the heady sense of political life beginning again. Over the next few weeks his misgivings were justified. The atmosphere of springtime on the Labour side, scenting at last a real possibility of victory at the next general election, was marred from Frank's point of view by the fact that Harold did not ask to see him.

The new leader was seeking out his old Keep-Leftist friends, asking their advice, but my father was not among those invited to dinner by the Crossmans at Vincent Square or the Castles at Hampstead. Wilson was aiming to create a British equivalent of Jack Kennedy's New Frontier in America, but poor Daddy, it seemed, had been excluded from the short list of comrades considered trustworthy.

27

'I suppose you've heard about Jack Profumo?'

Frank was sitting in one of the leather armchairs near the door of the tea-room when the other MP leaned over from the next chair with the expression of a man unable to keep a secret, and went on in a conspiratorial whisper: 'It's all round the Tory benches that Profumo's been sharing the favours of a model called Christine Keeler with a certain naval attaché at the Soviet Embassy.'

'So?' said Frank, affecting unconcern.

'So, he's been found out and George Wigg's on the scent, baying like a bloodhound. He says that quite apart from the honour of the Army and all that, security's at risk. You know the colonel when he gets his teeth into something.'

John Profumo was the War Minister in Macmillan's Government and Colonel Wigg, a leading figure in the Opposition, took a special interest in defence matters.

It is not difficult to imagine that my father must have felt a chill shiver of apprehension at the news his colleague gave him. For two years since those ominous brown envelopes arrived at the House of Commons he had been walking a knife edge, dreading that at any time their contents might fall into other hands.

Still no one was aware, so far as he knew, of his regular visits to the Kardomah Coffee House in King's Road, Chelsea, where he engaged in earnest conversation with an old friend from the Spanish Civil War. The Government had been in some difficulty over security matters since the Admiralty spy William Vassall went to prison. Two Fleet Street reporters had been jailed for refusing to tell the tribunal on the affair who had told them that Vassall bought women's clothes in the West End and was known to his colleagues as 'Auntie'. Although one of the typists in the office had decided that no one earning £15 a week could live in the style that Vassall did, and be honest, the sponsorship of two high-ranking officials enabled him to avoid the strictest part of the security vetting.

The Conservatives hated to be found wanting in matters to do with national defence and this was not the first time that the stiff upper lip had been seen to quiver. Brigadier Plumley-Greene fumed when he read in *The Times* that twenty-five men of the 1st Battalion the Scots Guards, instead of being on sentry-go outside Windsor Castle, had walked out and gone to London to air their grievances about excessive 'bull' to the *Daily Mirror.* Spit and polish was a Guardsman's lot in the brigadier's eyes. This was mutiny. The blighters should be rounded up and put in the glass-house. What had happened to the motto of the Scots Guards: 'Touch me not with impunity!' Their commanding officer is anxious that they should return so that he can discuss the matter with them . . . what namby-pamby drivel.

But the popular end of Fleet Street, still smarting over the imprisonment of two reporters for doing no more than their job, fell upon the Guards story as evidence of another crack in the great Establishment scheme of things presided over by the patrician Prime Minister, Harold Macmillan. Plumley-Greene was even more dismayed when he saw the Parliamentary report of John Profumo's candid admission to the House of Commons that there was something wrong at the Guards depot at Pirbright. The men who had mutinied were handled with kid gloves.

The brigadier might have been outraged to the verge of apoplexy had he known about the social life of Her Majesty's Secretary of State for War. At that time, long before wife swapping became the rage in the smarter suburbs, the upper crust in London were diverting themselves with Roman-style orgies. The names of various Ministers and apparent pillars of society were being bandied around Fleet Street, Westminster, Whitehall and the Inns of Court.

Now, according to Frank's informant in the tea-room, there was further trouble in store over laxness in security at high level. Rumours were flying round the lobbies that Profumo might resign after parliamentary approval of the Army Estimates within the next few days.

At twenty minutes to eleven on the night the House debated the Vassall business, George Wigg got to his feet and asked: 'Aren't we now in the middle of a new rumour campaign?' He invited the Home Secretary to deny the rumours relating to Miss Keeler, and then Dick Crossman jumped up to say that *Paris Match* was printing a full account of the War Minister's relationship with Christine Keeler.

The Home Secretary said that the Labour MPs were spreading rumours under the cloak of Parliamentary privilege and refused to answer them but the next morning, a Friday, there were huge headlines in the papers. When the House assembled at eleven in the morning Frank hurried in with the rest of the MPs, anxious to get a place on the crowded benches as Profumo was to make a statement. He told them that he had met Captain Eugene Ivanov only twice and Miss Keeler on half a dozen occasions socially at 17 Wimpole Mews, the London flat of Dr Stephen Ward, who was not only a highly fashionable osteopath with an entree to the grandest houses but an accomplished artist who had been commissioned by the *Illustrated London News* to paint the royal family.

Mr Profumo rounded on those who had attacked him and said he would sue them if they dared to repeat their allegations outside the House. Mr Macmillan patted him on the back as he sat down and that afternoon he and his wife, the actress Valerie Hobson, joined the Queen Mother at Sandown Park races as if nothing was amiss.

It looked as if the cracks in the Establishment had been papered over, yet the atmosphere in the House was uneasy and there was a feeling of resentment from both sides against George Wigg and company. My father must have felt some sense of relief though that the threatened witch hunt over Members' private lives seemed to have petered out. If so, his relief was short-lived. The bitterest English winter that anyone could remember was about to be followed by a damp and dismal English summer and a series of political catastrophes.

At the beginning of June, Mummy flew off to Nassau with her parents, packing me and Nigel up to the Lake District to spend the Whitsun holidays at a so-called adventure camp. It never stopped raining and to this day is associated in my mind with the odours of fetid plimsolls and damp woollens.

Daddy stayed in London working on a new book about nuclear war (it was never published, as it turned out) and shutting himself away from the world in our house at the edge of Regent's Park. He succeeded so well that when his mother telephoned to talk about the untimely death of Pope John he hadn't even heard about it.

He was, however, listening when the announcement that Profumo had returned suddenly from holiday in Venice to admit that he had lied to the House and resign his office was given out by the BBC on a Wednesday evening.

Frank at once picked up the telephone and called Esther, who had not yet heard the news.

'What do you think has made Profumo come clean?' she asked.

'I don't know,' said Frank. 'Perhaps he's scared that Dr Ward will start naming names and wanted to get in first. All the Top People have been busy rallying round Jack Profumo but Ward's been ruined by all these stories about girls being tied up and whipped at that little weekend cottage down at Cliveden. But it's not that so much that's put Profumo in total disgrace – after all, the upper crust isn't averse to a certain amount of snobbery with violence – no, it's the fact that he lied to the House that's finished him.'

'Keeler was Rachman's mistress before Ward introduced her to Profumo,' said Esther. 'Did you know that?'

'No, I didn't,' he replied. 'A charming liaison I must say. Have you ever met this chap Ivanov?'

'Oleg introduced him to me at a party once,' Esther admitted.

'He's a handsome, moody Slavic type, not someone I could feel comfortable with.'

'So you didn't go to bed with him?'

'Frank, don't be like that.' She sounded hurt by his sarcastic tone.

'I'm sorry,' he said, 'but it seems that in the best circles everyone's screwing everyone who's anyone. There's going to be a lot of high-minded disgust on our side over this. Quite apart from the security angle, it's got drugs, slum landlords and crazy black men like Mr Lucky Gordon chasing after the War Minister's tart. Christ, what a feast for Fleet Street!'

'We'd better not see one another for a while, except in the office,' she suggested.

'Right,' he agreed. 'It's better to play safe in the present climate. Our lot wouldn't be too kind to me, or you for that matter, if those photographs got into their hands. They're hardly suitable for the family album, are they?'

Esther laughed and told him: 'You're wonderful, you can get a laugh out of any situation. I shall miss our quiet little evenings together.'

'So shall I,' he said. 'But it's better to tread carefully. Sleep well, my precious.'

He was aware of a peculiar noise as he replaced the receiver and picking it up again, heard a slight buzzing followed by a click. It occurred to him for the first time that his telephone might be tapped. He did not sleep well that night and rose early to take a walk in the park.

The Profumos' town house was just around the corner and it was under siege by reporters, although there was no sign of their quarry. Presumably he would have to face the Queen when he handed in his seals of office, but in the meantime he had vanished. Frank crossed to the other side and hurried past the gaggle on the pavement, noticing that one of the reporters had provided himself with a canvas chair and a supply of sun-tan oil in expectation of a long wait and some sunshine.

He was destined to be proved right on the first and disappointed on the second anticipation.

By the time Dorothy returned to London with a deep Bahamian tan, the *News of the World* was full of Christine Keeler's life story, which she had sold to them for £23,000, and Stephen

Ward, the osteopath, had been arrested and charged with living on her immoral earnings. After his trial at the Old Bailey he took his own life. Perec Rachman was already dead from a heart attack but the scale of the vice and corruption fostered by his little empire was only now beginning to emerge. In the lurid exposés of the British *dolce vita* in the Sunday papers, no stone was being left unturned in case there should be something even more sensationally nasty lurking beneath it.

Mummy found it impossible to accept that her sort of people were involved in this sort of thing, so when she received a series of anonymous letters alleging that Daddy was the mysterious 'Man in the Mask' at a party of prominent people who had dispensed with the formality of wearing clothes, and that he had been photographed in obscene postures with a girl young enough to be his daughter she was absolutely horrified.

Frank was confronted with the letters over his morning coffee and toast

'What does this mean?' asked Dorothy, facing him across the table very coolly, displaying no outward sign of emotion. God knows what his reactions were as he read the first page, then another and another, but he, too, stayed calm.

'How long have you had these?' he asked when he had finished reading them.

'They started arriving last week and there's been one almost every day,' Dorothy told him. 'Actually, I burned the first one. What have you to say for yourself?'

'These pictures they talk about,' said Frank, putting marmalade on his toast. 'Where are they?'

'There were no pictures,' answered Dorothy.

'In that case,' he said, 'I suggest you burn the rest of these disgusting little missives and forget about it.'

'It's easy to say that,' she persisted, 'but they are written by a reasonably well-educated person who seems to have some inside information. What is all this about a man in a mask?'

'Darling, these sex parties have been the talk of the lobbies for months,' he told her with an air of long-suffering patience. 'All sorts of rumours are flying around. It seems the parties are quite exclusive and some people were particularly thrilled by a man who served dinner wearing nothing but a mask. The story was that he was a Cabinet Minister.'

'A Minister?' Dorothy was aghast. 'Who?'

'So many names are being mentioned,' said Frank. 'Anyway it certainly wasn't me. I don't get my kicks that way.'

Neverthless, I can imagine how desperately worried he must have been by the implied threat in those letters. He became convinced that MI5 was on his tail. First, there were those odd noises on the telephone, and secondly, he had the uneasy feeling that he was being shadowed. On several occasions, when walking in the street, he glanced over his shoulder to see a man staring with rapt attention into a shop window. A tall man with flat feet. A man with Special Branch stamped all over his trench coat, trilby hat and neatly clipped moustache.

Macmillan's days as Prime Minister and those of his government were numbered. The scandals of that dismal summer had created the conditions for Labour to win the next election after thirteen years in opposition.

Cruelly, after all those years in the wilderness, Frank Cole was compromised by his past. He had supported the Communists in the 1930s from idealism and disgust at the rise of unemployment and Fascism. He had never held a party card. Now, through his own moral lapse, he was being forced by the KGB into playing the role of a sleeper, the term used to describe an agent who only begins spying after establishing an impeccable reputation.

Perhaps it was a desire to release the tension or create a diversion which led Frank into an indiscretion which brought the wrath of the whole House down on his head. Certainly, at the time, there was no rational explanation for the folly which finally wrecked what was left of his prospects of office in the next Government.

Jack Harris was the unwitting catalyst, with another of his frequent scoops on the inner workings of the Parliamentary Labour Party. This story, that George Brown would be made head of a new Ministry of Planning, charged with bringing about the technological revolution when Harold Wilson eventually came to power, appeared on the front page of the *Evening Chronicle* on a quiet afternoon and was relegated to an inside page in the later editions. But its impact was out of all proportion to the modest headline. Where did Harris get his information? The Opposition Whips started making inquiries. Because of his former association with the *Evening Chronicle*, Frank was an obvious suspect.

In the midst of the hue and cry at Westminster, a letter appeared in the *Evening Chronicle*:

Of course leaks occur from meetings of the Parliamentary Labour Party. At every meeting at least a score of Members may be seen taking copious notes and later in the bars, leaking furiously. Every newspaper in Fleet Street has half a dozen or so MPs on its 'contact files': some are paid a retainer, some on what they produce and some do it for the personal publicity. And why not? This is a free society and the people have a right to know what is being decided in their name.

This letter was signed Frank Cole MP, and the effect was swift and salutary. A Tory MP drew attention to it in the House of Commons and his complaint was referred to the Committee of Privileges. My father was called to give evidence and the committee found his answers evasive. They then called the editor of the *Evening Chronicle* but he flatly refused to name the sources of his information.

Frank was censured by the committee for casting suspicion on Honourable Members. When he met Jack Harris in the Strangers' Bar afterwards he was still sweating.

'You were lucky,' said Jack, who knew very well that Frank was paid £50 a week by the paper to supply inside information. 'Remember what happened to poor old Garry Allighan in '47 for feeding the *Standard*? He was shown the door.'

'Sanctimonious bastards,' growled Frank, gulping down a double Ballantine's and glaring at other MPs at the bar who pointedly turned their backs on him. 'They all do it and yet they turn on me like a pack of wolves.'

'Look, Frank, we're very old mates,' Jack told him, putting an arm round his shoulder. 'I think that you've overreacted and you should try to calm down.'

Jack Harris had worries of his own. The circulation of the *Chronicle* had been falling and doubts whether London could sustain more than two evening newspapers any longer were hardening into certainty. The proprietor, Lord Edgbaston, had announced that losses on the *Chronicle* were increasing day by day and hinted that he was not prepared to go on picking up the bill indefinitely. In the circumstances, there were no potential buyers around and it was beginning to look as if the *Chronicle*, like the *Star* and the *News Chronicle*, might fold without warning one day.

Coming up to fifty, with a mortgage to pay and children still to see through university which he believed he owed them, Jack was worried about his job prospects if this happened and Fleet Street was again flooded with redundant journalists. As a political specialist he had narrowed his own market. He was already putting out feelers to other papers, even the *Daily Herald*, which itself was ailing. Frank Cole knew all this but offered no advice or even sympathy to his old friend, seeming to be immersed in his own troubles to the exclusion of everyone else's. Jack would have welcomed even a word.

Of course, he knew nothing of the deeper pressures that were on his friend, so he felt hurt and resentful when Frank reacted to his advice by shaking himself free and stomping out of the bar. Dorothy was less diplomatic than Jack in her comments on Frank's behaviour.

'You fool,' she told him. 'If you'd lain low for a short while it would have blown over. Why on earth did you write that idiotic letter?'

'I did what I thought was right,' he answered.

'Right or wrong, what does it matter?' she said wearily. 'You've committed suicide, politically. The best you can hope for now is to hang on to your seat on the Back Bench.'

Frank lost the Labour Whip and was dropped from the defence committee. When he was summoned to West Wickham by the local party to account for himself, Dorothy went with him, despite her harsh strictures. How seedy and rundown the party headquarters looked – the window with the flyblown photograph of Frank (which kept falling down and was sometimes left for days before someone thought to fix it in place again) and the tatty posters, curling at the edges. It was like something in a banana republic, only the slowly revolving fans were missing. 'Your local MP can be seen every Saturday morning between the hours of 9.30 a.m. and 12 noon.'

'How often have you failed to keep *that* appointment?' inquired Dorothy sarcastically as they went into the office.

'Whose side are you on?' he asked.

'I'm here, aren't I?' she replied. 'Playing the devoted little woman, as always.'

The committee room was upstairs, three rooms knocked into

one. They took their places at the bare deal table at the front, sitting next to Mr Rickett, the chairman, and facing several rows of unsmiling faces. Roy Bidwell, the secretary, and Frank's agent, Stan Taylor, sat at opposite ends of the top table. Stan was biting his nails nervously. He was a permanently worried man.

Mr Ricketts rapped on the bare surface with his chairman's gavel, cleared his throat and remarked how nice it was to see 'our Member of Parliament and his charming lady wife' in attendance. There was no applause, so Ricketts coughed again and plodded on with the dreary routine of a local committee meeting agenda, interspersed with dry points of order and appeals to 'Brother Chairman'.

After an hour or so of this he suddenly appeared to go rather red in the face as he began to stammer . . . 'motion before the Committee from Brother Bottle . . .'

Stan Taylor had warned Frank in advance that Brian Bottle, a senior shop steward at the Ford motor plant at Dagenham, was leading the revolt against him. Dorothy looked at Mr Bottle with obvious distaste as he stood up and launched into his address: 'I'm just an ordinary working bloke and I don't pretend to know much about defence and foreign policy and all that stuff that our MP is always on about on the box. All I know is that if he spent half as much time on the bread and butter issues affecting the workers and housewives of this constituency we'd all be a lot better off, because I'm not a Communist, but yes, I'm Left-wing and I believe in bettering the conditions of me mates . . .'

As Mr Bottle warmed to his theme, Frank could sense that he was carrying the audience with his down-to-earth Cockney approach.

' . . . I've got a wife and two kids and we pay a mortgage on our little terrace house. There's not much left out of the fifteen quid a week I earn at Ford's. My car's a six-year-old Anglia. What does Mr Cole know about people like us? Is Mr Cole the kind of man we want representing us at Westminster? It should go out from this meeting that he is not . . .'

Stan Taylor was biting his nails again. Frank shifted uneasily on his hard chair. He did not like the turn events were taking as Brother Bottle came to the point.

' . . . we have no confidence in our Member of Parliament

and he should be replaced at the next election by a candidate more in touch with the great mass of this movement of ours. I so move.'

He sat down to vehement applause and several others rose to speak in favour of the motion, including a certain Mrs Hopwood from Greentree Close, who related at length how letters to the Member about excessive parking in her neighbourhood rarely received an answer 'even though I always enclose a stamped, addressed envelope.'

Scarcely a voice had been raised against Mr Bottle's motion of no confidence when Frank rose to defend himself.

'Over the past thirteen years that I have had the honour to be your elected representative,' he told them in his sincerest tone, 'I have travelled, written and broadcast constantly with the single-minded aim of diverting tax-payers' money, which has been frittered away on rockets and bombs, to more constructive ends, such as new schools and hospitals, better homes and improved social services. This mission has taken up untold hours – as my wife, sitting here beside me, can testify – and if this has meant I have given too little attention to you, then I can only say . . .'

'However busy you might have been, Comrade, you still found time to visit a West End club with a lady who is not your wife,' called out Bottle.

Dorothy did not bat an eyelid at this but Frank flushed and said sharply: 'If Brother Bottle wants a bare-knuckle contest, he can have it. I might suggest to him that instead of wasting his time reading the gossip columns of the gutter press . . .'

'The *Daily Herald*,' shouted Bottle, to laughter, 'our own paper.'

'It's still gossip,' continued Frank, 'and I suggest, brother, that you'd be better employed improving relations at the place where you work instead of calling unofficial meetings on the shop floor during working hours and precipitating strikes which benefit no one. Why is there so much trouble at Ford's, Brother Bottle?'

'Because,' answered Bottle coolly, 'the management keep demanding more and more out of every man. We turn out thirty-three and a third Cortinas every hour – now they're asking for forty-eight an hour. It's soul-destroying work which you, Brother Cole, wouldn't understand because you've never done a shift on the assembly line. You're too busy making money out of leaking the Party's private business to Lord Edgbaston and your other mates in Fleet Street and preening yourself on the box. The top men in our own unions don't understand, either. They're out of touch with the men on the floor, just as you're out of touch with this great movement of ours . . .'

'Don't try to tell me what it's like being at the bottom,' Cole retorted, his voice rising. 'I was born in Camberwell. I went to school at Albion Hill Elementary in Deptford . . .'

'Was that before you went to Eton?' called out someone from the back of the room.

'You lot make me sick,' yelled Frank, oblivious to Dorothy's gentle tug at his sleeve beneath the table. 'I grew up in South London when times really were hard in the twenties, worse in the thirties when I became a Socialist.'

'You mean "we've never had it so good", is that it?' retorted Bottle. 'I think we've heard that somewhere before. It's not just money, you know, we're on about. As I said before, you wouldn't know because you don't have to clock on every day at the House of Commons and have your pay docked if you're late. You're like them in the office – they're part of Ford's. We're not, we just work there. We're just numbers.'

Dorothy at least could see that the meeting was behind Bottle and was unimpressed by Frank's exaggerated efforts to show that he was just a working-class lad at heart. But even a sharp rap on the ankle with the side of her foot failed to warn her husband, whose Cole blood by now was up.

'Jealousy and bitching seems to be your main occupation, Brother Bottle,' he snapped.

Suddenly the room was in uproar, with Ricketts pounding the table with his gavel and calling 'Order, Comrades, order!' It had little effect. Everyone was on their feet, all shouting at once, while Brian Bottle shook his fist at the platform. His words were drowned in the hubbub. Frank, struggling to regain his composure, took out a tin of Three Nuns tobacco and started filling his pipe but Dorothy noticed that his hands were shaking so much that half of the flakes fell on the floor instead of going into the bowl. His face was ashen.

The truth was that Frank had not expected such hostility from the local rank and file, such a virulent attack from the floor and such a violent reaction when he attempted to fight back. Bottle had put a spark to the tinder of their pent-up frustration at their Member of Parliament's lack of involvement with them over a long period.

It was obvious that, despite repeated assertions by politicians, the class war (in West Wickham at least) was far from obsolete. Mr Macmillan might have formed the most aristocratic government that Britain had seen in years, including a duke, three earls and a marquess, but the worlds of the arts, fashion and popular entertainment were aggressively working class. This left the middle class, to which my parents belonged no matter how much Frank might protest otherwise, on dangerously exposed ground. And within their marriage my parents epitomized the conflicts between the upper and lower divisions of the same social class.

Brian Bottle was unequivocally one of the callous and bloody-minded lower orders who viewed his so-called betters as merely cynical and corrupt. His motion of no confidence was carried overwhelmingly, but at the suggestion of Mr Ricketts, who still retained some vestiges of the old respect for middle-class Socialists, it was agreed to give the Member one last chance to mend his ways.

There was silence in the Rover driving home through the seedy back streets of South London, father's own, but Dorothy could not resist saying before they went to their separate beds: 'I knew that your playing around with that tart would land you in trouble. I have never been so publicly humiliated in my life, and you made it worse by descending into the gutter with that awful little man.'

'I had to defend myself,' protested Frank.

'The man's a Commie agitator,' said Dorothy. 'If you'd kept a dignified silence he would have hung himself.'

'It's easy to talk after the event,' replied Frank bitterly. 'You heard them – they were after my blood. I'm finished at West Wickham.'

'Nonsense,' retorted Dorothy, taking out a gold-plated compact and minutely examining her eyebrows in the little round mirror. 'You will fight back and regain their confidence before the election. It's a bore, but it must be done. Please though, tell Taylor to keep that Bottle creature out of my way or I might behave totally out of character and kick him in the balls.'

* * *

I suffered a lot at Bridgelands during that half from much spiteful gossip over my father's troubles at Westminster, which were widely reported in all the papers. I could hardly wait to get away for the holidays at the same rambling old house on the Isle of Wight that we had rented the previous summer. But it was not the same.

I remember hours spent sitting at the window watching the rain splashing on to the weed-grown terrace. Mummy was even more irritable than usual, always telling me to switch off the radio when I was listening to the Top Twenty, while Daddy was spiritually miles away, lost in his own reveries or sitting at an escritoire covering page after page in his almost indecipherable hand. He seemed to have aged overnight and we no longer talked as we used to on our long walks along the beach. Usually so dapper, he seemed not to care any more about shaving every morning, and the order for Scotch from the off-licence in the village mounted dramatically.

There was no television in our holiday house so I had to rely on my tranny for entertainment, listening to 'Saturday Club' and 'Easy Beat' on the BBC and Radio Luxembourg, rising and falling on waves of static. It was the sound of 'She Loves You' by the Beatles which was in my head as I returned to Bridgelands, after the summer we never had, almost with a sense of relief.

The school was housed in a Victorian stockbroker's folly, one half Rhineland schloss, the other half a perfect copy of a Loire chateau, and this schizophrenia was reflected in the attitudes governing its pupils. In Littlehampton and as far away as Bognor Regis or Worthing, Bridgelands' girls were known by their traditional chocolate brown uniform, velour hats and sensible shoes. It was also rumoured that they were not all that they should be, although many a local youth might have known otherwise.

As a progressive school, an interest in mod culture was not discouraged but a line was drawn at our doing our hair in the huge hollow bouffant style which was then in favour. Escaping to Brighton on the train on Saturday afternoons, the more daring of us bought Miners make-up in Woolworth's and gave ourselves deathly white faces with sunken black Dusty Springfield eyes, which we scrubbed off in the station loo before returning to school. My most prized possession, kept hidden in a locker, and smuggled in and out of school in a duffel bag, was a pair of slim shoes with Italian winkle-picker points and stiletto heels.

This sort of gear was part of our secret lives, together with after-lights-out conversations about sex and pills, the sort that prevented you having babies and the sort that turned you on and speeded you up. Some of the older girls boasted about their trips on amphetamines in the changing rooms after a brisk game of lacrosse.

We had an Indian summer that year as autumn drifted by with pale blue skies beyond the playing field where the leaves of the elms were beginning to turn reddish brown and gold. Even compulsory games seemed bearable as the Beatles' triumphant number one hit continued to soar across the firmament.

She loves you,
Yeah, yeah, yeah . . .

It was not a phrase our English mistress found particularly elegant but, as I said, Bridgelands was a progressive school and the older girls (from thirteen upwards) were privileged to be ATWRSG – 'Allowed to watch "Ready, Steady, Go".' This went out just after six on a Friday evening with the most popular groups playing and young swingers from the Scene Club in Soho grooving away among the cameras, lights and cables.

This was the high point of our week, our weekly fix of the records, clothes and dances that were in and therefore us, our chance to savour vicariously the mod culture of the capital which flourished at places like the Scene Club, the Mecca, the Hammersmith Palais, the Purley Orchard and the Streatham Locarno. Few of us had been to any of these places, but television conjured up for us a mock psychedelic experience which our elders could neither understand nor participate in. We are the young ones, the world is ours. Unlike our teachers, Cathy McGowan, the presenter of 'Ready, Steady, Go', was on our wavelength.

One Friday evening in November, just as the show began, our idol was brusquely interrupted by an unbelievable announcement. A grave face suddenly appeared on the screen and a solemn voice said simply: 'President Kennedy has been assassinated.'

There was a shocked silence and then one of the big girls, a sixth former, started to cry. Soon most of us were weeping.

Supper was forgotten and so was lights-out as we sat up with the entire staff watching the bulletins as they came in.

The President, so young, vital in contrast to our own faded neo-Edwardian leader, had been shot in full view of a television audience as he rode in an open car through the city of Dallas. Even though we cared little about politics, a shadow seemed to fall on our lives at that moment. Around the Kennedys and their court at the White House, Camelot had gathered, and now a bullet from a crazed assassin had shattered the illusion like a broken mirror.

28

Harold Wilson was on course to become the next incumbent of number 10 Downing Street, but for the time being it was occupied by the Earl of Home, appointed by a coterie of Old Etonians to become Prime Minister when Harold Macmillan fell ill.

'After half a century of democratic advance,' said Wilson, 'the whole process has ground to a halt with a fourteenth earl.'

Douglas-Home retorted blandly, 'I suppose Mr Wilson is really, when you come to think of it, the fourteenth Mr Wilson,' but his riposte, and indeed his very presence at the head of government, was out of tune with the times.

Sitting in the conference hall in Scarborough listening somewhat cynically to his leader's vision of the New Improved Jerusalem, Frank Cole privately admitted that you had to hand it to Wilson. He had kept his head down on the deeply divisive issue of disarmament and allowed Bevan and Gaitskell to fight it out over foreign affairs and the H-bomb.

Now he had found a way of by-passing the interneicine quarrels which had bedevilled the party for years by concentrating on an issue over which they could all agree. In the process, the traditional cloth cap of the Labour supporter could be exchanged for a microscope and a white coat. Brilliant. But Frank joined in less than wholeheartedly when the delegates cheered and clapped Harold Wilson's vague words about a technological revolution. He no longer wanted power in the way that he had Wanted it with a capital W when he first took his seat in the House of Commons.

True, he made an effort to mend his fences down at West Wickham, but it was a lacklustre effort and he felt little confidence in his personal future. In an effort to revitalize him, Dorothy decided upon an essentially 1930s tonic, a Mediterranean cruise. Daddy at first baulked at the idea, imagining palm court orchestras and stuffy cocktail parties for which one had to dress, make polite conversation and answer idiotic questions from the sort of people who were impressed by celebrity.

'I can't imagine anything less like a holiday,' he said.

'But it will do you good,' Dorothy insisted, showing him the brochures which she had collected from Thomas Cook. 'Sea air and sunshine will work wonders for you. And we'll take the children – our first family holiday together abroad.'

Nigel, released for the holidays from his captivity as one of the lowest forms of life at Harrow School, greeted the idea with enthusiasm. I imagined it would be the greatest bore of all time but refrained from saying so. P & O Orient with its memories of serving the Empire was as remote from my imagination as the rituals of crocodile hunters in Papua New Guinea. My mother's assurances that these days cruise liners catered for teenagers with juke boxes, hot dog stalls and rumpus rooms only served to add to my foreboding. Glossy brochure photographs showing couples in evening dress leaning against the rail watching the sunset might have seemed romantic to Dorothy.

To me the whole scene looked merely passé. People no longer travelled the world in ships, they went in jet planes. In any case, at fourteen I had reached an age where going on holiday with parents was more of an inescapable chore than a pleasure to be eagerly anticipated as it had been just a summer or two before.

'Frankly,' I told them, 'I'd rather go hitch-hiking in France or even go on a package holiday to Majorca – at least there'd be people of my own age to talk to.'

But Mummy ignored our whingeing and bludgeoned us into it. Of course it had to be P & O first class and she booked us on the *Canberra*, at that time a shiny new vessel encapsulating its owners' attempts to get with it and come to terms with the swinging sixties. It looked like a vast overgrown luxury yacht and its trendy young designer had given it rakish twin funnels set at the stern instead of midships and painted a bilious shade of yellow.

Its sheer size was impressive as we mounted the gangway, having left our baggage-laden Rover in the charge of armies of porters, but Daddy remarked that it totally lacked the dowager-duchess class of a Cunarder. Stewards in white jackets fussed around, ushering us to our splendid cabins with large windows looking out over the bows. Nigel and I had a stateroom to ourselves. It was novel, and although I was predisposed to find the whole experience the ultimate in mind-blowing boredom, I could not help but enjoy the departure with the band of the Royal Marines in white helmets playing on the quayside as we threw streamers over the side–'A Life on the Ocean Wave', 'Rule Britannia'. It reminded me of those old-fashioned Pathé News-reels they sometimes showed on television.

The next pleasant surprise was the navigation officer. We encountered him on a guided tour of the bridge, as we passed and exchanged salutes with the New Zealand Steamship Company's *Waranui*, bound north. Over the next two or three days as we rounded the Rock of Gibraltar and cruised along the coasts of Ibiza and Majorca, I draped myself all over the deck in my skimpiest bikini hoping to attract his attention. But whenever he passed by, handsome as the devil in his crisply pressed whites, he failed (to my intense disappointment) to give me a second glance.

When they were not fixed on some indiscernible landmark on the far horizon, his hypnotic Viking blue eyes invariably rested, I noticed, on the posterior of a raddled blonde of at least twenty-five who paraded herself daily in what were called hot-pants. I thought this very unseemly behaviour for an old woman like her.

I found it difficult to concentrate on anything other than the navigation officer. When we anchored in twenty-two fathoms off Cannes harbour near the aircraft carrier *Roosevelt* and a small fleet of other American warships, I hoped that he would be going ashore and that we might bump into him in a relaxed off-duty moment. I rehearsed introductory comments such as: 'How clever of you to find the way here' and 'I'm terribly interested in astronomy', but the opportunity to use them did not present itself.

The night after we left Cannes I was leaning against the rail contemplating the calm, moonlit surface of the sea when I saw mysterious flashes on the horizon.

'That's Stromboli,' said a deep voice at my side. 'It's a volcanic island.'

It was Him.

Of course, I could not think of a single intelligent thing to say except: 'What is our position?' And then, silly fool, I went scarlet all over.

'Darling,' said my mother, 'I do wish you'd join in things a bit more instead of lying there with your nose in a book all the time. Why don't you enter the sports?'

'I hate games,' I told her. 'I get enough of that stuff at school. This is supposed to be a holiday.'

'Nigel seems to be enjoying it,' said Dorothy.

'He's just a kid,' I replied. 'It's all right for him.'

Nigel was eleven, not even into puberty yet, although I caught him peeking when I came out of the bathroom with nothing on and hastily covered myself with a towel. I did not much like the idea of sharing a room with my little brother, who was at the nasty little boy stage, all sniggers and changing-room filth.

Although I stood head and shoulders above him, he and I were entered as Anthony and Cleopatra in the fancy dress competition. It was our steward's idea, enthusiastically approved by mother, who believed that it would get me 'into things', perhaps. Norman, the steward, devoted hours of his time to moulding a breastplate, helmet and shield for Nigel out of gold and silver foil and bits of cardboard. He wore mother's gold sandals which laced up above the ankles.

'That man's bent,' growled Daddy. 'He's got sweaty hands.'

'Darling, don't be prejudiced,' said Dorothy, laughing. 'He's a perfect treasure. Absolutely super and adorable.'

She liked being waited upon and having Norman was like having one's own personal servant. He brought the morning tea and the ship's paper to the cabin, cleaned shoes, ran errands. Frank was irritated by the man's fussing around every evening, brushing and laying out his dinner suit on the bed.

'I wish he'd lay *my* dress out for me,' said Dorothy, pulling a face.

I quite liked being Cleopatra, wearing false eyelashes and a black wig which Norman got from somewhere. He was fat and middle-aged and he did sweat rather. His hands seemed to touch my bottom more often than was necessary as he draped my robe (a borrowed P & O bedsheet) around me.

Nigel and I won first prize in the fancy dress and Dorothy was delighted, but it made her pester me even more to socialize. 'Try mixing with some of the other young people,' she suggested. 'You're not the only teenager on this cruise, you know.'

'They're all so *wet*,' I answered, and pointing out one of the reluctant youths who had been dragged along on this cruise by his parents went on: 'I mean, look at him. He's spotty and his hair's cut so short that his ears stick out and he wears socks *and* sandals. How square can you get?'

'He seems a perfectly nice, well-mannered young man to me,' said Dorothy, applying another coat of Piz Buin to her already mahogany-brown folds of flesh.

'Of course he's nice,' I exclaimed. 'Too nice by half. I asked him if he liked the Beatles and he said no, insectology wasn't his scene, but he's very into Scifi and would like to fly to the moon. I wish he'd go now.'

'What about the dances and parties – you should be having such fun,' said Mummy.

'I hate all that formal dressing up and shaking hands and all that stuff,' I replied, 'and the dances – when it's not Palm Court it's just too embarrassing seeing all those old fogies making fools of themselves trying to do the Twist.'

'Really, you're quite impossible,' sighed Dorothy, exasperated.

'I'm going for a swim,' I announced to escape further parental censure. As I picked my way among the deckchairs full of somnolent geriatrics I spotted the steward with the Elvis Presley haircut. I had noticed him before among the men using the crew swimming pool which our cabin windows overlooked. Now, as he bent over one of the tables with his tray, setting out glasses of gin and tonic and Martini with a tinkle of ice cubes, he turned his head towards me and winked. I pretended not to notice but from that moment the cruise became interesting again.

The crew, of course, were not supposed to fraternize with the passengers, but that evening just before dinner when he was serving drinks at the bar I went up on my own and ordered a Coca-Cola.

'Sign here, please, Miss,' he said, handing me a slip on the back of which was written: 'Meet me on A deck, aft, at 0100.'

An assignation. My knees turned to jelly at the prospect. The handsome navigation officer was dismissed as a square, as my attentions focused on the slim young steward with the black hair sleeked back with grease. I went to bed earlier than usual and lay awake listening to the regular breathing of my little brother and counting the minutes on the luminous dial of my wristwatch.

Just before one I slipped noiselessly out of the cabin and headed towards A deck, to wait in the shadows of the twin yellow funnels, trailing a plume of exhaust against the warm night sky. Somewhere far below the engines thrummed away while everyone except the duty watch slept.

Five past one, and still no sign of my admirer. Was he having me on?

No sooner had I thought it than he appeared around the corner of a stack of deckchairs, beckoning me over. He had laid a mattress on the deck, out of sight behind the deckchairs, and we sat down cross-legged and side by side. He told me his name was Kevin and offered me a cigarette, which I accepted even though I hated smoke.

I don't want him to think I'm just a kid.

He talked about himself and his hometown, Liverpool, and the Cavern Club, which the Beatles had made famous virtually overnight.

'Have you ever met the Beatles?' I asked.

'Met 'em? I've known the time when I lent Paul McCartney a couple of bob for his bus fare,' he boasted. 'And George Harrison's dad has often taken me for a drive – in his bus.'

I surmised that he must be joking but I could not be sure.

'Aye,' he went on, 'I knew 'em all before they went to Hamburg and started making it big. Saturday night at the Picton Lane busmen's social club – that was about their lot then. Johnny and the Moondogs, they were called, though they'd call themselves anything that came into their heads. John and Paul would sing and play as the Nurk Twins sometimes.'

That made me laugh, but I was impressed by Kevin's Merseyside connections.

'I've done a bit of performing with the old electric guitar myself,' he went on, casually slipping an arm round my waist.

'I've got the same as John Lennon started with, a Hofner "Club 40", semi-solid with two knobs on it.'

'I'd like to hear you play,' I said admiringly.

'Next time you're in Liverpool, drop into the Cavern,' he replied, dropping his cigarette butt on to the deck and putting his heel on it. I made a move to throw mine over the side but he took it from me. 'Never throw fag ends over the side – they might get sucked back in through a porthole and start a fire.' He ground out my cigarette end on the deck alongside his. 'You know, you're a good-looking bird. I've been fancying you ever since we sailed from Southampton. What do they call you?'

'Jenny,' I told him.

'How old are you, Jenny?'

'Sixteen,' I lied and he seemed quite prepared to believe me. He lay back on the mattress and pulled me gently down beside him, kissing me a few times. The dark Aegean water rippled past the rail and the sky above us was speckled with stars, a brochure description come true, for once.

'What are those islands called?' I asked, pointing to darker shapes against the lonely sea and sky.

'Pelago and Khelidromi,' he said. 'We're on passage through the Pelago Channel.'

The Greek names sounded funny pronounced with a Liverpudlian accent and I couldn't help smiling. His hand was now under my T-shirt and I wasn't wearing a bra.

'You've got a smashing pair of tits,' he said.

It was the nicest thing anyone had said to me and I positively purred. Some of the kinkier girls at school played around with one another after games or in the dorm but this was *much* more exciting. I relished the thought of telling them about it when I got back after the hols.

'Let's get into one of the boats,' suggested Kevin. 'It's more private, like.'

I eagerly allowed myself to be led down two flights of stairs to the boat deck, glancing anxiously around in case we were seen. But there was no one about. One of the lifeboats was swung inboard for maintenance and Kevin clambered nimbly up the side, pulling me up after him. Inside it smelt of pitch and canvas and saltwater.

'Take your T-shirt off,' said Kevin, and meekly I obeyed. My breasts, shielded from the sun by my bikini top, were pools of white amidst the darkness of the rest of my skin. I felt his lips and tongue on my nipples.

'You don't think I've got a bit too much?' I ventured, breathlessly. 'My boobs, I mean.'

'No, they're great,' he said. 'They really turn me on.'

And to show it, he deftly unzipped his fly and guided my hand towards it. Involuntarily, I recoiled.

'What's the matter?' he demanded. 'Don't you like it?'

'It's funny,' I said.

'*Funny*?' His male ego was bruised. 'What's funny about it?'

'I mean, it's so big.'

Heavens, if he sticks it inside me, I shall die.

Now Kevin's hand was inside my pants, caressing the soft curly hair between my legs, his index finger probing passionately. Then, just as I was going mad with desire, he suddenly asked. 'That old bloke you're with – is he your Dad?'

'Yes. Why?'

'Well, he's famous, ain't he? I've seen him on the box myself,' Kevin went on. 'What's he do for a living then?'

'Daddy's a Member of Parliament,' I told him.

'Christ!' exclaimed Kevin, vastly impressed. 'Me, Kevin Slattery, screwing an MP's daughter.'

When it was over and I was back in my cabin, taking care not to wake Nigel, I was not altogether sure whether I had enjoyed it or not. The preliminaries had been fabulous but the actual thing, with me on my back on the bare boards in the bottom of the boat and Kevin sprawled on top of me, was all brute potency and really rather disgusting.

On reflection, none of Bridgelands' biology classes and sex lessons had prepared me for this crude reality, yet notions of romantic love were démodé. Is that all there is to it?

In point of fact, I was still a virgin. Kevin had done his best to get my pants off but I instinctively thwarted him. Even so I still feared I might in some mysterious way become pregnant. Kevin seemed so experienced and mature to me. Actually, he was probably no more than eighteen, a virgin sailor for all his worldly-wise talk. The older generation had convinced themselves that sexual intercourse began, as Philip Larkin put it, in 1963 and that they had missed something. My generation fell for the propaganda.

Frank and Dorothy suspected nothing of my initiation when I cheerfully faced them over the breakfast table next morning, with our ship anchored off the seafront at Thessaloniki. What did they know about sex anyway? In any case, unknown to me, Frank had other things on his mind. One of the main items on the morning news from the BBC in London, relayed directly to our cabins with the chimes of Big Ben and the strains of 'Lillibullero', concerned the arrest of a businessman called Graham Moody on charges of spying for the Russians. Even in my state of euphoria, I noticed that Daddy looked ghastly, although I did not connect it with the BBC news, which scarcely registered in my mind at that time. He had been morose and out of sorts throughout the trip, complaining constantly that he hadn't wanted to come, it was Dorothy's idea and cruises were 'package holidays done up in dinner suits'.

After breakfast, which he hardly touched, he returned to his cabin and spent the rest of the day there smoking, drinking Scotch and listening to radio bulletins even though it was a gloriously sunny day and most of the passengers went ashore in the ship's boats. The temperature was in the nineties and after a day on the sun-baked beach Mummy and I were glad to get back to the air-conditioned comfort of the ship and a cooling bath.

'My husband has a tummy upset, he's staying in bed,' said Dorothy, explaining Frank's absence from the captain's table at dinner that evening.

The truth was that Frank had consumed the best part of a bottle of Johnnie Walker Black Label and was now comatose. It was just Mummy and I at dinner with the other guests of the captain. Nigel went to children's tea and it was in recognition of my adolescence that I was allowed to join the grown-ups. Dolled up in my first evening frock, full-length, turtle-necked, sleeveless, I looked round the dining room hoping for an admiring glance from Kevin. But he was not on duty that evening.

Enchanting Greek islands slipped by unnoticed in the darkness while the ship's band played hits from *South Pacific* and girls in imitation grass skirts and paper flowers danced the hula-hula. Next morning we awoke to find ourselves docked at Piraeus alongside an equally spanking Russian cruise ship. Stavros Niarchos had invited us to be his guests at his private beach at Glyfada and a gleaming silver-grey Mercedes was waiting at the quayside to take us there.

Frank looked slightly better but was still somehow distant and preoccupied. Even the discovery of the shipping millionaire's little oasis of green in the arid brown landscape failed to bring back his old sparkle, but I was captivated by it.

Mr Niarchos himself was not there. This was just one of his private beaches, we were told, and he was at this moment away on one of his private islands, slaving over a cool telephone, no doubt. We were given our own changing rooms and plied with cooling drinks and appetizers. I remember lying in the shade of a fig tree watching the gardeners watering the lawns and flower-beds while teams of small boys scoured the beach removing the tiniest bit of rubbish and debris, even pebbles. From a nearby kitchen came the tempting smell of fish grilling over charcoal.

Daddy started drinking again, ouzo this time, which I thought tasted like disgusting medicine, and spent a long time indoors on the telephone. Mother did not seem to mind because a rich young Greek was paying attention to us. His name was Adrian Aghios and he was quite good-looking in his oily sort of way, although I resented him eyeing my body up and down with undisguised lust.

If only Kevin was here, it would be heaven.

'One finds the most awful people on cruises,' Mummy was saying. 'It really is Butlin's afloat. The other day I was accosted by a really dreadful little man in lace-up shoes and *braces*. He actually went down to dinner dressed like that.'

'You should come for a cruise with me, dear lady, in my yacht,' said Mr Aghios smoothly. 'That's her over there.'

He pointed to a motorized schooner moored to a buoy just a hundred yards out from the beach.

'She looks super,' said Dorothy, ogling him like a flapper.

'Of course, it is nothing beside what my friend Stavros has,' replied Adrian modestly, and turning towards me: 'Do you like waterskiing and skindiving, Jenny?' He made even the word 'skin' sound lecherous.

'I don't know. I haven't tried it,' I told him.

Take your eyes off my tits, you revolting person.

'This sand is too hot even to walk on, it burns the soles of one's feet. Let's go out to the boat, it'll be a little cooler on the water, and we can dive and swim,' suggested Adrian.

My mother and brother eagerly agreed to this proposition, I less readily, while Frank was hauled out of his comfortable cane chair in the shade of a fig tree and persuaded to join us. Aghios ferried us to his yacht in an Avon inflatable with an outboard motor. We sat under a striped awning in the cockpit sipping Pimm's or lemonade and Adrian took some photographs while Nigel experimented with the Agfa 35-millimetre Mummy had given him for his birthday.

'What a pity the *Canberra* sails this evening,' sighed Dorothy. 'I should so like to spend the night here.'

We sat smiling at the cameras in our family group, showing nothing of the stresses which lay just beneath the surface of our comfortable lives, bolstered by power, possessions and position, although Mummy chided Daddy for not having shaved: 'That horrid blue shadow will show up in this light.'

Looking now at those banal family album snapshots of the four of us, lounging, drinks in hand, on a yacht in the Aegean, I cannot suppress a shudder. It has become a notorious family portrait.

'We're leaving for Santorini tomorrow,' Adrian was saying. 'Do you know it? Oh, well, we call it Thera, you know, from the son of Autesion who was called Thiras. He was Viceroy of Sparta.'

'I did Greek history at school,' growled Frank, and yawned.

Dorothy glared at him while the garrulous Greek continued unabashed: 'There are two lesser islands as well, you see they were formed by a gigantic volcanic eruption hundreds of years before Christ. It blew the top off the mountain and the sea poured into the crater through three cracks, destroying a whole civilization like the Minoans of Crete. It's very, how you say, picturesque – the main town is perched right at the top of a cliff above the harbour and the only way up is by a long, winding stone stairway. You either go on foot or you can hire a mule to carry you, there's no other transport. Actually, the last earthquake was in '56 and they're only just beginning to pick up the threads again.'

'It sounds an enchanting spot to visit,' said Dorothy.

'Then, gentle lady, come with me,' begged the preposterous man, kissing her hand. 'If we set sail now, and keep going all night, we can be there by tomorrow afternoon. Leave your cruise liner to the secretaries and shopkeepers.'

'Oh, Mummy, *could* we go?' pleaded Nigel. 'It sounds so exciting.'

'Why don't we?' cried Dorothy, clapping her hands and giggling.

'You've had too much wine,' grunted Frank, still in his

grouchy, grumpy mood. 'I'm going for a swim.'

'I'll come with you,' I said, and Nigel jumped up too, while Adrian dashed off down the steps to the main saloon and reappeared beaming over an armful of rubber flippers, goggles, masks and snorkel tubes.

'Here, try them on,' he invited us. 'They're all sizes.'

We had never tried snorkling before. It was like entering a new dimension, a cool green world where one came eyeball to eyeball with all manner of fishes and underwater creatures and drifted on the surface like flotsam, gazing down at the brilliant colours of secret gardens and grottoes.

Daddy's skin was still milky white, unlike the rest of us who were as bronzed as fisherfolk. He kept a T-shirt on while he was swimming, to protect his back from the fierce rays of the afternoon sun. He swam off on his own with his slow measured breast stroke. I could see his grey head bobbing among the languid ripples.

Nigel, having failed to get the hang of the diving equipment or master the breathing technique in five minutes, threw his mask and tube back on the deck and amused himself by practising dives from the poop.

Adrian Aghios stuck to me like my shadow, diving when I dived, drifting when I drifted, grabbing me on the slightest pretext.

'Hey, Jenny, look at this, an octopus, near that yellowy green rock, down there, can you see it?'

He called it an otcopus, one of his rare mispronunciations. Most of the time his English was faultless, but I tired of his wandering hands before I tired of underwater exploration and returned dripping seawater to the deck. Adrian disappeared below, calling out to me: 'Come and have a nice freshwater shower.' I ignored him.

Mummy was stretched out on a sun lounger, sound asleep. I touched her shoulder and her eyes opened behind the owl-like brown saucers of her Polaroid sunglasses.

'Where's Daddy? Why hasn't he come back?'

'Oh, darling, don't be neurotic,' she answered sleepily. 'I expect he's gone for a dip.'

'I *know* he went swimming,' I said, impatiently. 'He was with us. I watched him for ages, swimming farther and farther away. Now he's vanished.'

Dorothy sat up now and stared out to sea, shading her face with her hands against the glare.

'Are you sure?' she asked anxiously. 'Your father's not a powerful swimmer. It's not like him to go very far away, and out of his depth, too.'

A dreadful feeling of foreboding suddenly overcame me.

'Mummy, do something, please,' I cried out. 'Sound the alarm, quick. He must be in trouble. Are there sharks here?'

Hearing my shouts, Adrian Aghios came running and called out in Greek to people in other boats nearby. Then he went to the klaxon and sent blasts echoing about. The beach, one moment dozing in the sun, became in the next a teeming anthill with people dashing here and there shouting at the tops of their voices. Boats were launched and churned up the placid waters as they zigzagged across the bay.

Throughout the afternoon and into the evening they searched, while the brassy sun sank gradually towards the horizon. It seemed like a bad dream, our movements uncontrolled, our voices disembodied. Darkness came with the dramatic suddenness of the Aegean. They brought back no body. Daddy had simply disappeared.

We could hardly take in what had happened. Still in a dream, we allowed ourselves to be marooned among the oriental carpets and Grecian urns of the King George Hotel. The *Canberra* sailed for Southampton at 7.30 that evening with my black-haired Kevin. Ships that passed in the night.

I stood on a balcony overlooking Syntagma Square and watched Greek roués trying to pick up female tourists outside the American Express office and the *evzones* changing the guard. Even in the midst of my worry and shock over the disappearance of my father, I could not help being amused by their quaint ballet shirts, the bobbles on their shoes and their operatic gestures.

The sound of bouzouki music drifted across the square from the tavernas while in the room behind me Mummy sat in a Louis XV chair and cried. My little brother was crying. I silently chastised myself for the fact that I was not crying. This was before I gave up guilt for ever.

The next morning an English journalist in a crumpled khaki

safari suit with wine stains down the front came to see Mummy and ask a lot of questions. After that the phone never stopped ringing until we left three days later to catch a plane back to London. The papers at home were full of 'MP's Mysterious Disappearance' for a day or two, then it all died away and by the time I went back to Bridgelands our grief had become a purely personal affair.

Daddy was presumed drowned. My friends and teachers offered their sincere condolences but there were no tears as there had been at the death of John F. Kennedy. How very, very strange that the death of my own father should grieve us less than that of a foreign President.

'Poor Jenny,' gushed Miss Cartwright, who taught PE and history to the fifth and sixth forms. 'You were so fond of your father and he of you. It's a cruel loss.'

Back in London, Dorothy bore the legal and bureaucratic formalities with quiet dignity, accepting the necessity for an application to the High Court before death could be presumed in law. She wrote a long letter to Ralph Greedie in New Zealand and he replied: 'My heart goes out to you in your sad loss. Frank was a good man and a dear, kind friend of mine. If at any time you feel the need to get away from all your cares and sorrows my home is yours.'

How Esther Rutley reacted to the news of my father's disappearance we had no way of knowing, since she had disappeared from her bed-sitter in Lambeth, but it was kept from Grandma Cole, who at that time was in King's College Hospital with a broken hip. She had been trying to prune rambler roses on the fence in her beloved little garden at Amen Road and had fallen from her precarious perch on a stepladder. It was no use anybody trying to tell her that at eighty-four she was getting rather old for that kind of activity.

The general election that autumn seemed an anticlimax. The older ones among the girls at Bridgelands were allowed to stay up until midnight watching the results coming in on the television. Owing to the peculiarities of the British electoral system, Labour ended up with more seats than it had had since 1945 even though it received fewer votes. I could not conceal my jubilation as it became apparent that Harold Wilson would be able to form the next government, despite disapproving glances from the staff, except Miss Cartwright. She made no secret of her politics and had been driving around with a 'Let's Go With Labour' sticker in the back window of her Mini. I felt satisfaction, too, when the result from West Wickham came in. A Tory candidate had been returned with a majority of just a few hundred over the Labour candidate, Brian Bottle.

It now had to be explained to Jenny, up and about the ward at King's College Hospital with the aid of a tubular steel walking frame, why her son was not in the fray. Her reaction was one of blazing anger.

'Why wasn't I told?' she demanded of Dorothy.

'You were very ill at the time - we didn't feel you were up to taking the shock of such terrible news.'

'What do you take me for,' she said fiercely, 'a weak-minded old woman? I've had more suffering in my lifetime than you could ever imagine. I bore him on my own, raised him on my own - don't you think I had a right to know?'

The ward sister, alarmed by her raised voice, came over and said soothingly: 'Now, Mrs Cole, don't upset yourself. It's not good for you.'

'Stop treating me like a child, or an imbecile,' retorted Jenny. 'My only son presumed drowned in a foreign country - and I'm the last to hear.'

She turned to Dorothy and added icily: 'I never liked you, Miss Plumley-Greene, and after this I don't believe I shall ever be able to forgive you.'

Dear Granny Cole, always a fighter, constitutionally incapable of diplomatic evasion, how I loved her. Because of Frank's death we were closer than ever.

'The death of a loved one makes us realize that life moves irresistibly onwards,' she wrote to me that autumn. 'Sorrow like ours forces us to realize that there is no escape from change, decay, the unexpected, the tragedy and the comedy in our lives. None of us ever knows, however secure we might imagine ourselves to be, however rich we are, or important in wordly terms, what the next moment may bring. Never believe otherwise, my dear.'

In her declining years, the Catholic faith in which she was reared resurrected itself and she began to attend mass again after a break of many decades. Mummy, of course, was just as upset as we were but she derived comfort not from religion but from the unexpected downfall of the hated Mr Bottle.

'Your father held that seat against the Tories by the sheer force of his own personality,' she told me proudly, 'and he would have won it again despite the opposition from within of little people who were jealous of his success.'

Nevertheless, Harold Wilson's list of Ministers caused her more than a slight pang of regret.

'Denis Healey has got Defence, I see, and Harold's given Aviation to Stonehouse – your father might well have had that if things had turned out differently.'

The Plumley-Greenes were no more enamoured of the dynamic Mr Wilson with his pipe and his tartan-collared Gannex mac than they had been of Clement Attlee a generation earlier. They scoffed at Harold's preference for cigars in private and his ridiculous working-class affectation of liking his meals smothered with HP sauce, and being photographed with the cast of 'Coronation Street'.

The Plumley-Greenes, in short, believed that Wilson was a dangerous little demagogue who would interfere with the established order, encourage strikers and send England even farther down the drain. Dorothy shared, as she had always done, her parents' class attitudes. Of course, it would have been different if Frank had been part of the Government. She felt very sorry for herself.

'Jenny, how cruel life can be sometimes,' she moaned.

I was home from Bridgelands for the Christmas holidays and to cheer ourselves we went to Harrods to buy lots of frivolous presents, then took a cab to Fortnum & Mason's for tea at the Soda Fountain.

The telephone started ringing just as Mummy put the key in the door at Albany Street. She dumped an armful of brightly wrapped packages onto the marble-topped table and answered: 'Yes, Dorothy Cole speaking . . . Who's that? Jack! What a surprise, we haven't heard from you since Frank . . . What's that? Are you sure?'

The tone of her voice sharply changed, became cold, hostile.

'No, I know nothing whatever about it. Nothing at all. No I don't wish to comment. Certainly not.'

She put the phone down and reached out to me as if to stop herself falling.

'That was Jack Harris,' she said, so faintly that I could hardly hear her. She looked terrible. 'You know, Jack Harris, your father's old friend from the *Chronicle*. He's with something called the *Sun* now.'

'Mummy, what is it? What's wrong?'

'Your father,' gasped Dorothy. 'They say he's alive. In Moscow. Jack has talked to him on the phone.'

29

In a long interview in the *Sun*, the new title of the *Daily Herald*, born like the new Labour Government 'of the age we live in', Frank Cole described how he faked his own death at Glyfada simply by swimming away from the yacht and coming ashore a short way down the coast at another, less private, beach where he was unnoticed among the crowds. He had his passport, landing permit and five thousand drachmas in a waterproof money belt under his T-shirt. After drying out a little he hired a taxi to take him back to Piraeus. If the driver thought there was anything odd about a fare with no shoes on his feet, he kept it to himself.

At Piraeus, Frank walked through customs and immigration, but instead of boarding the *Canberra* walked straight onto the Russian ship berthed alongside it. They were expecting him following the long conversations he had had on the telephone that morning with the Soviet Embassy in Athens and, through them, with the KGB. A cabin was waiting for him, together with a wardrobe of clothes and a complete set of personal effects. They sailed a couple of hours ahead of the *Canberra*, heading for a port in the Black Sea.

'I deeply regret the pain and grief I have caused my wife, my mother and my two young children,' he was quoted as saying, 'but I had no alternative when I heard that Graham Moody had been arrested in London. Moody was my "agent runner" and I knew that I would be next on the list. M15 had been on my tail for well over a year. I want to stress that I gave away no military secrets for the simple reason that I did not know any. My role was to give the KGB inside information on the political scene at Westminster and to forecast possible changes in the strategic deployment of British armed forces. It is a relief to be free from the pressures which have been on me for the past few years. By faking my death I hoped to obliterate my past life and start a new one as a citizen of the Soviet Union.'

Graham Moody was eventually sentenced to nine years' imprisonment for selling secret information to the Russians. There was irony in the fact that the first report of Frank Cole's reappearance from the dead appeared in the paper which had launched him on his journalistic career in the 1930s, and ironic, too, that it was written by his oldest friend. Jack Harris sorely needed that prominent front-page by-line and the kudos that went with it.

Only a month or so earlier, the *Evening Chronicle* had finally folded, leaving many of its former employees out of work with little prospect of finding new jobs in Fleet Street. Jack happened to be at the Endell Street offices looking up old friends when the tip-off came that Frank Cole was alive and well in Moscow. The source of this information was never disclosed. But Jack telephoned a contact of his and managed to obtain the telephone number in Moscow at which Frank could be reached.

Through this lucky break, Jack was able to secure a place for himself on the political staff of the *Sun*. In his more reflective moments he recalled Frank's words when they were reunited after the war. Winners, losers and survivors. Now Frank Cole was the loser, while Jack Harris was the winning survivor.

Certainly, his scoop was the talk of Fleet Street bars for a day or two. No sooner had the early editions of the *Sun* arrived on its competitors' news desks shortly after 11 p.m. than reporters were sent to stake out our house. By midnight there was a little knot of them on the pavement, walking up and down staring up at the windows, or leaning against the area railings, gossiping and smoking.

At daybreak they were still there, but in significantly larger numbers. Occasionally, they rang the bell or pushed little notes through the letterbox asking for interviews. Mummy ignored them but, like the Profumos the previous year, we were under siege by the press in our own house.

When my grandparents called they had to fight their way through the crowd to reach our doorstep. Lady Plumley-Greene ploughed straight through the hacks like the *Queen Mary* on full steam. But she was not amused.

'My poor lamb,' I heard her saying to Mother on the other side of the drawing-room door. 'After all you've suffered recently, to have to put up with this vulgar harassment. I don't like to say this, but Poppa and I warned you from the start that Cole was not the man for you.'

'I tried so hard, Momsy,' wailed Dorothy. 'But now it's all wasted.'

'Breeding will out,' declared my grandmother. 'I suppose that slut of his will be joining him in Moscow.'

The photograph of Frank and Esther at the opening of the Establishment Club had been raked out of the files and was in all the papers, together with the family picture taken on the yacht at Glyfada. 'Frank Cole MP, pictured for the last time with his family on a yachting holiday in Greece on the day that he staged his own apparent suicide.' Adrian Aghios must have passed it on to journalists, though he hardly needed the money.

'They are welcome to each other,' I heard Mummy saying. 'I will not divorce him, though. I wouldn't give him that after all the sorrow and grief he has caused us. He's betrayed everyone. It's all such a mess. I've no idea how I stand with regard to insurance or the lease of the house or anything else. The lawyers and accountants are trying to sort it out and you know how expensive *that* will be. How could he do this to us?'

'How are the children taking it?' asked Lady Plumley-Greene.

'They don't know what to think, poor darlings,' answered Dorothy. 'Their confidence has been shattered.'

Then I heard the brigadier's voice, redolent of Cockburn's port and overripe Stilton: 'Dreadful business altogether, what. It's bad enough for a boy of that age to be let down by his father, and when the man's a traitor into the bargain . . .'

This made me so angry that I wanted to burst into the room and scream at him. What do *you* know about my father? You've always hated him. What right have you to say bad things about him? The thunder of blood rushing through my head made me miss some of what was being said.

'. . . bad enough at the club, but schoolboys can be perfect little swines to one another. I do hope young Nigel's tough enough to take it.'

'He must come down to us for the rest of the holiday,' Lady Plumley-Greene was saying.

What about me? Don't I have feelings as well as Nigel,

noticing the girls at school pointing and whispering, and the room suddenly going quiet as I come in? But instead of going into the drawing room and making them aware of me, I crept upstairs to my own room and sat on the bed staring at the dolls on the glass shelves above my dressing table. The dolls which Daddy brought me from all the countries he visited when I was a little girl.

How could he have just gone away from us like that, making us believe that he was dead? None of the papers that I read bothered to examine his motive for defecting to Russia: it was tacitly assumed to be political, given his background of being a man of the far Left, a fellow traveller with the Reds. Although an affair with Esther was implied, if not actually stated except in the outrageous print of *Private Eye*, it did not come out at the time that he had been blackmailed into cooperating with the KGB.

As I grew up in the 1960s when sexual mores were becoming more and more permissive, I would have considered it absurd that my father should have thrown away his position, his possessions and his reputation not from ideological conviction but because he had been secretly photographed having it off with an attractive woman who was not his wife. He had not been obliged to make any public statements about it, or tell any lies, yet like many men of his generation and class he was burdened by guilt over this liaison with a woman younger than his wife.

He certainly was not the first, or the last, prominent man to be subjected to pressure by the KGB once they had got something on him. My father's guilt was intensified in a curious way by the covered-up circumstances of his own birth, the lie of legitimacy that he grew up with. Now traitor was added to bastard in the calumnies against his name but it was not until several years later, when his papers and diaries came into my possession, that I discovered the true nature of the pressures under which my father finally cracked, and which I have set down for the first time in these pages.

At the time, aged only fifteen but wise beyond my years, I sensed that there was more to the affair than we knew. Hurt and resentful though I was of his deceiving us, I was relieved to know that he was not dead and gone as we had believed.

I know I will see him again now and I don't care what hurtful things Mummy, or Nanna or Grandpa say about him. He is still my Daddy and I love him, whatever he's done.

For the first time since that dreadful ominous sunbaked day at Glyfada, I wept for him. There in my room, overlooking the bare trees and greensward of Regent's Park, the tears came in a flood, splashing down on the pretty flowered pattern of my bedspread.

Like me, my grandmother Cole was unutterably thankful that Frank was alive and well, even if he was living in Moscow. Of course, she could not comprehend what had happened or why. She had been brought up to believe that patriotism and loyalty to one's monarch and country were the highest virtues, second only to the love of God.

Unlike Dorothy, when the inevitable pack of reporters arrived on her doorstep, she invited them in and made tea. She had only just returned to her home from hospital and could move about only very slowly, with the aid of a stick, but she insisted on playing hostess.

'My son is no traitor, as some people are claiming,' she told the impromptu news conference in her front parlour. 'He has worked hard in the cause of peace and he will continue to do so in Moscow as he did here in London. The real enemy of mankind is the H-bomb, whatever its nationality.'

'But he has admitted being an agent of the KGB,' pointed out one of the reporters.

'Young man,' said Jenny, with a dangerous glint in her sloe-black eyes, 'my son is no more a spy than you are. I should know. He has always followed the dictates of his conscience – fighting Fascism in the East End and in Spain in the 1930s. Before you were born, I dare say, but now it's all happening again right here. Just go outside the door and look around – see the swastikas scrawled on the walls. "Blacks Go Home". Well, young man, the Blacks are my neighbours and some are my friends. There's good and bad in every race. Some Jamaican boys were down here the other night chalking obscenities on *my* wall. I went out and talked to them and made them clean it up. They were not bad boys, just bored, with nothing to do and nowhere to go.'

Her faith in the human race, to say nothing of her grit, her stamina and her single-mindedness, was plain to see. The reporters stacked their cups and saucers neatly in the kitchen sink as they left. One of them who dared to come back, on the instructions of his editor, to offer her a five-figure sum for an exclusive series on the lines of 'My son, the Kremlin's Fourth Man in Britain', was shown the door.

Jack Harris came to see her in Amen Road, too, and was received (with another pot of tea, of course) as the old friend of the family that he was. His role in the affair was a difficult one. Having broken the story in the *Sun*, he was bound to follow up with further revelations and stay ahead of rival newspapers, but there was little he could write. After his initial coup, the Cole Affair became something of an embarrassment to him and he was frankly relieved when public interest in it began to die down.

Long before then Mummy decided that she had had enough of being in the limelight and cabled Ralph Greedie in Auckland: 'ARRIVING WITH JENNY BOAC FLIGHT 281 VIA KARACHI AND SINGAPORE AM WEDNESDAY'. Nigel was left behind with the Plumley-Greenes at the Oak House until it was time to go back to Harrow School.

My first view of Waitemata harbour and Manakau harbour was from the window of a Comet jet. 'Good morning, ladies and gentlemen, boys and girls,' said a disembodied New Zealand voice. 'We'll shortly be landing at Auckland International Airport. Please fasten your safety belts and extinguish all cigarettes.'

There below us lay a city built on gently sloping hills, surrounded by forests. The snow-capped mountains of South Island could be seen across the cerulean waters of the strait.

We seemed to have been flying for days and nights, relieved only by a short stopover in Singapore where we stepped out of the plane into the atmosphere of a blanket bath, scented with exotic flowers. I was not prepared for the shock of the appearance of the stranger who met us in the arrivals lounge at Auckland. The skin of his hand felt like parchment. How could Mummy bear to kiss that grinning slit in a face that was still a patchwork of grafts from those wartime repairs at East Grinstead?

Ralph could not have been friendlier. He stuck a pipe in his mouth and drove us the thirteen miles into the city with a continual stream of banter between pointing out the various sights.

'That's One Tree Hill – my house is up there. Just a bit of an old wood shack really, but the views are magnificent. I must take you up to Rotorua at the weekend. You've never seen anything like it. Geysers, boiling mud, spouts of steam gushing from the golf course. The Maoris lay on a bit of a song and a dance for the tourists. You'll love it, Jenny. Then after Christmas on Anniversary Day there's the Regatta, one of the biggest in the world you know, all the yachties take part. I'll be in *Spitfire* – that's my ketch, a fifty-footer and a real beauty. Wait till you see her. I'll take you deep-sea fishing as well. Marlin, shark, tuna . . . Extra good, young Jenny, extra good.'

I found him overwhelming, although he obviously meant well and was trying to put me at my ease. He just never stopped talking for a moment.

'. . . this is Queen Street and over there – ta-ra, ta-ra – the Greedie Emporium, selling everything from a hairpin to a motor mower . . .'

They were putting up Christmas decorations and a man on a ladder was arranging a group of papier mâché angels over the shopfront. He paused to wave at Ralph, and then wiped the sweat from his forehead. The sun beat down from a cloudless blue sky and the pavements were thronged with women in bright summer frocks. Harrods and Fortnum & Mason seemed to belong to another world.

It was the last place on earth I would have expected Mummy to be happy in, my mother who loved the social round of Ascot, Henley and Cowes, gossip about the royals, and being at the centre of things. When the actress Googie Withers was asked how she found New Zealand after a tour there she answered that it was difficult to say, it was shut when she arrived.

As Ralph Greedie put it: 'I'm afraid we're just a bunch of backward colonials out here. Every once in a while some bloke in pinstripes pops over here for a week or so, then nips back to report "It's all right, chaps, they're still there, keeping the supplies of butter and lamb going" . . . Of course, if there's another war, it'll be different again. We'll be included in the team. Awfully nice chaps these Kiwis, what. Just so long as we don't question the captain's authority.'

Mummy laughed. 'The same old Ralph,' she said.

I thought he was a funny old man too, once I had got over the way he looked. His 'bit of an old wood shack' on One Tree Hill turned out to be a gracious colonial-style mansion with manicured lawns lined with pohutukawa trees. His parents were dead and he lived there in bachelor ease, surrounded by every domestic convenience that modern technology could devise, from dishwasher to deep freeze. He had a cook-cum-housekeeper and a gardener, although the very idea of domestic servants was anathema to New Zealanders.

Yet for all their professed egalitarianism, and Uncle Ralph's proud assertions that 'there's no snobbery here – none of your Pox Britannica', the New Zealand Labour Party held coming-out dances for debutantes in long frocks and white gloves, to be received by party leaders in white ties and tails.

Mother, with her Roedean accent, her good breeding, her elegance and style, was able to dominate any social occasion at this level. And she did. When at coffee mornings, articles with such titles as 'The English Village Heritage' in the *New Zealand Herald* were discussed, Dorothy held the little circle spellbound with dissertations which might have come from the pages of *Country Life*.

In short, in New Zealand Dorothy could be the lady that she was. She felt at home there. It was not just the red mailboxes attached to the lampposts, or the policemen's helmets (white rather than black), white-painted cottages and winding country roads, or the green fields, but the fact that all Ralph's friends, although born in New Zealand, referred to England as 'Home' and were ardent royalists.

Week followed week unhurriedly as we drove in Ralph's vintage open Bentley along those country roads climbing into the mountains, admired quiescent volcanoes, swam from pink-coloured sands, watched Maori war-dances and bubbling mud, flashed across Auckland harbour in a plume of spray, spinnaker flying, ate egg and ham sandwiches washed down with sparkling pink wine called crackling. If you wanted to eat out you always took a picnic.

What was originally intended as a temporary escape, an extended holiday, gradually developed into permanent residence. Every time Dorothy said: 'We'd better start thinking about booking our passages home,' Ralph put his hand on hers and said: 'Not yet, stay a bit longer.' I was enrolled at a local girls' school.

The only happening that disturbed the peaceful tranquillity of our new lives was the news, briefly reported in the *Herald* and the *Auckland Star*, that the former British Labour MP Frank Cole had been granted Soviet citizenship and had been joined in exile by his former secretary, Esther Rutley.

None of Ralph's friends even mentioned it. There were no reporters hammering on the door for interviews, yet Mummy was furious.

'Am I to be hounded by memories of that man no matter where I go?' she cried. 'Is there no escape?'

'Easy, old girl,' said Ralph mildly, looking up from a report of an All Blacks rugby tour. 'There's no need to get your knickers in a twist. He's welcome to life in the good old USSR from what I hear of it. He must have a tile loose.'

'I thought you were supposed to be his friend,' I snapped at him. 'What do you know about life in Russia? I suppose you believe all that propaganda they print in the papers.'

Ralph put down his paper and raised his hand.

'Don't you dare lay a finger on me,' I screeched and stomped out of the room, slamming the door behind me.

Ralph thought with some justification that I was a spoiled brat, throwing his kindness back in his face, and mother made me apologize to him later. But I still thought that I would rather be in Moscow with Daddy and Esther than here in New Zealand with Mummy and boring old 'Uncle Ralph'. Or better still, I would rather have been back in what had become known around the world as Swinging London.

I was an inveterate letter writer, sending my aerogrammes winging halfway round the world to former friends and teachers at Bridgelands, to the Plumley-Greenes and even to my brother at Harrow, even though he rarely bothered to reply. Letters from contemporaries made me long for home, to be where it was all happening, buying mini-skirts at Mary Quant's Bazaar in the King's Road or jeans and hipsters in Carnaby Street, absolutely twentieth-century clothes. I looked at photographs of Twiggy, a six and a half stone Cockney sparrow with 'the ideal shape for a girl of the 1960s, narrow body, perfect square shoulders, long legs, small bust' and wished that *my* chest was flatter. Despite the beaches and the marvellous climate, I felt that I was missing out on the most exciting time for the new generation in my native city.

Playing my already dated Beatles discs, 'I Want to Hold Your Hand' and 'Can't Buy Me Love' over and over again, I yearned to lay my hands on new releases such as 'Help!', 'Day Tripper' and 'We Can Work It Out' and to listen to the fleet of pirate radio ships now operating round Britain's coasts, Radio Caroline, Radio London and the rest, pounding the airwaves with pop music, their DJs deriding the stuffy old values of the BBC. Here in New Zealand, Ralph sat puffing his pipe and listening to the sports news.

Just to infuriate me, he would smugly quote some lines from his favourite poet M.K. Joseph in the form of an ironic prayer:

> That we may never lack two Sundays in a week
> One to rest and one to play
> That we may worship in the liturgical drone
> Of the race-commentator and the radio raconteur
> That we may avoid distinction and exception
> Worship the mean, cultivate the mediocre
> Live in a state house, raise forcibly-educated children
> Receive family benefits, and standard wages and a pension
> And rest in a state crematorium.

This supposedly wry recitation was invariably accompanied by a ritual pipe cleaning. Uncle Ralph's wretched stinking stained pipe cleaners were left lying all over the house for his housekeeper to pick up and dispose of. How I hated Uncle Ralph. How I loathed New Zealand.

Meanwhile my proud independent old grandmother stayed on, living on her own in Amen Road on the fringe of a Black ghetto. Nigel was rarely allowed to visit her and I reserved for her my longest letters, which she unfailingly answered at similar length, in a firm round hand.

'There's a great row going on in the Government over immigration,' she wrote, 'and there has been much talk of faked passports, impersonation and what have you. Mr Wilson is playing a cynical game. Personally, I find the rantings of the racialists disgusting, so I have named three of my new cats (all black toms, by the way) Tyndall, Jordan and Webster after the leaders of the odious National Front.'

The headquarters of this organization at that time was a small shop and house in nearby Tulse Hill and Jenny took a delight in ripping down their poisonous posters bearing Hitler's portrait and the slogan 'He was right'. She claimed that her three cats squabbled almost as often as their three namesakes.

She moved unaided except by her stick around the streets among the West Indian 'rude boys' with their pork-pie hats, braces and fuzzy hairstyles, a tiny bent old woman with a deeply furrowed face and gnarled hands. They laughed at her. Gone were the days when she was regarded with respect in the district, the lady from number 35, the midwife who had brought so many of them into this world in the first place.

She made her way with painful slowness towards the supermarket in Balham High Road, although she found the little corner shops selling sweet potatoes, breadfruit, bluggoes, plantains, cassava, yams, callalou and okra more interesting. When she had selected her minute portions from the shelves and placed them in the basket on the trolley she made her way to the checkout and, balancing her stick against the counter, got out her purse to pay the assistant, judging each move with unhurried precision.

The deteriorating appearance of the district worried her and other long-standing residents who agreed that it was going down. Streets littered with rubbish and road signs half obliterated with graffiti from aerosol cans of paint–'Black Power Rules, OK'. Black prostitutes lounging on the steps of the crumbling terraces, once so respectably Victorian middle-class. The smell of weed or ganja being smoked and the sound of ska music drifting from open windows and around peeling doors.

It was as if she had been carried off to a foreign city without realizing what was happening. Many of the old people were afraid to go out, frightened of being attacked and robbed. Jenny simply said: 'No one's going to attack a poor old thing like me and if they do, they're welcome to what they can find.'

When she was attacked by someone who crept up behind her in Amen Road, snatched her purse containing a few shillings and ran off, she told the policeman who interviewed her: 'I don't know whether he, or she, was black or white. But if I'd caught the little thief I'd have hit him . . . or her . . . with my stick.'

The local health visitor ventured to suggest that she might like to think about moving into an old people's home, where she could be properly looked after.

'This is my home,' retorted Jenny firmly, 'and I shall die here. In my own bed, thank you very much.'

As the months and the years went by she went out less and less. The meals-on-wheels people brought her a cooked meal at midday – meat and two veg in a tinfoil container – and a home help was provided two mornings a week by Lambeth Borough Council. She was grateful for these services, seeing them as evidence of the social progress which had been made in her long lifetime.

She sat indoors most of the time with her cats, listening to the wireless. She had no television set, which she referred to rather contemptuously: People spent too much time watching the peepshow. Yet she accepted a neighbour's invitation to watch the funeral of Sir Winston Churchill, the coffin on a gun carriage drawn by ranks of white-capped sailors.

'I did not much admire him during his lifetime,' she wrote to me. 'I never really forgave him for his equivocal attitude towards us suffragettes. Still, at my age one learns the virtue of tolerance.'

At eighty-five, her eyes were as sharp and her ears as keen as they had ever been, but since her fall her joints had become a little creaky. She was grateful to Mr Adulyi, the Nigerian who now owned half the houses in the district, for driving her every Sunday morning to church in Brixton Hill and home again afterwards. He still had a white car, only a bigger and newer one.

Mr Adulyi was a good Catholic himself and it should not be suggested that his charity to an old lady was influenced by the fact that she was the holder of a freehold property which he would have liked to add to his growing collection of real estate. Whatever the weather, he made sure that Mrs Cole got to mass and holy communion.

It was the major event of her week and she looked forward to it, joining in the hymns, especially William Blake's

> And did the countenance divine
> shine forth upon our clouded hills?
> And was Jerusalem builded here
> among those dark Satanic mills?

The music reminded her of Sunday evenings when she lived in Effra Road and the organ of the Methodist chapel opposite, the clanking of the trams going by. When she went up to the altar rail so very, very slowly for communion, she remembered, too, as if it were yesterday, the day when old Father Foley placed the thin dry circle of the wafer on her tongue for the first time and Alice Baxter confided her desire to be a nun.

Gone to Christ years ago, I expect.

Words of prayers learned in childhood and never repeated for years came unbidden to her lips without need of rosary or missal.

> Jesus, Mary and Joseph, I give you my heart and my soul.
> Jesus, Mary and Joseph, assist me in my last agony.
> Jesus, Mary and Joseph, may I breathe forth my soul in peace with you. Amen.

It was difficult to pray for a happy death when images kept floating into her mind of her privileged and pampered childhood in that grand country house at Westerham. Even as the croquet mallet swung in the sunshine and the ball glided noiselessly through the hoop, fate was opening a crevasse at her feet. None of us ever knows what the next moment may bring.

Postscript

The Cole family album is by no means closed. There are new pictures, scenes, portraits to be added to its pages and there are stories to be told of the lives behind those bland faces, smiling for the camera, but I cannot write them. It is too close. There is too much pain in it. Frank Cole, as you may have read in the newspapers at the time, died in the Botkin Hospital in Moscow in 1971 while undergoing a heart operation. The specialists there had diagnosed a faulty mitral valve, the legacy of a boyhood tumble into the pond at Blackheath and the rheumatic fever which followed it, and were attempting to replace it with a plastic valve. It is an operation which seems now, in the days of whole heart transplants, relatively straightforward but was then in the pioneering phase.

Within a month of father's death, mother married Ralph Greedie in New Zealand. Stubbornly, she had refused to divorce Frank, gaining, I believe, some form of malicious satisfaction from the thought that he and 'that woman' were living in sin in Moscow. I was in my final year in the School of Social Sciences at the University of Sussex when the news of Frank's death came through. An Amazon in faded, patched jeans towering over this funny little old lady, I called at 35 Amen Road to comfort Jenny.

She seemed without grief, serenely resigned to death, more interested in making me a cup of tea. Later, as we sat in her cluttered front room looking out over the common, she went over to a chest of drawers and carefully took out something wrapped in tissue paper. The pungent vapour of mothballs temporarily overcame the pervading odour of cats and the fumes from the lethal paraffin heater in that airless room.

'Take care of it,' she said, pressing the parcel into my hands. 'It's really rather precious.'

My son Charles is nearly three and he never wore that beautiful, delicately worked Georgian robe that both Jenny and I were baptized in. Jenny died peacefully in her own bed, in the house where she had lived for nearly fifty years, just as she wished. It is too late now to dress him in the robe which his great-grandmother handed down to us, he has quite outgrown it.

Sitting on the rug at my feet, he is engrossed with a pile of plastic building blocks, humming to himself as he tries to perch one block upon another. The tune is easily recognizable: 'Spread a Little Happiness', which the Sting has been crooning over the radio all summer. How odd that this innocently banal little number which made my father fall in love with Binnie Hale when he was just a boy should be bubbling in the earpieces of Walkman sets more than half a century later. Charlie adores it.

He is a happy little chap with big velvet brown eyes and an enchanting smile which lights up his entire countenance, showing two wide, even rows of milk teeth. At such moments he is the mirror image of Malcolm and I become as liquescent as an ice cube in a rum punch. Mother had the surprise of her life when she set eyes on him for the first time at Auckland International Airport last Christmas.

In her letters she had been disapproving enough, heaven knows, of my single-parent status, having, it seems, forgotten that my two previous marriages were unmitigated disasters. I met my first husband at university and kicked him out as soon as I discovered I was pregnant. I couldn't bear to have the child of a man I had come to despise as vain and shallow and, anyway, I badly wanted a successful career, so I had an abortion.

My second husband was a surgeon in the Marines whom I met in Northern Ireland. He equated marriage with babies, as many as possible in the shortest possible time, and of course I failed to oblige him. The whole thing was a stupid mistake. I never wanted marriage or babies at all. I just couldn't see myself in the little woman role, washing nappies and making sure that hubby's socks were in the right pairs when they came out of the washing machine.

Then Charlie arrived.

Even allowing for my indiscretion, immorality or just damned carelessness, it would never occur to Mother that the father of my child might be anything other than white, Anglo-Saxon and (preferably) Protestant. Somehow, I never got around to telling her in my letters that Malcolm Makepeace, the man that I love, is black.

Not only is he black but he is Catholic – oh, God, why is it that we Coles are for ever falling into the arms of the Church of Rome however much we try to escape its clutches? – and also married to a lady of his own race. He hates her, but he stays with her.

Dear reader, you see why I don't want to talk about it? My mother, who has always terrified me and made me feel that in some way I do not quite come up to scratch, is less than impressed with my success as a television documentary director, a card-carrying member of the new elite of women. She would prefer to see me married to what she thinks of as 'the right sort of person'.

Clearly Malcolm is not the right sort of person and anyway he is already married, as I have said. He is strong as few men are, yet gentle and humorous, genuinely a good man, a caring man. I would love to share his faith but my intellect refuses to accept it as truth. Much as I would like to, I cannot believe there is a life after death.

The only meaning to life that I can see now is the creation of new life.

Through my failure to take a man's name, family history repeating the mistake of that other Jenny Cole so long ago, my son Charles now continues the Cole line. Will he grow up to be like his grandfather a Member of Parliament (there is a noticeable lack of black or even half-black faces on those green benches) or become Prime Minister? If there was such a place as heaven, I could see his grandfather and his great-grandmother and, yes, his great-great-grandfather beaming down happily on such a poetically just turn of events.

Jenny Cole

Brixton, London SW